Advance Praise for
# RED CLAY SUZIE

"Arresting debut...a vivid depiction of a unique childhood that feels universal in its longing."

—**Christopher Castellani**, author of *Leading Men*

"*Red Clay Suzie*'s Philbet Lawson joins Scout Finch (*To Kill a Mockingbird*) and Frankie Addams (*The Member of the Wedding*) in Southern literature's pantheon of outsider children. While Philbet finds unlikely allies in his small world, others ridicule his sensitive nature and deformed body. Philbet's roots are planted in the South's inhospitable red clay, but he grows up, honest to his true self. Read *Red Clay Suzie* and cheer on Philbet, a new literary hero."

—**Alice Leccese Powers**, writer and editor of the bestselling *In Mind* series

"A great new southern storyteller has emerged, and in *Red Clay Suzie*, Jeffrey Dale Lofton with his fastidious and keen eye has created a coming-of-age story unlike any other. It is a world revealed by the gay, misshapen narrator, Philbet, who with a pitch-perfect voice takes us on a weird, comical, and mysterious adventure story of the rarely explored world of a gifted and repressed gay childhood. It feels like a new and indigenous style. "*Red Clay Suzie* is a tour de force by a rare, imaginative, and important writer—a fascinating gay story of the South, and yet through the magic of this writer's skill, it transcends its own themes. This is a rare occurrence and a true triumph—a sunken treasure chest of fiction, so close to the heart you can sometimes feel it beating."

—**James Hart**, author of *Lucky Jim*

"An intimate exploration of people, place, and identity, *Red Clay Suzie* opens up the idea of the South into one that is more inclusive and real."

—**W. Ralph Eubanks**, author of *A Place Like Mississippi: A Journey Through a Real and Imagined Literary Landscape*

"Jeffrey Dale Lofton is a writer's writer, whose strong, authorial voice captures your imagination with an unshakable grip."

—**Willee Lewis**, PEN/Faulkner Foundation board member, editor of *Snakes: An Anthology of Serpent Tales*

# RED
# CLAY
# SUZIE

# RED CLAY SUZIE

a novel inspired
by true events

## Jeffrey Dale Lofton

PRESS

A POST HILL PRESS BOOK

ISBN: 979-8-88845-528-9
ISBN (eBook): 978-1-63758-577-1

Cover design by Nicole Caputo
Interior design and composition by Greg Johnson, Textbook Perfect

This book is a work of fiction. People, places, events, and situations are the product of the author's imagination. Any resemblance to actual persons, living or dead, or historical events, is purely coincidental.

Library of Congress Cataloging-in-Publication Data

Names: Lofton, Jeffrey Dale, author.
Title: Red Clay Suzie / Jeffrey Dale Lofton.
Description: New York : Post Hill Press, [2022] | Summary: "Philbet Lawson
   is born in 1960s rural Georgia with two inescapable strikes against him:
   he's gay and physically misshapen, both of which inform his every
   thought, unless he's thinking about cars, his obsession.  His world is
   populated by an ineffectual father; a devoted though fearful mother; a
   rowdy but popular older brother; his best friend, a Black boy who also
   understands the sting of being an outsider; boorish uncles who belittle
   Philbet for sport; a Grandaddy who is an oasis of wisdom and
   unconditional love; and Knox, the older boy Philbet idolizes to
   distraction. Over time, Philbet finds refuge in unexpected places and in
   unexpected ways"-- Provided by publisher.
Identifiers: LCCN 2022038555 (print) | LCCN 2022038556 (ebook) | ISBN
   9781637585764 (hardcover) | ISBN 9781637585771 (ebook)
Subjects: LCSH: Bullying--Fiction. | Self-esteem--Fiction. | Gays--Fiction.
   | Dysfunctional families--Fiction. | Race relations--Fiction. |
   Georgia--History--20th century--Fiction. | LCGFT: Autobiographical
   fiction. | Bildungsromans. | Novels.
Classification: LCC PS3612.O3826 R43 2022  (print) | LCC PS3612.O3826
   (ebook) | DDC 813/.6--dc23/eng/20220811
LC record available at https://lccn.loc.gov/2022038555
LC ebook record available at https://lccn.loc.gov/2022038556

**Post Hill Press**
New York • Nashville
posthillpress.com

Published in the United States of America
1 2 3 4 5 6 7 8 9 10

*To my beloved partner,*
*my cherished, perfectly imperfect family,*
*and my fellow fringies everywhere*

# Contents

**PART TWO**

**PART THREE**

# Author's Note

*Red Clay Suzie* is in a way a letter to my younger self, the boy who felt the sting of living and loving on the fringes. Dramatic license notwithstanding, Philbet's story is *my* story, which I wrote from the heart for everyone who has ever struggled like I did to find acceptance.

Through this child in rural Georgia, I want my fellow outsiders to know that bullies are paper predators who have no more power than you yourself give them. They are as scared of life as you, and once you understand that they lose their sovereignty, as if a gentle wind catches on the edge of them and lifts them away.

Know that whatever imperfections (real and perceived) your body has, it is beautiful; it is precious. Treat it with kindness and care so it carries you as far as it is able. Know that you should not give in to your inclination to hide, to withdraw from the world. Know that there will always be a caring someone you can trust somewhere in those concentric circles of humanity that surround and follow you through life.

My fellow fringies, above all else, know that it is the quality of your mind and heart that matters most. They, more than anything else, define you.

Oh, and yes, love, real love, is never wrong. Bravely bestow it on whomever is worthy of the gift. That is what I wish my younger self had known. That is Philbet's story.

# Breakfast at Tiffany's

W hy, you might be wondering, would I be using the title of the fabled story by Truman Capote for my introduction to Jeffrey Dale Lofton's own novel? Even as I type these words, the image of Audrey Hepburn, dressed for the film in her sublime Givenchy black dresses—one worn with the lacquered black straw hat, the other with upswept hair and pearls, unforgettably creating the persona of her role as the rather rackety Holly Golightly in the supremely stylish film of Capote's 1958 novella—is fixed in my head.

The answer is because I met Jeffrey, quite literally, when having breakfast at Tiffany's in July 2019. I had flown into New York from London the day before as a guest speaker invited by Cunard to join their iconic liner *Queen Mary 2* crossing the Atlantic to England on their celebrated Transatlantic Fashion Week.

While always happy to talk about "insider" memories of working with storied designers during the twenty-five years my husband and I ran our boutique public relations agency specializing in nurturing luxury fashion brands, that part of my life story came to an end in 2000. I stepped back from fashion to follow my personal dream of writing. At that point, I aspired to write biographies about legendary, pioneering names in the early 20th century fashion, retail, and beauty industries whose stories had been eclipsed or forgotten. Being passionate about libraries and archives, researching the letters, diaries, and magazines necessary to delve into first the life and times of Helena Rubinstein and Elizabeth Arden for *War Paint*, followed by Harry Gordon Selfridge for *Shopping, Seduction & Mr. Selfridge*, was a joyful experience.

Our embarkment day started with an invitation for speakers to join a group of Fashion Week voyage's specially chosen guests at Tiffany's recently opened, much vaunted Blue Box Café—an irresistible treat as the café already had a long waiting list, and what's not to love about having breakfast at Tiffany's?

In true American tradition, breakfast started early. Jet lag having kicked in—and being somewhat slow in getting organized—rather embarrassingly, my husband and I arrived to find the welcome speech already underway. Rescued by a resourceful waiter, we found ourselves at a table with Jeffrey and his partner Erich Parker, members of the enthusiastic American clientele on the previous year's sailing and "on board" on dry land to help explain to us newcomers the delights of the voyage.

We talked about opera (a grand passion of Erich's, who had sung professionally since childhood), traveling, London, the BBC, and our mutual love of dogs (*Queen Mary 2* has a kennel). Jeffrey and Erich were complimentary about both the Broadway musical of *War Paint* and the PBS television series *Mr. Selfridge*—adapted from my books—and were particularly interested in my transition from publicist to published author. For my part, I spoke of the personal issues involved in the change of pace writing entailed. Writing is a lonely occupation, but one where you are expected to leave the cocoon and emerge—blinking in the sunlight—to go on marketing and speaking tours.

In talking to these two charming breakfast companions, I got something of a sense from Jeffrey that there was an agenda underneath his gentle camaraderie, but obligations in Washington, DC meant they weren't able to join the crossing, and with hugs and a *bon voyage*, they said goodbye— our conversation about the art and process of writing cut short.

Then in March this year, Jeffrey wrote to me: "We talked of our pastimes, our passions, our pasts, but most of all we talked about writing.

Your career, your remarkable story, really inspired me. I have long imagined writing a novel loosely based on my childhood in the Deep South,
and meeting you and hearing your encouraging words has convinced me
to give it a go at long last."

The book you have in your hands is the result—Jeffrey's debut novel,
*Red Clay Suzie*. I can say with absolute conviction that his efforts have been
rewarded. And neither did he tuck himself away from life to write. Instead,
with astonishing determination, he wrote his book largely on the keypad
of his mobile while commuting to and from his work at the Library of
Congress. I believe we always absorb the atmosphere of presence and place,
and clearly Jeffrey's years working there have imbued him with a passion
for words. But to write a book—especially one as powerful as this—on
a phone seems such an achievement to me that I am finding it complex
pondering exactly how he managed to do it!

Jeffrey's novel is largely based on his own life growing up in rural
Georgia where, with masterful understatement, he readily admits: "I had
a bit of a tough time growing up both gay and afflicted with a skeletal
deformity—bullied and teased by classmates and extended family alike. I
have poured all these experiences into the book through my protagonist,
Philbet, struggling to understand life and love living on the fringes."

*Red Clay Suzie* is a descriptive triumph—not just in bringing the red
clay soil of Georgia alive to those of us who have not (yet) traveled to
the South, but in reminding us just how conservative and complex family
issues were back in the 1960s. In dialogue so sensitive you are vividly trans-
ported back to Philbet's childhood, his older self ultimately accepts the
pent-up frustrations on all sides, acknowledging that his family simply had
no mechanism for coping with anyone being "different."

Another of the curious coincidences that has emerged since our brief
but important time at Tiffany's and my reading of his book draft is that I
really do understand what Jeffrey means. I too grew up in a largely conservative family, where my father in particular was full of British "reserve"—for
which read "we don't talk about problems or scandals." Thus, in about
1962 when I was twelve and my much loved but fragile and hyperactive
older sister was admitted to hospital where she was incarcerated for several

weeks, I was never told why. I found out from a group of sniggering girls in the playground at our school who, when I walked past, said, "How's your sister getting on in the nuthouse? She's in Saxondale isn't she? That's a loony bin." At home that night, I challenged my parents to explain what was wrong; they did everything they could to avoid telling me the truth. Back then, mental illness was a stigma just too great to comprehend. They felt ashamed. My sister had many good years in her life to follow, but having bipolar disorder, she had many bad years too. She died in September 2019. I miss her every day.

So, I have a natural empathy toward the semi-fictional Philbet. And, I feel close to Jeffrey and have a huge sense of pride that in some way I may have helped unlock his latent talent—the start of his writing career. His is an extraordinary, beautiful book, and one that will remain with you long after you have finished.

I started this foreword by talking about Truman Capote—who himself took every inch of his Southern discomfort as background for his work. Like her creator, Holly Golightly had her own childhood demons to hide. For those of us who read the book, we don't know if she found her happiness. The film, of course, had a Hollywood ending. Producers think audiences want to be happy, and I guess—in the main—they are right. Certainly, Jeffrey has found his happiness in the end.

We are all so affected by our childhoods. Sometimes you have to be tough. You have to try not to give up. You have to be brave. Jeffrey has been brave to write this story. So, tuck yourself up with a yellow tomato sandwich—don't forget the mayo—and enjoy *Red Clay Suzie*.

*Lindy Woodhead*
Oxfordshire, England—2022

# PART ONE

〜

## CHAPTER ONE

# Keebler

The bell rang, and I looked outside and saw Daddy's truck sitting all the way at the far end of the circular drive, parked almost at the exit onto the main road. I only got picked up if snow or ice was coming, if something was wrong, or if someone was sick. I marched around the half-moon drive toward the truck, opened the door and climbed in ready to ask Daddy…and it was him, the boy from the GTO, in the driver's seat.

I felt a little tear in my heart, and whispered, "Daddy." I wasn't questioning where my father was or why my teenage obsession sat where Daddy should be, behind the wheel in Daddy's truck outside my high school. It was more like a statement: "You're my Daddy."

He flashed a big smile and said, "Hi. Um…I fixed your pop's truck, and I'm meeting him here to hand it off."

"You live just down the road," I blurted out.

Of course, stupid me just told him I was stalking him. Why would I know he lives down the road? Why would I care? My brother wouldn't notice a boy. Adam would see a guy on the basketball court and play one-on-one just because another guy was there and never ask his name or really even look him in the face. Only *I* would sit in a wrecked car in this boy's backyard to watch him come and go. Only *I* would wait, skip lunch,

3

or not do my homework just to listen for his car's engine so I could hurry out to hide myself next to the road to catch a half-second peek into his window to see his hand pull the shifter into second gear as he rocketed off somewhere.

I thought, and said, "God, driving this heap must be a letdown."

He laughed, "You're funny."

"Don't tell Daddy. I'm not ready for him to know." And he laughed again, bringing his hand up to slap the steering wheel. The ring on his finger made contact with the driver's side window, and an inch-long crack appeared. As we stared, it grew a twin leaf of a crack at a perfect right angle to the original.

"No, no. Crap. Brownie's gonna kill me."

Without thinking, I said, "That crack has been there for a week. I saw it last week."

"What? Why, why would...? It just happened. My ring hit it."

"I'll say I noticed it last week." Why was I doing this?

"You don't have to do that. It's no big deal."

"What about your dad?" I asked.

"Maybe I can find a replacement in the yard. We've got a scrapyard in back of the house."

"Yeah...." And I stopped myself from telling him I already knew that because I spent half of my life watching him from a totaled-out Oldsmobile a hundred feet from where he slept.

"Yeah, so maybe I can grab a replacement."

I knew he could. Three cars over from my 1973 Oldsmobile Ninety-Eight Regency hideout sat a grass-green version of Daddy's truck. It had no bed, as if someone took a big axe and chopped the back half—the hauling part—off.

I knew these windows would continue to crack once they started. This would be a full spiderweb by tomorrow.

Silence.

"So, what's your name?" he asked.

"Knox. I mean—"

"Knox? No way. That's my name."

"Yeah, um, Philbet. I'm Philbet. Um, I know you're Knox. Sorry. Daddy told me about the truck. I forgot. I thought you meant 'Did I know your name?'"

Daddy didn't tell me anything. How would I know his name? Why would I care unless I was obsessed with him? He smiled and then his face went blank, and he looked at me, straight at me. I couldn't read his expression, but I had never seen anyone look at me like that. Mama and Daddy looked at me, but only to check to see if I was still there, hadn't wandered off, or no one had taken me. Daddy had an unhealthy fascination with kidnapping—and property lines. Seething, but never doing anything about it, he was always convinced that the neighbors moved the property line stakes an inch or two during the nighttime every several months.

It's not easy to talk to someone about something that's important to you. Maybe you only get one chance at this, and you don't get what you want if it doesn't go well. And here I was having the most important conversation I'd ever had. And we weren't really saying anything—at least I wasn't. No words, only silence and stares.

I guess the look that was closest to his stare was how I imagined I looked at Knox when I stared at him from my hideout wreck as he worked and roamed the yard several car lengths ahead of me. But I was alone then, with no one around for me to hide my true feelings from, no one to ask why I stared at this boy. And he couldn't see me peering at him from the back seat of the hideout. But he could see me now, both of us in Daddy's truck. He stared at me like he was determined to win a dare that he could look the longest, that I would turn away first.

His stare was more than I could stand. I wanted to throw myself into his chest to hide my face and touch him. This was something new, something I didn't know existed. But it didn't perplex me. I understood. Sort of like someone spoke to me in a different language for the first time, and I understood what he said, but I didn't know how to respond. He didn't look at me like I was a scared kid. He looked at me like I was a person, an equal. Then he reached over slowly, his hand relaxed so casually that it seemed like he was about to dip it into a stream for a scoop of fresh water.

"What's this?" And he picked something off my chin just below my lip, and he put it in his mouth. "I like cookies too. Got any more?"

I did. He could have all the cookies I could get my hands on.

"Um, yeah, I…" And I pulled out my baggy with one remaining.

"Mmm, shortbread stripe. My favorite."

He took it, broke it in half, and handed one side to me. Then he downed his half in one bite.

"Thanks. You're a regular Keebler elf." And I had yet another nickname, one that wasn't created to minimize me and make someone else feel big. I felt like I was going to melt as I ate my half of the cookie, never savoring a bite of food more, knowing that he touched it. And I giggled a little, in that way that always drew fire from Uncle Kingston. But when I was near this boy, this kind and beautiful boy, I didn't care what anybody might call me or say about me.

But it's too soon for Knox. My story really begins twenty-five miles up the road and ten years earlier, when I was four.

## CHAPTER TWO

# Grandaddy's Tater Rule

Grandaddy's vegetable garden was perfect for carving out paths and roads for my fleet of Matchbox cars. The neat rows defined by mounds of soil were long avenues that headed any place my preschool mind could conjure. Each row looked endless, its perspective making it disappear before it actually stopped against the fence that followed the back line of the property, which abutted a railroad track. My miniature green 1968 Mercury Cougar was almost identical to Beau's real Cougar, which sat across the highway at Pick and Lolly's filling station every day Beau worked there. I could see it from any place I stood, whether I was at Adam's and my bedroom window, next door on Grandaddy and Jorma's front porch, or in the garden rows.

Ours was a small, insular world, but it seemed back then to go on forever. The axis was the two side-by-side plots of land that held Grandaddy and Jorma's house, our home, and the vegetable garden that connected them. And a twenty-five mile sunburst that radiated from that point was all I knew, all I wanted or needed. That was our universe.

The railroad cut that ran behind us to the east seemed miles deep with a treacherous path of rocky steps and complicated switchbacks hacked out of the jungley brush between the edge of our backyard and the track far below. In truth, it would take a rock tossed from our yard about three seconds to hit the track, so it wasn't actually miles deep, but it felt that big to my four-year-old eyes. The cut was the place where outlaws traveled, walking along in the dark of midnight, avoiding the law and good folks like us who were free to come and go as we pleased during the day. We, safe in our homes, were superior to those who had the law after them and couldn't live in real houses with actual roofs with all their things and toys around them.

The cut, a man-inflicted open wound in the red clay, separated us from colored town on the other side of the bank. From where I stood, colored town looked the same color as our side of the cut with the same patches of bare red clay on the banks, green and brown trees and bushes. But Adam said it was colored town because of who lived there. And sometimes there was a funny smell in the air. "Colored folks are burnin' their hair again," Adam would explain. I thought they must have an awful lot of hair because I smelled that smell a lot. But I never saw anyone on the bank on the other side, not any folks of any color. I wondered how far behind the line of trees on the top of the bank they lived, and why the kids never came out to play in the cut like we did.

Our house was sandwiched between the railroad cut and the highway—busy with cars during the day, but not much traffic at night. While the cut was our outback wilderness, our Times Square was Pick and Lolly's filling station and grocery store. It sat across the highway and about one house-width over to the left from our place and was the social center of our small community. You had to go there for just about anything, except for barbecue. The store up past Grandaddy's had exclusive rights to barbecue and green sherbet push-ups, but only Pick and Lolly's had bread.

I also couldn't understand why I never saw the colored kids at Pick and Lolly's, but they didn't come, not even to get candy. I know, because I looked out our door toward Pick and Lolly's a lot. I was looking for Beau, their son who was eighteen, grown up already, and the size of two people in one—Pick and Lolly combined.

Beau, so tall and big that it was a wonder he could come up behind me so quietly that I didn't know he was there, pick me up just by wrapping his hands around my middle and sling me up and over his head. Then he'd settle me onto the seat of his shoulders, only his ears or the underside of his chin or the curls of his hair for me to hold and keep myself up on my surprise perch.

How could a person so giant in my eyes raise a leg so big as his and touch his foot down again to the ground without me hearing? He must have cast magic dust in front of him that rendered him silent and invisible before each step as he sneaked up. Surely it was sold off a shelf so high in Pick and Lolly's that it would be years before I was tall enough to see it there, *Beau's Invisible Powder*, and know to ask for it by name.

When I looked for Beau, I looked for the Cougar. I didn't need X-ray vision into Pick and Lolly's to see if Beau was there. The Cougar was my sign. If the Cougar was there, Beau was there.

The Cougar was a machine from another world, with taillight bulbs that blinked each in turn, starting at the edge of the tag and *blink, blink, blink*, out toward the back fender to signal which way the car wanted to turn. It had headlights that lived under pop-up doors that only opened at night and when it rained. Beau sometimes took a break from the station and wiped a paste on the hood and trunk lid, and then rubbed it off, leaving it the exact color of the inside of a ripe kiwi and with a light metallic glitter that exactly matched the glint of the wet fruit. I knew about kiwis because my cousins Meg and Suzie brought them from Florida every summer when they came to stay at Grandaddy and Jorma's. They were older than Adam and me because Uncle Rudy was older than Daddy. Daddy's brother had kids before Daddy because he was older. Adam, when he grows up, will get married before me because he's older. And then he'll have kids before me too. That's the way it works. That's what Jorma said anyway.

Even now, years later, I can see Beau's green Cougar every time I see a kiwi, even an unpeeled one, because I know what's inside. And that childhood toy rushes back to me with a soft punch to the heart along with all the joy it brought me rolling it around the edges of the garden. When I think of it, I want to turn. I want to see Beau sneak up behind me and lift me over his head and settle me on his shoulders.

Adam had a whole set of Matchbox cars, too, because when I got one— begging every time we went to the store—he got one too. But he never played with them. I coveted Adam's because his were showroom-immaculate and not scratched up and loved up like mine. But he was four years older than me. I guess he had outgrown them by the time Santa Claus gave us our first ones in our stockings. I loved mine, the Cougar, from the first. I don't remember anything else I got that Christmas.

I didn't want to trade my Cougar for his, but I did like playing with his. It felt special. The differences in them fascinated me, mine with dings; his, perfect. It made me think of the difference between the Grandaddy I saw every day and the Grandaddy in pictures. I liked the Grandaddy I had now, the one with almost no hair on his head and eyeglasses of gold wire, but sometimes I wished I could have opened a door and found the younger Grandaddy, the one who lived before I knew him. The scratch-free Grandaddy.

On rainy days when we couldn't go outside and play, I sometimes sneaked Adam's Matchbox case out of our room; it was a little blue suitcase with a yellow panel right on the top, with a big racing car emblazoned across the side. My own cases were worn, dog-edged. I could see the panels between the plastic covering were just ordinary cardboard. Somehow seeing that surprised me again and again. Cardboard didn't feel special enough, but even that thought didn't dampen the allure of these cars. I did have some ideas on how Matchbox could improve their product line, though. I had no problems with the cars, but the cases…why not design them to look like miniature parking garages, with cars neatly lined up as soldiers in formation?

While I'd take my Matchbox Cougar to the dirt at Grandaddy's garden's edge, I'd never intentionally take it beyond to the red clay. If red clay touched it, the stain remained, marked forever. If you dug down too far in the garden, you hit it—red clay. Grandaddy said he spent years hauling in regular brown soil from outside the county, and he scattered white pellets from a bucket all over the place—regular fertilizer—and added cow poop and catfish heads to the base of plants—natural fertilizer.

After one play session outside, the Matchbox wheels no longer rolled, grit caught up in the wheel wells. The garden soil always dried out and could be shaken loose. But I had to be careful, especially after a tater digging, because that red clay was only a few inches below the rich brown soil. When I got the red clay up in the wheel wells, well that was just about death for a Matchbox.

That was the alchemy of red clay, I realized thinking back. When moist, it had the texture of silken butter about thirty minutes out of the refrigerator. When the beating Georgia sun leached it of moisture, it was either hard as a rock or powdery, slippery even in the heat of day, feeling almost liquid against skin. Stand barefoot in the clay with your eyes closed, and you'd have no idea if it's dry dust or hot-mudded after a sudden downpour that came and went so fast it had no time to cool the surfaces it wet. When overloaded with water, the clay was a chunky, creamy soup, getting everywhere, gumming up everything. It reminded me of teeth stuck in an over-heaped spoonful of peanut butter.

Grandaddy didn't want to hear anything bad about the clay. It was there when he came into the world and would be there when they lowered him into it. He had sort of a reverence for it, though he claimed we'd have starved without the rich, fragrant soil he'd hauled and hoed into the garden's earth. The garden used to be twice as big, but Grandaddy and Jorma gave up half the land—and half the vegetables—to Mama and Daddy when they got married.

"What did Grandaddy used to plant that he dut'n now?" Adam asked Daddy.

"He plants the same stuff, just half as much."

That didn't seem to square with Adam's new math. "Two times more people and half as many vegetables." He didn't quite shake his head, but I could tell he wanted to.

"Grandaddy and Jorma figured we needed some land to grow on," said Daddy.

Our house was a white cinder block two-bedroom that Mama and Daddy found in a catalog. They just pointed to it in the wish book, and after a $600 down payment and a $3,000 loan, Homeblock South came out and in seven days, it was there. Mama said it was *The Parisienne*, and she chose it over *The Greenbrier*, even though *The Parisienne* was one hundred square feet smaller, because she always wanted to go to Paris.

*The Parisienne* had the back door on the side of the house instead of on the back. Mama said she liked it that way. Still, Daddy called it a back door, and Mama went along with him. But Homeblock forgot to put the kitchen cabinets in, and there wasn't even a septic tank. I didn't know what a septic tank was, but Adam said you had to have one if you wanted to go to the bathroom. Adam knew about the septic tank because he was there—kind of. Daddy dug the hole in the ground after he got home from work at night while Mama, with Adam in her tummy, held the flashlight. And the dark green carpet that was in every room except the bathroom and the kitchen wasn't there at first either. For Christmas, Grandaddy and Jorma gave Mama and Daddy door frames, doors, and carpet. MawMaw gave Mama and Daddy kitchen cabinets. When I first heard that, I remember thinking Mama and Daddy must have been really good all year long to get such a lot of presents, though they wouldn't have been on *my* Christmas list. And I would have told Homeblock South to put all that in when they built the house in the first place.

The path from *The Parisienne* to Jorma and Grandaddy's house—an old gabled clapboard with what Grandaddy called gingerbread trim, which confused me to no end—ran smack down the middle of Grandaddy's garden. The lush, over-my-four-year-old-head plants were jungle-green and full of string beans, butter beans, lady peas, black-eyed peas, carrots, banana peppers, turnips, cornstalks, and my favorite, "ourish" potatoes.

They required digging in the ground, and you never knew if you were going to find a small, pebble-like failure that never took off or a big honking potato so large that all six of us could eat it as a whole meal if we ever ran out of food. And there were the ones that were so misshapen, so long and skinny, that they looked like one of Grandaddy's cigars after Jorma twisted it all up to spite Grandaddy when she was upset with him. Or they were amorphous blobs growing in on themselves, looking like miniature infants set out to scrounge on the ground, catching the dirt in their little fists, only letting go when brought in to the kitchen sink and sliced open, revealing the little pockets of once dry but now muddy abscesses. Grandaddy liked these misfits best of all—respected them even.

The first lesson I remember word-for-word, not even knowing it was a lesson, was in his garden.

"Hey, Philbet, whatcha got there?" Grandaddy asked. His smooth head eclipsed the sun and shaded me.

"I got six carrots and five potatoes."

"You got five taters already?"

"Yessir."

"Philbet, that's real good."

"But this one ain't any good," I said.

"What's wrong with it?"

"It's all ugly, all pinched up, and has rough spots on it."

"No, that's a good one. That's a fine tater," Grandaddy assured me.

"It's ugly."

"No, it's a good one."

"It looks rotted."

"That's the best of the bunch." His knobbly finger entered my field of vision. "See, this is prob'ly where a bug got after it, but that little tater said, 'You ain't gonna get me, bug. I'm stronger than you.'"

"Really?"

"Yeah. And see, that tater had to work harder than that big pretty one right there just to survive. And that means it's got more flavor inside and more vitamins, too, I 'spect."

"Why, Grandaddy?"

"'Cause it sucked up more minerals from the ground around it. It had to, just to fight off that bug and survive. That tater dut'n care that it's not as big and pretty as those other ones."

"I'll look for more ugly ones," I replied, grinning. Only later in life would I understand what he really meant, a wave of devotion and grief overtaking me.

"That's fine. I know you will," he said. "You're about the best tater digger I've ever met, and I've known a lot of 'em."

I liked helping Grandaddy. Before he moved on, he bent over and stroked the back of my head, pressing my hair down. I was suddenly aware of how much heat it had soaked up from the sun.

"Hey, let me see that carrot you got there."

"Which one?" I asked.

He pointed to the one I had set aside from the others. I handed it to him.

"Philbet, see, you can apply the tater rule to carrots too. See, this little carrot was growin' down into the ground, and it come up on a rock."

"How you know?"

"On account of how it's shaped. Had to be a rock we missed and left in the row. Couldn't've been a root. And that carrot turned and growed sideways to get 'round that rock. But it kept on and dit'n let that rock stop it."

"What about peaches?"

"Yeah, if a peach has a spot on it looks like you doodled on it with a brown Crayon, that's where a worm tried to get in."

Now in on the rules of the game, I continued: "And that peach said, 'You're not gettin' in me and ruinin' me, worm.'"

"That's right, boy."

"And that works for all plants...tomatoes too?"

"Yep, it works for any living thing. People too," Grandaddy said.

"And dogs too?" I asked. "Is that why ol' Luke has only one back leg, but he can still walk?"

"Um, yeah, I guess. I guess it is."

Excited because I understood, I added, "He told that car that it wad'n gonna stop him?"

"You got it, boy." Then he swung wide his arms, and I went in for a hug.

Maybe there was something in the dirt that caused my problem. Maybe. The vegetables and me. Butter beans would produce pods with an under-formed bean next to a hefty, hearty one, as if two twins grew next to each other and one took the nutrients for both of them. String beans produced large, gorgeous husks that hung so straight from the vine, they looked like green crystals on a candelabra, so perfect that a picker had to stop and admire the sheer health and heartiness of it. But some of them were nothing but pith on the inside, dry as a pixie straw. That was the way of string beans.

Grandaddy gently, in his tender way, taught me the rule of potatoes and carrots and even ol' Luke almost fifteen years ago. It's the first of his many lessons I remember, loving guidance to last a lifetime, to help me make it on my own.

## CHAPTER THREE

# The Green Milkshake Cure

"Boys, get up."

"Wha…? Mama? Mama?"

The overhead light in Adam's and my room popped on in the middle of the night the same way it did when the electricity was restored after having gone out during a thunderstorm.

"Y'all get up. Grandaddy's sick."

"Wha…?"

This must have been about 1968 because I already had the 1968 Mercury Cougar Matchbox car. It was on the little table that sat between Adam's bed and mine. That's where I parked it every night. There were also two glasses of water on the table, one for Adam and one for me. And there was the Br'er Bear lamp that Aunt Pinky made for Adam and me in her ceramics class.

Aunt Pinky's real name was Beatrice, but she hated her name. She was Beatrice for the first three years of her life, back before Grandaddy had scarlet fever and still had hair on the top of his head, back before she was an old lady herself. Grandaddy said Aunt Pinky would take a mouthful of milk or a mouthful of the nearest anything and stick her lips out like the pucker on the metal fish at the fountain in front of the courthouse and spit whatever it was in her mouth out just like that fountain if anybody called her Beatrice.

My own Daddy was Phil. Not Phillip. Phil. Whenever he went to a counter and had to produce proof that he was who he claimed to be, he'd be asked, "Phillip, right?"

"Naw, just Phil. Mama and Daddy were too poor for the extra letters."

It was a similar story for Uncle Rudy, the boy who grew up between Aunt Pinky and Daddy. He wasn't Rudolph. He was just Rudy. Both Aunt Pinky and Uncle Rudy lived all the way down at the bottom tip of Florida. Daddy said they moved down there after the war so that they could get jobs picking oranges. I guess they got tired of picking peaches and wanted a change.

Aunt Pinky's set-jawed demand to be called Pinky did not save her from the long-held and specifically middle-Georgia pronunciation of "aunt" as "ain't." The sister of one's mama or daddy is an aunt. And it's pronounced just like the little insect that can lift and carry many times its body weight: the ant. But when one is addressing that aunt, when the word "aunt" is part of her name, it's pronounced "ain't," as in, "Ain't Pinky, that's about the best lamp I've ever seen." In my family we said "ain't" about as much as we said "fixin' to."

And similarly, "uncle" was pronounced "unca." That meant Uncle Vance was not only the man Jorma called that "heathen fruit from Boston who grows orchids" who Aunt Pinky followed to south Florida, he was "Unca Vance."

Jumping into a car to head to Florida with her new husband and her adopted name was likely how she set herself apart as the girl and woman she actually was on the inside, instead of the Beatrice that Jorma and everybody else wanted her to be. And I liked her, mostly because we didn't see her much.

When we did go to Florida to visit—Daddy, Mama, Adam, and me—all four of us slept in one bedroom at Aunt Pinky's. It was tight in there. At breakfast, she'd only give each of us one piece of toast, and Adam and I had to share one packet of grape jelly that came in a little white plastic pot smaller than a box of matches. And she didn't keep them in the refrigerator like we kept our jelly. Aunt Pinky kept those pouches in a bowl on a shelf above her stove to keep them out of little-boy hands; good thing, too, because I had a real strong urge to pull back the foil lid, lick the little bit of jelly that clung to its underside, which had a bunch of grapes stamped on the front side, and then use my fingers to get every last bit of jelly out of the tiny tub. That high-up shelf did something else; it warmed that store-bought bite to a temperature and consistency that turned it into a near homemade-like delicacy, the exact warmth of a batch of Mama's jelly just holding on to the last bit of heat from the canning.

So, I guess you could say Aunt Pinky was jelly-stingy, but when I turned my head on my pillow so I faced the table that separated my bed from Adam's and looked at that Br'er Bear lamp she sent to us all the way from Florida, all I could whisper to myself was, "Ain't Pinky, that's about the best lamp I've ever seen."

And it was. It was the best lamp ever. Br'er Bear stood on what looked like a big mud road, brown mud, and that mud road made it impossible to knock him over. And many a night I dreamed of walking alongside Br'er Bear in a cartoon-like world just like we saw in *Song of the South* on the Sunday night broadcast of *The Wonderful World of Disney*. Under the lamp-shade just above Br'er Bear's head and walking stick was a small, yellow bulb that cast the softest shadows across the room when it was turned on, shadows with ill-defined edges like the ones that fell across the soft, green grass in the backyard, not the hard-edged shadows on the red clay of the driveway or the railroad cut.

Mama always turned on the Br'er Bear lamp when it was time for us to get up. She never turned on the light in the ceiling unless one of us spilled the glass of water set out for us. Or, I should say, when I spilled *my* water. Adam never spilled his, but he had four years on me.

For a while, Mama took away my real cup and gave me my sippy cup from when I was little, and, you know, that sippy cup looked like some-body had taken the comb that Grandaddy kept in his shirt pocket and stuck it right down in the top of the cup to poke holes for you to suck out the water. After I didn't turn over the sippy cup for one month—thirty days, Adam said it was—Mama let me have the regular cup back, and I didn't turn it over ever again.

I didn't like the overhead light. One reason was because it had what looked like stalks of wheat in the etched glass shade. If you really stared right at it when the light was turned on and then looked at the white wall, you could see that wheat just as clear as if you were in a field. But I thought wheat was a stupid thing to decorate the ceiling light bulb cover. Why wasn't there something more interesting there instead of wheat? What about a car or a cloud or the sun? It was the light shade in the ceiling, so a cloud or the sun would have made sense, kind of an apology from the room for blocking the sky from view.

And the other reason I didn't like the overhead light was because when it came on in a pitch-black room, you couldn't see right away. You'd think you'd be able to see everything when the light came on, but it was just the opposite. The Br'er Bear lamp wasn't as bright, but you could see immediately. It was perfect for getting up in the middle of the night.

The overhead remained on as Mama switched on Br'er Bear. I heard the click, but the ceiling light ate up the soft yellow glow. Mama came over and picked me up and set me on the ground by the bed. I bent my legs up to keep my feet from having to do their job, but Mama kept lowering me until my shins met the carpet. Mama always lifted me up again to encourage my legs to straighten, extend to the floor, wave me around as she would float a wet sheet in the wind before clipping it to the line. But not tonight. My knees met floor.

"Look at me…both of you," she said. "We have to take Grandaddy to the doctor. I need you two to be big boys and stay here."

"What's wrong with Grandaddy?" Adam wanted to know.

"Adam, you watch Philbet. Get up and put some clothes on."

Adam chased her into the hallway. "What's wrong?"

"I don't know, Love, but it'll be okay." Then she whispered something to Adam that I couldn't hear.

"Put this on, Philbet." And he put a shirt and pants on my bed.

Mama got on her knees. "Stay right here. Do. Not. Go. Outside. Only let MawMaw in. You hear me?"

"Yes, Mama," Adam said.

"Philbet, do you hear me?"

"Uh-huh."

"Do what Adam tells you to do."

"Lock the door until MawMaw gets here. She'll be here any minute." And Mama hugged us into her, stood up, and left.

Daddy, Mama, and Jorma drove off to the hospital with Grandaddy lying in the back seat.

Adam stood at the bedroom door and with a flip of his hand, Br'er Bear alone showed me the path from my bed to the hallway.

"C'mon," Adam said, soft as a night light.

I followed him down the hall and could feel the green of the carpet cooling my every step. Red or gold carpet wouldn't have been as cool or soft, I figured. Adam stood at the window. Mama's car was gone already, and the driveway was darker than it usually was at night because the chrome of her bumper and the windshield weren't there to catch the falling moonshine.

The house was quiet except for the soft sound of a whir from the heater vent. I knew what that sound was. One time, Adam opened the big air vent in the wall and told me to climb in. I did, and he shut the vent on top of me. Through the narrow vent cutouts I could see the green carpet and the chair covered in nubby tan fabric. All I could hear was the soft, scratchy, rhythmic tap of a sticker on the side of the vent flapping in the warm breeze of the heat. I heard the same sound now. It sounded like the tick and scratch of a record where the needle keeps circling, catching a groove every time the record makes a rotation. It said, "The song is over. Pick me up, and switch me off."

"Kneel down and pray." Adam's words broke through the tick from the heater vent.

I wanted to know where everyone was. "When are they comin' back?"

"Get down. We have to pray."

What else would an eight- and four-year-old do in the middle of the night when everyone else had left?

"MawMaw will be here in a minute," Adam reassured.

I went to the window to watch for her.

Adam began, "Dear Jesus, watch over Grandaddy and make him well. Bless Grandaddy, Jorma, Daddy, Mama—"

"I'm thirsty."

"Grandaddy's sick!" Adam burst out. "Pray with me, or he's gonna die."

I crouched down. "When will MawMaw be here?"

A car without its headlights on went down the highway. "Its lights ain't on," I said. But I could see it, touches of it, the pinpoint glint of the moon and Pick and Lolly's Gulf sign bouncing off the car's side mirror, its bumper. The reflection was weaker, duller than that off Mama's car, which was a constant and not a passer-through like this car already down the road and past the unincorporated town sign.

I can remember thinking those touches of light, the reflections, reminded me of lightning bugs, how they came and went just as quickly, and how I loved running around in the backyard to chase the lightning bugs just as it got dark at the end of those long summer days that lasted longer than any day does now. I was invisible, fearless running full out without thought or worry of the clothesline post or abandoned rakes in the grass. The slight chill of the dark along with the breeze that came from running back and forth the length of the backyard fence washed me with air so cool that it bathed my insides with strawberry Kool-Aid. The feeling was a triumph over the heat of the day. I felt night-kissed, and I told Mama so. "I don't need a bath, Mama! I love you, Mama! I love you, Mama! I caught you a lightnin' bug, Mama!"

Those nights were the reason mayonnaise jars existed. And lightning bugs battled to live in my jar. Those nights were the memories against which I'd measure the rest of my life, the lessons that taught me how happiness and love felt. I imagined myself invisible in the night, just like the lightning bugs, just like that come-and-gone car. So invisible that nothing bad could find me.

Adam held me for a minute, but it couldn't have been because I was upset. I wasn't. Adventures didn't upset me, not back then. Not yet.

Adam told me to be still. "It will be okay. MawMaw will be here soon. She'll make you a milkshake."

"I want a green one."

"I need to check on the animals and make sure they didn't get out… but I'll wait till MawMaw gets here."

"Don't go out there. Soap Sally'll get you." Thinking it was more funny than scary.

"We have to take care of things now. Nobody's here…it's up to us."

A blue Coronet pulled up, and MawMaw was there. When she came in, she pulled us both to her, so tall she had to bend in half to hug us. I liked her so much, almost as much as Grandaddy. Her lipstick was always on her front teeth like it was so tasty she couldn't just leave it on her lips, had to have some to taste. And her hair was flat on top because it always touched the ceiling of her Coronet. I was not allowed in the front seat when I rode with her, not like with Mama who had me stand in the seat next to her, held there against the seat behind her shoulder, protecting us. Adam used to stand behind her shoulder, but he rode in the back seat now.

He went outside to check on the animals. I wanted to give him a jar of lightning bugs to help him see out there, but I didn't have any.

"MawMaw, I'm thirsty," I said. "I want a milkshake. A green milkshake." For as long as memory served, green milkshakes were my favorite.

She led me to the kitchen, poured milk into a glass, added vanilla extract, put her hand on the top and shook it. A true milkshake—shaken milk. I went to the counter, pulled open the box of food coloring, and selected the yellow and blue. Two drops of each and a finger stir turned it green, my favorite color. No matter what, green milkshakes seemed to make everything better.

"Can I have a sandwich? Peanut butter jelly?"

She stared at me. "A what?"

"A peanut butter and jelly sandwich."

She looked at me like I was her schoolteacher and had just sprung one of those pop quizzes that Adam talks about from school, one she wasn't ready for. She picked up the phone and called Aunt Ease.

"I don't know what he wants." Handing me the phone, "Here, tell her what you want, and then she can tell me."

"Hello? Aunt Ease? I want a peanut butter and jelly sandwich." And after a moment, "Okay. She wants to talk to you."

I handed the phone back to MawMaw, and she went limp, dropped the receiver, and fell to the floor. It was like somebody just told her it was naptime, and she'd better get to sleep. What else could it be? That's all my four-year-old self could imagine.

"MawMaw, you want to get into bed?" She didn't answer me.

I picked up the phone and said, "Aunt Ease, MawMaw's gone to bed." And hung up with no further explanation.

Then I sat down next to her. "You want a pillow? You want some of my green milkshake? It'll make you feel better."

She didn't say anything. It was the middle of the night, so it made sense to me that she was asleep. I pulled our "African" off the arm of the sofa and covered her up. I get a little wistful now looking back on those early years lived in innocent isolation, not knowing, for example, that what we called "Africans" everybody else called "afghans." I wasn't sleepy, so I turned on the TV. One station was just shimmery, but the other one had a cartoon playing. I'd seen it before, but I watched anyway. It was an old cartoon, a hand-drawn one that was so crude the lines of the characters wiggled, unsteady as individual cell after cell flipped in rapid succession to create the illusion of movement. A bird, a caricature of a bird, tried to blow up a balloon. As soon as he blew air into it, the air forced its way back into him, the balloon deflating while he expanded and floated upward like a Thanks-giving Day parade float. The light from the screen reflected off MawMaw's legs that pointed out across the floor, straight toward the television screen. I could almost see the outline of the bird bounce off the tight sheen of her stockings.

Then MawMaw woke up abruptly just as Adam was coming back in. She rolled on her side and pushed herself up off the floor. She looked around the room, getting her bearings, and said at last, "Where's your mama?"

"What?" Adam asked.

But MawMaw didn't say anything.

"Mama's gone to the hospital with Daddy 'cause…'cause Grandaddy got sick," Adam said, trailing off like he wasn't sure if what he was saying was really so.

"I don't know. Maybe I need to go to the hospital myself," MawMaw said, sort of halfway between a question and a statement of fact, like she was looking at a piece of sweet potato pie and wondering if she should have it.

"You don't have to go, 'cause Mama and Daddy are there with Jorma and Grandaddy," I explained, but I thought she knew that already.

"MawMaw?" Adam walked toward her like Aunt Ease did that time we put a big rubber snake in her sewing chair. She didn't jump like most people would if they saw a snake. She kind of slowed down and walked around it, at a distance, trying to figure out if it was a real snake or a fake one. "MawMaw, are you sick too?"

## CHAPTER FOUR

# Tomato Sandwich Air

A few days later, MawMaw was in the hospital and Grandaddy was out, like they had switched places. And once he was home I wanted one of his pretend spankings, but he didn't spank me like he usually did. He seemed different. I couldn't puzzle out how, but just different. I wondered if part of him was still back at the hospital, if when he got up from the hospital bed a layer of him stuck to the sheets and stayed behind.

He called me Philbet when he came back, "Philbet, hey little man." And he hugged me into his leg, moving his arm so slowly, almost as if he stuck it in a big tub of pecans and stirred them around with his hand, studying my upturned face and looking at me the way he'd inspect the pecans—studying each shell for worm holes bored in through the dark brown husks.

He didn't even wink at me, and if I didn't know better, I could swear he didn't even know me. He didn't call me "Whoop" like he always did. That was his special name for me, the name he called me the first time he saw me every day, whether in the morning or late in the afternoon. The first time he'd see me, he'd say: "There's old Whoop. Come here, Whoop, you need a whoopin'!"

It was his and mine, not his and Adam's or his and anybody's. It was his and mine, and it never failed to make me laugh until it felt like all my breath had left me. First, he'd grab me, then pull me between his legs, bend me over one knee, and close the other knee on me, trapping me like the rickety turnstiles at the county fair. It was the safest feeling being caught there, not able to move, not wanting to ever be set free.

Then he'd spank me by slapping his thigh, big pops that sounded like he'd blown up paper bag after paper bag and popped each of them just as his flattened hand smacked his thick cotton work pants. Each pop had me wanting a full breath of air and squealing with giggles. It was ours, just ours. His and mine, and this was the first time I'd seen him after the hospital, and he didn't call me Whoop.

In some ways, this was the moment when the best part of my young life slipped away…the time before knowing life had an end.

The best feature of the garden was the center path, where no vegetables grew. Nothing grew there, not even a blade of grass. It was straight and narrow, as if Moses himself came to part the garden on his own, allowing us to cross to the other side. And the peddle car Santa Claus brought me tore that path up, a fire-engine-red peddle car that I loved as much as green lime sherbet. Mama said I peddled that car a million miles along that path between our house and Jorma and Grandaddy's big gabled house, wearing out that path between us. I'd park it, diagonally, like Mama parked her car in town, up against Jorma and Grandaddy's back steps, but they weren't exactly steps.

Daddy said Jorma and Grandaddy's back door used to be in a different place. I asked, "Daddy, who moved it? How'd they do it?"

"Me and Grandaddy and Uncle Rudy closed off the original back porch when they built onto the back side of the house." And then I could see it. The new living room jutted out into the backyard and underneath were steps. They started at ground level, just next to where I parked my peddle car, and went up about six steps, ending at the underflooring of the living room, looking just like the steps in a swimming pool that lead up to break the surface water at the shallow end. I knew because I opened my eyes under the water when we went swimming at the Callaway Community Pool down near where MawMaw lived.

Just like it was yesterday, I can hear Mama telling me to stop doing that because the chlorine would make me go blind, but Adam did it too and he was okay. Here, in the dark cool of what used to be the porch steps, I imagined Grandaddy's feet magically appearing from the living room through to the steps—just as though he was stepping into the pool. But all I really saw were spiderwebs and bugs.

Daddy was too big to climb up in there, but I could, up and around and past empty flowerpots, some of them filled with dirt but without life, as if they'd been there since the living room moved in on top of them, blocking the sun and rain, dooming their occupants to a dark, thirsty end. I could wedge myself up in between the last step and the flooring. I think it must have been just about right above me where Jorma's and Grandaddy's chairs sat, facing the television, Lawrence Welk or a baseball game playing.

Near their chairs there were two windows—the kind that separate the inside and outside of the house—inside the house, right there in the living room. They were wide open, with lace curtains between the living room and Jorma and Grandaddy's bedroom. Daddy said they used to be windows to the outside before they built onto the house.

There was always a candy dish on the table just inside the living room below the window. My favorite was the pink, white, and brown coconut squares. They were the same color and shape of the Neapolitan ice cream that Mama always bought at the store. It was really just strawberry, vanilla, and chocolate ice cream in stripes for people who couldn't make up their minds.

I liked to guess which color I'd get more of in my bowl, and I'd decide just before Mama set the bowl down in front of me. It was usually more of the brown chocolate when the container was new and more of the pink strawberry when the container was almost empty. Mama reckoned that was because she was right-handed and scooped from the brown chocolate side first, and then, as there was less and less ice cream, most of what was left was the pink strawberry from the left side. But she'd always buy a carton of green lime sherbet for me. I liked green so much, I had convinced myself that lime sherbet was my favorite flavor...but it wasn't. I liked it, but I liked the pink strawberry better. If strawberries were green, I reasoned, that'd be the best ice cream ever.

The television was always on at Jorma and Grandaddy's. I didn't like their shows much, but I loved being there in what I still describe as tomato sandwich air. The tomatoes didn't grow in the garden. They were out directly behind the house and next to the barn, and last summer, I had walked barefoot right by four big black snakes that had taken up under the concrete slab at the barn door. Jorma was yelling at me the whole time to look out and "come back here," but she was always hollering, so I didn't listen. Luckily they were garter snakes and probably more scared of me than I was of them.

None of us ever wore shoes in the summer, and that saved on shoe leather according to Mama, but it also made our soles tough as Grandaddy's hands. We could walk over anything. The only time I remember wearing shoes during the summer was after I stepped on the cigarette Miss Paula flicked behind her and just under my foot. Boy, that hurt.

When I recollect those summer afternoons and early evenings, they were never too hot, but all cool breezes and dewy grass next to the garden where Grandaddy had been watering. The shade of the pecan trees was like being in a room outside with only the breeze for walls. And we always had sweet tea and tomato sandwiches. I liked mine with mayonnaise and yellow tomatoes. Everybody else liked red tomatoes, and that must have been all right with Grandaddy because the yellow tomatoes were hard to grow. What the birds didn't eat, the bugs did. But I think Grandaddy used to go to the peach stand down the highway and get me yellow tomatoes because there were always yellow tomato sandwiches whether it was Saturday, Sunday, or any day. Most everyone else but me liked a little salt and pepper on their red tomato sandwiches, and Daddy liked onion on his too.

It was the most delicious, easy, comforting thing in the world to run around with half a sandwich in hand, stopping long enough at the TV trays set up in the backyard to gulp some sweet tea from one of Jorma's aluminum cups, the colors of the rainbow. I always got the green one; Adam, blue. Those afternoons were part of a calm that seemed to radiate up from the soft grass and dirt patches of backyard ground and the cool wooden floors of the house, as if there wasn't a problem or care anywhere near us. At least I didn't know of any.

And when the ground got too hot, Daddy would give in and pile us into the truck, and Adam and I took turns sitting in his lap "driving" our sky-blue Chevy C-10. At three, four, and five years old, it felt like I could do anything. At the time, I didn't pay attention to the fact that my 10:00 and 2:00 hand positions were shadowed by Daddy's hand at about 7:00, ensuring we didn't veer off into a ditch.

And when we arrived at our destination, the real fun began. Being about the smallest four-year-old ever, I fit perfectly on the steering wheel of the truck. This is how it worked. I'd climb up on the steering wheel like it was a miniature set of monkey bars. I'd wedge both knees into the steering wheel at about what Adam called 4:00 and 8:00. Then I'd hold on with my hands at about 11:00 and 1:00. If Adam were there, he'd grab the wheel at about the 3:00 position and give me a spin to get me going. The wheel would spin around and then spin clockwise and then counterclockwise, back and forth, like the tub in Jorma's new washing machine. It was better than a ride you'd find at the Meriwether County Fair if the Meriwether County Fair had rides. Instead, they just had crafts and funnel cakes. I did like the cakes, especially the way my mouth watered just by closing down on the powdered-sugar crust.

But the best part of Ridin' the Steerin' Wheel was when Adam wasn't there to spin me, and I had to rock back and forth to generate enough momentum to spin around on the wheel. I imagined I looked like a gear in Jorma's glass-fronted clock that sat on the table beside her TV chair. Mama said it was a clock for over the mantle, but nobody ever went in that room with the fireplace and the plastic covers on the furniture. Same seat covers as in MawMaw's blue Coronet. The little nubby dots on the plastic slipcover were fun to push down. They always sprang back. It was fun on par with popping Bubble Wrap.

Sunday afternoons were the best time, for me anyway. I wish I'd somehow sensed it, but the truth is I didn't have even an inkling of Mama's dread of the coming Monday morning when Jorma, her mother-in-law, would make her daily commute down the path between the garden rows and sit at the kitchen table. Jorma would watch Mama from the time it took to wash Grandaddy's two breakfast dishes to the time she reversed her journey to start making Grandaddy's dinner…a roughly six-hour visit.

"Georgia *Mae*, but Georgia won't, can't, refuses to, dudn't want to give me one minute's peace," I heard Mama say into the telephone one day.

# CHAPTER FIVE

# The Beau Tree

Roman Meal bread came in a translucent orange sleeve, and it cost more than the white bread we ate the whole time I was living at home. It fascinated me, looking exotic compared to the day-old Sunbeam white bread we got at the Colonial on the days we visited MawMaw in Warm Springs. Grocery shopping was Mama's excuse to get in her black 1960 Ford Galaxie 500 and head twenty-five miles south to Warm Springs. Mama was wonderfully vague when Jorma asked when she planned her next trip. Mama changed her game plan following Jorma's sudden appearance early that morning as we headed to Warm Springs.

"I don't know. I need to make a list of what we need. Can I get you anything?" Mama was a strategic thinker.

And then Mama, Adam, and I would be in the car at dawn the next morning. When Jorma appeared at the back door two minutes after we returned, Mama would walk right by her with two brown paper bags of food and say without stopping, "You know, I stood there in the kitchen last night and realized I was out of everything."

I really stared at the Roman Meal bread there in the one aisle of Pick and Lolly's the first day I spotted it, taking it in. Lolly came up next to me with her cigarette between her pointing and middle finger. Her hand was down in front of her leg and held in the manner you would approach a wary dog—presenting the back of the hand forward. Sometimes she'd lazily sling the other hand across her waist, tucked under the elbow of her smoking arm, hand splayed wide as if she was getting ready to pick your pocket.

She said, "Whatcha lookin' at, Philbet?"

I pointed to the bread, "It looks different."

"That's Roman Meal. It's for people who are dyin'."

I thought she said "dyin'" anyway. I never saw anyone buy it, and there was always plenty on the shelf.

"It tastes pretty good," she said. "Makes a real good tomato sandwich. Holds up to mayonnaise pretty good too."

Lolly had black hair that looked like she left the curlers in and put hairspray right directly on top of those curlers. There weren't curlers in it, but not one hair strayed from her shiny helmet. And she had a gravelly voice, kind of like she swallowed some sand from the sandbox in our backyard. I can't remember much about Lolly beyond that. I can't see her face in my memories partly because she was gone so soon.

You see, Lolly was putting gasoline in an old lady's car one day. Lots of cars had the gas cap right there in the smack middle of the back of the car behind the tag. And the lady backed right over the top of Lolly while she was putting gas in the car. Just like that. I mean, I didn't see it happen, but when Adam told me, I tried to picture Lolly up under a car. Was she completely under the car like ol' Luke was when he crawled under there to get some shade on a hot day? Was she half under like Daddy was, his legs sticking out from under when he was undoing the oil cap? Was the tire on top of Lolly? Did she just get her head bumped and sort of go to sleep? Adam loved breaking the news, but he was short on details.

Up to that point I'd never heard about somebody not going to the hospital to die. I didn't know you could do that. I thought you could only die in a hospital. But Mama said Lolly died right there at the gas pump. I remember having to rethink the whole death thing. I knew you didn't have to be in a hospital to be born; Adam told me the iron bed in the barn was the bed Daddy was born in. He was born in that bed up in Jorma and Grandaddy's house before they built out the room on top of the back steps.

I don't know what happened to the mattress, but the head and foot board were stacked against the barn wall with Grandaddy's ropes and cords tied to them.

Every time I saw Roman Meal bread after that, I thought of Lolly, and I wondered why she'd been eating that bread. If she knew it killed you, why would she eat it? She could have had the regular white bread we always ate. She didn't even have to pay for it, I bet, because she already owned everything in the store.

After Lolly died, nobody called Pick and Lolly's "Pick and Lolly's" anymore. It was just "Pick's" or the "fillin' station." But other than Lolly not being there and the different name people used, nothing else changed much. The bookmobile still pulled up in the paved parking area every Wednesday morning.

And boy, did I love the bookmobile. It smelled of syrup in there among the shelves, the kind of syrup that we used on birthday mornings and came in a bottle shaped like a lady. And it smelled like a Christmas tree, my chin involuntarily lifting to catch a breath of cedar that hung in the air alongside the syrup at a point just above my head. I imagined the cedar bushes just across the road that Grandaddy planted when Adam and I were born—the larger one from when Adam was born, the smaller one for me. I loved taking *Curious George* back to my room, opening it to the first page, putting my nose to the place where the first page was stitched in, and taking a big sniff. Syrup and cedar always met me and made me think of visits to the bookmobile at breakfast time during the two weeks Adam didn't have to go to school at Christmas break. While Mama and I read the books, the syrup and cedar faded, but if I went off to do something like take my bath, the smell was there again as soon as I entered the room.

One Wednesday morning, the bookmobile wasn't in its usual spot. It was farther down Pick's paved lot, off to the side near the place you put air in your tires. In its usual spot was a big flatbed truck with a purple 1969 LTD with a black vinyl top on the back of it.

Pick wasn't there as much after Lolly died, but when he was around he wore a dark blue hat like the one you see on French men, and he always had on dark blue pants and a short-sleeve white shirt with galluses. Everybody except Pick and Aunt Ease called them suspenders, and Pick and Aunt Ease didn't even know each other because she lived twenty-five minutes away in Warm Springs seeing as how she was Mama's sister, not Daddy's sister. She might have bought gas there when she came up to visit, but I don't think she and Pick talked about galluses.

Well, that purple LTD was wrecked on the front end. If you had looked at it head on, you probably couldn't tell it was purple, but the back end was as perfect as the day it was delivered from the factory. Pick said the man who drove it was a thirty-five-year-old businessman from Atlanta, but he didn't know if he was hurt or not. The flatbed driver was transferring the car south for insurance reasons, he said. To my child eyes, that car looked about twenty feet off the ground up on that truck.

Pick and Lolly's son Beau walked out, and he didn't seem too interested. It was just a thing. Pick and Beau were tired of cars, maybe even tired of life since Lolly was gone. I didn't see Beau ever shining his Cougar anymore. They stood there looking like their picture in the newspaper a few weeks earlier, the one of Beau standing next to Pick outside the store. I remember when the newspaper man took the picture. I just happened to catch it when I was standing at the side door staring at Beau's Cougar.

Mama helped me cut out the newspaper article that talked about Beau enlisting in the Army to head off to Vietnam. But I only kept the picture and threw away the article because the picture showed me all I needed to know, and I couldn't read yet anyway. Pick wasn't smiling or wearing his French hat in the picture. Instead, the hat peeked out from between where Pick's hand mashed into Beau's shoulder, holding Beau next to him. Beau was smiling, but almost like Pick was squeezing him too hard. And tall as Pick was, Beau was taller by a head. Pick always looked so tall, but I think he might have shrunk since Lolly died.

I can remember Daddy telling me Beau would get killed over there, and I didn't understand why Beau wanted to go all the way over there to Vietnam if somebody was just going to kill him. I figured he didn't know somebody was going to kill him, but I didn't want to say anything in front of Pick.

So I followed Beau back into the store, and I told him, "Beau, don't go over there. Daddy said somebody over there is gonna kill you."

He didn't say anything; he just looked at me with a blank stare.

"Do you know who? Who wants to try to kill you?"

Beau stood stock still, and his mouth was open a little like I said it was snowing outside, but it was really a hundred degrees, and he was trying to decide if he heard me right.

"I figured you didn't know."

He stared.

I continued, "So, I made this for you," handing him my drawing of Beau surrounded by pine trees and then holding up another, identical drawing. "And this for me. As long as you have yours and I have mine, that person over there cain't kill you."

He got down on his knees and looked right into my face with that same stare. Then he slowly pulled me to him and gave me a big hug. He must have gotten tired of holding his breath because I felt one big exhale blow by my ear. And I thought he'd crack my ribs he hugged me so tight. I guess this is how he felt when Pick squeezed him in the newspaper photograph.

Then Beau stood up, smiling like he didn't really want to smile. He was a big ol' tree with legs bigger around than I was, and they were brown and rough and looked just like pine bark. He always wore flip flops, and the top of his feet spread out like the part of tree roots that radiate from the trunk before going underground.

"And I'll say your name every night when I say my prayers," I added.

Even his arms looked like tree limbs, and his chest under his tank top was textured—not smooth, something you could grab onto and get a foothold to climb up. I felt small next to him, but small in a good way, just like you feel standing under a big tree when it rains.

"And don't eat Roman Meal bread, whatever you do."

"Don't you worry, Philbet. I'll come back. Alive."

And I believed him. He wouldn't lie to me. I didn't think Daddy would lie either, so Daddy must have heard wrong.

He took a bubble gum cigar off the shelf, a green one.

"Open up, mister." And he held it out for me to chomp.

The cigar had a powdery coat that made my fingers feel and taste like sweet chalk sticks. One good lick, and they were back to the fingers I knew. But the sticky, sweet was still there, dried in the small creases in the pads of my hand, there until supper.

Beau took one, too, and bit it in half.

"First one to blow a bubble wins."

Yep, Beau was steady, just like a big tree. I wanted to reach out with my sticky hands and hug him, like when you press yourself into an old pine just to soak up the sun that's warmed it all day. If I could have figured out how to do it, I would have climbed in like he had a hollowed-out part and nestled inside protected, peeking out like a little brown owl.

## CHAPTER SIX

# MawMaw and Jorma

When I looked out the window of Mama's Galaxie 500 on the way from Alvaton to Warm Springs, I was trying to see if the sun that fed Grandaddy's garden was the same sun that lit the pine thickets that hugged MawMaw's house.

"Mama, is that the same sun we got in Alvaton?"

"Yes, Sweetheart. There's only the one."

"Hmm," I said because that's what Grandaddy said sometimes when he was thinking.

Grandaddy's garden and our cinder block house stood in the direct sunlight all day long, while MawMaw's house down in Warm Springs was shady and cooled by the pine trees. But as I think back, Mama looked brighter under the Warm Springs pines than she ever did in Alvaton with nothing but the breeze between her and the sun.

Mama, Adam, and I were getting into the Galaxie to head down the highway on one of Mama's Warm Springs escapes when Jorma appeared, and then I understood.

"I thought I'd come and go with you to the Colonial."

Silence.

Then Jorma said, "Need bread."

"Oh, Jorma, they got bread at Pick's," I said, thinking Jorma had forgotten. I didn't want her to wait all day to get her bread home.

Jorma and Mama looked at each other, and the point of Jorma's elbow rested against her hip while her stubby forearm bent upward and off to the side with her tight fist plopped right at the end. Her pocketbook hung in the crook of her elbow, still as a leaf on a tree in the windless heat of July. Mama's right foot was up and on the floorboard of the Galaxie, and her car keys stuck out of her hand. In a game of rock, paper, scissors, Mama's keys were surely more powerful than the rock of Jorma's fist.

Mama was just tall enough so that the window frame of the door floated between them, blocking Mama's mouth from Jorma's view. Mama said something softly, and Jorma either heard it clearly or decided it was a "Get in" because that's what Jorma did.

"Good try," Mama said to me as her soft hand on my back lightly nudged me away from the front and into the back seat. "You and Adam both ride back here today."

MawMaw and Jorma were my models growing up for how family matriarchs behave, and they couldn't have been more different. They had only two things in common as far as I could tell back then. MawMaw was Mama's mama, and Jorma was Daddy's mama, and of the four of them, only Mama and MawMaw seemed to even like each other. The other thing was, I never saw either MawMaw or Jorma wear a pair of pants, only dresses.

As I think back, Jorma was the celluloid negative to MawMaw's bright, color photograph. Jorma was short, round, and always in a small-print, faded cotton dress with a faux leather belt that was sun-damaged crackly, the underlying plastic showing through the broken surface of the leather grain. She usually had a Kleenex, a peppermint, and toothpicks held together with a rubber band stuffed in the left sleeve of the sweater of the day, which she had crocheted herself. The one she wore most often was exactly the same color as my crayon called "flesh," but it wasn't the color of everybody's skin. Daddy's arms looked more like the crayon called "copper," especially if he came in all hot from the sun. Some days the Kleenex and peppermint would remain stuffed in her sleeve all day, but you could bet money Jorma'd suck on her teeth for an hour straight after every meal, pulling out one of those toothpicks like it was dessert.

In contrast, MawMaw was very tall and all awkward angles in her bold, solid-colored housecoats, unruly hair, and apple cheeks that framed a broad mouth full of teeth. She was sweet and warm and always hugged us with words and kisses that made me think she wanted to squeeze us in half with love, but the squeeze wasn't that tight, as if she didn't have the strength in her body to match the strength of her love. She seemed like a feather caught on the edge of a tree limb. You could reach for it, climb up to it, but you knew that a breeze was just about to catch it and blow it away before you could get to it.

I always wished my grandmothers had liked each other more. If they had, maybe Mama and Daddy would have liked each other too. It was hard to imagine MawMaw and Jorma in the same room together, but they were. I remember a visit down to Warm Springs in particular. An audio cassette recorder for me and a Polaroid camera for Adam arrived on the same Christmas Day in time to document the event. The cassette recorder was the size and shape of a cigar box with a red plastic button the only color in what was otherwise black and feathery silver plastic. Adam's very first picture from the Polaroid was soft-edged in the way a painting suggests images instead of recording them exactly, and in it I hold up the recorder to Jorma and MawMaw to capture what they said to each other. The grainy image brings to mind the seam of where the soft grass of the yard meets the hard and cracked edge of the sidewalk, and their voices on the cassette confirm it.

Jorma's voice scratched my eardrum like the grate of chalked slate against chalked slate. MawMaw sounded like she was forever sucking on a butterscotch candy, as if she hesitated before speaking and was afraid her candy would jump out of her mouth if she spoke too quickly.

"MawMaw and Jorma, say som'um in the recorder."

"Get that thing away from me," Jorma snapped back, and at the same time MawMaw said, "Oh, fun," but so softly that I didn't hear it until I played the cassette recording back later. It sounded like "orphan" instead of "oh, fun," but I knew what she meant.

MawMaw never seemed to make a move that had any intention behind it. I remember her standing in the kitchen, but not cooking, not really standing either. She half-leaned against the counter. There were chairs in the house, but she never sat in them or in the front porch metal chairs with the backs that looked like a seashell. In contrast, Jorma was strong of body, maybe strong of heart, the one that pumped her blood. But her feeling heart…well, it just seemed like she kept it in the pie safe next to her peach hand pies, not too hot, not too cold, but spoonfuls short of sugar. Kept it so cold it didn't pump out love like MawMaw's did. All growing up, I heard people say Jorma was mean, but it wasn't that. She wasn't mean. She never hit us. She just kind of ignored us. And when we accidentally crossed her field of vision and locked eyes with her, she looked at us like we'd stepped in dog doo and tracked it inside.

And then she'd do something that on the surface seemed warm and grandmotherly. Jorma baked, but she didn't go to the trouble of telling you she made the pie for you—at least she didn't walk up to you and tell you. She didn't walk in from the kitchen wiping her flour-caked hands on her apron, declaring with a smile, "Peach hand pies for anybody who wants one!" Nope, the pies were just there in the pie safe, every bite as bitter as a raw lemon. Her peach hand pie crusts bore the markings of her weapon of choice, a fork. Oozy peaches ripped too soon from the tree bled from the fork-crimped, charred edges.

Even her sweet tea was bitter, a result, according to Mama, of boiling the water in an aluminum pot, of drinking it from aluminum cups, and stirring in sugar when the tea was too cool. And Mama said one time, when she didn't know I could hear, "She prob'ly spits in the sweet tea to save on the water bill."

## CHAPTER SEVEN

# A Car for Everyone I Ever Loved

"Mama, can I have cinnamon toast and a milkshake?"

Cinnamon toast was my favorite, but it took more time to make than regular toast because Mama had to put four pats of butter on each corner of the bread. And if the butter was too cold, the bread ripped. Mama always took the butter out of the refrigerator first thing on cinnamon toast mornings. Then she'd sprinkle the buttered bread with a mixture of cinnamon and sugar. One time, she bought cinnamon and sugar from the store already mixed, but that was expensive, so from then on she mixed her own and kept it in the container the store-bought stuff came in. But she had been out of her homemade mixture all weekend, and she was short on time trying to get us in the car and off to Warm Springs before Jorma made her usual Monday morning appearance at the kitchen door.

On some level, deep down inside, even as a little kid I sensed my parents' marriage was an unhappy pairing. I clung to anything that seemed to hold things together. I decided that Mama and Daddy liked each other better for a few days if we had cinnamon toast on Sunday before church. If we didn't have cinnamon toast before church, they didn't get along as well all week long. I thought that if we had cinnamon toast that morning, then it might not be too late for us to have a good week. I didn't have to have cinnamon toast for myself, I just wanted to help Mama and Daddy and Adam and me like each other more. But Mama scolded me for always wanting special things that take too much time.

After we left and got to MawMaw's, I saw the sugar bowl and some toast on the counter. When everyone went to the other room, I climbed up on the counter by opening the cabinet door and stepping up on the shelves, then put one foot in the pulled-out drawer like I was a mountain climber. I stuck a finger in the butter, then in the sugar bowl, and poured cinnamon from the spice drawer over my finger. I stuck that in my mouth and took a bite out of the toast. Now at least I'd had some cinnamon toast and everything would be okay. But when I stepped into the drawer to get down, the drawer slid off its track, sending forks, knives, and spoons to the floor with a sharp, tinny crash.

Mama ran in, MawMaw just steps behind her, and yelled at me to get down. It was one of only four times Mama ever spanked me. Just the memory still stings today. And it was no pretend spanking. Afterward I was humiliated and ran outside the house in the shadow of the snake bushes and just waited there until it was time to go home. I hated disappointing Mama and making things worse than they were.

I was still embarrassed when we got home that night, so I walked up the garden path instead of peddling my car. Walking just felt right. When I got to Grandaddy's he was working on his white Galaxie 500. He must have known I was blue because Grandaddy had an open Coca-Cola on the ground beside the car and the Coca-Cola crate next to him just ready for me to climb up. That car seemed gigantic to me with its distinctive fins. Nineteen-sixty was the transition year when those '50s-era boat-like cars with aeronautic fins turned into more streamlined silhouettes—still with those fins that looked to me like they had the power to flap on their own and lift that Galaxie 500 aloft. The little half-moon-on-their side taillights looked like Grandaddy's eyes did when I called up to him and he squinted over his wire-rimmed frames, a little like Santa Claus if you looked at him real close up.

I think this is why I loved cars so much. They made me feel closer to Grandaddy. And if I could, I imagined I'd have a big garage and in it a car that reminds me of every person I ever loved, starting with a 1960 Ford

Galaxie 500. I'd paint one half black and one half white to remind me of Grandaddy and Mama. But I'd only have one Galaxie, 'cause having two seems greedy.

Grandaddy brought me bubble gum cards that had pictures of cars on them, Detroit's version of baseball cards. There were classic cars and race cars and even a Model T. My favorites were cards with custom cars. A 1947 Ford painted green with yellow and orange flames erupting from the hood down the side of the doors. A deep purple 1957 Cadillac convertible that belonged to Elvis. The card description said Elvis bought it off the lot white, but he took a handful of grapes, squeezed them on the hood and said, "Paint it that color."

Grandaddy also bought candy cigarettes, especially the paper-wrapped kind that provided one good puff of powdery sugar. After that, it was just a thin, round cylinder of gum. There were also hard sugar sticks approximating the size and shape of a cigarette with a red-food-color-stained tip, as if any cigarette you ever saw burned cherry red. I was not yet five, and even I knew cigarettes were either orange or silvery black on the lit end. And these sugary sticks stuck in your teeth when you chewed them. It didn't strike any of us that they were a clever marketing ploy to get young people to start smoking. To me, at least, they were simply Grandaddy candy—a way to share something with him.

As I think about it, Grandaddy was more concerned with getting me through childhood than he was about encouraging smoking. And with his health beginning to fail, he must have felt the pressure of limited time. Sometimes when I am quiet and just sit, it washes over me how he worried and fretted about me…about all of us.

But my brother Adam was the least of his worries. Adam was most like Grandaddy—happy, confident, and with more common sense than anyone needed. He could work out the solution to a problem before I'd fully grasped the problem itself. And he could build anything. Adam truly lived in the moment, fretting about nothing that he couldn't do something about.

He popped his friend, Cade, in the mouth with his fist when Cade called me *girly* one day. They didn't hang out for a while after that, but they were friends again before too long. I didn't care about what Cade thought anyway. If I couldn't hang out with Adam and Cade, I'd always be able to go see Grandaddy, like this day that had started off so bad in MawMaw's kitchen. But when Daddy got home, Mama didn't tell him about me climbing on MawMaw's kitchen counter, and we had pork chops for supper. And Mama and Daddy didn't fight that week, so I was glad I did it.

## CHAPTER EIGHT

# A Perfect Comeback

Before I started school, summers seemed to last a lifetime. No schedule, no place to be. Actually, the summers were just like the rest of the year for me, but since I didn't have a schedule or have to go to school yet, Adam's schedule was my schedule. And when he got all excited and came home with end-of-year celebratory cupcakes and the papers he had squirreled away in his desk all year, it was time to go swimming and eat dipped ice cream from the drugstore counter and go down to Warm Springs a lot to see all of the cousins on Mama's side of the family.

Adam and I liked to play Guess What Kind, a favorite when Mama went to get her hair fixed, and she let us sit in the car instead of going inside. Well, first we'd go in with her, get a Coke and M&Ms and go back out to the car. One of us would sit with our back to the open window and listen for cars coming down the road and guess what kind of car it was based on the sound coming from the engine. A GM sounded different from a Ford, which was more sewing machine-like than the GM. The GMs were solid sounding, but when their transmissions had a lot of miles on them, they sounded like somebody had a hammer chipping away at a cinder block. When that transmission went, it was like somebody had dropped the cinder block into a spinning clothes dryer.

At first, Adam was the master of Guess What Kind, but I eventually got so good I could beat him. The first time I won, he really should have, because the car was one neither of us had seen before. It said, "Volvo" on the back, and Adam guessed "Ford," since it sounded more like a sewing machine than a sewing machine. It was the funniest looking thing. It pulled up next to us, and this man got out and went into the hair salon. He was as odd looking as the car. He had hair that was two colors. Black from his scalp to almost the end of each strand, with just white on the ends, like somebody had dipped every single black hair on his head in white paint.

The seats in his car had what looked like ladders on the back of them, right behind where your head would be if you sat in the seat. And the seats were this brick-red color that looked odd with the yellow paint. There was only one other yellow car in the whole county as far as I had seen, and that was Uncle Kingston's Ford F-100, which was more the color of white corn. But this car was like one of the butterscotch candies from Jorma's candy dish. It was like a school bus sideswiped it and got yellow paint all over it. It was uglier than a Ford Falcon, and that's pretty ugly if you ask me.

"He's funny," Adam said.

"Yeah, his hair is weird," I agreed. I didn't see him do anything funny, but he did have hair I'd never seen on another living soul. Anyway, I was more interested in his car than him.

What was this Volvo? I'd never heard of such. It was a four-door station wagon, but it looked smaller than the station wagons I knew. And it had two license plates. One was the regular Georgia tag, white with blue letters and numbers, but the other underneath it was longer and thinner, like the tag was made of biscuit dough and someone just stretched it out. I was intrigued. I'd never considered that there were brands of cars I had never seen. What else was out there? Were they as odd looking as this one?

"Adam, where'd he come from?" I'd already decided that this yellow box of a car was a boy.

"He's Miss Laura's son. He's a hairdresser from Atlanta."

I was talking about the car, but I didn't say "I meant the car." Instead, I imagined the man who had just run inside standing at the row of beauty parlor chairs, his hands in rubber gloves putting ladies' hair in curlers. I couldn't figure it out. In my little world, a man who cut hair was a barber and wore a white jacket with pockets to hold his comb and scissors and lollypops if you were good and didn't squirm too much.

"He's a pillow biter," Adam explained.

He was a beautician instead of a barber, and he bit pillows. I didn't know why someone would want to bite pillows. But I didn't know why Scotty Pickler ate paper either. I guess he liked the taste of it. Daddy liked to eat gizzards in his rice, but I thought they were gross. Adam said gizzards were for grounding up rocks that the chicken ate, and I thought chickens must be the stupidest animal ever if they ate rocks. But Daddy liked Red Man chewing tobacco, and that was really gross. He'd snort and chew it and spit it on the ground or in a cup he kept in the truck or by his TV chair.

Then Mama came out with her hair less high than usual, and we left.

"Mama, you don't look finished," I said.

"I'm as finished as I'm gonna get today, Sweetie Pie."

Mama's driver-side door was still a new sound to me, more of a rubber mallet if you smashed it on a tree trunk instead of an empty coffeepot slapped down on the back of the doorstep, which is how the Galaxie's door sounded. Mama and Daddy had traded in our black Galaxie 500 for a chocolate-brown 1969 Pontiac Catalina just the week before. The Catalina was a girl because it came with a name tag in the form of a blue and white license plate with MAW-444 stamped on it. MAW had flecks of gold in her brown skin that made her sparkle in the sunshine. She had belonged to Walton Talley, but Walton didn't pay the bills on her, so Mabie Motors took her back and sold her to Mama and Daddy. I loved her because she was like a living room on wheels.

The right back seat was my spot, and the left back seat was Adam's. The backs of the front seats had lines that ran up and down in the design of beadboard. I knew it immediately because beadboard was in Jorma and Grandaddy's bathroom. They also had a clawfoot tub that looked like somebody had chopped off a lion's feet, painted them white, and stuck them on the bottom of the tub. And the tub had the metal showing through right where you'd put your hands on the side to help stand up after your bath. Jorma always had soap in there that was either pink, blue, yellow, or green, but Aunt Pinky brought her some soap from Florida that was brown. It looked dirty, which didn't make a lot of sense for a bar of soap to look dirty when it was supposed to make you clean. Jorma must have thought so, too, because she never used it. That soap sat in a dish on a shelf for as long as I'd been going in there. Well, that brown soap was the exact color of Mama's repossessed Catalina.

The change was just fine with me because the Catalina had air conditioning and head rests on the back of the front seats. Mama hung this little trash can around the back of the headrest so that it dangled off the back seat in front of me. This way, if I was eating candy, I could put the wrapper right into the trash can, which was a good thing since I liked candy, and Mama said I was vice president in charge of keeping the car clean. One time I even had to throw up after I took some awful medicine called Tedral that Mama said would taste like licorice candy. The only problem is I hated licorice. But Mama didn't even have to stop because I threw up right in that trash can.

The weekly trips down to Warm Springs were always fun, and I enjoyed seeing familiar landmarks along the way. First there was Bit's peach stand, which went by out of the left window before the car even had a chance to warm up or change into a higher gear. That's where they had yellow tomatoes in season. Next, came the big cow pasture that doubled for a parking lot when the Meriwether County Fair was going on once a year. Then it was a boring patch with the same trees after the same trees. Finally, we turned off to a curvy gravel road that took us to MawMaw's as though we crawled through a pine thicket just off the highway and climbed out the other side to a soft, cool, secret opening. But every rotation of the new Catalina's wheels made the familiar twenty-five-minute journey an epic event.

Sometimes Mama'd leave us there for a few days. When we stayed with MawMaw, we'd only come inside after it was pitch black.

"You have to stay out after dark or else you cain't see the fireflies," we reasoned with her.

And then mosquito-bumped and thirsty, Kool-Aid-thirsty, we'd finally respond to her twentieth call, her version of the metal triangle dinner bell,

"Adam? Philbet? Y'all come on in now, okay?" Asking, not telling us, her voice half breath and half hollow, like a rotted-out tree stump that just needed one good stomp to crush it.

She was sick, but we didn't know it. Mama must have thought we'd make her happy. "Y'all be good to her." "Help her out." "Don't make a mess, and if you do, clean up after yourself."

If she'd told us MawMaw was sick, I bet we wouldn't have even gone outside to play. I wouldn't have, and Adam was even better than I was, so I know he would have stayed there and watched television or helped her shell peas or stir the oatmeal. Oatmeal would stick really fast, and I always stood in a chair at home and stirred for Mama so she could do other things and not be tied to the stove.

The most specific direction we got was to "Use one bath. Philbet, you get in first and when you're done, Adam, you get in. Don't waste water on two baths. And wipe out the tub with your towel when you're done. Use one towel between you." That was it. "And hang up the towel so it's dry in the mornin'."

One day, Adam and my cousins were talking about who was going to marry whom when we all grew up. Adam, already very popular with girls interested in him both here in Warm Springs and back home at his school, was a catch. Nobody could argue his appeal, rich as J. Paul Getty if ease and good looks were the currency of the realm.

He coolly, comfortably soaked in the attention, the transition from little boy to slightly older little boy effortless, as if a coach just out of sight whispered instructions in his ear. It didn't hurt that he was "all boy," as Mama and Daddy called him, and everybody liked him. Jeb, our cousin, the same age as Adam and across-the-road-neighbor to MawMaw, was less so and without Adam's smooth, tan skin and tousled hair or that easy way of navigating through life. Jeb's gift was being happily unaware of it.

One summer day cousins Greer and Robin were in the yard, barefoot and taking in the pine shade. Who would pair up with whom? When the speculation turned my way, I was embarrassed by talk of Carleen and me as a couple. She was from down the road and Greer's best friend. And I had no interest. None.

"Maybe you'll marry Carleen!"

"She a good kisser?" I asked, without knowing what else to say.

"Touch her boobies," Jeb said.

"She your girlfriend?"

"Why don't you have a girlfriend, Philbet?" Robin asked.

In my defense, I was at the age when boys typically don't like girls, but I didn't know that. All I knew was I had to defend myself and not let them commit me to any alliance with Carleen. I mean, she was okay, but she was a girl.

"You're gonna marry her!" Greer shouted.

I thought I had the answer to shut them down completely. The perfect comeback. I mean, it could never happen, but I just knew I had won the argument before I even opened my mouth.

"No, I'm not gonna marry her. I'm gonna marry a boy!"

I still remember the silence, raised eyebrows, and opened, slack mouths all the way around for about five seconds. And then the loudest screams and laughs I had ever heard. I didn't exactly know what I had said that was so wrong or funny even, but I knew it was bad, something that wouldn't go away for the rest of the summer. I tried to rethink my logic up to the point of blurting it out, but I was overcome by confusion and maybe even subconscious shame. But I had to say something.

"Well I didn't mean it! I know I can't marry a man," I practically yelled out.

They laughed again, and it was torture.

I looked at Adam, and he said, "Okay, leave him alone. You know he was trying to make a joke," saving me, I hoped.

Then he added, probably because Jeb was such a "mean little shit" as Adam called him, "If somebody was gonna make me marry Carleen, I'd marry a man too."

"Yeah, you dumbasses," I turned on my heels and stalked off.

Adam followed me after a few minutes, "You can't say stuff like that."

"But you say 'dumbass' all the time."

"No, that thing about marryin' a man," he explained.

"But you can't marry a man. I was joking. It's just that I don't like Carleen."

"Just don't say stuff like that," and he was off down the driveway, tossing a rock in that mud puddle at the curve. It was the best mud puddle, just the right, soft dip to ride through with your bike. Didn't have any rocks in it, and it held water like a lake for at least a day after rain since the clay was so dry and hard-packed.

I was a little kid. I didn't know what "stuff like that" was.

Mama said boys my age didn't *have* to like girls. I didn't know why Adam and Jeb didn't know that. Then I heard them coming, Jeb and Greer and Robin. I ran ahead across the road to MawMaw's and slipped into the snake bush just next to the front door before they rounded the driveway. They walked by just feet away and were headed to the front door, talking about me. "Little weirdo." "He's a funny little shit." "Daddy said he's a mama's boy."

I almost jumped out to remind them that Jeb ate Boone's medicine from the vet, and just last summer wet his bed. I heard MawMaw tell Mama when they didn't know I was around. When they went inside, I crawled out of the bush and crouched down low enough to climb under the windows so they couldn't see me if they looked out. When I got to the other end of the house, I darted between the cars and down into the ditch and back across the road to Jeb's house.

The chain-link gate was never closed because Veralynn ran into it with Uncle Kingston's new 1969 yellow Ford pickup when it was a week old and had forty-nine miles on it. I know, because Uncle Kingston said words worse than dammit and hell. The gash on the side of the truck turned from a bright tin-gray color to a dark, jagged line that turned the color of a bloody scab within two months. But you could barely notice it because that truck always had a clumpy spray of red mud blown back up on its side, as if Uncle Kingston kept it dirty just to hide the evidence from the run-in with the chain-link fence.

When I got to the fence, I saw my next hiding place, Jeb's tree house. It was all old, rotted boards nailed to three scraggly pine trees next to Boone's pen, no grass, weeds, or even pine needles anywhere to be seen. Nothing seemed to grow back in that corner of the yard, and nobody seemed to care. Cast-off planks nailed to the tree trunks made do as a ladder to the treehouse, which was only a platform that you could see through like the rusted-out running board of Uncle Harp's Jeep. Mama told me to stay out from up there, but I didn't want to be with them the rest of the day. I was mad at them.

# CHAPTER NINE

# Measure Twice

"Jeb's treehouse is crap," Adam muttered.

And it was. Adam wouldn't even go up there.

"I ain't gonna break my leg fallin' through. It's rottin'."

"Rotting" was one of those perfect Southern words. Adam loved it and used it often. I think he liked it mostly because it gave him an excuse to drop the final "g." But a good Southerner didn't need an excuse. Those Gs, the last letters at the end of "-ing" words, were an effort too far—energy we could put into doing something else.

"Rottin'" and "rotten" were pronounced the same, only distinguished from each other by context. When Adam said the treehouse was rottin', he meant it as condemnation, as much as a statement that the boards were in decay. A rottin' treehouse wouldn't be allowed in our family, the way I figured it. Grandaddy or Adam would rip up rotten boards and replace them. Even if there wasn't money for new boards, they'd find some somewhere.

But there was no treehouse in our backyard, not even a rottin' one. Jeb at least had a treehouse, crappy as it was. And it hid me that day I wanted to escape from everyone and the embarrassment of having said I'd marry a man one day. Rotten or rottin', those boards held me and protected me and nobody bothered me there the rest of the day.

Adam had a fort in the top of the barn, out behind the cinder block house in Alvaton. The steps up into it weren't like stairs you find at the courthouse. The only building I knew that had a second story was the courthouse. Nobody in the family had a house with a second story, but if somebody did have a house with a second story, I bet they'd look a lot like the courthouse steps, which had smooth little dips worn into the granite from all the years of people walking up and down them.

But that dip was so smooth, it looked like it would hold a pool of water better than any mud puddle. I imagined gliding down the steps on my bike, feeling the perfect indentations while spraying water out beside and behind me. I didn't know that stone as hard as granite could rot just like wood did. And that wearing away of the steps was a rottin' of some kind, else it wouldn't wear away like that. Nothing lasted forever—not wood, not stone, not a lot of things.

The steps up to Adam's barn-top hut were wood, and they were more a ladder than courthouse or house steps. And that ladder climbed up the outside of the barn. I was scared to climb them because they looked so far up, and you had to step off the ladder at the top and into an opening. Just thinking about it made my stomach feel wiggly like Jell-O. Adam didn't care. I even think he liked that I didn't come up. It gave him some time alone, a place of his own. It must have reminded him that I hadn't caught him yet, and I never would because I was younger.

It was the day after I told everybody that I would marry a man instead of a girl when Mama said, "Sweetheart, what's got you so sad?"

"Nothin'."

And she hugged me like she knew it wasn't nothing.

"Where were you all day? I couldn't find you."

"In the treehouse."

And Mama must have thought I wanted one of my own because that Friday, Daddy said, "Do you want a treehouse, son?"

I did, and Adam did too.

We got out Daddy's tools and two saw horses and hauled them behind the barn just next to the railroad cut. That's the only place in the yard that had trees on account of the whole backyard used to be part of Grandaddy's garden. There weren't many boards, and Daddy started drawing on one of them. It was a sketch of what the treehouse would look like.

"I figure we need two boards we can cut into three-foot strips. That's our steps. And the platform will be about…." He pulled his measuring tape out and held it up into the tree like it was a fishing rod that had got its line caught when you tried to cast it out into the pond. But he wasn't trying to unhook his line, he was cipherin'. That's what he called it.

"About six foot by six foot'll fit right up in them branches there. That's gonna be about…huh, if we use plywood sheets, that's about three sheets. And then we need the supports. Don't wanna nail in the tree if we can help it."

"You gonna build it like it's a deer stand?" Adam asked.

"Yeah, just not as high up. Don't wanna kill the tree. Ain't gonna nail into it."

Then we went off to the lumber yard to get all the wood. And on the way it came to me that boards were just dead trees to wrap around a live one.

We got as far as the steps the first day. Daddy measured the three-foot lengths, which he rested between two pine trees, but nailed into posts he buried deep into the ground.

"Why you keep measurin' the wood, Daddy?" I wanted to know. He was so patient, like when he had to slow down and let me steer when we were out on the dirt road going to church.

"Son, wood don't grow on trees—"

"Yeah, it does," Adam interrupted.

"I mean…it costs money, and money don't grow on trees. You hafta make sure you're careful. Measure twice and cut once. 'Cause once it's cut, it's cut. If you cut wrong, you're in trouble."

After the ladder was done, we put the tools away for the night.

"We'll do some more tomorrow, first thing," Daddy said.

Years later, the ladder was still there, leading up to a place that never was.

## CHAPTER TEN

# Good Grits

The simplest little thing can change everything—like stepping on gum, digging potatoes outside in the garden, standing in line for the school bus, cutting a board an inch too short, or going across the street for a loaf of bread. It was that last one that got us, but good.

I wanted cinnamon toast, and Mama told Daddy we only had two end pieces, so he said a bad word, put on his boots, and went across the highway to Pick's. He had worked all week, and Saturday morning was the only day he didn't have to get up early and do anything, but now he had to go out in the rain because "Cereal ain't good enough for Philbet."

He wasn't gone long, and then there was a sound in the distance. It was a new sound. Sort of like when Adam smacked air-filled brown paper bags to make me jump, or when Grandaddy missed a nail and hit the very edge of the shed's tin roof, or how MawMaw's Coronet's door pops when she opens it on really cold or really hot days. It sounded like all of those things, not just one.

But it wasn't Adam because he was still asleep, and Grandaddy just fixed the shed, so it couldn't have been him.

Mama heard it too, but when she looked out the side door she didn't see MawMaw's car in the driveway. Mama's face and chest looked as though she had just taken a breath, but held the air in. It was an expression I'd never seen, worried and hopeful all at once. I thought maybe she just wanted the bread so she could finish making breakfast and get to her sewing. Then it sounded like thunder and lightning at the back door, banging and banging. It was Pick. He said something that I didn't understand, and Mama just ran out of the house in her robe and bedroom slippers, leaving the grits on the stove.

I looked out, but even with the lights that illuminated the parking lot, all I saw was Mama run into the store. I remember thinking that Daddy must not have any money on him, and everybody knew you could get arrested if you take something without paying. But Pick wouldn't call the sheriff on Daddy. And Mama didn't take her pocketbook. I pulled a chair up to the stove and stirred the grits because they stick fast if you don't stir them. My chest hurt, like I swallowed one of Daddy's fishing hooks.

The house was quiet, nighttime quiet. When I looked around, I thought something that shouldn't be here was going to slide into view from one of the doorways…a ghost, or maybe Soap Sally. I had the grits pan handle in my hand, ready to sling it at her. I would aim for her eyes so she couldn't see to find me. I just knew she was here; I could feel something bad staring at me.

I'll never forget what happened next. Mama came running back with an "Oh, God" expression on her face, a gape, and soaking wet right through to her skin. She put her coat on over her wet robe like she needed to go someplace really fast. She had come out of the rain, but she moved so quickly that she looked like she'd just stepped out of the shower and realized that very minute when she picked up her towel that she needed to be someplace, so she just put on her clothes, wet and all, and was ready to head out.

"Mama, I stirred the grits, but I don't know how to turn them off."

"Never mind that. Go wake up Adam and tell him to get dressed right now." Her voice was thin and pinched, but loud. "You get dressed too. Both of you. Go to Jorma and Grandaddy's. No back talk now. Go get Adam."

I pointed to the grits.

"Go! Just go!"

I jumped off the chair, running as fast as I could into our room to get my brother.

It wasn't until after Adam got up and we went to Grandaddy and Jorma's that I remembered the grits on the stove. Adam left to make sure everything was okay, while I stayed with Jorma. She pulled a paper bag of Hershey's Kisses out of a cabinet, and I made a note of that so I could get some later when her candy bowls were down to the hard cherry suckers, which I liked even less than the gizzards and rice that Mama made for Daddy.

Adam came back shortly and said the stove eye was off and the pan of grits was in the sink.

"Did I burn 'em?" I asked.

"They were fine," he said, "just floatin' in the dishwater."

I was glad to hear I hadn't burnt them, but it made me turn cold, just like that feeling I had earlier in the morning when I thought Soap Sally was about to grab me off the stool and take me down into the railroad cut to boil me into lye soap. Mama would never throw away good grits. I knew something was wrong if she did that.

"Jorma, what's wrong?"

"Just hush up, Philbet, and eat your candy."

And then, softening her birdcall voice into a soft coo I'd never heard before, she said, "Go sit at the kitchen table."

I started to go and then stopped. I'm not sure exactly why. Something told me that once I went through the kitchen door, I'd never come back out. Part of me would always stay trapped in there with the smell of fried catfish and overbaked peach hand pies turned bitter.

"Go on. I'll be right there," Jorma showing her version of a smile.

I could hear her talking to Adam behind me as I pulled out my chair, the scrape of the metal legs almost covering what she said.

"Sit next to him. And don't cry."

I didn't cry either. If Adam could sit there and not cry, I could too.

Jorma poked a toothpick in and out of the holes of the salt and pepper shakers that sat dead center of the kitchen table. The table was never free and clean of anything, even when Jorma wiped it down. She'd move the pepper sauce and napkins from one end of the table to the other and wipe where they'd been, and the same with the salt and pepper. Mama always took everything off our table after we had eaten and made sure it was dry after she cleaned it before she put anything back on it.

"Air dryin' is the best way to make sure you get rid of all the germs," Mama always said. She thought Jorma's cleaning was substandard.

I focused on the toothpick going in and out of the salt and pepper shakers, trying as hard as I could not to hear whatever it was she was going to say.

"He's gonna be okay," she said. And that was it.

"Who?" I asked, knowing something had happened to Daddy, but wanting to be sure.

"Phil…your daddy."

"What's wrong?" I asked.

She didn't say anything.

I looked over at Adam. Then I said, "I'm not gonna cry. I promise. But I know somethin's wrong if Mama threw out a whole pot of good grits."

Finally, she said in a measured way, "He had an accident at Pick's, but he's gonna be okay."

"Jorma—" Adam said.

"He'sgonnabeokay," Jorma said really fast.

"What happened to him?" I demanded. I wasn't crying, so why wouldn't she tell me?

I went to stay with MawMaw, and Adam stayed with Jorma and Grandaddy. Adam could feed the animals, and he could dress himself. I could dress myself too, but I didn't like clothes. I liked being nekkid and running around in the backyard when it rained, just running in circles, catching the rain in my mouth. It was so much fun to run so hard that I thought I'd burst. At the end, I'd lie down face-first and lick the grass, so thick it was an outside carpet with not a weed in sight.

I was too much trouble to stay with Jorma and Grandaddy. Nobody said that, but I knew. Everybody was nicer than usual, and MawMaw took me to the Dairy Queen every day at lunchtime for a hamburger. She even let me stand in the front seat behind her shoulder while she drove, just like Mama did. The Dairy Queen put chili on their burgers, but it was different from Mama's chili. It was really smooth, and Mama's was chunky with meat and beans. I liked Mama's better. But those hamburgers were good, with cooked onions, and the man at the counter asked if you wanted pickles or not. I got 'em the first day, but not after that.

The combination of being at MawMaw's, a place I knew pretty well, but being there without Adam had a strange effect. I almost forgot about Daddy and Mama and Adam. Nobody visited me, not even Grandaddy. It seemed like forever since MawMaw came to pick me up—at least as long as the summer break when Adam wasn't in school. I got used to being at MawMaw's. But not so used to it that I would eat this new kind of smooth chili.

The Dairy Queen had milkshakes too, and these were more like melting ice cream instead of the sweet green milk like Mama made. They didn't have green ones, only chocolate, vanilla, and strawberry. I liked them, at least the strawberry one I tasted that MawMaw got, but MawMaw made a real green one for me when we got home instead of getting me one from Dairy Queen. I ate my hamburger in the car. She made me sit in the back seat when I ate because she had a plastic slipcover on her seats, and because I couldn't stand behind her shoulder in the front seat and eat my hamburger.

She had a little trash can that had sandbags on each side of the bottom that flared out like little saddlebags that they throw over horses on *Gunsmoke*. Those little sandbag saddlebags held that trash can down on the hump that ran between the two-foot wells. Grandaddy said that little hump in every car is where the transmission runs from the front of the car to the back wheels. And that made sense to me. It sure did take up a lot of foot room if you were big, but it was perfect for me. My feet rested right behind the trash can with just enough room. Plus, the trash can was perfect for holding my fries.

"Philbet, you put your fries right in there. That trash can is just for show; never been a piece of trash in it."

So, that's what I did, and if I dropped a fry, it was already in the trash can. And if I dropped anything on the seat, it was okay, too, because of the seat covers. They were clear, so I could see she had cloth seats. Mama liked vinyl seats, since you could wipe them down. I guess that's why MawMaw liked the seat covers. They had a design with nubbies raised in a square pattern of pie-shaped pieces. I pushed down on them to flatten them, and they slowly sprang back to their original, nubby shape. I held races on our trips between town and MawMaw's house. She drove slower than anybody I ever knew, even Grandaddy, who was just about the steadiest driver ever. So I could have lots of nubby seat cover contests by the time we got home.

I'd poke the nubbies in a line, and wait to see them spring back. Sometimes the very last nubby I pushed sprang back immediately. Sometimes the first nubby I pushed sprang back last. There wasn't any pattern; they just came back to life when they wanted to. Sometimes I worried because I'd push a nubby in, and it wouldn't pop back out by the time we got home. I'd worry about it until we got a chance to get back in the car, but they always popped back out by the time I saw them again.

One day we went to Mr. Selby's house, and I sat in the car while MawMaw went in. He lived in a big house that didn't look like a big house. It was brick, the color of Brach's caramel candies, but Jeb had been there to play a long time ago, and he said most of the floors were below ground. MawMaw said it was built on a hill, and the front looked like one level, and the back had three levels.

The driveway was black asphalt just like the highway between Alvaton and Warm Springs, which had to cost a lot of money. I didn't even know who you'd call to put in a driveway like the highway, but the best part was the parking spots. There was a whole parking lot that was in the shape of an airplane on account of Mr. Selby was an airplane pilot. You drove down the center part of the plane where the aisle was. And then you pulled off into spots that were where the wings were on a plane. I'd never been on a plane, but Jeb had flown to Texas one time.

Sometimes we didn't go get hamburgers for lunch. I thought maybe MawMaw wasn't hungry and forgot it was lunchtime. So I reminded her, but she didn't always answer. One day I asked her for peanut butter and jelly, since we weren't heading for the car to go to Dairy Queen. I'd rather have had a tomato sandwich, but I knew she didn't have any tomatoes, and she looked at me with a very sad expression. Everything had been fine at breakfast, but then she took a nap on the floor and afterward changed her dress and watered her plants, so I thought she must have felt better.

MawMaw kept falling down and taking naps on the floor just about every day. She only did it when I was around. I guess she figured she could take a nap with me there, but anyone else would probably tell her that if she wanted to take a nap, she should lie down on the bed instead of the floor. But I didn't care. Sometimes I took a nap too, right there on the floor curled up next to her. But now I wondered if I had done something wrong.

All she said was, "Neck." I didn't know what that meant, but she kept pulling at the skin on the side of her neck, and the skin didn't pop back into place like the skin on Mama's neck did. It kind of stayed pulled out like the toilet paper does when you're trying to find the end of it but you're in the middle of the roll. And skin like that made me think how old she was. I bet she was about the oldest person I knew. I wondered if she'd just looked in the mirror, seen her neck skin, and realized she was old.

Then she picked up the phone and said, "Who is this child?"

Aunt Ease must have been on the party line talking to somebody because a few minutes later she was at the front door.

"Mama, you tired? You need to lay down?"

MawMaw pulled at her neck, but she didn't say anything.

"I don't think she's tired anymore, Aunt Ease. She had a nap on the floor."

"The floor?" Aunt Ease repeated.

"Yessum, she napped right there in the hall yesterday, and she napped over there in front of the washin' machine this mornin'. I laid down with her even though my nap time is after lunch."

"Mama?" Aunt Ease kind of whispered.

And MawMaw said, "Louise, it's okay."

Aunt Ease sat down at the kitchen table next to MawMaw, reaching out to take MawMaw's hand into hers. But Aunt Ease's hand pulled back a little, too preoccupied to complete the caring gesture. Then she said, "Thank you, you're doing a good job lookin' after MawMaw."

She was looking at MawMaw when she said that, but I think Aunt Ease must have been talking to me. Then she glanced over and down at me, smiling in that thin-lipped, forced way grown-ups sometimes do.

"I thought she was lookin' after *me*," I replied.

"She, um, she…. Philbet, we're all lookin' out for each other."

Not long after Aunt Ease left, cousin Veralynn knocked on MawMaw's front door, but only after she had already come inside.

"MawMaw, you home?"

Veralynn goosed me in the side when she saw me, like she always did, and it made me laugh so hard that by the time I got my breath back, I forgot to tell her that she had it backward—you're supposed to knock first and then come in. But Veralynn would have just laughed and flapped her hand at me like she was trying to shoo a fly off the kitchen counter. To cousin Veralynn, everything and every situation was light and gauzy. She drove barefoot, which Adam said was against the law. But she didn't like shoes, and she didn't have any on when she walked in that afternoon. When she came through the door, she was wearing a bathing suit top and some jeans I remember Mama had embroidered for her. Her skin was the color of sweet cream speckled with pumpkin- and caramel-colored freckles in an almost perfect pattern that looked like the material in the dress Mama wore to cousin Owen's wedding.

Mama said it was called Dotted Swiss, and it came in all kinds of colors that she used to make into prom and bridesmaid dresses—mostly pink, green, yellow, or blue with little fuzzy white dots. But one day Mama dropped her purse in the fabric store, and when she bent down to pick it up she found a bolt of some special Dotted Swiss, creamy-colored with amber dots, peeking out from under the table. I could see from her face that this wasn't ever going to go into anybody's prom dress. It was for her. She made into a dress for herself, and just looking at it made me think of Veralynn's freckles.

Veralynn stayed all day, and we played, and she made me a sandwich. When Aunt Ease returned, she and MawMaw went out in Aunt Ease's car while Veralynn and I carved out a path for Matchbox cars in front of the house. Veralynn had the emerald-green Ford pickup truck that had a see-through camper top that covered four plastic dogs that fit in the back. She didn't play with the dogs and the camper because I told her they get lost easy. I put them back in the Matchbox case for safekeeping.

When Mama came to pick me up later that day, I remember I didn't want to go. It was kind of like I forgot about her, because I hadn't seen her since that morning she ran out the back door in her nightgown and came back all wet from the rain. I ran to the back of MawMaw's house and hid in a closet. I thought Mama would follow me and tickle me like Veralynn had earlier, but she didn't. I crept out to see if Mama was waiting to surprise me on the other side of the door, but she wasn't there either. She was still by the front door. I heard her say to Veralynn, "Louise called. They said MawMaw's been having strokettes. Lord, help us."

I wasn't sure what strokettes were, but from the sound of Mama's voice and her asking for God's help and all, I recall thinking that they must be bad. So, I slipped back inside the closet and waited for Mama, and I decided when she found me I'd make her laugh so she'd feel better. And while I waited, I wondered if she'd tell me what a strokette was and what really happened to Daddy.

The hems of MawMaw's dresses hung just above me in the closet, an enveloping bower that reminded me how much I loved MawMaw and loved being in her house, those two houses that got turned into one. The family that lived next door moved away, and MawMaw started living in both sides of the house.

MawMaw had two of everything. Two bathrooms and two kitchens. And her closets had two doors. You could open one door, and if the door on the other side was open, you could see right through into the other room. It was just like when Mama would take us to the library, and Adam and I could be on different aisles, pull books off the shelf and whisper to each other. One time, I rolled my Matchbox car right through the shelf, and Adam caught it on the other side.

But Mama ran around to the other room and climbed into the closet just as I was trying to escape. I turned around, dug my way back into the dark of the closet, and she followed me through, hunching down under the clothes and over the shoes on the floor. She caught me breathless just as I stepped out of the closet and into the room. Then she picked me up with both arms pinned against me, and she kissed me all over my face as if she were on *Truth or Consequences* and the challenge was to cover every square inch of my face with kisses in under fifteen seconds, and she was determined to win. Her lipstick smelled so good, wax and perfume and something that kind of made it hard to breathe, like something from a factory.

And then we went home with me standing on the front seat beside her, behind her shoulder, just like always. When we got there, it was kind of like walking through that closet to another side, another room. The last time I saw Daddy he was going to get bread, and Mama was wet from the rain and looking really scared. Now, back in our kitchen, Mama was all shiny again with her makeup, and Daddy was on his recliner with a big white patch over his ear.

"Hey, boy."

"Hey, Daddy."

I didn't know what to say. I wasn't sure where everybody had been. Jorma told me Daddy had an accident, and we all had to stay out of the house while he got better. I studied him. It was like he had an earache.

He reached one arm toward me with his hand stretching out, like he was about to pull off a bunch of cotton candy, not pinch off a mouthful, but grab a fistful. And then his hand closed and opened and closed and opened. He was peering off into space, like he was looking at something and nothing at the same time. I turned to see what he was looking at, because I thought maybe he spotted a fly and wanted me to hand him the swatter. I didn't see a fly, so I walked closer thinking I would figure out what he saw or what he wanted. He grabbed my shoulder and pulled me over and hugged me real tight. Then he let me go, snorted like he had something tickling his nose and wanted to blow it out without using a handkerchief, and he just stared at the television.

"They got me, son," he whispered.

"Who?" I whispered.

He didn't say anything.

"They did, they got you?" I tried again.

"Half inch one way or the other, and I'd be dead."

## CHAPTER ELEVEN

# In One Door and Out Another

*ead?* I stared at Daddy, not understanding.

Mama walked in. "Phil, don't scare Philbet."

"I'm just talkin' to him, goddammit!"

The TV was on; I could hear the evening news. Already forgetting the start of our conversation, Daddy was on to another topic. "I hope they don't draft you and Adam."

He took a swig of his beer, but it was empty. Maybe he was reaching for a new beer, a draft beer. There're three kinds of drafts, I'd learned. One is when you get a wind inside the house because there's a hole someplace—usually so small you can't see where it is, but you know it's there because you can feel it. It never goes away completely. Jorma and Grandaddy's house had lots of drafts.

When it's cold outside a draft makes it cold inside. But when it's hot outside you don't get the same cool breeze. I bet that's how they thought up the air conditioner that's in the window. If a draft can cool the room in the winter, let's put a motor behind it and make our own draft in the summer. And that's what an air conditioner is—an electric draft. If you opened a door to the other side of the house in the winter or fall or spring, it was like you walked inside the meat cooler over at Pick's where they hang the deer just after Daddy skins it. But if you walk back in there during the summer, it's like you put your face inside the hair dryer down at Miss Nita's beauty shop.

Another draft is the kind of beer some people get when they go to a bar, and the bar's run out of beer in cans or bottles. Daddy went to a bar when he was in the Army, and I remember Adam telling me about Daddy getting a draft beer. They got the glass out of a refrigerator instead of off a shelf because they wanted the glass to be as cold as the beer. And then they turned on a water faucet, but beer came out instead. I wish they could do that for green milkshakes. That was before Adam and I were born when Mama drove up to South Carolina one weekend all by herself to see Daddy.

Adam told me about another kind of draft and that was when the Army comes to get you and makes you fight in a war. I never asked why Daddy got a draft beer instead of one in a can or bottle, but I worked it out in my head that you must get to drink draft beer after they draft you. If you're not drafted, I decided, you drink it from a can or bottle.

I liked the draft beer idea better than the draft where they come get you. How could the Army just come and get you? It sounded like the prisoner men in white suits and blue-striped pants we saw on the side of the road picking up trash. I wondered if the prisoners were drafted into prison. *Lord*, I thought, *let me get to twenty-seven before they try to draft me because Daddy said that's when you're too old to be drafted.*

But Daddy talked about the draft all the time. I wasn't sure, but I thought the draft is why he started buying more guns. He always hunted, and he always had guns, but he bought more guns now. They were rolled up in sheets under every bed in the house, and he even had a gun rack in his truck. Most daddies had gun racks. And there was a pistol in the handkerchief drawer, weighing down the handkerchiefs when you reached in for one.

The gun promised to me for my twelfth birthday was propped in the corner of the room where we watched television. It was a thirty-aught-six. I didn't know what that meant, but it was mine. I got to hold it when Daddy was there, but I didn't like holding it. I didn't want to shoot somebody on the other side of the wall, but Daddy said the walls were cinder blocks and the bullet wouldn't go through them. But then I worried that the bullet would bounce off the wall and hit us. The thirty-aught-six had brown wood that was pretty, like it was polished with Pledge, and it reminded me of the wood on the arms of Grandaddy's TV chair. But the metal barrel looked cold and *was* cold. I didn't like it. I remember worrying about where I'd keep it when I grew up and had to take it to my house.

I could already tell that Daddy was different, and it was more than just the bandage on his ear. He was quicker to anger, more agitated. He followed me outside as I rode my pedal car up the garden path. "Go find Adam, son," he said. "I need to tell y'all about watching out around you and what to do if somebody takes you."

*Takes us where?* I wondered. I didn't understand him. I decided I'd earned a candy break, and Grandaddy and Jorma always had candy in their dish. It was the only thing Jorma had over Mama.

I went in and didn't see anybody, but you didn't have to ask before you took candy. It was for anybody, just like the toothpicks at the cash register over at Pick's. There were two candy bowls in the house, both in the living room. I always went over to the main candy bowl—the one on the table next to the kitchen door—because it had a bigger selection. Most of the candies were Brach's, but if Grandaddy got any Hershey's, he'd put them in the main candy bowl. Adam would scoop up the Hershey's as soon as he knew they were there, but I would leave at least one Hershey for somebody else.

Well, there weren't any Hershey's that day, so I went to the smaller bowl, which was next to the window that looked right into the bedroom next to Jorma's bed. There were identical tables in each room on both sides of the window, both with lamps sitting on big, white crocheted covers. The only difference was the living room side had a candy bowl, and the bedroom side had a water glass with teeth in it. If you came to visit early enough, you could see Jorma's teeth in the glass floating there, looking like they belonged to a big fish who was going to come swim along and open up and snap those teeth in his mouth. I just knew that if I lowered a fishhook down in that glass one morning, those teeth staring up at the ceiling would bite that hook just to get out of that glass. I just knew it.

"Jorma, how'd you get them teeth?" I asked.

"From eatin' candy," she said.

And I thought, maybe Jorma got trading stamps from the candy store. I figured it was like that time when Mama and I put stamps in a book and took it to a store and exchanged it for an ice-cream maker. But I didn't remember seeing any teeth in the catalog when we were picking out the ice-cream maker. We almost got an electric ice-cream maker, but that took two books of stamps. The hand-crank model took only one. My job was to sit on the ice-cream maker while somebody else cranked it. My shorts were always wet afterward, but I didn't care because we got homemade ice cream.

Still, it made me wonder how many books she needed to get a set of teeth. I would have helped her lick the stamps and fill in the book. And I really don't know why she didn't put a candy bowl on her side of the window. Every now and then you'd see her hand reach through from the bedroom side and pick a piece of candy out. You'd hear the wrapper crinkle, and then she'd reach for another piece in about a minute. I found one brown, white, and pink candy, which I grabbed before a hand came through the window and snatched it away. Jorma reaching her hand through the window and grabbing candy reminded me of our piggy bank. It was a black box with a place to put a penny on top. When you wanted to insert money, this green hand, which *had* to belong to a witch, came out of a secret door, grabbed that penny, and pulled it into the box. There was a secret door on the other side of the box where you could get at the pennies. It was about the spookiest bank I'd ever seen.

Then I heard Adam. At least it sounded like him, but like he was pretending to be Walter Cronkite announcing the news. "An armed robbery on the morning of January 4 at a Gulf Station on Highway 85 left one man dead and another critically injured with a head wound. No arrests were made following a police investigation."

I froze, just the instant before I started to unwrap my candy. All of a sudden, I thought I shouldn't be here. Had I heard him talking about something I shouldn't be hearing? I caught myself just before I asked out loud, *Who got shot? Who are you talking to?*

I had to think, so I sneaked out of the house and crawled under what used to be the back steps, remembering to jump over the loud board just next to Grandaddy's chair on the way out. I couldn't understand why everybody was so different. It was like Mama had walked through a door and come out the other side as someone else, like when she picked me up at MawMaw's and crawled through the closet. She was laughing as she chased me, but by the time she'd come out the other side, she sighed. Then she kissed me a whole lot and said, "Let's go home."

And Daddy acted so weird, staring at something in front of him that I couldn't see. And he hugged me. Daddy never hugged me. And then Adam was pretending to be Walter Cronkite. He was different too, changed like Mama and Daddy. They all looked the same, but they were different.

## CHAPTER TWELVE

# Swing Time

And then I realized that Daddy didn't have an earache. He must have
been shot in the head, right in his ear. That's what Adam was talking
about in his TV announcer voice.

"Maybe they shot the gun near his ear and made it bleed," I thought
out loud. 'Cause if he got shot in the head, I reasoned he'd have died.

I remember thinking it through from the beginning. First, Daddy went
over to Pick's for bread. Then Mama went over there and came back really
upset and without her bedroom shoes. Then I woke up Adam, and we
went up to Jorma and Grandaddy's. Grandaddy took off over to Pick's as
soon as we got in the house. I didn't ask what was wrong because I was
afraid it was too terrible to ponder.

I stopped thinking things through when I saw Grandaddy's feet walk
up to the edge of what used to be the steps into the house. And his feet just
stood there parked alongside my little peddle car, and he must have shifted
his weight because his feet moved just a little bit apart from each other.
And for the first time that day, I laughed—not an out-loud laugh, but a
secret laugh—because Grandaddy didn't know I was there. His little foot
shift and the pause that came after meant Grandaddy was going to take a
wee outside, and Jorma wouldn't like that.

Grandaddy was as likely to take a wee off in the railroad cut as he was to reach up and pull a dead leaf off the low limb of the pecan tree. He didn't see any reason to go all the way up the steps to the house when he had to go, what with the cut right there. Adam would go wee off the cut too, and behind the barn all the time. I did it once outside, but I got some on my shoes, so I went to the house from then on.

But the feet just stayed there, and no stream appeared. I saw his hand appear, and it set a Hershey's Kiss on the lowest step. And the feet stayed. Then the hand appeared again and set a Brach's chocolate, white, and strawberry coconut chew on the step next to the Kiss. Then his feet disappeared.

I just watched the candy. Then I slowly climbed down. As soon as the sunlight turned my hand from gray to pink, he said, "Come on out and give me a hug."

I hadn't seen Grandaddy since before I went down to stay with MawMaw that morning Mama came into the kitchen soaking wet and told me to go wake up Adam. Was Grandaddy different too? I picked up the candy and opened the Kiss on my way over to him, and as I leaned slowly into his leg, he put his hand on the side of my head, making my chewing muscles tickle as his fingers pressed on them. I ate the Kiss and the coconut chew in one mouthful. That was a good candy combination, and I decided Hershey's and Brach's should be friends and mass produce it.

He leaned down and whispered with a grin, "I think somebody needs a whoopin' for eatin' my candy." And he grabbed me and trapped me over his one knee, closed his other leg on me and slapped his leg about twenty million times. It was the most fun whoopin' I'd ever gotten.

"Hey, son."

"Hey, Grandaddy."

"I missed you so much," Grandaddy said as he tickled my side.

And I hugged his leg because my throat was suddenly dry with coconut and love and relief. This was not a different grandaddy. This was Grandaddy.

"It'll be okay," he said as he patted my head. "Let's go swing."

He pushed while I sat in the swing. We didn't talk for a while. As I remember it, I just felt the wind on my face and his hands on my back at the point you feel you weigh about zero pounds and the pull of life and the world leave you alone for a second. When I was at the very highest point, weightless, I heard Grandaddy say, "I want to talk to you about what happened to your daddy."

And I knew that it was bad, but I knew it was okay. Grandaddy would make it okay, even if it wasn't.

## CHAPTER THIRTEEN

# When Daddy Was a Recliner

Grandaddy explained you could get shot in the head and not die. And Daddy had gotten shot in the head real close to his temple, and when I asked how close, he said about the length of an M&M—a regular one, not a peanut one.

"That's close, Grandaddy."

"Not close enough to matter."

And then Adam banged out of the back door and walked over to us. "Mama wants us home."

"You go on with Adam. I'll see y'all later."

Adam headed toward the path while I ran over to get my peddle car. I peddled faster than I ever had because I wanted to get a good look at Adam. I wanted to see if it was really him and not a different him.

I caught up to him at the corner of our house, right outside the window of our room where the chain-link fence post was up against the house and had a swish of powdery white paint from where I missed the house and got paint on the fence. That was from when I asked Daddy to let me paint one block, just one block, so I could say I helped paint the house too. He let me, and he didn't fuss at me when I missed the block and got the fence instead.

"Adam." He kept walking. "Adam?"

He stopped and looked over at me, and his head tilted as he let out a heavy breath.

And then I hugged him, and he hugged me back.

And Adam pulled me back by my ear and said, "Little weirdo." But he didn't say it like I was a weirdo. He said it like it was okay that I hugged him. I cried a little, but he didn't know.

Mama was standing in the door when we came up, and she said, "Y'all play in the yard and stay out from Jorma and Grandaddy's." Then she turned into the dark of the house behind the screen door.

Mama had never told us not to go up to Jorma and Grandaddy's. Grandaddy liked us. He'd always let me have a drawing pencil, and even if Jorma wouldn't hug you, she always put more candy out in the candy bowl. And she'd give you sweet tea that tasted like mouthwash. Mama's tea was sweet, like sweet tea should taste. But I still drank Jorma's tea because it was hot some days, even in winter.

More and more, Mama was busy after Daddy got sick. She decided she was going to work. She didn't want to, but we needed the extra money. Something happened one day that has stayed with me, something that helped me understand how money weighed on Mama's mind. We were at the grocery store. Restless, I climbed up on the side of the buggy full of groceries, and it flipped over. It wouldn't have been too bad, but Mama had just put a gallon of milk in, and it exploded all over the floor. The floor looked perfect and glossy white, like milk at the top of a floor-size bowl of bacon, apples, rice, flour, saltines, eggshells, and collards making up the worst cereal ever—with a can of peas as the prize inside.

That week Mama had to pay for stuff we didn't get…not only milk, but eggs and broken bottles of juice. I didn't mean to turn it over. I wasn't that heavy. Mama didn't yell and that made me feel worse. I almost started to cry. She moved in slow motion, picking things up and putting them back in the cart as they dripped. It was like she was setting wet dishes in the drain, dripping dirty, cloudy water instead of clean.

Miss Driscoll came up behind Mama, gently touched her on her elbow and said, "Here, let me do it."

Mama just stood there, looking away at a shelf of canned pineapple like she was searching for a library book she didn't really want. And I just wanted to be home and stand inside the closet of Adam's and my room. The closet was next to the door that went out in the hall, and when the door to the room was open, it was up against the door to the closet. You could hardly hear anything in there with the two doors between you and the rest of the house. You couldn't even hear Daddy yelling for Mama.

There was a box of photographs in that closet, and if I took a flashlight with me when I went in, I could look at the pictures. I liked one in particular when I was sad, like I was on the days I did stuff like turning the shopping cart over. I looked at a picture of Daddy sitting on the couch with his leg propped up on the wall. He looked like the man on the television who was in the Olympics with his hands on these rings hanging from the ceiling and his bent legs at this angle while he was midair. Daddy wasn't an athlete in midair, but he sure did look like it if I put one finger over the back of the sofa and one finger over the wall where his feet touched it.

I didn't know how he thought it was okay to put his feet on the wall. If I ever did that, he'd tell me to get my feet down. But Adam was sitting in his lap, and his legs were propped up right on top of Daddy's, like Daddy was a big ol' chair. And they looked so happy. It must have been a bad weather day because the sky outside was dark gray. I liked that picture, even though it made me sad. I'd been all through that box, and there wasn't a picture of me sitting on Daddy's lap with our legs propped up like that, smiling. And I thought, *It's never going to happen now because Daddy seems like he's never going to be happy again.*

I wanted Mama to be happy again, too, instead of staring at cans of pineapple on the shelf while Miss Driscoll picked up our groceries off the floor.

## CHAPTER FOURTEEN

# God Bless

I don't know if MawMaw timed it so nobody was around the day the strokettes turned into a full-on stroke, but she was alone when she died. I like to think she planned it that way, not wanting to bother anybody. When Veralynn visited late that afternoon, she thought MawMaw was taking a nap sitting upright there in her seashell-backed chair on the front porch.

Mama, Daddy, Adam, and I drove away from MawMaw's graveside service in the brown Pontiac Catalina, and leaning over the front seat from the back, I said, "Now we can stick knives in MawMaw, and she won't feel it." Adam grabbed my collar and pulled me back so hard it knocked the breath out of me. I didn't know why I said it, and I didn't really understand why I shouldn't have said it. It just struck me that morning, just leaving her grave, that nothing could hurt her now. I didn't really want to stick a knife in her, but if we did, or if the doctor gave her a shot—she had gotten lots of shots because she had been so sick—then she wouldn't feel it. Not now.

But one day, it was probably a week or maybe a month later, I knew. I knew how much what I said that day driving away from MawMaw, the last time Mama would ever see MawMaw, must have hurt Mama. Sometimes in life you come to understand something long after it happened. And just the sudden knowing can scare you in a way because it makes you wonder what else you didn't know and still don't.

I first realized it when I walked up to the closet in MawMaw's house, and Mama was standing in one of the kitchen chairs she'd dragged into the closet to reach something on a high shelf. She was just standing there with her arms folded down on the shelf, her face in her arms. She was making a sound I'd never heard, almost silent, but I could hear what sounded like a grumbling tummy, but it was coming from where her heart was. And she was shaking like she was cold. It was a private moment that no one was supposed to see. I don't know what she came across up there on the shelf…a photograph? One of MawMaw's hats? Or maybe she just remembered that her mama was gone and that she'd never see her again. She would never have an excuse to pile Adam and me in the car and head down the road before Daddy's mama showed up.

At first I backed out of the room, not knowing what to say, but then I went back and stood there, looking up. I still didn't know what to say, but I thought that I should stay in case she needed a hug—like the tight ones she gave me when I cried.

But she didn't notice me. I started to pull on her pants, but then Daddy yelled for her, "Mama!"

She looked up and said a dirty word, I guess not knowing I was there.

"What." But it wasn't a question. It was more like, "I hear you, but I'm not coming to you."

He called her a lot. He never seemed to need anything when she was standing next to him, only when she was on the other side of the house. And he'd keep calling if she didn't show up or if she didn't answer him. Sometimes I hated him. He had his own mama, and Mama wasn't his mama. She was his wife. I ran into the living room and said, "She's not your mama. She's my mama. You've got a mama, and her name's Jorma."

"You little shit runt. You better get out of here before I tear you up." But he was laughing and hit me with the newspaper, so he must not have been too mad.

He yelled after me in a high voice, "She's my Mama. She's not your mama," as if he was on stage in a play acting like a girl, and I was feeding him lines.

When we all rode together in the truck, I had to ride next to Daddy, and then it was Mama, and then Adam got to ride by the door. Mama put us in this order because Adam was older, and he and I always fought when we sat next to each other. When I said my prayers at night, I said our names in the same order that we rode: "Dear Lord, bless Adam, Mama, Philbet, and Daddy." But later on, I reordered us in my prayers: "Daddy, Adam, Mama, and Philbet." I figured I couldn't bless myself first, but I wanted to be the farthest away from Daddy and the closest to Mama. I didn't want Mama next to Daddy either, so I put Adam in between them.

I went back in there where Mama was standing in the chair. I didn't know what to do, so I just held onto her pant leg and stood there.

"Mama?"

If Mama lost MawMaw, maybe it would cheer her up to see her daddy. If I misplaced my Cougar, another Matchbox would do for a while.

"Yes, Sweetheart?"

"Mama, where's your daddy?"

She didn't answer. Then at last she said, "He's in heaven like MawMaw."

"Oh. Did MawMaw see him when she got there?" I asked.

"I don't know." Mama climbed down and sat in the chair.

"Why wouldn't she go see him when she got there? Didn't she know he was there?"

"I don't know, Sweetheart."

"If you knew he was there, she must have known it too."

"I guess."

"Maybe he'll see her at the grocery store, and then they can live together in heaven. Or maybe they'll see each other at church. Or at the post office."

She just took a deep breath, and she made a sound that wasn't quite a word when she breathed out.

"What was your daddy like?"

She looked off at the cuckoo clock, and the bird came out of his little hole. The clock was just like the one Jorma and Grandaddy had, even down to the little pine cones that hung from chains you had to pull on every day to keep the clock going. I didn't touch them because I might accidentally pull the clock off the wall.

But I got to touch the pine cones one time when Grandaddy was there, and they weren't real. They were heavy and made of metal and didn't stick your hands like real pine cones. If you threw one in a pine cone fight, you'd break a window.

"He…" she thought out loud. "He smoked. Smoked cigars."

"Like Grandaddy used to?"

"Yes, like Grandaddy."

"Was his name Grandaddy too?"

"Papa," she whispered.

"That's good, because when I pray for him now, God won't get confused who I mean."

Mama smiled and kissed me about ten times all over my face, but she was crying a little bit too. I couldn't tell if I was helping or if I was making her sadder, but if she kissed me it must have been helping a little.

"What else about Papa?"

"Well, he drank. I wish he hadn't, but he did."

"What'd he drink?"

"Kool-Aid." She finally smiled and laughed a little under her breath. I *was* helping.

"What else about Papa?"

"He was tall. He looked more like Aunt Faydra in the face than Aunt Jimmie Ann and Aunt Bert. You never knew Aunt Bert."

"Did Aunt Bert have a mustache like Aunt Jimmie Ann?"

"A little one."

"What else about Papa?"

"He was quiet. He was sitting in his car…."

"What kinda car?"

"Um…I don't know. He was parked at the washerette washing Adam's and Jeb's diapers." Mama let out a big breath without having taken in a breath. "And he had a heart attack right there in the car in the parking lot."

"And he died?"

"Yes, Sweetheart."

"When?"

"Um…nine years ago."

"Are Jorma and Grandaddy your parents now?"

"No, Sweetheart. I don't have any now. But I've got you and Adam."

How could Adam and I be her parents? I didn't have any money to give her for lunch or school milk.

"You and Adam are all I need now."

Then it made sense. She didn't want me to watch her like she watched me when she was afraid I'd run out in the road without looking both ways. She just needed somebody to love her back.

## CHAPTER FIFTEEN

# Junkyard Quiet

I didn't ever go into the woods when we were in Alvaton, since we really didn't have woods, just the railroad cut. But after MawMaw died, we went down and stayed at her house some.

"I'm taking the boys down there so I can help Louise clean out Mama's things," Mama said to Daddy.

"You need to be home."

"I can't keep house here and clean out Mama's stuff. The sooner it gets cleaned out, the sooner it gets sold," she said flatly.

"You go down during the day."

"Do you want the money?"

"How long will it take you?" Daddy wanted to know.

"I won't know until I get in there. She had so much packed away."

So, off we went to MawMaw's house, and Daddy came down on weekends.

And I loved being there, especially during the week when it was mostly Mama and me. There was so much to explore. I went out back, sneaking through the pine trees, and all I could think was to stay out of the pine straw. Red bugs lived in the straw, and if they got on you, they dig in and make a permanent red bump. Mama would know I'd been in the woods if she saw the bumps.

The woods were full of people's secrets. A discarded chair with a coffee mug on the arm and a milk crate ottoman. That was all. No trail to or from it, as if a spirit, tired from floating through the trees decided this place was as good as any to set up a lounge. Nothing distinguished the spot, not that Adam and I could see. We never moved the mug, as if we were trespassing in the home of someone who left their door open, and we had wandered in. If we'd moved it, the resident would know we'd been there. Or maybe it was out of respect and an over-awareness of Mama's, "You keep your hands off other people's things."

There was an impromptu dump just off a dirt road about a mile in from Raleigh Road that really fascinated me. Unlike the recliner, this spot changed dramatically from one visit to another. This wasn't a place where bags of daily trash were left. This was a place for heavy duty stuff like refrigerators, stoves, swing sets, and even a car.

There was a rusty old Willys Jeep with rotted out tires that sat nose to nose with an old rowboat in an almost kiss that made them look like mismatched lovers. Adam figured it was dumped, but I didn't think so. I figured it died there, lumbering along over the wood's floor when it just rolled to a stop, wondering if the owner would let it rest for a while. The driver, stepping out and more hungry than concerned about the Willys, had decided to walk a mile to the main road in search of lunch. He'd return later to see to the Willys after lunch, but one day ran into the next, and another passed, and another. And then the ice storm came, and it was too late, a nuisance now. The Willys was best left where it was, its only consolation the boat. I found what people left behind somehow exhilarating.

I knew the woods well because Adam and our babysitter Lori cut a trail for the motorcycle—a Honda SL70. It was turquoise and intended for one person, but Adam and I could both ride at the same time since I weighed so little. One day when Adam and Lori went back to cut the trail, I sneaked into the edge of the woods and walked around until they got back. There they were, both on the bike, and they weighed too much. I told them so, and Lori got off. But now I knew they rode like that all the time. *Some babysitter*, I thought. I was the real reason Mama hired Lori, since Adam was just a few years younger than her. What if something happened to me while I was alone? One day I turned on the stove, but nobody except for me noticed, so I turned it off.

The trail cut was within twenty feet of Finley's dog pins, and even over the motorcycle engine and under the helmet, you could hear the pinned-up dogs going crazy. But today they didn't make a sound. I wasn't even trying to be quiet, but the pine straw is like a freshly swept floor. If it never rained, I swear you could put a recliner and television out there and stay all the day and night. Wouldn't that be something? Sit right there with a motorcycle path right between you and the television, and never be disturbed all week long until Adam rides the SL70 by around noon every Saturday, and then back through on his way home after riding around the old moonshiner's shack and along the edge of the soybean field. I could even jump on and join him and hop off again in the afternoon. But I'd never live in the woods this close to Finley's dogs. They barked at night, and I'd never get to sleep. And Soap Sally might get me.

Soon I was at the back edge of the junkyard. It had barbed-wire fence in some places, chain link in others, all of it rusted. Get a cut on that, and it'd be a tetanus shot from the emergency room. Mama would even make Adam get one, just like the one he'd gotten when Jeb accidentally stuck him in the foot with a pitchfork. It was an accident, but Jeb was "supremely stupid" according to Mama, so I believed it.

But that first time I climbed over into Finley's yard was easy. Pushed right up against the barbed wire there was a dark green, rusty 1960 Impala with its trunk lid up, looking like a sleepy lizard with its mouth open waiting for a bug to light inside. It was so quiet there in the woods...always quiet. No one knew where I was, and it made the part of my stomach just under my belly button hot and soupy, like anything could happen.

His yard was bigger than MawMaw's because Finley had taken pine trees down farther back than she had. I bet his backyard was about twice as deep as MawMaw's. Her yard didn't have a fence, and it was a good thing it didn't because we'd have to go in and out of a fence with the SL70 every time we went into the woods. That was another difference, the plants. In the months since MawMaw died, Daddy had dug up bushes from all around the county during the weekends and planted them in the yard, honeysuckle and azaleas, all the colors you could imagine.

"Curb appeal is important if you want to sell a house," he'd always say.

For every plant Daddy had, Finley had a dog, and those dogs had run that ground bare down to the red clay. A patch of grass didn't have a chance. The one tree was growing right up through where the engine used to be in that old 1960 Impala.

## CHAPTER SIXTEEN

# Looking in a Fun House Mirror

I always thought my name was kinda funny—not ha-ha funny, but odd funny. Philbet. It isn't even a name. It's shorthand from Daddy, Phil, and from Mama, Betty Tom. Mama's daddy was named Thomas, not Papa like she said. Adam told me that. He told me that Papa wanted another boy, and when Mama turned out to be a girl, he decided to name her Tom anyway. That's how they got Betty Tom.

My name, I figured, was sorta like a nickname, but not the kind that wounds you, that holds up a misshapen image in front of you like a fun house mirror. Although I never really liked it, my name reminded me that Mama and Daddy had liked each other once. They liked each other so much they put their names together and gave it to me. But I wish they'd given it to Adam instead of me because he's cool, and if anybody said anything like, "That's a stupid-ass name," he'd have punched 'em.

But Adam had to be Adam because he was the first boy. He was the first, just like Adam was the first man. In my young life I earned four nicknames. The first two came early, during the same year from two different uncles. Like those uncles, the nicknames played a huge part in shaping how I saw myself, not to mention how I imagined the rest of my family and every other person saw me.

*Mama's boy* and *sissy* weren't words I heard often. I did hear them, but not from my uncles. They had other names for me. I wasn't even a sissy, not even the bottom-of-the-social-order sissy that everyone in the South recognized. So I never thought of myself as that, never considering that I belonged to them, which might have provided some comfort, some camaraderie with other outcasts because there were other sissies around. There was a boy at church who probably would have welcomed me. Nobody actually called him sissy to his face, but I heard the giggles and whispers behind his back. He had an identical twin brother who was like him, but not like him. And their physical similarity only made their differences more striking. There was the sissy one, who was like a test pie that their mama made on Saturday, not quite right and under filled. His brother was the real pie that their Mama made on Sunday morning before church, perfect and bubbling with apples and cinnamon goo because she had a chance to practice the day before. No one wanted a dry, underfilled pie.

I looked to where they sat, two pews ahead with the mama, daddy, and the perfect boy seated in a row, evenly spaced shoulder-to-shoulder. Looking made my throat hurt a little, as if I stuck the tip of my tongue into the cinnamon jar and then got some of the chalky dust down my windpipe. That was because the sissy child was next to them, but about a shoulder-and-a-half-width away, breaking the perfect equal-but-close distance and signaling to anyone paying attention that though the sissy was right there on the same pew, he was alone.

And it dawned on me right there in the church that all those whispering kids called me the same names when I wasn't around. And I expect he, a fellow outcast, thought I kept my distance from him because I didn't want to be associated with his kind. Or maybe he kept his distance from me because he heard them talk about me—each of us longing for a friend, but too afraid and hoping we were not like the other. But I was his kind, and he mine. The truth was, I didn't even think he'd want me as a friend. I was worse than a sissy.

Starting at about five years old, Uncle Calvin started calling me Tittysack, which back then I didn't understand. He never used Philbet. Ever. I heard one word, one name: Tittysack. I was much older when it dawned on me that he was calling me a titty sack, as much a signal that he hated women as it was a derogatory name for me. The mere mention of words like *titty* had a paralyzing effect on my parents. We didn't acknowledge or talk about anything related to the body or sexuality or vulgarity. I was too young to understand the words, but I knew this wasn't okay. Mama and Daddy screened things out they didn't want to think about.

Even so, I kept expecting Mama or Daddy to say something. But Uncle Calvin's titty name met no reaction, much as polite, cultured company might go on with whatever they were doing if someone passed wind. No reaction—not a raised brow or sideways glance when Uncle Calvin started in. And that both hurt and puzzled me. Mama usually would come to me before tucking me in at night and hug me and hold my face in her hands and tell me I was a good boy, a strong boy, whom they loved. Daddy would occasionally say, "How are you, son?" emphasizing the last word to reinforce that was who I was, or who I should be.

At least Uncle Calvin called me Tittysack in front of everyone. I'm surprised he didn't give up, getting no rise from anyone. But Uncle Calvin didn't hide the hulking bully he was, and I probably would never have been struck by his boldness if it weren't for Uncle Kingston, who timed his insults to fall on my ears only, premeditated, testing my reaction before he used his nickname for me in earshot of others.

It was Uncle Kingston who nicknamed me Suzie. I actually had a real cousin Suzie, but she was on Daddy's side of the family and lived all the way down in Florida, so I don't think Uncle Kingston had ever met her. But the first time he called me Suzie, I excitedly turned around really fast expecting my Florida cousin to jump from behind the door and say "Boo!" Suzie and Meg, her older sister, had just written a letter to Adam and me, and Mama read it to us. I liked the way they had written a note on the back of the envelope with one big S that served as the first letter of all three sentences:

S uzie and Meg are excited.
aturday is the day we plan to arrive to begin a week-long vacation.
ee you soon!

I was excited too. They were older, and they'd sit on the swing just like normal, and they'd let me sit on one of their laps, so that when we went forward and they leaned back in the swing, it was like I was flying, only backward. And they always brought kiwis, mangos, and lychees. They were so good, that I'd rather have mango than M&Ms.

But when I turned around I didn't see Suzie, and she wouldn't be at Uncle Kingston and Aunt Ease's house anyway, a whole twenty-five miles away from Grandaddy and Jorma's house.

He meant *me. I* was Suzie.

No one else was there, just him and me. The smell of slightly burned cornbread and simmering turnips was coming from the stove. I think that's why it always smelled like a cat had gone to the bathroom in there, but they never had a cat. To me, their house looked as odd as it smelled. It was a straightforward red brick ranch, with one long roof. But at one point, there had been a carport cutout toward the left end of the house.

At the very end of the left side there was a storage room that ran the depth of the house, but so narrow it was like a bowling alley almost, only wide enough for a washing machine and dryer to sit side by side. And it had lots of shelves with boxes and clothes piled up everywhere. It smelled like chocolate chip cookies and cat. But it was cool and damp and not a bad place to explore. There was always something new thrown in on top of the old, and it looked like the county dump with the whole family discarding something daily. Nobody ever knew where I was if I hid myself away in there, and there was always a quarter or dollar stuck in a pair of unlaundered trousers.

To the right, just off where the carport used to be, were stairs up to the kitchen and a window, but it was an outside window just like the outside window at Jorma and Grandaddy's. Aunt Ease always kept that window open, looking right over her kitchen sink at whatever we were doing in the room below, the former carport. They had closed it in, making a big room that was almost a full floor level down from the rest of the house.

There Uncle Kingston sat in his recliner spitting his chewing tobacco into a cup with the juice running down one side of his mouth. It made him look like a really old puppet with that line separating the chin from the head. A mean old puppet.

"Suzie, turn that TV to channel eleven."

After I realized cousin Suzie wasn't going to jump out and surprise me like it was a party, *my* party, I figured he was talking to me. So I changed the channel, and he said "Thank ya, Suzie," settling the matter. I was not sure what to do, so I stood there watching channel eleven for a while. Then I just walked into the storage room and climbed over the hill of dirty clothes and sat there. I had a Matchbox with me, and I just ran it back and forth over my knee, sad but not sure why exactly.

It dawned on me years later that he probably thought it was a clever way of calling me a sissy, sort of like pre-code films of the 1930s masterfully used double entendre to make risqué references that would never pass the muster of movie censors in films later in the decade.

They started looking for me later that night, calling out my name, as I lay motionless, isolated in the storage room just feet from where they were. But I needed time alone. I just lay there in the storage room, not wanting to talk to anyone, but I knew Mama was upset. I waited until the search crew was somewhere else in the house when I climbed out into the former-carport-now-den and plopped on the sofa near where Uncle Kingston still sat in his recliner, and never even glancing my way, said, "Suzie, turn the channel to six."

## CHAPTER SEVENTEEN

# Ain't Novella

My Aunt Novella was "Ain't Novella" when spoken to, just as Aunt Pinky was "Ain't Pinky" and all my other aunts were "Ain'ts" as well. I heard Daddy call Aunt Ease "Hain't Ease" a bunch of times, I think because she was always sniffing her fingers, which bothered him something awful. Maybe it was Daddy's contraction of *hateful aunt*.

Aunt Novella was Uncle Calvin's wife, and she always started every visit with "You don't let 'em sit on the floor with his knees pointed in and his feet out?" Apparently, this seating position had the same mythical risk of crossing one's eyes. Where the eyes would stick instantly, the knees would bow inward in time.

I always thought Aunt Novella was so pretty, a sort of sour and pinched version of Elizabeth Taylor. Dark hair without the violet eyes, but she was striking and expressive and curious. She came by to visit the Christmas after MawMaw died, when Mama, Daddy, Adam, and I went to stay down in Warm Springs in MawMaw's house.

"I don't wanna stay down there at Christmas," Daddy said.

"Phil, I got so much to do. While school's out, and I don't have to get Adam ready every mornin', I can go through a lot of stuff."

But I didn't see Mama do a lot of going through stuff that holiday. I saw her standing in rooms by herself. Or looking out of the windows into the backyard covered in dead pine straw and red-mud patches where grass didn't take. Daddy sat in front of the television with some sports thing going on or reruns of *The Rifleman*. When the rifleman shot his gun on the television, I remember wondering if Mama was looking out the windows, thinking some deer hunter was on the edges of the thick pine trees where MawMaw's backyard met the woods.

I didn't think about MawMaw much except when we visited her. But when I did think of her when we were at home up in Alvaton, I thought of her in her house alone. I didn't envision her having visitors or ever going out on her own to the store or to church or to Aunt Ease's house or to anywhere. But I was wrong. Those first weeks of staying in MawMaw's house after she died helped me realize the life that went on in Warm Springs when we weren't there.

I learned that Aunt Novella visited MawMaw a lot. Aunt Novella said so when she came by to see Mama while we were staying down there that Christmas. As soon as Aunt Novella came in the front door, she turned her head to the right, like she was trying to hear something in the next room, and she poked her pointing finger just inside the shiny hair behind her right ear. She did it every time she came inside the front door, not just this front door; she did it at Aunt Ease's house, and when she came to see us in Alvaton too. As soon as the finger got inside her hairdo, the right side of her mouth moved up toward her ear like she pushed a button back there on her head, and it activated a half-smile.

I didn't notice she did this until Daddy said, "Novella's got a redbug livin' up behind her ear—"

"Phil." Mama would stop him.

"She checks to make sure it's there every time she comes in from the outside. Needs a leash for it so it cain't get away."

Her hair was always pulled up with little curly wisps coming from what would be the sideburn on a man. And she had on dangly earrings. As soon as she came in and poked her hair, she sat down and started talking to Mama while I sat in the floor with the Hot Wheels racing strips I got for Christmas. These were plastic tracks you snapped together end-to-end, the top section above the rest so gravity provided the thrust the cars needed to go barreling down the track. The most exciting part was a loop, which often was the end of the run because the cars derailed. The loop reminded me of the Mindbender rollercoaster at Six Flags. The loops terrified me. A waffle cone filled with mint chocolate chip ice cream melted, forgotten in my hand as I heard stories of phantoms—ghosts of men who worked on building the coaster come back to stop the cars mid-ride just at the top of the loop.

That day I was in my usual pose, knees together on the floor with my feet splayed out either side of me. Aunt Novella bubbled, "He shouldn't sit like that. He'll ruin his knees." She sometimes revisited her opening statement in the middle of a conversation.

Mama didn't say anything. She just commented on how much I liked cars, couldn't get enough of cars. Played with them in the floor. Played with them in bed. Played with them in the dirt.

Aunt Novella stood, came over determined to get me to sit properly, and scooped me up from behind just like Grandaddy did with ol' Luke before he stuck his snout down into the wasp nest for the second Sunday afternoon in a row, as if his nose being so swollen and dry for six days in a row wasn't enough to teach him that wasp nests will get you good.

I was surprised because she didn't ever hug Adam or me. She suspended me in air, her hands digging into my chest. Her fingers moved a little, pressing on me, letting up, and pressing again like she was testing the Charmin.

She asked, "What's wrong with this child? His che—"

"Novella." Mama cut her off.

Nobody said anything, and nobody moved.

"You want some cake, Novella?" Mama asked.

Aunt Novella's fingers tickled my chest in response as if the cake was hidden in my shirt.

I couldn't see Aunt Novella's face, but I could see Mama's. She wasn't shiny and pretty like she had been just the minute before.

Mama said, "Put him down, *now*," very quietly.

"But something's wrong with his—"

"Aw, no there's not." She stood up and goosed me out of Aunt Novella's hands, a crane frozen mid-lift with me the cargo. "Go get that Matchbox car and show Aunt Novella. Green is her favorite color too," Mama said, trying to distract me.

I knew the one she meant. It was my favorite one of all time, a green Mercury Cougar with red interior and doors that open, the one just like Beau's except for his didn't have red interior. It didn't work on the Hot Wheels track because it was a Matchbox. The main difference between Matchbox and Hot Wheels were the wheels. Matchbox wheels were almost like real miniature tires, connected with a metal bar. They didn't roll that well and rusted if they were "loved too much"—Mama's way of saying I played with them all the time. Hot Wheels were wider, like the tires you see on race cars on the television, and they were connected by a wire. They rolled like oil on smooth glass and were perfect for the Hot Wheels track.

When I returned to the living room with my favorite Matchbox of all time, Aunt Novella and Mama were quiet, looking at me. It was like somebody told them Mrs. Dunson was burning trash out back of her house because I swear they were holding their breath.

"Here it is. I think the seats should be white. The red seats make it look like Christmas."

"Uh-huh. That's nice, dear," but Aunt Novella was studying me, not the car. "You can get a real one like that when you grow up." The tips of her long fingernails came up under my chin and tilted my head to the side. "He has the most beautiful face, Betty Tom. I always said he should have been born a girl."

# PART TWO

## CHAPTER EIGHTEEN

# Wonky Me

When Aunt Novella left, I didn't want to dance when *The Partridge Family* came on television. It usually came on just after I finished my bath, and when I heard the theme song, I'd jump out of the tub, wet, without a stitch on and gyrate around the living room pretending I was fresh out of my partridge eggshell, singing at the top of my lungs with David Cassidy.

"Mama, look at me! Take me to California, and I'll make us a lot of money. I can dance!"

Even Daddy thought it was funny. If I could make him happy, I could entertain anyone.

I was also a student of acting, having broken down the nuances of on-screen kissing and how to make an entrance like I was on a fashion runway. The folks on Mama's shows kissed all the time. They looked at each other, then got closer, turned their heads at angles sort of like a dog cocks his head when you talk to him or offer him a treat, but then hide it behind your back. Then they'd put their lips together and move their heads back and forth, sort of like windshield wipers. I got Mama to practice with me, but we didn't touch lips. She leaned over, and we stuck out our lips like fish, and then she moved her head one way, and I moved mine the opposite way.

Fashion models held their arms straight down by their sides and put their hands straight out, sort of like they were leaning back on the kitchen counter, but there was no counter under their hands, only air. Then they just walked around real slow.

I had done my research, and I understood show business. We wouldn't even have to buy a product to sell like Pick had to. That meant we had no overhead. That's what Pick called it, and if we didn't have overhead, we could keep all the profit and not have to pay anything. But that night after what Aunt Novella said, I didn't care. Something was wrong. Something must be wrong with my body.

I walked into MawMaw's room to the closet that had two doors going from her room to the room next to it, and I opened the door so I could see the long mirror there. It was just like the mirror in Mama and Daddy's room in Alvaton, the one Mama looked in before we went to church. I couldn't see high enough into any other mirrors in the house. I pulled my shirt off and looked. What was wrong with me? Maybe there was something that adults could see, a special sight you got when you grew up. But I didn't know what it was.

And then, I saw it. I had seen it before, of course, but hadn't thought anything of it. The middle bone in my chest, the one that the ribs connect to was turned so that it faced to the left. I didn't know what to call it, but I knew what the ribs were called because we ate them a few times over at Uncle Calvin's. Adam told me they were the pig version of "these bones here" and grabbed his sides.

"There's meat on 'em if you're a pig," he explained, "and you can eat 'em."

The bottom of that center bone poked out, with skin tight around it like I was holding a finger right up against a deflated balloon. The ribs on that one side pressed in like they were trying to touch my back. This must be what Aunt Novella meant. I didn't know it was wrong, I just thought it was different, like my blond hair when Mama, Adam, and Daddy all had brown hair and Jorma and MawMaw had silver hair, and Grandaddy didn't have any at all. I didn't know chests were supposed to be one way or the other. If somebody had asked me, I guess I would have said chests can be flat on both sides like Adam, poke out on both sides like Mama, or poke in on one side and poke out on the other like me.

The morning after Aunt Novella's visit, shucking my pajamas after breakfast on my way to a bath, killing time staring at the television at the end of *The Beverly Hillbillies*, I suddenly and for the first time wondered if they really could see me. Elly May, Granny, Uncle Jed, and Jethro waved to me, ducking and peeking through the closing credits on the screen. I usually waved back because I knew them, but now I was afraid they could see me without my shirt. It had made me happy before to think they saw me and waved at me, only me, while everybody else watching just saw them there, standing as the credits rolled.

When I'd been sad in the past, it never occurred to me that I wouldn't be happy again. Now, I thought that even if something great happened, I wouldn't be as happy as I would have been earlier…that my happiness level for all time had been set lower, like turning down a thermostat, or an oven that doesn't ever quite run as hot as you want. It was like I had a sad streak in me, which are good in cakes but not in people.

Mama always made cakes for birthdays, Thanksgiving, Christmas, Easter, and school events like the school fair—half fundraiser and half parent-teacher conference. Mama made a pound cake like always, and she put it on a Tupperware cake carrier with her name written on masking tape that she put on the bottom of the plate and the inside of the cover. Both smelled like vanilla that had seeped into them from all the pound cakes they'd carried over the years. Aunt Novella gave her the cake carrier as a wedding present, so it was older than even I was. I liked Mama's cakes 'cause she under baked them. There was always a gluey, moist streak running right through the bottom sitting just inside the brown crusty bottom layer.

"Why do you call it a sad streak, Mama?"

"Well, if you press a finger on top of a piece of just cut, still warm pound cake, a little sugary and buttery batter seeps out. It weeps a little."

I felt the moist cake in my mouth each time I took a bite, and I thought it must have been sad because it didn't get to be what it was supposed to be. Close but not exactly right. Mama said the heat of the pan cooked the outside to a buttery brown crust, but that saggy sad streak was batter that came close to cooking through, but not quite. "If you have a sad streak, you've got a moist cake."

And she was right. The goo stuck in the rough places in your teeth, just like her homemade communion wafers did. Cold grape juice went best with the communion wafers, 'cause the preacher said so. A glass of ice-cold milk went best with a gluey, gooey pound cake's thinnest layer of yum.

It made me think of when the Highway Department digs out the embankment when cutting a road out of the side of the hill—years of the uncovered earth exposed to the air, the elements, and the eye. Sometimes the clay isn't the pure red variety through and through. Sometimes there's a thin vein of something else running in it, separating the red clay into different layers. Sometimes you could see a silvery hard layer. But if you touch it, it's not hard. It's weak and flakey. It's gypsum, soft as wet chalk. *Weak.* I guess that's me, I thought. I've got a sad streak running right through me.

Mama's main job, what she cared most about, was protecting us. I guess Daddy felt the same way, but his way was waking us up at night to ask if Finley's dogs barking was keeping us awake. Our eyes full of sleep and creases between our eyebrows in confusion, Daddy wouldn't wait for a response. Then, after he'd awakened us a few times, I think Adam and I felt sorry for him and somehow obligated to tell him that the dogs did keep us awake. So we'd say they did. And after a while, they *did* wake me up, or worse, prevented sleep at all as I anticipated another yelp in the distance.

Then more and more, I started to hear other things when we went back home to Alvaton. One was best described as a "cuh," which came from inside the room Adam and I shared, small with two twin beds, a toy box that had lost its lid, and a dresser.

"Mama, he's 'cuh-ing' again." It was Adam's breathing I heard. It wasn't snoring, just that click in his throat as the soft, moist tissue allowed his breath out.

When I got tucked in for the night, my sheet and blanket had to be folded back in a very particular way. "Mama, fold the sheets so they come up to my ear, and angle it down over here so just my neck is above the covers." And then after Mama moved me to my own room, I couldn't go to sleep unless the light was on in the living room. I could see the living room door just through my bedroom door and across the hallway. I had to see that light while I waited for sleep to take me. If I woke up and the light wasn't on, I'd call out "Mama! Mama!" Tired as she was, she always got up, turned on the lamp, sat there, and waited for me to go to sleep before she went back to bed.

I had pictures from the newspaper on the wall above my bed. In the night, unable to sleep, I'd lie sideways in bed with my feet up on the wall, tracing with my big toe the rough edge of the tape that held up the photographs. For some reason, for a time, I was fixated on Janet Mabie. She was dark-haired and had really sparkly eyes that were angled like a cat's. My favorite clipping was of her smiling in her high school tennis outfit just after she won a tournament. Her sisters and one brother all looked the same, except Laurel who had blonde hair. Their daddy, Spit Mabie, was the most successful businessman around, owning a GM dealership. If you owned a Chevrolet, Pontiac, or GMC, it came from Spit's. On rare Saturday afternoons Daddy would take me there and let me run around the lot and sit in new cars, dreaming of the day when I'd have one of my own.

By this time, fresh out of kindergarten and a rising first grader, I was a GM man. My beloved 1968 Mercury Cougar was still a joy each time I saw one, and my Cougar Matchbox remained my favorite of all time, but the GM lineup in the early '70s was sublime, with beautiful, graceful lines. They were so glorious that I didn't want 1973 to come. The majesty of cars from the late 1950s that devolved into the abomination of those that came in the early 1960s was a harbinger, a caution.

My favorite car at that age was the 1971 Monte Carlo, having the longest hood on an American production car. It was elegant and almost smiling with its open, round headlights and broad, shining grill, though my former paramour, the 1968 Mercury Cougar, was an alluring contender still. While the 1968 Cougar held a never-to-be supplanted place in my heart and eyes, the Monte Carlo bewitched. The years 1969 and onward were a tragic time for Fords and Mercuries. It was like the mastermind behind the beautifully-proportioned designs had died, leaving lesser family members in charge.

Even though I had my true loves, I now and again flirted with other cars that captured my imagination. It was the opposite for Mama. She never strayed from her true loves—Adam and me. It showed in different ways. After I realized something was wrong with me, awakened from that dream that life was carefree, I noticed that she worried all the time, especially during the warmer months when kids were out in shorts and T-shirts, the boys often with no shirts at all. On those days, I wanted more, not fewer, layers.

She sewed custom shirts with darts and angles that camouflaged my deformity, and the net result was I was a little fashion plate, even in the summertime. Stiff linen shirts had a natural wrinkly quality, and that provided the illusion of dips and hollows and waves on the fabric's surface, masking my imperfection. And the winter was the best because I really did have a body for clothes. That is, I definitely looked better in, than out, of them. Layers and layers of fabric between the world and me. Covering my chest, camouflaging it, didn't comfort her or ease what I later came to understand as her guilt.

"Should have just stayed nauseated," she said, not an old person's ramble, but like someone who doesn't realize they're thinking out loud.

The only difference now was that she wasn't alone in worry. I joined her. My knowing didn't reduce her load by half…it increased it times two.

## CHAPTER NINETEEN

# Motor Magic

A s much as Mama's worry preoccupied me at times, I couldn't help but notice that something new was going on at the small house down the street from MawMaw's, which sat a few hundred feet through the pine trees. Finley and all his dogs left, off to where nobody knew or cared, and we didn't ask. This was great news because the dogs didn't bark at night, and it was almost funny seeing Daddy have nothing to react to. But it was sad too. I bet those dogs wouldn't have barked so much if they had been able to run around instead of staying in a pen all the time. Every now and again one would run though the yard, looking like it was as happy as a dog could be. They must have been starving for what I longed for behind the wheel of a car—nothing but the air holding you back.

The new family put up a big handmade, wooden sign with a drawing of a brown wrecker on it with a red car hooked onto the back, and underneath it read "Brown's Body Shop." They started hauling in one wrecked car after another on a real-life version of the wrecker in the sign. I wasn't able to watch on weekdays, but from what I remember Daddy saying, they'd bring a couple of cars every few days to the shop, and he wasn't happy about it.

"They haul all them damn wrecks in here, and they'll leak gas into the ground, and it'll be in the well water before you know it."

But I was fascinated and wanted to study each car. And, had I gone down there, I could have, because it was like the cars were on display for a little while in the front yard, a calling card for snooping neighbors. But I didn't go down to Brown's. Ever since I found out my chest was different, my spirit of adventure seemed to have dried up. But one car came and went under its own steam, my ideal dark green 1971 Monte Carlo. I couldn't see who drove it.

Aunt Loodie, who lived all the way down in Talbot County, knew all about Mr. Brown. Daddy said Aunt Loodie was so nosey that if you lost a fart in a windstorm, she'd find it. Mama didn't like when he said that, but that didn't stop him from saying it. He said that Aunt Ease smelled her fingers a lot too. "I don't know what she's been doin' with those fingers, but she smells 'em like they're covered in either roses or dog shit."

Mama always stopped him with some version of "I wish you'd be more clever in a more clever way."

Well, Aunt Loodie reported that Mr. Brown went by Brownie, and he wasn't married. He moved from down in Waycross, but she said, "I don't know why yet, but I think he was in a bad divorce, and they ran him out of town."

Daddy said, "When Loodie says she doesn't know and then gives you the answer, it's because she pulled that answer out of her—"

"Phil!" Mama stopped him.

But I didn't care why he was there because he had a Monte Carlo in my favorite color, which until then I'd only seen standing still on the car lot or staged with happy couples frolicking near a shiny new one in the car books that lined the shelves at the dealership. Sometimes I'd see a car in town and rub my hand along the vinyl strip that ran the length of it from tip to tail, protecting it from the unforgiving edges of other car doors opening against it. Running my hand along the chassis made me feel as if a piece of me had rubbed off on it, and it on me. Sometimes a blinker was embedded in the front or rear tip of the car, the pointing finger of a wiser, older friend who knew the way to go and pointed in that direction with every even-timed, flashing blink: "This way. This way."

I know it sounds odd, but back then I trusted cars. Still do, I suppose. I wanted to climb inside each of them and take a nap, my cheek flat against the vinyl of the back seat, stuck there in the humid, dripping-wet summer afternoon air. But I couldn't climb in. They belonged to somebody else. The only way to let them know I longed for their comfort, their protection, was to caress their painted skin, running my finger-tip along the curve of a chromed bumper or the loop of a door handle. Each touch letting the car know that I saw it, wanted to give it the gift of my cool hand during a Georgia-hot summer afternoon.

And even if it was a car I didn't want to ride in—a Pinto or a Corvair—I felt like it could see me through its headlamp eyes. I knew it, recognized it, and was convinced we were communicating through those brief touches. And when a car really entranced me, I longed to see who drove it. Because in some way, I had to be kinda like that person. Beau chose a Mercury Cougar, so I knew that Beau was like me. Cars signaled who around me was kin, something I couldn't explain but trusted in nonetheless.

I couldn't wait until the day I could drive. I just felt that a car would take me toward something, or someone. Had I known then what I know now, I would have been saved a lot of heartache.

## CHAPTER TWENTY

# Mama Won, Daddy Zero

Even though MawMaw was gone, Mama liked being in MawMaw's house across the street from Aunt Ease. Aunt Ease came over to visit every day just like Jorma came down to visit every day after Grandaddy went to work. But Mama smiled when Aunt Ease came in, and they sat down at the kitchen table together before they started going through boxes and closets.

"I want to move here," Mama said to Aunt Ease. They didn't know it, but I was hiding in the snake bush under the open window.

"What will Phil say?" Aunt Ease asked.

"I don't think I want him to move here, permanently."

"Betty Tom."

"What?"

"He'll never let you go," Aunt Ease huffed.

"He will."

"No."

"How much would I need to buy everybody out?" Mama asked.

"I have no idea."

That weekend, I overheard Mama tell Daddy that we could get the house for less than it's worth since nobody else was there and because all of her brothers and sisters had houses to live in.

"We have a house," Daddy replied.

"Mama's is bigger."

"Don't need a bigger house."

"The boys need their own rooms," Mama pressed.

*I'd like my own room*, I thought. I could put car posters on every wall.

"No, they don't."

"Philbet cain't sleep. He calls my name at all hours. *My* name, not *yours*. I have to get up and referee, not you." Mama said getting louder and louder. "I put Philbet in the TV room some nights, *not every night*, because he's not getting along with Adam."

"Put Philbet back in that room with Adam. He'll sleep when he gets good and tired."

"No, he won't. He'll wait until he sits at breakfast and fall asleep over his cinnamon toast. It dud'n help when you go in there and wake 'em up when they're asleep to ask if they're asleep!"

"Stop!"

"Why do you do that? Let 'em be." Mama smacked her hands together on *be*.

"I. Said. Shut. The. Hell. Up. Goddamit!" And Daddy smacked his hand on the table on every word.

"If you wouldn't go in there and make'm as crazy as you are—" Mama not letting up.

"Shut up, goddamit, shut up. Shut up!"

Silence.

And Daddy went out the back door. I peeked around the corner and saw Mama standing at the sink with her hands on the counter, like she was trying to get strong enough to pull herself up. Like she needed to climb up there to get a bug off the ceiling.

A thud against the cinder block wall from the outside made her look up, and Daddy's face popped up in front of Mama through the open window just above the sink. It scared me, too, but Mama is the one who jumped back, and when she did her hand knocked a glass off the counter and onto the floor. The splitting glass was the same sound as an open-handed smack across a cheek. It must have felt like that to both of them—a slap—but it didn't change anything. Daddy didn't ask her if she was hurt.

All he said was, "I want my goddamn TV room back. I cain't even watch my goddamn TV when I want 'cause you got Philbet in there. Put him back in that room with Adam. Do it, or I'll put him back."

And his face disappeared from the window. I couldn't see if Mama had cut her foot, but if she had, there'd be a bloody smear on the floor. I peeked around the corner a little more, and Mama was quiet. No blood. She was just still on the floor. I went in the kitchen to where she could see me.

"Mama?" I looked around the corner.

"Don't come over here. Glass."

"Mama?"

"It's okay," she said.

Daddy came in. "You alright?"

That's when Mama saw her moment, "The schools in Warm Springs are better."

"I went to the school up here. They're fine."

"They'd be the only White kids in the whole school if they go up here. You wanna do that?"

"They ain't all Black."

"They'd be the only White kids in the school."

And Daddy whispered, "Goddamit." And he walked out the back door so quiet and slow it was like he was trying to sneak up on somebody.

Mama stood up and walked toward the door. "Phil." She turned back to me. "Do. Not. Touch. That. Glass. You hear me?"

"Yessum."

"Phil."

Daddy stopped on the side stoop with his back to the door, looking out toward Pick's store.

Mama said to me, "You stand right in that spot and tell Adam not to come in the kitchen until I come back and clean up that glass. You hear me?"

"Yessum."

Then she said as she went through the door toward Daddy, "We'd only have to pay four parts out of five since Mama left the house to all of us in equal parts." And they walked into the backyard.

I stared at the broken glass on the floor, wishing I were a magician on the television and could make the glass come back together and not be broken any more…back to a full glass from two minutes earlier before Mama and Daddy started yelling at each other. It scared me, scared me like I felt sometimes when Adam held me down and tickled me. I thought about getting the dustpan from under the sink like I knew Mama would do. I liked to help. It made me feel like I was doing something to make things better. But Mama said not to, so I didn't.

And then I thought about MawMaw's house, and I remembered what Mama just said. I wondered which room MawMaw left to Mama, and which rooms she left the others. I figured the kitchen was for Mama because none of the others ever had anything good to eat when you went over to their houses. Aunt Ease surely got the living room since she loved her own so much. Uncle Calvin must have gotten the bathroom. I wasn't sure why, I just thought he belonged in a bathroom.

But that Monte Carlo. I'd move down to MawMaw's house just to see that car, graceful as a leopard running in slow motion like in those TV nature shows, then a minute later, taking off like it was spring loaded. If we moved, I'd be a neighbor. I might get a chance to ride in it one day.

When we visited Warm Springs, it became my number one project to stake out the scene and see who got in and out of that car. They parked around the back side of the house, and I didn't have any way of seeing when it took off. All the angles from the yard where I watched the road were wrong, and when I did see it, all I could make out was a hand, an old man's hand, on the steering wheel.

One day in town it was parked on Main Street, and I tried to get Mama to let me stay in the car while she went into the bank, but she said I needed some new shoes because Adam ruined the ones I would have gotten from him. I touched the driver's door handle as I walked by. By the time we got back to the car after shoe shopping, the Monte Carlo was gone, and a Pinto was in its place. *I'll hate Pintos and these shoes as long as I live*, I remember thinking to myself.

Back at MawMaw's house, I scouted every possible location to get a good look at the Monte Carlo. I even went into the woods and tried to see the back of the house from the trees, but I couldn't see the parking place from anywhere. I took to sitting in the snake bush, waiting for the sound of the car turning onto the road, protected from view so that I didn't look like I was just standing in the front yard for no good reason. And the kitchen window was always wide open. I could even hear the chicken frying.

Daddy said, "I don't want to move, goddammit."

I didn't think I really wanted to either. If we moved down here permanently, there'd be a twenty-five-mile asphalt road between Grandaddy and me instead of a dirt path through the garden.

Mama said under her breath when he went out the door, "Don't wish for that too hard."

Mama wanted what she wanted more than the rest of us wanted what we wanted, and she had a plan. The decision was made with no going back as soon as Mama got a job.

Mama said to Aunt Ease one day while I sat outside in the snake bush below the kitchen window, "He can't keep up like he did before he got shot."

"I thought he was okay."

"Louise, be serious."

"Well, he's always been an ass." I imagined Aunt Ease sitting there with her coffee, sniffing her fingers.

"He's not good for the boys," Mama said, and I wondered what she meant. He wasn't bad for us in the way eating too much watermelon is, or like being in pine straw without getting checked later for ticks and redbugs.

"He's fearful. He's afraid," Mama said.

Why was Daddy afraid? The man who shot him in the head was in the jail and had been for a while.

"Um, more like totally nuts," said Aunt Ease.

"No, really. I'm being serious. He's…he's weak."

They were quiet.

"Well, he did just get shot in the head." I'd never heard Aunt Ease take up for Daddy before.

I wished they'd talk faster and not breathe so much.

"I remember," Mama started and stopped, "when…between Adam and Philbet…."

"I know," Aunt Ease said.

"Well, Jolie came down to check on me after the delivery. I was so sick. I was so sad, Louise." Mama said.

"I know."

Mama was much quieter, "I've never been so low, and Jolie wanted to take Adam for a week so I could rest."

"Yeah," Aunt Ease said.

"He wouldn't let her. I was so tired. I…my bones weighed a thousand pounds."

"Well wud'n it better for you to have Adam around if you…?"

"Why are you makin' excuses for him? YouhatePhil." Mama said it so fast I thought she was calling Aunt Ease "hateful."

And just like that Mama and Aunt Ease seemed to run out of things to say, even though it seemed like to me they had plenty to talk about.

"He won't even say anything to Calvin or Kingston when they tease Philbet."

"They're mean as hell, you know that," said Aunt Ease.

"Well, Louise, I'm not afraid of either of 'em. And if you aren't gonna tell Kingston to stop callin' names, I will. If I have to I'll drive my car down through that pasture and T-bone his goddamn tractor while he's on it."

Aunt Ease made a "humph" sound.

"Don't roll your eyes at me. Go back across the road and tell your husband to stop callin' my boy names. I heard him do it, Louise!"

"He won't stop."

"Louise, look at me." And they were quiet, so I guess Aunt Ease looked at Mama.

"Do it." I wish I could see Mama right then. She didn't sound like the Mama I knew.

They didn't say anything for a while.

"I need to get a job. The boys are going to both be in school. We need the money. There's nothing in Alvaton unless I want to pump gas."

"He ain't gonna like that."

"Too bad," Mama said.

And Mama had a job before I could manage to see who drove that Monte Carlo—a job that left me breathless. She was the new receptionist at Mabie Motors, which meant she'd be working in the showroom big enough for three full-size cars, just steps away from the fenced-in lot where all the new cars sat ready for buyers to pick their favorite. If Mama was going to be spending time away from Adam and me, I couldn't have picked a better place for her to be. Daddy's job was halfway between where we lived and MawMaw's house. Mabie Motors was only a few minutes from MawMaw's, so we had to move. It only made sense. I couldn't get the grin off my face for days and days.

The excitement didn't last long. The day we were supposed to move to MawMaw's house, the cinder block house in Alvaton was almost empty, and I walked from room to room slowly as Mama and Daddy and Adam moved really fast, just as people in old movies seem to move faster than real people do.

"Mama, when did we move into this house?"

"Philbet, I'm…I…I have work to do." She frowned.

"Where did we live before here?"

"We lived in the white house Sharon lives in by the church." And then she disappeared out the front door with a box in her arms.

I followed her, not remembering ever living in Sharon's house. "I don't remember that, Mama." I was suddenly as bereft as I was when Daddy and Grandaddy took ol' Luke off and never came back with him. His doghouse just sat there by itself without ol' Luke. That's what the house looked like without furniture, like ol' Luke's empty doghouse.

"Sweetheart, I'm so busy." And then she crouched down. "You didn't live there. Your Daddy and I lived there before you were born." The soft side of her hand brushed my ear, and she was up and off.

I went into the room Adam and I shared for as long as I can remember, and the only thing left was the toy box. I was just in the way. That's what Adam kept saying. So I climbed in it. I fit perfectly. If there wasn't room for me in the car, they could just put me in the toy box and put us both on the back of the truck to go down to Warm Springs. I stayed right there in the toy box when Grandaddy came in. He sat on the edge.

"Son?"

"Yessir."

"What's wrong?" Grandaddy asked.

I didn't really know what was wrong.

"Can you look up?" Grandaddy tapped gently on the side of the toy box.

I looked up at him.

"I guess I'd be scared if I was moving. You scared a little?"

I didn't want to be scared. I really wanted to live next to the Monte Carlo, but I'd rather live next to Grandaddy.

I shook my head, thinking I wouldn't be able to talk if I tried to because I thought I had chalk in my throat.

"We can visit every Sunday," he promised.

"Are we going to go to church with you still?"

"I don't know. We can talk to your Mama and Daddy about that."

I always sat next to Grandaddy, and on Communion Sunday he'd grab two little wafers and give one to me. Grandaddy always slipped one to me, and I let it melt in my mouth and get soft before I chewed it. The wafer turned back into gooey dough and got caught in the rough little mountains that made up the surface of my back teeth. If I'd looked in the mirror, I bet it would have looked like snow on the caps of mountains.

Then he'd give me half of his holy Welch's.

I didn't know why I could have Welch's grape juice at home out in the open, even if the preacher was standing right in front of me, but I couldn't have the little half mouthful of grape juice in the church.

"When you get saved by God, you can have your own grape juice," Grandaddy would whisper in the pew.

Now, he said, "I'll miss seeing you every day, but your Mama needs to move to be near her sister. Your Mama just lost her own mama, so she's real sad right now. She's sadder than you or me. Now, stand up."

I did. He put his hand on the back of my head as if it were a signal that he'd said all he came to say, and he expected me to be a little more grown up when he left. He didn't say that, but he had a way of letting you know that your end of the bargain was to be strong, maybe stronger than you knew you could be. And I knew I could do it because I didn't want to let him or Mama down.

Then, he pulled a pencil from his shirt pocket and picked up my blue plastic Matchbox carrying case. The thin plastic skin was curled back at one of the corners, revealing the separating cardboard underneath, and Grandaddy wrote something on it and turned the case around toward me.

"If you ever need me, if you ever want me, you pick up any telephone and dial the zero. Okay?"

"Yessir."

"And when the operator answers you say…what do you think you should say?"

I looked at him.

"I want to talk to Grandaddy."

"That's right. That's part of it."

"What's the other part of it, Grandaddy?"

"Tell 'em you want 'em to call your Grandaddy, and he'll pay for the call."

"Okay."

"Tell 'em to reverse the charges."

That sounded like the operator would owe me some money, but I didn't dwell on that part.

"And then you call out these numbers that I wrote down here on your Matchbox case. What are those numbers? You can read 'em, I know."

"Yessir, I know my numbers."

"Okay, read 'em for me."

"Four. Zero. Four. One. Three. Two. Five. Four. Three. Two."

"Come here," and he pulled me to him as I crawled out of the toy box.

And softly, while I rested, melted against him, he said, "I wrote that number there 'cause I know those cars won't ever be too far from you, Philbet. But I want you to study them and be able to say them from memory, whether the case is with you or not."

"Yessir."

"Do you know why?"

"Why what?"

"Do you know why I want you to memorize my telephone number?"

"'Cause if there was a bad thunderstorm and the lights went out, I couldn't see to read the numbers in the dark."

He laughed, as if his laugh surprised him.

"You know, that's about as good a reason to memorize than any I can think of. Just promise me you'll do it."

"Okay, Grandaddy. I promise."

"You'll be okay. I wouldn't say you'd be okay if you weren't going to be." And then he winked.

## CHAPTER TWENTY-ONE

# Jess Station

That first week of first grade was a trial. Well, it was actually an adventure to start off. Mama had put off getting the vaccinations, but she had to get them so that my paperwork would be okay when I went to school the next day...the very first day of first grade.

I already knew all my letters and could write whole sentences. I was a first-grader after all. I could even read some, mostly by sounding out the words. I didn't always know what they meant, but I could read! I could read any car label, not because I had memorized what kind of car it was from sight, but because I could read it. When they came out with the new car models every September, I could even tell what the new models were, even if they didn't look anything like their previous year's. And I could even read the nameplate on new models. That's how I learned about the Monte Carlo. It was brand new for 1970 in late 1969.

So we hauled down to the county health department for vaccinations. Adam must have planned it. Mama was so focused on getting my vaccinations that she didn't figure on Adam outmaneuvering her. We pulled into the parking space at the health office, and Mama and I got out. Mama set me on the pavement, stuck her thumb in her mouth and rubbed my chin, and turned around at the sound of a thud.

Adam had about two inches to finish rolling up the back window after having tossed her pocketbook out onto the ground. Mama lunged for it as Adam turned into a boy-sized spider and jumped around to each door lock to slap it down flush with the door.

Mama's keys were still in the ignition. He knew that we had come there mostly to get my vaccinations, and I still had no idea what they were. Mama said Adam might need some vaccinations too. I was so anxious about going to school the next day that I didn't even think to ask what a vaccination was. When I saw him push her envelope of papers out through a slit in the window on the other side of the car from where Mama stood, I knew something was up. Mama must have realized I figured it out at the same time I figured it out because she turned her head to me and said, "It's okay, Sweetheart."

I picked up one foot slowly, as if I'd just realized I stepped in gum, and she continued, "Don't. I can catch you."

"What's a vaccination?" I put my foot back down.

"Philbet, go pick up those papers your brother threw out the window." I did as I was told.

One paper got loose, and I chased it, stepping on it with my foot. The place where my foot smashed it into the pavement made it rough, and I could feel the imprint where my new school shoes had pressed it into the pavement.

"You think a vaccination hurts? Just wait," Mama said through the closed window to Adam. He was up on his knees in the very center of the back seat, as if he were in a cage at the zoo trying to stay as far away from the wild animals that roamed freely all around him.

"Mama, look, did I hurt this?" I realized that there was another rough patch on the paper.

Over her shoulder as we went inside, she warned Adam, "Be in that car when I get back and unlock the doors before my hand touches the door handle."

She stuck her head out through the Health Office door as soon as we went inside, and called, "Don't talk to any strangers!"

"Mama, I stepped on this. Did I hurt it?"

"No."

"Did somebody step on it here too?"

"No, that's a seal. That makes it official. That's your birth certificate. It proves you were born…it gives all the details. It will tell the school tomorrow that I'm your mama and Daddy is your daddy and the day you were born…that kind of stuff."

"Oh." That made sense.

I held the papers as Mama talked to the lady at the counter. Since I could read, I started to study my birth certificate.

"Father's ahk-you-pay-shun. In-jun-ear ade. Mama, it says Daddy has an ahk-you-pay-shun, but it doesn't have your ahk-you-pay-shun."

"Um, my occupation is to take care of you and Adam."

"Where does it say that?"

"It's…it's just something everybody knows," she replied.

"Number of…? What does that mean, Mama?"

"Um."

She didn't answer.

"Mama, under other children there's Adam and Jes-tay-shun-ul. Who's Jess?"

"That's not a person. That means, um…."

I'd never known Mama not to have an answer, except for that time she opened a can of pineapple and found what looked to be baby corn inside.

"Let's get the vaccinations and go home. We can look at your birth certificate at home and talk about it. Okay?"

"Okay. Are we going to get Adam's vaccinations too?"

"They won't just give them to me. They have to give them directly to him. We'll come back to get his. We need yours today so they'll let you in school tomorrow."

I was kind of sick the whole first day of school. Not *sick* sick; I was *scared* sick. Plus, I was upset with Mama for not telling me what a vaccination was before we got to the Health Office, and I wanted to know where my other brother or sister was. I didn't like being upset with Mama; it didn't feel right. I kept repeating to myself "jess-station-birth." Could that mean Mama gave birth at the Esso Station in Greenville on the way to the hospital? I wasn't sure, but that was what the birth certificate called it. I sounded it out.

If Mama had had another baby, I wanted to see it—meet it. I wanted to know if it was a brother or sister. I wanted it to be a sister. I decided it *was* a sister. And I named her Jessie…Jess for short.

## CHAPTER TWENTY-TWO

# My Nowhere Sister

One reason school scared me was that Adam didn't give me any clues on what to expect, except: "Don't go in the girl's bathroom." And then he said, "Oh, in the lunch line, check out the bottom shelf. If they have chocolate milk, that's where they'll try to hide 'em."

Adam was right, there was a lot of regular sweet milk on all the shelves, but if you crouched down and looked, there were some chocolate and strawberry milk cartons on the bottom shelf back behind the others. I got both a chocolate and a strawberry, sorta like melted Neapolitan ice cream, but not a sweet milk. The lunch lady let me have both of them, but only after I gave her an extra nickel.

I didn't want any lunch, just the milk. I couldn't eat. My stomach was all rumbly 'cause I was still thinking about Jess and wondering where she was. I mean, if she didn't live with us, who fed her and where did she sleep? When they called Mama from the principal's office after lunch, they blamed it on the two milks and the mixing of chocolate and strawberry on an empty stomach. I thought they must have never heard of Neapolitan ice cream, which made me kind of sad for them.

I lay on the school's hallway sofa with cushions like hay bales covered in leather so fake that even I, a first-grader with a sick stomach, paused to notice. It felt like long hours there outside Principal Pratt's office waiting for Mama to come pick me up, there on display for other students to see me and categorize me as the sickly, scrawny kid, and for teachers in their continual scan of the grade school landscape to make a mental note of my face so that they could slide me into their delicate/weak file as soon as they had a name to put with the face. I wondered if I did the right thing by calling Mama instead of Grandaddy on his phone number that I memorized the very night he wrote it on my Matchbox case. But I called Mama and repeated, "Four. Zero. Four. One. Three. Two. Five. Four. Three. Two." over and over to myself until Mama arrived.

I don't remember arriving at Warm Springs Elementary that first day. All I remember is the increasing excitement and anxiety leading up to day one. If my nerves got the better of me, I'd imagine a bubble of protection moving along with me, encasing me just like a baby bird shell, but thinner, protecting the new life inside. But after I learned about Jess, the shell seemed even more delicate than before, quicker to break.

Mama sometimes drove us to school in the mornings. Or we'd take the bus. Freckle-faced cousin Veralynn, already graduated, sometimes got paid to pick me up, usually sitting outside in the circular drive in her little light blue VW wearing her swimsuit, hair still wet. She was fun, always asking how the day was and having a comment that was too grown up for me to understand. She wasn't trying to be too grown up because she *was* grown up. But she talked to me like I was grown up too. I felt a responsibility to understand what she meant, but I usually ended up trying to hide that I didn't quite get it.

But on that first day, it was Mama who came to pick up her sick boy. She walked into the school's hallway, a thin, black, shadowy stick blown in by the wind as the door creaked open. Her face came into view the farther she got away from the bright outside and the closer she came into the dark hallway toward me. She felt my forehead and then kissed the top of my head.

"Can you make it through to the end of the day?"

"No'm."

To herself, she said, "Maybe it was the vaccination."

Then to me, "Okay, let's go home."

She grabbed my bag, and I followed her. The door she had just come through was slowly creaking shut, slow as an old man's leg. She didn't have as far to push it open because it hadn't quite shut. The door handle was broken and just hung loose and heavy against the door. If you lifted it a little and let it fall back against the flat of the door, it sounded a lot like the door knocker on Aunt Novella's house.

When Mama and I got outside, I asked, "When did my sister die?"

Mama stopped right in front of me so fast that I thought maybe a car was coming up the drive as she stepped off the curb. But she wasn't looking both ways. She was looking straight ahead, across the street, at something I couldn't see. Or wouldn't have understood, even if I could see it.

She turned around. "She didn't die, Sweetheart."

*She was alive?* I thought.

"Really? Where is she? Where's Jess?" I couldn't believe I had a sister.

"Um."

I didn't understand why Mama didn't know where she was.

"Jess? Let's talk about it when we get home."

But I didn't want to talk about it when we got home. If I had a sister, I wanted to know where she was and why she didn't live with us. I mean, we could turn the little TV room into a bedroom for her.

"Does she have light hair like me?" I asked.

And then mama just stood there as still and plastic as a mannequin from Belk Department Store. Just as if somebody had picked her up off her stand and carried her sideways out the front door without paying for her or the clothes she had on. And she cried without even closing her eyes or making any kind of sound at all.

"Mama?"

But instead of answering me she threw her pocketbook at the building and her lipstick and change made a twangy thwack as it went everywhere. I was not sure if I should go pick it up, but after about a minute I did because she was too big to climb under the overgrown holly bush near the classroom window. And as I stood up, my new first-grade classmates whose desks were near the window had turned their heads and were looking directly at me.

I bet I didn't get all the change. Grandaddy said he put all his paper money in order starting with the dollar bills and then the fives and tens and twenties with the one-dollars on top, with all the faces going in the same direction.

"Line up your money so you know how much you have," he said. "That's showin' respect. And if you respect it, it'll respect you." And he always had his hand in his pocket, gangling his change like he was sifting through a bowl of freshly shelled pecans. And on Sunday, he'd let me slip my hand in his pocket and pull out whatever change I could and put it in the collection plate.

So if Mama spent so much time looking after Adam and me, shouldn't she be spending time looking after Jess too? Why wasn't she with us, and why didn't Mama know where she was?

Suddenly afraid, I said, "Mama?"

And she stopped being frozen and came over to me as I climbed out from under the holly bush. She picked me up and got waxy lipstick on my cheek and tears on my ear.

But still, I had to know. "Did the thieves come up from the railroad cut one night and steal Jess?"

Mama breathed in and out really slowly. I had a pack of her Certs in my hand, and I peeled back the gold paper to loosen the very first one from the roll for her. And she smiled while she took it and put it in her mouth.

Finally she said, "No. I was gonna have a baby, but it didn't come to live here."

"So where is it?"

"It was never born."

"Yes, she was. You said the paper said something, Esso Station birth. Was she born at the Esso?"

And she took the Certs and pulled one out, kissed it, and put it to my lips. I loved Certs, and I loved the ones that tasted like Mama's lipstick even more. Sometimes, if there was some red on the Cert she gave me, I'd take it out of my mouth and rub it against my lips. That way, once the Certs was dissolved in my mouth, I had one last sweet lick on my lips, and they were perfume-waxy to remind me that Mama gave it to me.

"The paper read *gestational birth*, which means she didn't quite get born."

I took out my Certs and held it in my fingers because I couldn't really talk with it in my mouth. "Well when's she going to get born?"

"She…she was growing inside my tummy. Babies start off in their mommy's tummies."

I knew that. I wasn't a baby. "Yessum."

"And she should have stayed in there longer, but she decided that she wanted to come out of my tummy too soon."

"Yeah?"

"And she wasn't alive by the time she got out of my tummy."

"Couldn't you tell her to stay inside like you do me?"

And Mama hugged me to her.

"Oh, I guess she was stubborn like Adam. I told him to come out of the car, and he wouldn't. "

"And you tried to get her to stay in?" I asked.

"Yes."

"And she wouldn't?" I guessed.

"Yes, Sweetheart." She kissed me on that soft line where my forehead and hair meet and whispered, "Something like that."

## CHAPTER TWENTY-THREE

# The Fear of Misstep

One morning Mama pulled into the school's circular drive and stopped. School had already started. We'd just come from Dr. Oren's office. I'd been out of school a lot, more sick in my head than body, even if you counted my chest. But I couldn't bear being there, for PE class especially.

Physical education class was fun at first, during kindergarten anyway, but I started to hate it after a while. Early on we just ran around and played on the monkey bars and slide. I even reenacted The Banana Splits down in the pine trees. I can't believe they let us wander off into the woods next to the school. But then we had to play games they organized for us. Kickball was okay, but I always felt this anxiety over wanting to play well. Baseball and football were torture. And when it rained, we had to play basketball inside. There should be a law forbidding anyone from forcing a child to participate in sports when they don't want to.

I could see everybody in my class from where Mama stopped her car in the circular drive, and a couple of them came to the window to look out, seeing me get out of the car with Mama. Starting on that first week of first grade, I moved through each school day with a fear and paralysis so intense that I sat stock still in my desk, not engaging with anyone, silently watering and grooming the hedge of protection I'd cultivated about a foot around me in all directions. I was paralyzed with the thought that eventually, maybe soon, I would misstep so monumentally that I would never recover. Certainly never matching among my peers the status, the comfort, and the acceptance Adam so effortlessly achieved.

I tried to remember Grandaddy's tater rule when I got scared of being found out, of somebody seeing my sunken and twisted chest, of becoming known around school as Tittysack or Suzie. Some days, it worked, but other days were tougher. That's when I would think of Adam as my advisor and protector. But Adam was spending less and less time at home. I don't know where he went, but Mama said he was getting older and didn't need watching all the time like I did.

Adam had caught the car bug like me, but not as bad. Mama said we both used to teethe on little plastic, generic-looking cars. The wheels were one piece—two miniature tires connected by a small crossbar axle, a minuscule barbell sized for a flea. It snapped into grooves that looked like the teeth of a comb, the kind that Daddy gave him to stick in his back pocket and to slick back his greased hair on '50s day at school. It was also the costume Adam wore on the last Halloween he dressed up. I'd always been with him on Halloween, and his costume informed what I did. That year, he didn't want me to have a '50s-themed costume because he had one.

Mama said I could be a hippie, which is what the greasers turned into after JFK died. I didn't know what that meant, but I liked having a long-haired wig and carrying around bubble-gum cigarettes. Adam took one of them and put it behind his ear, but when he came back home there was a real cigarette in its place. The next year he didn't dress up and told me it was stupid. Then he handed me his '50s jacket.

It was too big for me, but he rolled up the sleeves. It still covered me almost down to my knees. Then he stuck a real cigarette behind my ear. It wouldn't stay. My ears stuck out away from my head I guess, so instead, he cut a small circle from yellow construction paper and stuck a pencil through the center to make a hole. Then he drew wavy lines radiating out from the opening in red and orange markers. It looked kind of like a bloodshot, yellow eyeball, but when he stuck the tip of the cigarette through, it looked just like that cigarette was on fire.

"Stick this in your mouth and pretend you're a cool dude. When you get to the door, take it out of your mouth like this," he demonstrated using the tips of his thumb and pointing finger. "Don't do this," he extended his pointing finger and the finger next to it with the cigarette held between. It looked like the fingers the scouts use when making a promise.

"Only girls and sissies hold cigarettes like that," answering my unasked question. I was afraid to hold it at all after that, afraid I'd make a mistake and everyone would instantly know.

My first-grade desk was several seats back in the row, and a girl sat just in front of me. She had blonde hair so fine that it reminded me of the silks from an ear of just-shucked corn, the silks in perfect order barely disturbed, like the way Grandaddy shucked corn. He was slow and calm, and he didn't make a mess at all. Daddy was messy, almost like he hated every single piece of corn. He showed that corn what was what by ripping the husk and snapping the little stalk off like he was trying to break its neck, the corn silks flying like blood splatter. But her corn-silk hair was perfectly straight and combed down to where it was cut very high up on the nape, like a little swimming cap. The base of her neck was soft and downy like the throat of a chick.

I was really confused because Mrs. Anderson called her "Julie" sometimes and "Sandy" sometimes. Now, lots of folks had two names. Like Mama—Betty Tom. I had a teacher named Donna Jean. People try to make a special name so that their child will be special, at least in one way. That's why you get so many crazy names in the South. But Sandy Julie or Julie Sandy didn't sound right to me. It was an even odder name than Uncle Percy Needham. His name was Percy Needham Rutherford, but they called him Percy Needham. Even Aunt Jimmie Ann called him that, and she must have gotten tired of that long name morning, noon, and night. Then Julie Sandy dropped her book and bent over to pick it up, and there was another girl at the desk in front of her. There were two of them. They weren't twins. They kind of looked like each other from the back of their heads, but not so much alike that you'd mistake one for the other.

I was so confused and scared. I wanted to be home with Mama, helping her. Just last Saturday, I was napping on the bed next to Mama, who was at her sewing machine. It was one of those perfect naps when you are so comfortable you feel like a half-melted caramel left a little too long on Grandaddy's dashboard, liquidy on the top of the bedspread. I woke up a little when Mama covered me with a towel from the jumble of clean-but-not-yet-folded laundry. I wasn't cold, but I guess you're supposed to have a cover over you when you sleep so that the monsters don't grab your toes. I pushed the towel off, and Mama put it back over me. I pushed it off again, and it became a game pretty quickly—for me at least. I wasn't asleep, but I think Mama thought I was. She kept putting the towel back on me until I giggled. Then she called me a little stinker.

I wanted to be home. Not at school. I didn't want to be where I was so nervous that I didn't notice that the one girl who sat in front of me was really two girls. I raised my hand, "Can I be excused?"

And I set off to the bathroom, taking my bag of Keebler elf-made shortbread with chocolate stripe cookies with me in my pocket. Those are the best cookies ever.

The bathroom was horrible, but at least nobody was around. The bathrooms in my school smelled like ours at home just after Daddy had been in there. Some of the commodes didn't have the seat part, so I couldn't sit there. I figured nobody had gone to the bathroom on the flat-topped heater under the window, so that's where I sat to close my eyes, eat my cookies, and pretend I was at home next to Mama as she sewed.

About that time, a boy came in and went up to one of the commodes, pulled down his pants all the way to the floor and took a wee. That was just weird. I wouldn't pull my pants all the way down in front of somebody, even to go wee. You don't have to do that. Daddy showed me how to leave your pants buttoned, and how to pull the peepee out through the zipper. You don't even have to undo your belt. But I didn't like to wee that way, and Daddy finally told me that I could loosen my belt, undo the button and zipper and then wee, but only if I didn't let anybody see my peepee.

And I didn't understand. I asked, "You mean, they shouldn't see me *peepee* or *see* my peepee?"

"Both. You shouldn't let them see you go peepee, and you shouldn't let them see your peepee."

Mama didn't say peepee when she was talking about weeing, and she'd say "thing" when she referred to the peepee itself. It would have been easier to follow the rules if Mama and Daddy had the same rules. But I think both of them would have agreed that I should not let my fanny hang out. And here was this boy showing his fanny. I thought his daddy must not have told him about first-grade boys' bathroom etiquette.

He turned around then, with his shirt pulled up and held under his chin so that he didn't wee on it, I guess, and with his peepee in full view to me and anybody else who might have been there. And he proceeded to pull up his underwear, then his pants. He pulled his shirt down and tucked it in, zipped, buttoned, fastened his belt, and then stood with his arms hanging slack by his side, but sort of in front of him like he was standing on an incline.

"Hi," he said.

"Hi."

"I'm James."

"I'm Philbet."

"Want to meet in the playground at recess?"

"Sure."

Staring at my cookies, I figured I should offer him one, but he just went to the bathroom, and that was dirty.

He continued staring, so I offered, "Want a cookie?"

"Yes, but I can't. Bye."

Then he reached over and took a whole lot of toilet paper, wadded it up, and wet it at the sink. He looked up and threw it straight up like a bottle rocket takes off. It just missed hitting the ceiling and landed on the floor next to him. He picked up the paper and threw it in the trash can and walked out.

"Bye," I said, mostly to myself, wondering why he did that.

With a cookie half in my hand, half in my mouth, I didn't know what to make of him. My eyes went to the ceiling, which I hadn't noticed before looked like the inside of Mama's freezer before she set pots of hot water in it to loosen the ice. It was covered in toilet paper, little squat stalactites like we saw on our one-day holiday to Lookout Mountain that summer, cut short because Daddy was afraid we'd left the stove on. Mama said she could call Aunt Ease to go across the road to check the stove, but Daddy pointed the car home.

"The house will have burned up by the time we get there," she'd mumbled under her breath.

Five hours later we were home, but not before a quick look inside a mountain that showed formations growing up from the ground, put there over many years as the dirt inside the water dripping down eventually formed what looked like big, spikey cow pies hanging upside down from the cave ceiling and rising up from the cave floor.

I returned to class, saving two cookies for later. Grandaddy said it's always good to be sure you save a little for later. That applies to everything, no matter what it is.

## CHAPTER TWENTY-FOUR

# James

Later that day, I saw James again at the very edge of the playground. He was sitting on a metal post that had managed to shake free of the chain-link fence it once held up. The fence drooped on the ground behind him, looking like a roll of toilet paper unrolled lazily against the boys' room floor.

"I still have cookies. Want one?" I offered.

"No thanks," he replied.

I sat on the concrete blob that used to anchor the fence post into the ground, the hole that once held it just behind us. It looked like that one spot ol' Luke dug up time after time in Grandaddy's garden. Grandaddy swore there wasn't a bone buried in the garden, but Adam said Grandaddy's garden was probably on top of an old cemetery. Grandaddy told Adam, "Stop tellin' tales."

James and I just sat there, not saying anything. So I ate a cookie. I kind of felt like I knew how Mama felt when Jorma came down and sat at the kitchen table and just stared at her all day long. Only, James wasn't staring at me. He was just looking at the ground and poking it with a stick.

Then he looked up. "Your daddy whip you with a stick or his hand?"

"Um, he dud'n really ever whip me."

"Yeah? Huh."

"What about yours?"

"Oh, if he ain't got a stick he'll use his hand. But my mama's always got a switch by the door. Got one in every room."

"Jorma's got a fly swatter in every room."

"Who she?"

"My grandmama, my daddy's mama."

"Oh, so she must use that fly swatter on you."

"No, she dud'n hit us either. She kills flies with it."

"I got a joke," he said.

"Okay."

"Time flies," he said.

*That doesn't make sense*, I thought.

"Time flies," he said again.

"Is it my turn?" I asked.

"What do you mean?" he asked.

"I don't get the joke."

"See, you can hear it two ways. Lots of old folks say that time flies, and that means it goes by real fast. They're old."

I listened.

He continued, "But the joke is that you are supposed to time house-flies as they fly by, just like you'd time how long it takes somebody to run from here back to class. You know, like, how long it would take you to run there."

I laughed.

"See, you get it."

"No, I don't get it," I said. "It's funny because that's a stupid joke."

"Aw, what do *you* know?" But he laughed too.

Then he asked, "You got a brother and sister?"

"Just a brother. You?"

"Naw, it's just me," James said, not giving any clues if that was good or bad.

"My sister died," I said.

"Aw, man. That's rough."

And then I felt guilty and like it was true, but kind of not true because I didn't know if she was a sister or a brother. I figured God would get me if I didn't tell the truth.

"I mean, I think it was a sister. She, or he, died before I was born, just a baby. I don't know if it was a boy or girl. Mama dud'n talk about it."

James looked over at me as though he were still listening to me tell the story, except I wasn't saying anything. He finally shook his head slowly up and then down once.

Silence.

"My grandaddy whips me every mornin'," I said, "or he used to."

"Mean, huh?"

"No, Grandaddy's the best grandaddy ever."

"Don't sound like it."

"Oh, he's just playin'. I'll show you. Um, here, bend over my knee."

"Do what now?"

"Bend over my knee here. That's what he does. He'll grab me and bend me over his one knee and then he'll close the other knee on me," I demonstrated with my jacket pretending to be me, "and then slap his leg here."

James didn't look as though it sounded like fun.

"He does what now?"

"He pretends to whoop me. He dud'n really whoop me."

"Why?"

"'Cause he's playin'. Playin' like he's mad at me, but he's not."

"It ain't gonna be so funny when he pulls you down and gives you a good beatin'."

"He calls me Whoop. That's his name for me."

"Y'all White people are some weird-ass folks."

"It's fun. He wouldn't beat me." And I wanted to ask him about his grandaddy, but I thought maybe I shouldn't because maybe his grandaddy beat him.

I wanted to reach out and touch his hair. I bet if I did, I'd pull back a little tuft like it was chocolate-flavored cotton candy. Adam told me that colored folks' hair wasn't like White folks' hair.

"Their hair ain't one long string like ours is," he explained once, "it's little bitty pieces only about as long as an ant with little hooks on the end that hook together."

*If it's a bunch of little pieces…?* I didn't know how to ask my question, but if the hair didn't connect to the head, how did it grow? Adam must have read my mind.

"Things in the air, like dust blow by and get caught on the little hooks of the hair, and it makes it look like the hair is growin'."

But James's hair didn't seem like dust—it looked dark like when you wake up in the night and everything is quiet except for the whip-poor-will singing off in the woods. And, for now, for today, I liked being at school because James and his cotton-candy hair made me think of the whip-poor-will, and that made me think of all those whoopings I got from Grandaddy who was only twenty-five miles up the road.

And then Mr. Blanton walked up. "You boys get over there and line up to play kickball," he said, and I decided I didn't like Mr. Blanton.

## CHAPTER TWENTY-FIVE

# Sharing Cookies

I finally asked a year later, on the first day of second grade, "I know you like cookies. I've seen you eat them in the cafeteria." I said this after James turned down a cookie again. He never took one, not one time.

"Yeah, I like cookies," he said.

"Why don't you ever want my cookies?"

He didn't say anything.

I pretended I didn't ask the question and moved on. "We've got woods around our house."

"That sounds cool."

"Yeah, they're cool. Folks dump stuff back there, and there's one part that looks like a livin' room."

"What'cha mean?"

"There's a recliner and a table next to it where it looks like somebody sat there drinking beer. There's empty beer cans. Just like you walked up on somebody's house and they left the front door open. Want to go see them sometime?"

"Yeah, maybe."

"And, maybe you can come over on Saturday and have lunch with us." Thinking just as I was saying it that I should ask Mama before I invited him over.

"I don't know." And then he said, "I don't know" again as if he wanted to say something else but could only think of the same thing to say.

"Okay." Kind of relieved because I didn't know if Daddy would take to James, him being Black and everything.

"I'd like to," he hesitated. "My mama told me not to take any food from White…." He kind of trailed off.

This was the thing that James and I hadn't talked about at all, him being Black and me being White.

"She didn't say I couldn't eat with a White boy, but she told me not to take food from White folks."

"Why?" I asked, genuinely confused.

"I don't know. We don't really know any White people."

But I knew what he meant. Daddy knew Walter, and they laughed when Walter came over, but Walter never came inside. Daddy talked to him from the porch, and then Walter would go on down the road.

"Daddy dud'n trust White people," James explained.

That was fair. "I don't think my Daddy trusts Black people," I replied.

Adam and I used to stand at the back door of the house in Alvaton before we moved and call the folks across the street at Pick's names, names Mama told me not to use. But I'd heard Daddy say it. And, truth is, I hadn't told Mama that James was Black.

I didn't think she'd care, but I didn't think she wouldn't. Daddy would care.

I'm not sure how I knew, but I did. I remember Uncle Harp saying one time, "They like havin' their own church. They don't wanna go to church with us."

Daddy said that smell from when we lived in Alvaton was when the Black folks burned their hair, the same thing Adam had told me, so it must be true…but why would anybody burn their hair? On Greer's fifth birthday, her hair got down over the cake when she went to blow out the candles, and her hair caught on fire, suddenly making a halo over her head. Uncle Harp was fast and started clapping his hands all around her head and put the fire out. It looked like they were in the circus doing a trick.

And her burned hair smelled like something rotten. Adam told me that one time Aunt Nedra got mad at a boyfriend she had before she married Uncle Do, and she put raw shrimp in the seat cushions of his 1963 Mercury Comet. You'd have to be pretty mad to put shrimp down somebody's car seat because shrimp cost a lot. Mama wouldn't ever waste shrimp that way. I bet Greer's burnt hair smelled like rotten shrimp in the crease of that Comet's seat because shrimp stink even before they rot. So they must have really smelled bad after a day or two in that hot car. No wonder James's daddy didn't trust White people.

And then, he reached over and took a cookie out of my baggie and put it to his mouth.

# CHAPTER TWENTY-SIX

# Stronger Together

Year after year, James was my only true friend at school. We spent the first three years playing *Banana Splits* in the woods, which we could do because *The Banana Splits* weren't Black or White. We'd meet in the playground, set a plan for the day, and decide which cartoon to act out. *Speed Buggy* was my favorite, a talking dune buggy with headlamps for eyes. It seemed most cartoons were versions of *Scooby Doo*. Speed Buggy was even the same color as Scooby. But mostly we just walked, whacking the bushes with limbs that fell off the pine trees from all the kids who climbed in them, pulling them apart in their locust-like invasions of the woods. I didn't climb. I looked for corners of the woods to skulk around so that we could escape the organized sports. Sitting in the woods with our hidden snacks, we had the best talks.

"Wait, how many grandaddies do you have?" I asked.

"Three."

"How'd you get three grandaddies?" I couldn't believe I didn't know James had three grandaddies after all this time.

"Granny liked my new grandaddy more than she liked my old grandaddy."

"So she's got two of them?"

"No, fool, my daddy's mama was married to my grandaddy, but she ain't married to him anymore. She married a new man, and he's my grandaddy too. My mama's mama and daddy are still married."

"Oh."

"How many grandaddies've you got?" James asked.

"I have one."

"Where's your other one?"

I remember thinking I didn't need more than the one I had, and I couldn't imagine a better one. "We lost him."

"You don't know where your grandaddy is? That's an extra Christmas present you ain't gettin'. Birthday present too."

"No," I replied. "He died. He was at the washerette to clean my brother's diapers. He died right there, sittin' out front in the car, and didn't even finish the diapers or anything."

James didn't say anything, so I asked, "Which one do you like best?"

"Prince. My mama's daddy. He's not crazy. He takes me fishing and for hamburgers and milkshakes. Plus, he's just nice."

"He sounds like my grandaddy," I said.

"Plus, Grandaddy knows how to hold onto his woman. I respect that. This new grandaddy hasn't proven he can hold onto Granny. And he's crazier than my real grandaddy, so I ain't betting any money on him." James made sense. He was like Adam in that way. That's one reason I liked him so much.

As much as I hated PE, I was active in some school groups, especially industrial arts. I made a table out of one sheet of plywood. It was really a box with openings on the side with a place to stick in newspapers. The very top and bottom were just equal size pieces off the edges of the sheet. Then one extra piece with the identical dimensions of the top and bottom was split right down the middle, and I had to cut curved pieces out of one end so that it looked like I had two pizza paddles that they used down at Pizza Hut to put the pizza in the oven and take it out. The piece left after that was cut right in half and then in half again. It's hard to describe. I made the pattern myself, cutting it out of newspaper.

James made a bowl. Glued seven boards on top of one another, changing the direction of the grain every layer, making them stronger together because the grains are actually the weak spots. After the glue dried, he took that big cube of wood and put it on a lathe, dug out the inside, and scooped it out like the seeds in a cantaloupe. He rounded off the outside to be bowl shaped. "It's a fruit bowl for Mama," he said.

*My* mama has my table to this day.

## CHAPTER TWENTY-SEVEN

# Thrice New

It was a big day for all of us, but for different reasons. For starters, school let out early. Daddy and Adam picked me up, and we went straight to Mabie Motors, where Mama met us in the parking lot.

That was the day Adam got Radar, a hunting dog. In the end, though, Adam didn't hunt with him much. There are two things I remember about the day we got Radar. President Nixon resigned, and Daddy drove his new Cheyenne S-10 pickup off the Mabie Motors lot with Adam sitting next to the door and me in the middle. Mama waved to us as we drove off since it was the middle of the day, and she had to stay at work.

The truck's interior was caramel colored, almost the soft tan of a mature buck's hide. But the outside was two-tone burgundy and white. I liked each of the colors individually, but they didn't go together. It looked like GM painted the outside and then realized they'd used up all the burgundy cloth and had to switch to light brown. But I forgot about the mismatched colors as soon as I sat inside and looked out the windshield, which seemed twice as big, expansive I'd say, as the old 1965 Chevy pickup. I was in awe. And there was a thick blue band across the top of the windshield, which Daddy said was for the glare. The Cheyenne had power steering, and that meant I couldn't ride the steering wheel anymore, but I was too big anyway. I hadn't done that in years, probably not since the Christmas Aunt Novella asked Mama what was wrong with me.

As we drove off the lot, I glanced back at the sky-blue Chevy pickup that held such great Ridin' the Steerin' Wheel memories while Nixon spoke to us over the new Delco radio, his voice tight as if he held the foil from chewing gum wrappers between the back teeth in his mouth. I was half listening, more interested in the new truck, but Daddy started talking about shame, and how Nixon should be ashamed. Shamed in front of the whole world.

My attention remained on the details of the truck, especially the wood grain metal strip across the dash. It looked fake. It *was* fake. I could see the individual dots of brown and black and touches of yellow and orange that created the wood pattern. Fake. Pretending to be what it wasn't in full view of anyone who rode in the truck or to any automotive voyeur like me who sideways glanced into every car he passed, already knowing the pattern of the cloth and even the transmission in most cases, as fewer and fewer larger cars had manual transmissions.

We headed north on our day of acquiring new things. I didn't remember ever traveling that far on this road. We stopped at a house that sat right on the highway, and we walked around the back of the house, looking over our shoulders or, in my case, walking backward to soak in the sight of the new truck with its front tires cut at a sharp angle. That angle made it look as though it were a deer frozen on the side of the road, just waiting to bolt as soon as it saw or heard anything that spooked it.

A litter of bird dog puppies stumbled over each other trying to get their mama's attention. Small yips here and there reinforced how small and vulnerable they were, each a variation on the others in shades of cream and over-cooked beef liver. Adam chose the floppiest-eared one for his new bird dog. Its new name, Radar, showcasing his expected proficiency detecting and pointing to the birds they'd hunt for years to come. A new truck, a new puppy, and a new president on the way.

Radar's pen was in the very back corner of our backyard, opposite side from where the body shop sat through the woods. It was a big pen, half in and half out of the woods. There was a clean dirt path worn all the way down to the red clay, all the way around the inside of the fence.

Adam took Radar hunting, and they came back with some birds, just one or two, which Mama cooked like they were really small, meatless chickens. It was about that time that Adam stopped coming home right after school, which increased tension in the house. He was spending more time with his friends than he did at home or out in the field with Radar. As time went on, either Mama or Daddy took Radar's dinner to him, quickly slipping inside the gate, trying not to let him out. I didn't ever go feed him because I always let him out, never mastering the timing of scooting through the gate fast enough. The smallest of all of us, I opened the gate the widest, I guess.

Radar was a running dog, and he must have felt like a prisoner in that pen, getting out so little. But he wouldn't have understood the concept of prison, him being a dog, but I just knew he felt something was amiss, a dog's version of a person feeling unfulfilled, longing for something he didn't and couldn't have.

As much as Daddy complained that Adam was being mean to Radar, as much as Mama and Daddy paid for dog food over the years for a dog that wasn't quite a pet or a successful hunter, we didn't do anything about it. Radar died in that pen years later, his legs twitching like he was chasing birds in heaven.

## CHAPTER TWENTY-EIGHT

# The Season of Wright

My favorite candy probably remains so because I had it only once, and memory has made it all the more delicious for its uncommonness. I tried it while I was over at my friend Wright Finch's house.

I saw him the first day of fifth grade and couldn't stop watching him. It was the first time I met someone and noticed how comfortable he was. Whether he was in study hall, on the playground, or in class taking a test, he seemed like he was lying on a sofa with a Pepsi in one hand. It was like he enjoyed whatever it was he was doing, no matter what. Before Wright, I'd only known Adam to be so quietly confident and self-assured. It was intoxicating.

But more than that, when I stood next to him in the lunch line, he smelled like Grandaddy's garden after the rain. Not after Grandaddy waters the plants with the hose, but how it smells just after the rain stops. It was the kind of rain that isn't cold and stinging like on a dark, fall day and not those sudden hot-shower bursts in the summer. He smelled like the garden after the kind of rain that is barely warm, body temperature warm. It's so comforting that if you stand out in that kind of springtime rain, you almost don't know you're getting wet. And the plants are happy as they kind of spring back up just opening their eyes as the water stops dripping over them. Grandaddy said plants like wet feet.

When Wright was there next to you, that's what came to mind, except it was even better. He smelled like wet garden sprinkled with cinnamon. It's about the best smell combination in the world. One day, I was standing in the lunch line in front of James and behind Wright, and I leaned forward to get my nose as close as possible to the back of Wright's shirt to get a whiff, when James said, "What's wrong with you?"

"Um…I don't know whether I want pizza or a hamburger," I stumbled, as I tried to listen to what Wright was saying to Linder Ray in front of us.

I didn't want to be Wright's friend instead of James's. I wanted to be friends with both. Most people had more than one friend. James did, but I really didn't. I didn't feel lonely, but I wasn't part of a pack like most of the kids. Living out in the country, my pack was more Adam, Jeb, and my other cousins. And I had James at school. He had other friends, and everybody always slapped his hand way up in the air as they walked by. James gave me one quick shove, and my face landed right against the soft part between Wright's backbone and his shoulder blade. He turned around to me at exactly the same time I spun around to stare at James.

James smiled and said, "What?"

Wright was smiling when I turned back to him, "Yeah?" But he was smiling with his eyebrows raised up real high, and not like he was going to hit me, but more like he thought it was funny.

"I'm sorry. I…I slipped."

"He's super clumsy," said James shoving me a little.

"Stop it!" I turned and yelled.

James and I never fought, but at that moment I was so mad at him, I didn't ever want to speak to him again.

"You okay?" Wright asked both of us.

"Yeah, I'm sorry."

"No problem. I'm Wright." And he stuck out his hand to shake it like adults do. He wasn't going to hit me.

"Philbet."

"Hi," he said.

"Hi," I said.

"Hi," James said.

And then James turned to Ridley in line behind him. He just turned his back. James was being a brat, but he was still my best friend and always would be. He never one time didn't stand with me in the hall.

But Wright was really nice and fun, a friend to everyone, and that's likely why he befriended me. But James didn't like him, and I couldn't tell what Wright thought of James. He sort of looked at James like the preacher looked at people who only showed up to church on Easter, Christmas, and funerals. James and I didn't really see each other much outside of school. He lived in town, and I lived out in the country on a paved road so rough in places that it may as well have been a long stretch of packed red clay.

Red clay is a funny dirt. It can make for the smoothest road, or it can be as rough as a dried-out creek bed. I figured the quality of the road was due to the combination of the clay, rocks, and moisture content. In my experience, red clay that was well trod and mostly dry could turn into a smooth, easy-to-travel path that was hard packed and solid on the base with a sandy-soft surface. Lots of rocks in a patch of a red clay road make it wash away into the weedy ditch on either side. It's sort of like when you stand on the beach's edge and the tide rushes in and rolls out, and the sand around your feet washes away, leaving you on a smaller foundation, unsteady and dizzy as the whole wide ocean runs away from you.

Once Mama and Daddy were home at night after work, we didn't go out much. Wright lived even farther outside the city limits, on the grounds of a retirement community where his father was the preacher. Mama worked there, too, as a secretary, after she left her job at the car dealership to make more money. Since Wright lived so far out of town, he was more a friend on the weekend. It worked out since he and James weren't buddies. They sort of tolerated one another.

Wright offered to teach me how to play golf, so Mama and Daddy got me a used set of junior clubs for Christmas that year. According to Wright, there was a special way to hold a club. It sounded complicated, and when I couldn't figure it out, Wright stood just behind me, his arms making a sort of cage, his hands on top of mine around the club.

"All you do is link your pointing finger," Wright said as he squeezed my left hand, "with your pinky." Then he squeezed my right hand, and he turned his mouth toward my ear to say, "See." It wasn't a question; it was a command. It all made sense for the first time, and I tried to concentrate on the one-link chain he made of my fingers and not give in to my impulse to let go of the club and turn around to face him.

Days out on the pine straw-edged course were escapes for just the two of us. The farther we could hit the ball, the longer we got to walk with each other before stopping. Maybe it was my lack of skill, or maybe it was on purpose, but I usually hit the ball into or onto the side of the pines. That was my favorite place on the course, the edge of the woods where it met the green, the pine straw barely covering the closely trimmed grass looking like Mama sprinkled cocoa powder on top of a green milkshake she made just for me. And when I'd get a swing wrong, Wright would come up and reposition my hands on the grip.

Wright lived next to the course, so we could use it often, sometimes being the first ones on the links if I spent the night, which I did a few times. He had bunk beds, which were almost as cool as a treehouse. And he had this great candy, which his mother—he had a "mother" not a "mama"—got up north where she was from. It looked like real rocks, not the rainbow-colored nuggets that were so clearly straight sugar, but actual rugged dirty pebbles and larger bird-hitting-sized stones, ones with grit caught in their rough, creviced surfaces. Inside was chocolate and a creamy nougat, so good I can still feel the tooth-breaking crunch, and so sweet it was almost savory.

I wished I had been able to get one of those rocks to give to Grandaddy. He would have gotten a kick out of it. If one of these chocolate rocks got in the way of a potato in Grandaddy's garden, that'd be the happiest potato ever, gooey and chocolate-centered, a tater digger's find of a lifetime.

No matter how much I concentrated on playing well to impress Wright, I simply wasn't a golfer. The lack of muscle development in my twisted chest and scrawny shoulders prevented that. But it didn't matter. He seemed to like encouraging and helping me. I'm sure he did. But looking back now, I realize we were enjoying it for different reasons.

When I was with Wright, I felt awake. Not the opposite of being asleep, but the opposite of being me. I felt safe. I felt like those summer days were forever days, the times from years earlier when I didn't live by my own summers or seasons, but instead waited for Adam's school to let out so that we could run around in the hot Georgia sun from morning to sundown, about 9:00 at night. Sometimes Adam and I'd explore the railroad cut, sometimes the backyard, sometimes up and down the path between our house and Jorma and Grandaddy's. We usually ended up drinking Kool-Aid in the shade of the pecan trees that had broad sun-soaking leaves like a tall ceiling over the whole of Grandaddy's yard, the small pecan shells watching us, giggling to themselves over how they'd choose just the right moment in October to drop down and crack us on the noggin.

There was a community center on the grounds near Wright's house as well, and he could get us in, so we saw *The Big Bus*. I was nervous once the movie started because it was really a grown-up movie. That bus was like a clown car version of a bus with lots of people and even a swimming pool and a bowling alley. It went across country with all these crazy people and even almost went over a cliff.

The summer was coming to an end, and we wanted to memorialize our friendship, so we decided to make a time capsule. Wright and I took our movie tickets, a golf ball, some coins with the date stamped, that perfect candy, and two letters we'd each written to each other. We found a metal box at his house and buried it all in a deep planter on the top post of a stone wall that overflowed with ivy.

Wright scaled the side of the stone, and I tossed a spade up to him. He dug out the planter—and this was the coolest part—"Toss up the box," he called down, "at the same time I drop the spade. I'll catch the box as you catch the spade."

I wish someone had been there to take a photograph of the box and spade passing each other mid-toss. I wondered if a photo would capture which direction each was headed, with cartoon swoosh lines flowing behind in the direction each moved. This whole time-capsule idea was more of an emotion than a thought, a longing, I think. Were I an inventor, that's what I'd create—a camera that shows the future, the direction people and their hearts will travel. Then I'd know if I was going to do something stupid before I did it. I could keep and protect friendships. I could protect Mama and Grandaddy, Adam too. And I'd have known not to lay my insides bare to Wright.

## CHAPTER TWENTY-NINE

# They Just Knew

If there was no school, I'd get up early and ride to work with Mama. When we got there, Wright wasn't always awake, but I'd sit on the benches at the tennis court, spectator to nothing, in the early morning sunshine.

When Wright got up, he'd walk over, eating toast.

"God, I need some coffee," he'd mutter.

In my experience thus far, the children of preachers were rebellious, doing and saying things I wouldn't. Drinking coffee was for grown-ups. We headed over to the cafeteria, and he got his coffee, breathing deeply and feeling his stomach like one of my uncles who was stiff and achy. He didn't put anything in it or even blow on it. It had to be hot because I saw steam even in the August heat.

"Ahhhh. Want some?"

I did not. But the next morning I joined him in a cup, mine loaded with so much milk that the temperature went from scalding to barely warm, and enough sugar to make the top of my mouth pucker.

"You'll get used to it."

I didn't believe him.

"When I grow up, my woman'll bring me coffee in bed."

"Yeah," I replied, thinking about what he'd said, something I'd never thought of before.

"I'm gonna give her a lot of kids."

"Who?"

"My woman. I'm gonna put babies in her stomach."

"Oh, yeah." I felt really sad all of a sudden, hopeless, and thinking something else was wrong with me. His woman. I didn't think I'd ever want a wife like Wright did, and I wondered how he knew he wanted that. Adam seemed to want it too. It wasn't even a question for him, I don't think. He just knew, like it was a part of him, like it was a part of Wright. Like it wasn't a part of me. But maybe next year. Maybe then, I'd like a girl and want to marry her one day, want to talk to her a lot, and want to hold her hand and kiss her.

*She'll think I'm a weirdo*, I thought, wondering if I could manage to hide my chest from her. If I changed my clothes when she wasn't in the room, maybe. And if I stayed covered up in the bed, or wore a T-shirt, maybe I could hide it. Or I could lie on my side and bunch the covers up around me. Maybe I could hang a towel around my neck when I came out of the bathroom. The more I thought about this yet-to-be wife, the more I worried about the day she'd appear, me lovestruck and spending all my waking hours trying to hide myself from her so she wouldn't know I was deformed.

Lovestruck? The thought of it didn't excite me. It was a rite of passage that eluded me while everyone around me seemed already past it, ready for it, obsessed with it. The only person who might understand was Greer, underdeveloped, but wanting to be full-figured like her mother. Time was on her side. My chest would never blossom. Greer's would.

## CHAPTER THIRTY

# Don't Tell Daddy

James had never been to our place after school, mostly because Daddy didn't know he was Black. Mama knew and had known ever since she met him and his mama at school.

"Where're your friends, James and Wright?" Mama asked.

"There's James and his mama. Right over there," I said, pointing.

"*That's* your best friend?" she said almost to herself, heading over to them.

"That's James. Wright's my best friend too." But she had already set out to meet James.

"You're James's mother?" Mama asked instead of stated.

"Yes," James's mama replied, but her *yes* was more of a "Yes, and what's the problem?"

"Philbet, you and James go and get a sno-cone."

We were off. "Why do you think Mama wants to talk to your mama?" I asked James.

"'Cause I'm Black, and you're White."

All Mama said when we headed to the car was, "Don't tell your daddy your little friend is Black."

"Why?"

"You want to keep your friend?" Mama asked.

"Yes, Ma'am."

"Then don't tell him. Don't tell anyone."

"Adam—"

"Don't tell him either," she said.

"He already knows," I admitted.

"Adam knows?"

"Yeah. And Veralynn. She gave him a ride home one day when she came to pick me up."

Deep breath. "Why didn't you tell me he was Black?"

"Why does it matter?" I asked.

"Why didn't you tell me?"

We stared at each other.

"I thought you would make me stop being his friend."

"Why *is* he your friend?" Mama asked.

Without sass, but truly curious, I asked, "Why shouldn't we be friends?"

Mama sighed deeply.

"Because he's my friend. I like him. He's nice," I finally answered.

"No little White boys are nice to you?"

"None that are nice to him," I explained.

"Don't sass me."

"I'm not sassing, Mama."

Mama didn't usually stare, but she was staring straight at me now.

"Why isn't it okay?" I wasn't poking. I was asking.

She didn't say anything.

"Wright is my friend too…but he doesn't really like James. Why does it matter, Mama?"

She waited a moment before answering. "You have to be careful."

## CHAPTER THIRTY-ONE

# The Letter

After the summer ended, I was kind of sad because it had been so great, almost like those magic days before I went to school, and Adam, Mama, and I spent the summer going to the playground any time we wanted.

Mama liked the summer back then, too, because she only had to get Daddy off to work, and Adam and I didn't get up so early. So, she could go back to bed for a thirty-minute nap after Daddy left and before I got up. And then Adam, Mama, and I could go and do what we wanted to. Mama liked to go swimming, and Adam and I did, too, at least before I knew my chest was wrong. But I think Mama liked to go because she had a really good figure, and she had this bathing suit that was white with brown swirls and these little loops that decorated the V-neck and the place where her arms and legs came out. It had a padded part built into it up top that kept its shape even when she wasn't wearing it. The whole thing was very soft, and everybody said she had the best figure of anybody. She didn't ever say anything, but I know she liked hearing it.

None of my aunts were as pretty as Mama. They were all jealous, I think. Mama even looked better than my teenaged cousins. They wore these ugly, scratchy-material dresses and plastered their hair down with hairspray when they went out on dates, and it made their hair look like the outside of Aunt Novella's Christmas ornaments that had what looked like spun red silk wrapped tight around these balls. The string came off one of them, and it was just a stupid old Styrofoam ball. Aunt Novella didn't throw it away. She just cut off the loose string and hung it back on the tree. Her skin was all dry and rough like that double-knit fabric they made dresses out of, so her fingers always snagged the soft string on the Christmas ornaments and pulled it out.

When the next big break after summer rolled around, Wright and I were spending a lot of time on the golf course. I was getting a little better, and by this time Wright was pretty good. The best part of it was when we got to use a golf cart. We weren't even old enough to drive, but they let us have a golf cart. I rode, and Wright drove. I liked closing my eyes, pointing my face out the open space that would have been a door had we been in a car. I'd open my eyes and shut them, open and shut, open and shut, watching the grass zoom past. It looked like a big sheet of sour apple goo before they cut it into tapes. I was tempted to jump out, face-first as the cart rolled past, to taste the green to see if it tasted like sour apple candy.

As Christmas break began, I was so excited, thinking I was in for a shorter version of the fun summer Wright and I shared. I wrote him a letter on the last day before the break and slipped it into the vent of his locker door. It was a cool letter. I wrote out a letter and then I took a second piece of paper and wrote the same words as the first letter, but all over the paper and in a random order. Each time I wrote a word, I put a small number under it, like a puzzle that Wright could decipher by putting the words in order according to their number.

But Wright didn't acknowledge my letter, and he didn't write me back. I thought because the letters we wrote during the summer weren't supposed to be dug up and looked at until we were sixteen, this letter would be a fun reminder that we had letters to open in a few, long years from now. In my letter, I told Wright I couldn't wait to get together over the Christmas break, and that I was really glad he was my friend. The second day into the break I called him.

"Wright?"

"Yeah?"

"What's up?"

"Nothing," he said flatly.

"Want to get together?"

"I can't," he replied.

"Oh, okay. Tomorrow?"

"No, my grandparents are coming to stay, so I can't."

"Oh, okay." Grandaddy and Jorma were coming, too, but I didn't have to stay with them the entire holiday.

"Want to get together after they leave?" I offered.

"They're going to be here the whole time."

I was hoping to meet them. He talked about them a lot. I thought they might have brought some chocolate rock candy.

"I see. Okay."

He didn't say anything.

"Did you get the letter I left in your locker?"

I heard him breathe.

"Yeah," he yawned.

"Did you decipher it?"

"Yeah."

"Cool, huh?" I couldn't wait any longer to know what he thought.

"Yeah. Well I got to go."

My face got really hot, and it must have been red. "Oh."

Then he blurted out, "Philbet, just *talk* to me. Boys don't write letters to each other."

How could writing a letter now not be okay when we had letters to each other stuck in a box and buried next to the tennis court? I didn't understand, but I was getting mad at him a little. I thought about the sour apple candy tape I'd put in the envelope with the pre-Christmas holiday letter, shut my eyes, and ached at what he must have thought. I put the candy in because the sugary, glittery perfection of it reminded me of the smooth grass carpet of the golf course, both blemish free in a way that only a factory-produced product can be. Neither the candy nor the grass showed the perfect imperfections of the beans and peppers of Grandaddy's garden, a thought that hadn't occurred to me in my excitement over writing my time-capsule letter. If I'd tried to talk to Wright more about this on the greens, I think he would have said nothing, handing me a golf club, as if I had forgotten why we got together.

"Use your back, not your shoulders." I can hear him saying, the way he'd said it so many times in the past. "Put some power behind that swing! Power comes first, Philbet. Then you learn how to steer the ball where you want it to go, without taking time to think too much about it."

All of a sudden, I didn't like that manicured perfection anymore. I wanted Grandaddy's garden. I wanted to see an abandoned washing machine or a junked-out Oldsmobile on blocks with no tires. I had no interest in playing golf, and I didn't think I'd ever want to again. I felt bad that Mama had gone to the trouble and expense to buy me a set of junior clubs. I felt guilty and sad and hurt and confused all at the same time.

## CHAPTER THIRTY-TWO

# Grow, Manicure, Repeat

Not knowing exactly what to do next, I got a ride over to the retirement community from Mama and just started walking and thinking. It was times like these that I missed Grandaddy the most. I mean, I missed seeing Grandaddy every day, but I *really* missed him when I was feeling like the world would never fall into place for me. I wanted to ride my little peddle car like I used to up the garden path to Grandaddy's from the white-block house we moved from all those years ago. As I'd peddle by, I'd hold my non-steering hand out to brush the floppy green leaves covered in dancing beads of water and imagine the plants sprouting little lips to kiss the droplets in.

Before long, I found myself at the groundskeeper's shop and just stood there, hoping someone would come out or walk up behind me and go inside so that I didn't have to knock. I hadn't thought much about what all went into maintaining the golf course, but my walking and thinking about Grandaddy's garden made me wonder, so I knocked. A woman came to the door who had an orange scarf wrapped around the same color hair, so messy it looked like a bunch of spaghetti sauce and noodles bursting out at the corners. And the inside of the creases around her eyes were so white compared to her suntan that it looked like she had fake Halloween wax Dracula fangs taped to each side of her head.

"Hey there, little mister."

"Hi."

"Whatcha need?"

"Um, I don't really need anything. I...I've played golf here a few times."

"Yeah?"

"Yes, Ma'am."

And she laughed like I had told one of Uncle Kingston's jokes about dog doo or something.

"The course looks perfect," I almost whispered.

"Thank you."

"Why does it have to be so perfect?"

"Huh?"

"It's so perfect. It kind of doesn't look real."

She didn't say anything. She kind of cocked her head like Radar did when you stood at his fence and told him dinner wasn't for a few hours yet.

"I mean, it's all real. It's grass mostly, and a few trees." I tried to be clearer.

"Yeah." She smiled and cocked her head the other direction. "I don't know what you're askin', son."

"I don't either. Sorry."

"Are you okay?"

"Yes, Ma'am. I'm...." I stopped. I missed Wright already, but I didn't want to say that.

"My Grandaddy said grass is a waste, and, I mean, I know you work real hard to get it so perfect...." I stopped again.

"Yeah...it's hard work."

"But you can't eat it, and I think that's what Grandaddy means."

"No, you can't eat it," she replied.

"But it takes a lot of water."

"You're not one of those Earth-lover, airy-berry-nuts-and-fairy folks, are ya?"

"Um, I don't think so." I wasn't sure what she meant.

"Did you want me to do something?"

She made me think of MawMaw, so sweet and patient trying to understand me, but totally not getting what I was saying. I didn't know myself what I wanted. The question I hadn't been able to form was a more difficult question than asking for a peanut butter and jelly sandwich or green milkshake. What I wanted was to ease my loneliness.

I felt outside myself, and it made me think of those folks on *Phil Donahue* who talk about out-of-body experiences. I floated to her door, hoping she could tell me why the grass wasn't useless, wrong, indulgent. I wanted her to say that the grass was there so that Wright and I could be together, walk all Saturday morning and afternoon long, side-by-side with our golf clubs so that we could talk and laugh. But she couldn't do that. And I guess she didn't need to because I knew the answer even though I didn't know the question.

"Want a cookie?" She *was* like MawMaw.

"No, thank you."

And I turned to go.

"What's your name?"

"Philbet."

"I'm BJ."

"I like your name."

"I like yours too," she said.

Silence.

I turned to go.

"Fake, huh?" She stopped me.

"More perfect than fake."

"Nothin's perfect," she said.

I knew that. If it was perfect, Wright would still be my friend.

And because I was feeling sorry for myself and didn't want our conversation to end, I added, "I kind of want to lick the grass. It looks like sour apple tape."

She thought that was funny because she snorted a little. "I wouldn't recommend that," she said.

"I'm not really going to do it."

"Come around here with me." She pulled on my sleeve.

I followed her around the shack, and it was like Grandaddy had been there to clean up her garden to get it ready for spring. There were neat rows, and plastic covered part of the ground.

"How's this? Better?" she asked.

"Yes, Ma'am. It's like Grandaddy's been here to get the garden ready for spring."

"Yep, you gotta do the hard work to get it to grow. I love my little garden."

"What's your favorite?" I asked.

"Potatoes."

"Mine too," I agreed. "Why?"

"Hmm. I like surprises, and you never know what you'll dig up."

"The ugly ones are the best ones."

"Yeah, I think so too," she agreed.

"You know why? Grandaddy told me."

"Why?" she asked.

"They have to work harder to survive, so they have more minerals and nutrients, and they taste better."

"That sounds about right."

"Well, thank you for showing me."

"Come back if you want," she said. "I'll be here. You can help me dig taters."

I kind of wanted to hug her, but I didn't. I guess she had to grow the golf course so that she would get paid, but she had her garden because it ensured that she could eat. Or maybe she just liked growing something that was real, like when the crops come in, and you've got beans to shell and peppers to put up, and so many vegetables you don't even notice when a worm gets brought in too and set on the kitchen table.

Grandaddy kept the garden because we needed to eat, and if the money ran out, we'd always have the garden. He had faith that the rain and good weather would always balance out to do their part if he did his, which was to plant, weed, and fertilize. But he also pulled dead leaves off the plants because dead leaves and stalks pulled water away from the good part of the plant. He made sure floppy pea vines were staked and off the ground so they didn't rot or get bugs. And he always picked the fruit when it was time, even if we had enough sitting on the window ledge cooling in the breeze. We could always give the extra to somebody if we had too much. But he also kept the garden because he loved it, and he loved us. I went back to the groundkeeper's door and knocked.

"Hey there again," BJ smiled.

"I didn't mean to be rude. I was just interested to know why you work so hard on the golf course."

"'Cause I like to eat," she said.

"But you have the garden."

"Yeah, but if the grass doesn't grow, they'd make me move."

"So, why do you have the garden?" I had to know.

"It feeds me in a different way."

## CHAPTER THIRTY-THREE

# Coming Clean

I rode to work with Mama one day when I didn't have to go to school. I hadn't told her I wasn't going to spend time with Wright, but I wasn't. I wanted to visit the places Wright and I used to hang out. I didn't have my golf clubs, but I went to the green and walked along the tree line. I found three stray golf balls, but I didn't keep them. I threw them out on the green for somebody else to find. I didn't think I'd be playing as much without Wright, which was okay with me because I don't think I liked it that much. I did like being out there on the green carpet, but I didn't need to hit a ball to have a reason to do that. The movie theater door was unlocked, so I went in and sat in the back row because Wright and I always sat in the very front row.

After a while, I walked over to Wright's house so I could leave him his Christmas present.

His mama came to the door, and she said, "Come on in. Wright and Adam didn't say you were coming?"

*Adam who?* I thought.

I went in the kitchen to put Wright's Christmas gift on the counter, and I saw that postcard again. That whole year Wright and I were friends, there was a postcard stuck to a message board by the kitchen telephone, like a lost letter at the post office just waiting for the addressee to finally walk in and claim it. It was posted from Brussels, dated April 5, 1964, addressed to Prudence, his sister. Wright wouldn't have been born yet, and she would have been a baby, I guess. Little Miss Prudence Finch.

"Dear Prudence, we are missing you, our sweet angel, and will…" but a picture of Wright and Pru was tacked up on top of it, covering the rest of the note written in sweeping cursive. I ached to get a peek at the rest of the message, as if the thumbtack was a magnet, and my hands were cold steel. I forcibly held my hands at my side. But this day in particular, I wanted to rip it off the board and walk into the next room and stick it in my brother's face. He and Pru were sitting in the next room, right next to each other. Seeing them there when I walked in was a big surprise to say the least. I didn't even know they knew each other. He didn't say he was going to be at Wright's house.

They were intertwined like one of those games you can play with your fingers with one continuous loop of string. But the intertwine was all knots, not knowing where one knot began or ended or how tight it was. Wright was on a chair nearby with a bag of chips on his stomach, unconcerned. And he talked to Adam like he'd known him for, I don't know, all his life. They even looked like each other: brown hair, legs spread wide, half-open smiles. The only real difference was Wright didn't have his arm around Pru with his thumb caught in her belt loop.

I sat there and quietly fumed.

"Why?" I asked under my breath. I didn't finish the question because I didn't know what to ask. I was so surprised, so confused. It just felt like I should have known. There were so many girls around, but Adam was here…in my friend's house with his hands all over my friend's sister.

The house was cool and had dark, knotty pine paneling all through it, except for Pru's room, which you had to go through a short, dark hallway to reach. It was almost a wing of its own, a built-on room that was about half the size of the entire house. It had white plaster walls with her bed in the corner and a whole sofa and a door to the outside. It was self-contained, except for a kitchen. I wondered why their parents didn't take that room and put Pru in the room next to Wright's.

"I can hear my parents doing it." Wright smirked. "I'm gonna do it when I get married."

It didn't bother him when his parents did it. It didn't bother him to see Adam and Pru right here in front of him practicing before doing it, leading up to it. And they *would* do it. Adam did it with Cindy last year, at least that's what I heard at school. And here was Adam, right in my territory, with both Pru and Wright drinking him in, worshiping him.

*Why do you keep a post card from when you were a baby on the wall? Are you a baby?* I said in my head, but not out loud. I felt crazy, unreasonable. I was so mad Adam was there, and I wanted to do something to ruin it for him. Wright was my friend, or at least he had been. This house was mine to visit, not Adam's. I wanted them to stop touching each other and to stop Wright from being Adam's new little brother.

*Why don't you just be Wright's brother instead of mine!* I screamed inside. And I thought they heard me for a minute because first Adam looked at me, and then Wright, and then Pru. But I didn't say it out loud. I know I didn't.

Adam said, "Let's go."

And we went. I was mad at Adam; I was mad at Wright; I was mad at myself for being mad with them. Everything was so easy for Adam. When he kissed Pru, I'll bet he didn't think about whether or not she wanted him to kiss her. He just kissed her because he wanted to. But she wanted him to because she wouldn't have asked him over if she didn't like him. She wouldn't sit on the couch with him with his hands on her if she didn't like him. I bet she'd even come over to have lunch at our house some Sunday. Mama said I could invite a girl to Sunday lunch when I got a girlfriend. But I wouldn't know what to say to a girl, especially at the table with everybody looking. She'd never said I could invite James or Wright over for lunch.

I couldn't understand why sometimes it felt like Adam was pulling away.

At times like that, I would wish for my sister…the baby on my birth certificate, the one I'd named Jessie. Jess and I would talk about boys. With Adam off doing his grown-up stuff and Mama and Daddy out looking for him, I bet Jess and I would have stayed home together, maybe making cookies, getting the whites off the eggs so we could put fake facials on each other. If Adam and I had a sister, she'd understand because she'd like boys too. And Jess would tell me what it's like to kiss one. I couldn't tell Adam I wanted to kiss a boy. He'd tell Mama and Daddy.

The next time I saw Wright was at school during gym class. He didn't smile. He kind of looked over his shoulder at James and me as he ran past us, playing a game with the other boys. Coach Sammy smiled at me a lot, and at James too. But then Coach Sammy would bark like a dog at us if we didn't run fast enough or if we could never get the ball in the hoop on rainy days when we went to the gym instead of outside. Rainy days should have been easier. Staying inside should have been an excuse to do inside activities, like read or draw or sit. But rainy days were cage days, like catfish caught in one of Uncle Kingston's wire traps. I was always on the bottom down where the trap settled into the muddy pond floor and unable to see daylight because other fish were more aggressive and stronger than me.

That's how they carry the fish from one lake to another over behind Uncle Kingston's. They push all the fish to one corner of the pond and then take a big vacuum that sucks up water instead of air, and all those fish get pulled up in that vacuum and dumped into a big bucket on the back of a truck. They drive over to the other pond and shoot them out a big tube with the fish wiggling like I did when Jeb used to hold me down and tickle me. I always wondered what would happen if a baby fish didn't get pulled over in the net, or maybe the baby fish was so small it went through the hole in the net while its mama got pulled away trying to get back to her baby.

The Matchbox cars distracted me, hypnotized me during those days when I could not bear school, those fish-in-a-big-ol'-cage days. I didn't even have to look at the Matchbox. Just holding it in my hand in my pocket was enough for some measure of comfort. I felt close to home with the Cougar in my hand, imagining I was not in the gym, but back in my room at home, enveloped. James hated those days as much as I did, ignored and shunned almost as much as me. He was standing near me, Wright a few feet away from us.

I didn't say anything.

"Dude, move!" James said as Wright backed into him, elbowing him as he caught the basketball.

"Hey little man, it's cool. Just playin' here," Wright responded. And then to me, "Tell your bro to cool off."

I was in the middle, silent.

James turned away. "I know he doesn't like me," James said. "That works both ways. I don't like him either."

I was surprised. Wright never said anything bad about James. Come to think of it, he never said anything at all about James.

"Okay, guys, basketball. All of you are skins." Coach Sammy drew an imaginary circle in the air, and I happened to be standing in the very center of it. "And the rest of you are shirts."

I panicked and went up to him and asked, "Coach Sammy, do I have to take my shirt off?"

"Yep."

"What's wrong?" James said walking past me, voice low so that Coach Sammy wouldn't hear.

"Don't want to show your little-girl titties?" Coach Sammy yawned. "Afraid these boys'll get all excited by your little breasteses?"

And the crowd began to circle, forming a pen around me, trapping me in with the coach who was a feral but slow-moving cat that didn't have to use its speed to pounce on me. He moved slowly because I couldn't move. He knew he'd already caught me.

"Tell you what. You come over here and show me what you got under your shirt, and I'll tell you if you can keep it on."

Everyone was looking.

"No," I said.

And Wright said, "God," clearly irritated.

"It's okay," said James.

"Take your shirt off," Coach repeated.

But I couldn't do it.

I stared, ears hot and full of rushing water. I stood there and looked at him, knowing that if I took my shirt off, everybody would see me and pick on me. It would be unbearable.

Nobody here knew what it felt like to be misshapen. Nobody knew.

"Go get a fag belt." He must have meant a flag belt, but I went anyway. A flag belt was for flag football, but I guess they'd know the flag meant I was on skins and not shirts.

"Philbet, what's with you?" Wright asked. "Don't be so weird."

Suddenly somebody in the room screamed, a loud, ear-aching, high-pitched scream.

Then I realized it was me. I screamed. It was like I burst.

Everybody looked, some right at me, some with their bodies turned away and heads turned over their shoulders as if everybody was in quiet conversation in groups of two or three, and they stopped whatever it was they were talking about mid-sentence when I screamed. I'd always kept out of the way, kept quiet, almost invisible. Mama's notes helped get me out of PE most of the time, but today was too much—my breaking point, my turning point. I flinched, as if to run, as if I had come face-to-face with Bigfoot out in the middle of the pine trees behind the house and my instinct was to run, but I caught myself before I bolted and kept still.

For a few years I had swum slowly and quietly, largely unnoticed into the midst of a school of sharks. I had observed them without them seeing me, but today I pulled out a knife and stuck it in my mouth, tightening my tongue and lips on it as I pulled it out, blood gushing out into the water. I wasn't invisible anymore.

James grabbed me by the back of the shirt and pulled me off the court and toward the lockers. "Come on, man. Come on."

He was twice as big as me, so it was either be pulled along, or let him pick me up and move me. He could have.

"Philbet, just calm down, man. You actin' crazy." He led me out of the gym, glancing over his shoulder to see if anybody else was coming. No one was. He sat down in the hallway.

To himself, "That was bad. That was so…. What is wrong with you?"

"You don't know what it's like."

"What what's like?" James asked.

"Never mind."

"Tell me."

"I'm such a weirdo," I said more to myself than to him.

"Man, you can't tell me anything I haven't already heard."

"I bet I can."

"Okay, try me. You don't know half the stuff my crazy-ass family does."

"Like what?"

"My Aunt Dee eats washing starch. Big blocks of corn starch. She just eats it while she's doing laundry."

"Why?"

"Hell if I know. Says she likes it. Reminds her of being a little girl."

"Does it make her sick?"

"She ain't never sick," James replied.

"Does she cook it?"

"Breaks it off and eats it like a mouse eats cheese." He nibbled at his fingertips for effect.

"My Aunt Ease smells her fingers all the time," I replied. "Daddy said they either smell like roses or dog doo."

"Maybe she eats washing starch too."

"She must be eatin' it because her laundry looks like crap."

"Got a cousin with no toes," James added to his list.

"Where's his toes?"

"It's a girl," James explained. "Never had any."

"How does she stand up?"

"She does okay. She stuffs toilet tissue in her shoes. She wears high heels. She said no missin' toes are gonna hold her back."

"I got one," I said. "My aunt gives my uncle weird gifts, like a pot with sausages floating in apple juice."

"I like sausages and apple juice."

"The pot was a chamber pot," I said. "Folks used to go to the bathroom in them before they had bathrooms. She thought it was funny 'cause it looked like poo and wee."

"This is why everybody thinks you're a little wierdo. Say shit and piss like everybody else."

"I don't want to."

"Why'd she give him fake shit and piss in a pot?" James asked.

"She thought it was funny."

"It *is* funny."

"No, James, it's weird."

"No, Philbet, you're uptight."

We just sat there, looking at the doorway, thinking Coach Sammy would come through.

"I think we got out of playing. Thanks, but you didn't have to act like a fool," James said.

"Aw, leave me alone."

"Philbet, I'm kidding."

"I just ruin everything," I blurted out, on the brink of crying.

"No, you didn't."

"Just leave me alone, James. Okay? I just want to hide."

"Yeah? Screaming like a stuck pig won't help."

"I didn't scream like a pig!"

"You did, but it's okay. Okay?"

I felt so stupid. I didn't say it out loud, but I said it in my head a lot.

"Philbet, tell me what's wrong." James was trying to help.

I took a deep breath and began to lift my shirt, but I stopped and looked toward the door. I walked around the corner where James could see me, but anybody walking in couldn't. I sensed someone standing nearby as soon as I lifted my shirt halfway up over my stomach. I couldn't see who it was, but James could. Coach Sammy appeared from around the corner and tossed a piece of paper at me, "Get your ass to the principal, and give him this."

The note read, "Screaming like a girl."

## CHAPTER THIRTY-FOUR

# My Refuge

Long after kids my age gave theirs up, I still had my toy box. It was the one I crouched in the day we moved from Alvaton to Warm Springs, the one Grandaddy perched on as he reassured me it would be okay, that *I* was okay. It was big and at the foot of my bed, not a big lump forgotten in the corner of the room like the toy boxes of my peers. It was full of toys, some I didn't play with any longer—toy cars, and my beloved car books.

September was a month of magic. New television shows started, and the new car models debuted. With the cars came the car books. It would have been a perfect month if school had not begun at the same time. I had an extensive car-book library dating from the early '70s, all carefully stored in one compartment of my toy box. They were more promotional pamphlets than books, most featuring Chevrolets, Oldsmobiles, and Pontiacs. I got them because Mama brought them home from Mabie Motors, one or two at a time.

I imagined her going on a coffee break, checking to see if anyone was looking, then quickly, quietly taking a pamphlet or two. Or she'd spot one that a customer had left on a chair and stroll by to lift it as if she were straightening up the show room. But instead of returning the out-of-place promotion to the rack, she'd take it back to her desk as if she had forgotten she had it in her hand, carefully slipping it into the over-sized pocketbook she kept under her desk. Mama, a small woman, preferred big handbags, as if she might one day need to carry around enough food and fresh clothes for us if there was an emergency. But there was hardly ever anything in those bags, except now and again those treasured booklets.

I begged her to bring them home. I longed for all of them that very first day in September, but they dribbled in over the course of months, always, in my mind, because Mama had to sneak them, which made them more special somehow. But looking back, I think she knew that they would be more exceptional to me if they appeared over time, giving me a chance to study them individually, like Christmas packages opened one at a time, stretched out over the course of an entire Christmas day.

In the other toy-box compartment was a fleet of toy cars of varying sizes, all makes and models, some plastic, some wood, and some metal. One was even made of foam, a foam-filled pillow for lying on the floor. I was on the floor that day, my face horizontally smashed against the dusty carpet. This was my world, the only place that mattered. The school gymnasium didn't exist here. I stared at the fleet all scattered out across the floor, cars in profile, at an angle, as if they were staged along some dewy meadow or on the beach or in a chic cityscape, all posed for a car-book photo shoot. They looked perfect. I had long ago memorized how to position them across the room, tricking the perspective so they all looked the same size. The dune buggy, twice as long as my feet, had to go all the way against the closet door on the other side of the room. The lime-green Mustang was closer to me at about the edge of the bed leg. The closest was a crudely carved Flintstone car that Grandaddy got me the very first year they held the Meriwether County Fair.

But they weren't the same size, and I didn't treat them the same either. I loved the Mustang the most because it was the Ford version of the Mercury Cougar.

The Mustang also had a chrome-finished bumper and taillights that hooked into slots cut out of the green plastic form of the car. The front grill and lights were the same. I left the shiny bumper half on, half dragging the carpet. I imagined fender benders and conversations with the driver who ran into me. We'd exchange insurance information, and I'd wait for the wrecker, like the one that hauled in cars down at Brown's, to take me to a garage.

Everybody in my imaginary conversations was earnest and interested. "That's awful!" "What will you do for a car while it's being fixed?" "Will they Bondo or press the dents out?" And then I imagined my family in the car with me. "Everyone is fine. Just a fender bender."

Adam and I had miniature drag racers, mine green, his blue. Other than the color, they were identical. The chassis was hinged at the back bumper and flipped up to reveal a black frame, the skeleton that held the insides of the car together. A prop, sort of the same type of rod that holds up a real car's hood, could be lifted to hold the blue or green chassis aloft. A silver-tone engine was the centerpiece, gleaming like a diamond in a flip-top ring box.

One day, Daddy walked into my room and stepped right on top of mine in his work boots. It was totaled, an insurance write-off that the driver surely couldn't have survived. If I'd taken it down to Brown's yard and placed it close enough in the foreground of real wrecks, it would have looked like a real totaled car in a photograph.

I dreamed about it, or had nightmares, really. My subconscious was working out a solution to my continual worry over being found out—that I was the guy who didn't want a wife one day. I'd daydream, imagining myself losing my beloved spouse in that tragic accident, leaving me behind too heartbroken to ever find another wife, this in the service of living my life without anyone knowing I was someone they didn't really know and wouldn't want to know or love if they knew me, the me inside.

Wright must have gotten a glimpse of the me inside, because since my meltdown in the gym, he hadn't spoken to me. He didn't even look at me, so he didn't have to pretend to smile either.

## CHAPTER THIRTY-FIVE

# Black and White

Dr. Oren's office was in an old house, which had walls covered in once white but now grayish shingles about the size of a sheet of notebook paper. Each shingle had a curvy bottom edge that reminded me of ocean waves. I always wondered if the top edge of the shingles were curvy, too, but the shingle above covered it, so I couldn't tell.

The house never seemed to change from visit to visit, until one day it did. The top edge of a shingle by the front door had fractured and fallen away, leaving the straight edge of the shingle below visible along with the wood of the actual house, which was no longer the bright honey yellow of freshly milled timber. It was gray, light deprived, as if it had soaked up all the sadness and sickness of those who went there to get better.

The shingles were asbestos, fire retardant, a mid-century development in fire prevention. That's what Daddy said to me one time when he brought me to Dr. Oren's. But to me, it looked like a house covered in fish scales, one of those big monsters of a fish that lived so far down in the sea that only robot-piloted submarines could capture photos. One fish I saw in my science book had a little antenna sticking out its forehead, and that antenna curved out in front of the fish's mouth, holding a little light at the edge of it like a little fishing pole. When littler fish came up to look at the luminous glow—something they must not have understood being so submerged in the inky black darkness of the deep sea—the big fish opened its jaws and gobbled up the smaller, nosey fish that had swum right up to its mouth.

Every time we walked through what used to be the front door of that house-turned-doctor's office, I looked at the copper loop that sprang out from the scaly wall over the front door. It bent with the weight of a light fixture that looked like a Mason jar screwed in under a yellow glowing light bulb, which stayed lit morning, noon, and night, season in and season out. But this monster, this house, had two mouths, one here in front and one all the way around on the side.

The side door into Dr. Oren's office didn't have the fishing lure-like light arching out to draw in patients. It was just a door at the top of steps, no porch with a roof to protect anyone entering from rain, no swing and chairs to sit in if you got there too early. There was nothing to welcome, nothing to beckon. Instead of the light, there was only a small tin sign, which I'd never seen because I'd never been to that door. I figured it was the kitchen. Our side door at home went into the kitchen.

Mama parked on the street that lined the side of the house. I could tell she was irritated we hadn't gotten to Dr. Oren's earlier. She liked us to be the first ones in so that they'd call us in first, and it was already after 8:00 a.m. I saw James go in the side door. I didn't realize he even went to Dr. Oren. And I couldn't understand why he'd be going in the side door where the kitchen most likely was.

I followed Mama up the sidewalk to the front and inside. It felt like what I imagined 1940 to look like. The books and the magazines were all at least twenty years old. And the furniture was covered in the same inflexible fake leather as the sofa outside Mr. Pratt's office in elementary school. It was hard and stiff in the winter, especially if you got to the doctor's office early in the morning and were the first to sit on it. In the summer, any exposed skin stuck to it. There were the beginnings of cracks along the edges of almost all the chairs, and the foam was so dry rotted that every time Mrs. Jarvis plopped down, the cracks spit out floaty bits like a hay-fever sneeze. The nurses wore actual nurse uniforms, ones that they'd probably had for forty or fifty years, looking soft-edged and thin-seamed from over-wear and many washes in scalding water, which is the only way to kill germs. I wondered where James was. He couldn't have already gone in to see the doctor. There were several people in the waiting room, and they would have been here before James.

"Did you have any homework to turn in today?" Mama asked.

"No, Ma'am," I said, but I did. I just didn't want to do it.

Was I sick? I was sick of PE. Some days I couldn't face it. And it was going to rain today, and that meant inside sports. My favorite way of staying home from school was when I was really sick. I swear, I think I bit my fingernails just to get every single germ I could in my mouth. If I could get away with it, I'd lick every door handle I could get my tongue on, even the bathroom door at school. Instead, I touched everything that I thought might get me sick. Grandaddy said that if you get sick and can get well without taking medicine, it makes your body stronger naturally. Well, I should be Mr. Universe because I got sick all the time and didn't take any medicine. If Mama gave me something to take, I spat it out before swallowing if I got the chance.

The other way to get to stay home was to say I hurt, or more specifically, that my chest hurt. Sometimes it did, but it's hard to describe just how it hurt. It's more a hurt in my head, but not like a headache. I became pretty good at getting out of school, staying home at least one day a week. Mama always wrote a note. The days I didn't have to go to school were like having a full summer break right in front of me, all crammed into one day. June was 8:00 in the morning. July was noon. August was 5:00 p.m. And having to go back to school after a holiday…the worst.

The receptionist called my name to go back to Dr. Oren. As I went through, she called James's name too. I saw him walk through a door on the other side of the reception desk, from a room I'd never been in.

"Hi. What you in for?" he said.

I shrugged my shoulders. "You?"

"Mama made me come. Got a cold."

"You going to school?"

"Not if I can help it. You?" he asked.

"I hope not."

"See you," James replied.

"Bye…. Hey?" I asked.

"Yeah?"

"What's in there?" I wanted to know.

"That's the colored waiting room," James explained before I could say anything else, following the nurse to an exam room. When I went back to school the next day, James wasn't there.

## CHAPTER THIRTY-SIX

# You Don't Have to Know

"I didn't know there were two waiting rooms," I said to James out on the playground after his return to school.

"Yeah, there are two waiting rooms at the dentist too."

"Why?"

"'Cause White people are triflin'," James replied.

"They're what?"

"They want everything for themselves," he explained.

"No, they don't."

"Yeah, they do."

"Not everything," I said.

"What do you mean not everything?"

I didn't know how to answer.

All I could think to say was: "I'm not a racist."

"Hmmph."

I didn't know what to say to that either.

"I know you're a White boy, and I'm a Black boy. We're different." James didn't smile when he said it.

We stared at each other.

"I've never been to your house," he said.

"I've never been to yours either," I replied.

"Philbet, you don't know there are two waiting rooms because you don't have to know."

"Well, yeah I do. What if I went into the wrong one?" Even as I said it, I knew it was wrong, knew it sounded lame.

"You can be friends with a Black boy, and I can be friends with a White boy. But we…we don't do anything to change anything," he said.

"What do we do?"

"Don't ask me." James was genuinely baffled.

"Want to come over to my house?" I asked.

"You want me to come over?"

I didn't say anything.

"I guess you don't," he replied.

"I…"

"Yeah?" James had thought about all of this more than I had. I could tell. How could I admit that I was afraid if he met Daddy, he would think I'm weird? And I guess I was worried Daddy wouldn't want me to be friends with him anymore.

"That's okay. I don't really want to come over."

"Why?"

"I don't think I'd like your family," James said.

"Why?" I asked.

"Because I don't think *you* like them."

## CHAPTER THIRTY-SEVEN

# Team Mama

I don't know if it was Daddy or me who first stopped liking the other. He made sounds when he ate. Sounds that could not, *should not* come from a human. He smelled the food at the same time he ate it, worse than a wild pig in the woods. And his chewing was messy and staccato, like some entirely new musical genre imagined by a wild beast, and the instrument he played was a mouth full of sloppy food, with a half-stopped-up nose as back-up vocals. It was horrible to behold, and I hated him for it.

"You don't love him. Make him leave. We can make it on our own," I said to Mama one afternoon.

Silence.

She was such a good seamstress, she could make enough money at it if I helped her somehow. There was a picture in the living room of Mama and Daddy on their wedding day. Mama had a skirt and matching jacket. It was black and white in the photograph, but the suit hung in the closet. It was pale yellow with raised nubs, which were almost but not quite orange. The inside lining was blue-green. Mama said it was dyed, but I couldn't understand how it got dyed to be yellow and almost orange on the outside and blue-green on the inside. I wonder if she wanted a white wedding dress, or if getting stuck with him was such a disappointment that she dressed the part. Mama and I were a unified team, and Daddy was the other side. Adam was neutral. I think Mama disliked Daddy as much as I did.

She tried different ways to make extra money over the years, wanting to be financially independent, I guess. When she sold Avon I said, "I am beginning to need deodorant." I didn't, but I ached to buy something from the catalog, and with Mama's discount it only cost about twice as much as deodorant in the drugstore. And then there was Townway cookware. I had dreams of the Townway sales board naming Mama the top salesperson each week. She really was one of only a few trailblazing saleswomen in the whole country. Almost all the sales teams were men, with their wives as backup. The men went into homes and demonstrated the cookware, while the wives stayed in the kitchen and cooked a full meal for the other couples who came to the dinner. The menu was a meatloaf, potatoes, carrots, and a pineapple upside-down cake, all cooked in stacked pots on one burner.

Mama cooked a "minute steak" in front of a group of three couples one night. I was her backup. She heated the pan, put in a Delmonico steak, turned it over one minute later, and turned off the heat. The steak came out a few minutes later, perfectly cooked. The homes we entered, dragging in our cookware and prepped food, fascinated me. I liked looking at how other folks lived. And if the house had an accommodating layout, I could sometimes sneak out of the kitchen while everybody was in the living room. I'd peek into their bedrooms and bathrooms and imagine their lives there, wondering if they were happy. Wondering what they talked about when they were alone as a family without Mama and me there making dinner and talking to them about cookware and trying to sell them something. I'd look at their bed and think about how they had a private life with the world shut out behind their locked front door...a world of their own. An Adam and Eve who wanted to populate their own little world with their own things—a favorite pillow, shared secrets, children. How did these two-person, private worlds start out? How did a man and woman start their own world? How would I start a world with someone, with my own Adam? Not my brother, but Eve's Adam.

Mama and Daddy didn't seem to have a world away from the other world. They seemed to want to move to another world, and not together, but apart from each other. Daddy liked to pile us all in the truck on Sunday afternoons and go off on the country roads to search for honeysuckle, which he'd dig up while we were parked on the side of the road. Adam and I had to take turns standing at the very edge of the woods pretending to wee. We weren't allowed to say "pee," and certainly not "piss," but Daddy said "shit" about every other breath. If anybody drove by while Daddy was out in the woods stealing a plant, they wouldn't think anything was up, just that we had to stop to wee.

Ever since Adam got bigger and stronger, he went into the woods with Daddy to help haul the plant out and throw it over into the bed of the truck while nobody was looking. Mama increasingly rode shotgun, usually staring out the car window as lookout. With Adam hauling Daddy's booty, I was designated wee-er. In a funny way, this version of a family outing united us, each with a role to play, the perfect job for four people about our sizes and ages.

But those trips to the woods became more and more infrequent, as Adam stayed out several nights a week and didn't come home until early morning. One of those mornings, the last one as it turns out, Daddy paused and took me by the shoulders before he and Mama headed out to look for him.

"Philbet, don't do us like Adam does us. Don't do it. He's killin' Mama." And with that, Daddy took his keys off the hook, and he and Mama were out the door, in his truck, and off to search for Adam. Well, I didn't want to kill Mama. Adam didn't want to either. Daddy sounded like he was in a soap opera. But Adam was a trial. That was so.

Why didn't Daddy do something like make Adam stay home or take his car away if he didn't like what he did? Daddy wielded guilt as parental control, and it just made me think Daddy didn't know how to be a daddy. If Grandaddy had said to one of us, "You stop doing that," I bet we'd stop. I sure would stop, not because I was afraid of him, but because… well, I'm not really sure why I'd do something Grandaddy told me to do, but I just would.

And I was going to try to be good, super good, but I already did that. It kind of hurt my feelings when Daddy said that. It was like he was blaming me for something Adam did.

And as soon as the dot of the truck's taillights disappeared, Adam swerved into the drive from the other direction. He came through and gave me an uncharacteristic hug. He smelled like a cigarette, kind of. Mama would not like that. He went to the fridge and drank the rest of the pitcher of Kool-Aid, which Mama had just made that night using the last of her sugar. She might get mad because she sure did get mad when I dropped a whole pitcher of Kool-Aid on the kitchen floor that one time, the floor covered in pink juice just red enough to look like Mr. Arvin had butchered a pig on the kitchen counter and washed the blood-pink water off onto the floor.

"Mama left a plate in the oven," I said.

He pulled it out and ate.

"They're out lookin' for you," I warned him.

"So?"

Adam just never seemed to worry about anything. Then instead of falling face-first into bed like he usually did after his nights out, he took a shower and put on a tie. He was in his car and off before Mama and Daddy returned. When he came back about noon, he smacked his enlistment papers down on the table next to Daddy's TV chair. Adam had joined the Navy, and that was the end of the honeysuckle bandits.

I wondered if the four of us would ever even ride together in the same car at the same time again.

Adam had only two weeks at home before reporting for duty. I didn't know what to say to him when he was home and not making the rounds to say good-bye to his friends. He seemed to understand I was at a loss, already missing him because the night before the Navy recruiter came at 4:00 in the morning to pick Adam up and put him on a plane to boot camp, he came to my room and said, "Let's go for a ride." He took me to get Krystal hamburgers. We didn't really talk. It was tough enough just getting the Krystals to go down because my throat felt tight, narrower.

The granite rocks Daddy had poured over the red clay drive in front of the house popped under the weight of the car tires as we pulled slowly in.

Adam turned the key to silence the motor and said, "I'll…come back." Those were his words, but I heard an unsaid, "miss you" there in the quiet before he spoke. He put his hand on my shoulder and squeezed. I thought he'd snap my shoulder off, but I don't think he knew how much pressure it was.

The next morning he was all smiles, but the smile looked like a not very good painter put it there. He was so scared, the same eight-year-old little boy left in charge to take care of me the first time they took Grandaddy to the hospital in the middle of the night. About twenty minutes after they drove off the telephone rang. It was Adam calling from a pay phone up in Greenville. He'd left his orders at the house. Mama always said her secret prayers just loud enough so you could hear them, and we'd all heard her say a few times that she was afraid she'd never see Adam again once he left the house for the Navy. I chose to believe he left his paperwork behind just so we'd have to get in the car and take the folder of military papers to him. Then Mama's prayer would be answered, if only technically. She got to see him again after he left the house. It set Mama at ease, more comfortable than she'd been those two weeks leading up to him leaving. She got one more hug and kiss and said, "We'll see you at Thanksgiving." And she was okay.

It's one of the kindest things I'd ever seen. He did it for her, but it must have been tough on him, too, having to say goodbye twice and then turning away to face the unknown.

## CHAPTER THIRTY-EIGHT

# I See You

The very next Sunday, Mama said we were going someplace different and not to the woods to dig up honeysuckle. "Phil, you can go if you want to, but we're going to the antique store in Woodbury." He cussed and walked away.

Mama didn't tell me this was Beau's store. It was a surprise. I hadn't seen him since we moved to Warm Springs. Ten years? I figured he was at Pick's. I hadn't thought about him in a long time and felt bad about it because he was always so nice to me. I had a box of paper cigar bands from all the bubble gum cigars he gave me, just like Grandaddy had the cigar bands from all the cigars he smoked.

When we got to Attic Antiques, Beau gave Mama and me big hugs and said he couldn't believe how big I'd gotten and asked me how old I was.

"Thirteen."

"Gosh, you're growing up."

And he asked about Adam. Mama said he'd just gone off to the Navy, and he hugged her again. I don't know how he knew to do that. She didn't cry or anything.

And then someone else walked in, so we started walking around looking at stuff.

The antique shop was like somebody had gone through Mama's, Jorma's, MawMaw's, and all my aunts' houses and took one each of their most favorite pieces of furniture, and some of their clothes too, and arranged them all together here in this new house with price tags on everything. A hat hanging from a pie safe looked just like the one Minnie Pearl might have worn. I recognized that pie safe. It had belonged to Lolly. It had to be her pie safe because it had the same red edge on all the corners. I'd seen her get flour out of it I don't know how many times. It was a wonder to me. I had no idea anybody would want all the old stuff we had and lived with every day. But Lolly was gone, so she didn't need it.

A pie safe was almost a playground to us. When I was little, Adam used to lock me inside Jorma's. I was a willing and eager prisoner. And, anyway, I knew as soon as Jorma saw me in it she'd make me get out so I wouldn't be captive too long. There was one good "Boo" in it before I was released. The flour sifter that came built into it was long gone, and Jorma set a bowl on that hole so that it looked intentional, like the carpenter built in a space for the owner to set out fruit or something. When I was in the bottom cabinet, my head fit perfectly through, and if I balanced it just right, the bowl stayed on my head when I came up through the hole. I bet I looked just like I was in a skit from *The Carol Burnett Show*.

There was also a gun cabinet, but it didn't have any guns in it. It was full of brooms decorated with ribbons, propped upright like they were a row of rifles. And they weren't sweeping brooms like they had at the Dollar Store; they looked like a bunch of straw just pulled out of the field, like a witch's broom. Mama said they weren't for sweeping. "Decoration," she explained. "Faye's got one hung next to her stove near the back door."

Well that was about the stupidest thing I'd heard in years. Why would Faye hang a bunch of straw wrapped up with a ribbon next to the stove? That's just asking for a fire, I thought. But Faye wasn't too smart, and her taste level was what Mama called "a swing and a miss." Mama said, "Brooms are for sweepin', not for decoratin'." And I agreed, saying so, but not loud enough for Beau to hear me. I loved it when Mama got a little catty.

But I liked Beau's shop. Being around all this old stuff instead of the new furniture they sold down at the mall made me feel at home. He had a sign on one chair that read "Do not sit." and a sign on a cabinet that read "Please ask for assistance." I figured that was just like at Jorma's house. She didn't have a sign, but everybody knew not to go into the last door off the living room that was built onto what used to be the back porch and steps. Sometimes I peeked in anyway when I was really little because it interested me so. It was supposed to be a bathroom. Daddy said Jorma and Grandaddy didn't have a bathroom in the house until they built onto it. And they had space for two bathrooms, but they only finished off one.

In the unfinished bathroom, there was a hole for where the commode went, but there wasn't a commode. They had a bunch of boxes and lumber in there. It was a good place to go when you got too hot running around outside because it was really cool in the summer, but it got really cold in the winter. Every now and then I sneaked in and ate candy or hid from Adam. It was a good place to go when Mama and Daddy weren't happy. If I ever found a treasure, I vowed I'd hide it down the commode hole.

I came around a row of chifforobes, and that man who came in earlier was standing behind the counter, so I figured he worked there. Maybe some of the furniture in the store belonged to his mama too. Then I saw the man touch Beau's back, down low in the place where Daddy sometimes gets an ache after work.

And I thought, *Beau hurt his back. I bet he was lifting this furniture on his own.*

But something was different. Then the man slid his hand down Beau's back right into his back pocket. My chest got really hot. I must have looked like the snack machine dropped two bags of chips instead of one. Eyes not too wide, but my mouth definitely a little too slack. Beau looked over at me just as the thought formed in my mind. He smiled very slightly and then winked. He didn't wink like Grandaddy winked. It wasn't like, "Boy, it'll be okay." It was more like, "You see me. I see you."

"Come here," Beau said, sort of gently.

He put his right hand on the back of my head the way Grandaddy did when he wanted to talk just to me. "Philbet, old friend," but Beau wasn't looking at me. He was looking at the man, and his left hand was on the man's head, but not the way Grandaddy did it. It was identical in movement, but different. "This is Dean, a new friend."

"Philbet, it's good to meet you," Dean said. I looked at Beau's hand on Dean's head, instead of at Dean's eyes.

"Hi," I responded blankly.

"Philbet and I go way back," Beau said.

"Yeah?" Dean asked.

"Yep."

And I didn't know what to say to them. I was embarrassed because I saw the man, Dean, touch Beau. It seemed private. But it was an accident that I saw. I just looked at the wrong time.

"Philbet, it's okay," Beau reassured, reading my mind.

"Okay?" I said vacantly.

"You okay?"

"Yeah."

I'd never been in an exchange between two people so full with something, with hardly a word passed between them.

I didn't know what to do. Beau did. He turned around and picked a frame from the cabinet behind his desk. A child's rendering of a boy encircled by pine trees, and the one nearest the boy had a set of eyes and then another set of eyes lower down the trunk, as if nestled, blinking out from inside the tree.

"Oh, you're Philbet," Dean realized. "Come here."

He came from around and hugged me, kissed me on top of the head.

I was paralyzed, hoping Mama hadn't seen that, a strange man hugging me, kissing me. When I could move, I whipped around and saw Mama facing the other way across the store.

"You brought him back," Dean said.

I didn't understand, uncomfortable here with Beau and whatever was going on. What would Mama say if she saw this stranger hugging me? What would she do if she saw Dean touch Beau's butt? Actually, I really wanted to know. And I wondered what it would feel like for someone to touch mine, my butt. It seemed like something you should get permission to do beforehand because that could go wrong.

While I stared at Dean, confused, Beau said, "I carried your drawing folded up in my pocket all through the war."

# PART THREE

## CHAPTER THIRTY-NINE

# Enter Knox

Months later, something changed. I saw something new—a beast of a car flew by and turned off our road into Brownie's. It was alive. And it wasn't on a wrecker. No wrecker would ever get this one. If it ever cracked up on the road, it wouldn't be a fender bender. Nope, this car would disintegrate into beautiful green dust, leaving no carcass to rust in the lot of a body shop. And if it ever cracked up, I'd be there to breathe in that dust, the car then a part of me.

A 1972 dark green Pontiac GTO with hood scoops. It was the absolute hottest rod I'd ever seen or could've dreamed about. I could tell by the way it paused mid-flight that it was a manual shift, almost scraping the pavement from the surface of the road when the driver mashed the clutch, pulled it into the next higher gear, let the clutch out, and floored the gas. When that car tore off down the road, the deep grill looked like it could suck up the pavement as it went over it, spitting it out as gravel through the low-slung, squinting red line of the taillights.

I could feel it in my ears, feel it in that place between skin and muscles. I wanted to drive that car, one day when I could drive a car.

The blackened grill set back inside what seemed a foot into the engine cavity reminded me of the beautiful bull I saw on a poster over Mr. Dannon's desk when Mama went in to see him during one of our Warm

Springs days. The bull was in mid-charge, his nostrils flaring, headed toward a man in purple pants and vest with a hat that looked like Mickey Mouse, but after somebody chided him and his ears weren't so perky. And the man held a red cloth up to this bull, so close that the bull could just reach out and snap up this fellow in one bite.

At first, I only watched for the GTO from the edge of the road. I could hear him start up all the way over at Brownie's. The person who cranked it revved the engine, but there didn't seem to be an urgency, never a hurry to take off and fly by. It just roared, and each time it did I involuntarily closed my eyes and felt the imperceptible and single shake of the car's body as the engine roared. That GTO had been still for too long a time, asleep all day and now awake, but held to its spot in Brownie's yard by the press of a single foot against its brake pedal.

It wasn't Brownie. I knew it wasn't. It couldn't be. Brownie knew how to fix cars, but he didn't know how to touch them. The person behind the wheel knew that push and pull, the tension between taking off like a rocket and the anticipation that came before. And though I hadn't managed to catch sight of the driver, I knew that person was a boy. I sensed he was.

I always had time to get outside and stand behind a tree near the road before he peeled out, his tires squealing. Was he over there letting the engine warm up until the idle settled into a rumble—*intending* to take off real easy, but unable to because he just had to let go and rocket down the road? Starting off too fast'll wear out your timing belt, and that's expensive to replace. But based on how fast he took off, he didn't care about timing belts.

I liked to think that he turned the key and imagined me. Me hearing his engine, my heart suddenly pumping twice as much blood with my feet tingling and my two smallest fingers numb all at once. Me slowly peeking around to see if Mama or Daddy was between the door and me. Me trying to walk softly, though the tingling in my feet had swapped for the numbness in my hands. Maybe he waited, giving me time to get into place by the tree to watch him. By the time he pulled out, I was there. Breath held, mouth open.

Every time the car blew past, I missed seeing who drove it, but just knowing he was in there planted a question in me that I wanted answered in the worst way. Adam called from boot camp, even though he wasn't supposed to call until he graduated. Mama and Daddy weren't at home, so I took my chance and asked.

"Adam, what's it like?"

"What's what like?"

I lost my nerve. "Never mind."

"Aw, c'mon," he said.

"What's kissing like?" I could barely get the words out.

"Huh," he said, and laughed.

God, why did I say anything? "Never mind."

"No, I'll tell you."

I waited, wanting to know what it felt like. I wanted to experience it, not tease myself about something that would never happen.

"It's like jumping out of the tire swing over the river."

That was the stupidest thing I ever heard.

"You just let go, and when you land, you're all wet and happy, and you think you can do anything."

That's what it's like? That's it? That's all?

"You like a girl?" he teased.

"No," I said with true conviction. I hadn't even seen who drove the GTO, but I knew that one day I was going to kiss him. And just Adam and everybody else wait and see if I didn't. And that boy's gonna kiss me back, and he's gonna like it even more than I will.

And wouldn't you know that as soon as Adam hung up the GTO called, and I again positioned myself by the road and behind the veil of a pine tree limb. The conversation with Adam either made me a little taller or a scooch shorter because this time I could see through the passenger window as he perfectly timed it to pass by the tree as his hand, a young and tanned boy's hand, pulled back on the shifter with the slightest dip in acceleration, quickly picking up speed to make up for the time the clutch reduced his velocity, and off he went.

The hand of the boy who drove the car belonged to Brownie's new son, his stepson. Aunt Loodie only came to visit when she had gossip to spread, and she made a special trip just to tell us, "He's up here to work in the garage. Name's Knox."

"Knox," I whispered.

"Just what you need, another hotrodder to add to the Evans boys," Aunt Loodie continued. "They'll tear that road up. Look both ways before you go out."

*Knox,* I whispered again, this time inside my head.

## CHAPTER FORTY

# My Obsession

My chest hurt. It was exciting, and it was a letdown. Where did Knox go? When would he come back? I wanted so much to ride in that car with him. Sit next to him. Close enough to smell him and the goldenrod blowing in the window, sneezing from it, gasoline, my skinny legs sticking to the bucket seat at the edge of my short pants, my hand gripping the armrest.

One day on Main Street, Mama happened to park right next to his car. I felt like someone poured fresh wet cement right out of the mixer into my chest. I got out, careful not to bump his door with mine. And I could see the gear shift knob, although it was a shape I couldn't make out. It was glossy wood. There was some color too. I wanted to go back and lean in the open window, but that would expose my secret, my private yearning.

I took that fleeting image of the inside of his GTO with me the rest of the day until I could save that memory, sketch it into my journal, the one I secreted in my hideout that sat in Knox's backyard in plain view of Knox's stepfather's garage and just steps away from Knox's bedroom window. Disfigured Pontiacs and Chevrolets that populated the graveyard around me were my subjects, my figure models.

They were broken, but the images I saw changed as I transferred them to paper. The cars began to heal, their forms much like they once were right off the factory floor. In my drawings, though, the trims, the lines, the tail lamps, and the headlights took on new shapes and angles. Cars with meek visages grew courage. Angry grills grew gentle. Inelegant proportions shapeshifted into what I thought the vehicle should have been, aspired to be. I found that there was magic in this. The cabin of the car I selected for my hideaway, my hut, was in great shape and well-sealed against the elements. What should have been the front was nonexistent, but from the dashboard back, it was untouched. A 1973 Oldsmobile Ninety-Eight Regency, dark brown with a cream-colored vinyl roof, the interior brown velvet cushions that looked like they floated above the actual seats. I pulled on them, and they were sewn down, but they were soft, softer even than my bed at home.

I loved sitting in the driver seat, pretending to steer, but unable to reach the peddles. I hesitated, touching the automatic buttons on the door. I didn't think they'd work, but if the windows went down and I was unable to get them back up, I'd have to abandon the Ninety-Eight for another hideout. This one was perfectly arranged so that it was only about two steps to the barbed-wire fence, and I could see the body shop without being seen. No one had come near my hideout since I had begun using it. I was convinced it was the perfect home away from home. At first, I stored my journal under the seat, but if water got into the car it would pool on the floor. Damaged cars could look sound, but at the same time be horribly out of alignment, destroying factory-tight seals. The glove box was safer and had the added benefit of hiding my journal from anyone who walked by when I wasn't around.

Every day in ninth grade, all I could think about was either getting home or getting to my car graveyard. I certainly found it preferable to roaming around like most boys my age, getting knee-deep in the marsh of bulrushes, catching frogs. These cars were my natural habitat, a setting that fed me, calmed and protected me.

I carried a flathead screwdriver with me each time I visited the junk-yard, a hunter and gatherer. A warrior who stalked through the lot for cars that had intact nameplates, the quarter-inch thick metal stamped out with the make and model of the car, electro-plated to a shiny gloss, sometimes pocked with the beginnings of rust. The Cutlass was a favorite; I loved its curvilinear lines. And the actual impala in mid-leap was so graceful, it made me wonder why the name was assigned to a such large, lumbering family sedan. Wasted. It better suited a bucket-seated coupe with four on the floor, built to outrun the rest of the pack. Who made these decisions? Who had the job of making up car names and designing the grills, taillights, and nameplates? The grills were like mouths in either smile, grimace, or frown. The headlamps eyes, with an angry slant or a rounded innocence.

That logic didn't follow for the back of the car, which didn't look like the back end of a person. The rear looked like eyes as much as the front, sort of like Mr. Dowd who came to class every Halloween in costume, but a few minutes into class he'd put his mask on his head backward, which made him look two-faced. Cars were kind of like that with red eyes that revealed the alter ego and usually darker half of the car's soul, as if they were saying, "Be grateful I didn't run you over."

I wanted to do that, make cars. That would be the best job ever. But I had no idea how you got that job. Maybe you had to live in Detroit.

## CHAPTER FORTY ONE

# Faking Normal

Mama never stopped fretting about my chest. So finally, when I was fourteen, she took me to a thoracic surgeon. This doctor was all the way up in Atlanta, and her office was in the tallest building I'd ever been in, but she wasn't up on a high floor. I was kind of disappointed we didn't get a chance to go up higher. I didn't like heights, I didn't think, but I was curious what it looked like from high up. Linder Ray was the tallest girl in our class, and her voice was soft as a fuzzy that grows out of the top of a dandelion after the flower dries up. She took a plane ride one time, and she said you can see swimming pools from the plane. She said they look like your Mama dropped a turquoise earring on a shag carpet. I couldn't imagine a swimming pool looking as small as an earring.

The doctor didn't come in at first. This man came in who I thought was the doctor, and he gave me the weirdest gown to put on. It started off like any cotton robe, with two regular armholes, so I put it on. And then, he told me to put it on backward, which didn't make sense, but I did it. Now, what looked like it should be open at the front was open at the back. Then he read the folder about me and said, "No, you were right, put it back on the way you had it."

And I was embarrassed because he and Mama were right there. I didn't want them to see my chest. I tried not to cry, and I don't think the man noticed that I did a little. Mama noticed because she knew me and could tell when I was crying without actual tears coming out. She got up close to the man so that he turned the other way and started asking him questions. She's about the best mama there ever was.

Then he stood me against a wall that had a bullseye projected on it from what looked like the school's movie projector. He told me to move this way or that and then stand really still and don't breathe. And then I heard a big click, sort of like a stapler, a big stapler. After that, Mama and I waited in another room, and I still had on that robe. I was getting tired of sitting there because I didn't have much meat on my rear end, and that metal table was hard. My butt got kind of tingly, like when your leg goes to sleep when you sit on top of it folded under you.

Finally, the doctor came in, but she didn't really look me in the face. She was reading from the folder the man had given her.

Then she said, "Take the robe off please," with a quick smile and a nod. I didn't move.

"I'm Doctor Proctor." And that was about the funniest thing I'd heard in a while.

She said, "Yes, that usually breaks the ice. It's nice to meet you."

Mama thanked her for seeing us and asked if she could help.

Then she started talking about my condition in more detail, and my ears started to feel hot, and I heard what I thought was a swarm of bees.

"Philbet, are you okay?" Dr. Proctor asked as she walked over and put one hand on my forehead and another on my wrist.

"Lie down for a bit."

I must have dozed off for a few minutes, and when I woke up, they were talking, but they didn't see that I was awake.

"We'd make an incision at his collar bone," the doctor said, gesturing to her own throat, "just about here where the thyroid cartilage is, and it would go down to the base of the sternum. We'd have to make horizontal incisions as well to gain access to the bones, the ribs and sternum mostly. And then we'd break all of them, reset them, pin them together, and close."

Mama didn't say anything.

"We need more tests to understand the condition of his organs…if they're currently in the general position and area they should be in, if they're functioning properly given the confined space. There is also the matter of balance. He has a slight scoliosis, and I'd need more tests to confirm this, but I believe the muscles aren't underdeveloped as much as they are absent. There appears to be no muscle at all over the ribs on the right side of his chest."

"What do I do?" Mama asked.

"Think about it. You asked me if the medication you took during your pregnancy caused this? I don't know. It's possible, certainly, but it's more likely a congenital defect due to a gene you or your husband carry. If we looked back, we'd probably find cases of this on one or both sides of your family. I've seen this before, though only once. What I do know is that you love your son very much, and the decision you make will be the right one."

Mama's mouth was tight, but quivering a little, and she just stared at the doctor.

"I know this seems drastic. So think about it carefully."

"How much will it cost?" Mama asked quietly.

"It depends. If his organs are functioning properly, and if there are no limitations on his mobility, this might be cosmetic. If we find a medical need, insurance will cover most of it."

"How much could it be?"

"Um, I'm not really sure. I'm going to send you to get more tests."

But when we left, Mama went up to the counter and talked again with the nice lady she'd spoken to on the way in. I heard the receptionist say, "tens of thousands."

The next week, Mama took me to the prosthetics shop over at the state VA hospital, and I shook Mr. McMinn's hand. He and Mama were the exact same age and had gone to high school together. He stayed late after work one day just so we could go see him. And he called her Tomcat. She turned red as a beet when I looked over at her, but she didn't say anything and didn't look at me.

She just said, "Phil and I really appreciate you helping us out here." And she told me to take off my shirt. She hadn't told me why we were there. I took my shirt off for doctors, and the one time Mama made me show Aunt Ease, but I didn't know this man and was suddenly embarrassed, frozen.

"He's going to see if he can make something you can wear under your shirt that will make it look like you don't have this…problem."

He smiled, like he felt sorry for me. He must have been a nice man to do this, and Mama was trying to help. I took off my shirt and tried to ignore the bright light in the room. I looked at all of the paraphernalia hanging from the ceiling and the fumes of wood, glue, and something that smelled like burning.

Mama said, "I was so sick when I carried him, and the doctor gave me this medicine for nausea. That's what did it. The doctor said maybe not, but I just know it."

She looked to be in such pain that I forgot I was half naked in front of a stranger. Mama started to cry. Mr. McMinn turned and hugged her, which was another surprise. Mama knew him really well. She put her hand on his chest, flat on it, like it was a warm place for cold hands. She looked like her pain would never go away.

I didn't ever think before of what my condition might mean to anyone else. It was *my* body. *I* was the one who had to go to school and deal with the fear of being found out. I always thought I caused my chest to be curved in, given my habit of wedging myself in between mattresses and headboards and tightly down the crevices of sofas when I felt unsafe, unsure, wanting to feel the comforting embrace of wood, metal, and fabric against my body.

I was *sure* I had done it to myself, ever since I saw the man at the Meriwether County Fair twist and fold green vines, securing them so they dried out and remained in that shape for making furniture. We had a chair made from what Daddy said used to be a vine like Tarzan swung from in the movies. I was mesmerized and convinced I had inadvertently molded my weird little self into my sunken, twisted condition, bones and ribs growing inward, forgetting they should bow out to protect my heart and my insides.

Mr. McMinn sat down in a chair and studied my chest. Next, he reached out very slowly, like he wasn't sure if what he was about to touch would hurt me. He looked up at me really quickly, smiled, stood, slapped me on the arm, and turned away. Mama was looking at me when I glanced over to her, and she smiled as if caught doing something she didn't want anyone to see.

Mr. McMinn returned with a piece of something pink. It looked like a supersized piece of Bubblicious. Then he turned away and went to his refrigerator, pulling out a paint can. "This is going to be cold," he said, and mashed a bunch of goo on me. It was clammy and reminded me of when the dentist puts the tray with that awful wet chalky glop in your mouth to get an impression of your teeth. When he had a good amount of goo on my chest, he packed it down, holding my back with one hand while he shaped my wonky side to be symmetrical with the pectoral muscle on the good side.

"That will dry for about fifteen minutes, so try not to move," he instructed. I stayed stock still the whole time it hardened. When he was ready, Mr. McMinn gently lifted the cast off my chest. He held it up and it was me, the small part of me that shaped how I saw *all* of me. Mr. McMinn then told Mama to bring me back the following week.

As we drove home, Mama and I were quiet. I was remembering one summer after we moved down to Warm Springs, when Adam and I were playing in the stream behind the house in the middle of the piney woods. He flung a mound of clay at me, hitting me squarely in the chest. He regretted it immediately and said, "Philbet, I'm sorry."

"It's okay," I said, slinging a handful back at him, but missing him because I don't even throw like a girl. I don't throw at all. He took off, leaving me there completely covered in clay. With no one around, I took off my shirt and took it to the stream below for a quick rinse. Red clay does not come out once it's in clothes, but if I didn't try then Mama would be upset.

As I let the shirt drag in the cool, crystal stream, the idea hit me. I went back up the embankment and applied a scoop of mud directly to my chest and started to mold it. The clay dries pretty quickly around the edges, so you have to work fast. Looking down, I saw what others saw, a boy's full breast, albeit in clay, symmetrical and strong. I was whole. I put the shirt on over, pressed it down, mesmerized by how it fell, resting on the equally proportioned sides of my chest. I had a new body, as if I had been reborn a few minutes earlier, but this time remade in the image of all the males around me. In that moment, nothing separated me from the other boys. This is what Mama wanted for me.

A week later, we were back at Mr. McMinn's. Mama hugged me, smiling. "You can wear this to school, and you'll be normal." I thanked her, hugging her back. I shook Mr. McMinn's hand, smiling brighter and wider than was believable, but inside, I felt like someone had stuck a pin in my chest rather than put a prosthetic on it. Mama didn't think I was normal.

Later on, at home, I pulled off the prosthesis. As it released its hold, my skin puckered out, separating from the prosthesis like the skin that came off the deer flesh when Adam and Daddy gutted one. I guess it looked more like the squirrel that Davey Dodd brought to science class, which Mrs. Savant and Davey skinned right there in front of us. Mrs. Savant said she was going to take it home for her husband's dinner. That made Davey really mad, and he got her back by stringing a fishhook over the light fixture to hook her wig and pull it off her head in class. He almost did it, too, but the light fell instead. The bulbs popped when they hit the floor. Davey was a little hellion, but in his defense, those light fixtures were probably older than Grandaddy.

But that squirrel giving up his skin and that prosthesis slowly, stickily giving up its hold on my wonky chest looked just about the same. And there isn't anything better to remind you that you're exposed and unprotected more than seeing something get skinned in a classroom, or pulling a piece of fake chest off your real chest, because your real chest looks and feels like someone took out the ice-cream scoop and made a double pass when your arms were tied behind your back.

It made me sad that Mama'd probably planned this for a long while and had gone to a lot of trouble to convince Mr. McMinn to stay late after work to carve me a new chest. I needed mineral spirits to clean the glue off of me and then off of the prosthesis. I smelled like Daddy's kerosene lamps, and I wondered if I'd catch fire if I put a match to my chest. Tossing my new chest into my sock drawer, I jumped headfirst onto the bed and fell asleep, crying for just a minute first.

## CHAPTER FORTY-TWO

# Longing

A nd this is where my story, my journey, picks up from that day when I was fourteen, and I climbed into Daddy's truck outside school only to find the boy of my dreams, my Knox, sitting behind the wheel. The day I became Keebler. The day I fell in love with the boy and not just the idea of him. And after that ride home from school, whatever else was going on, Knox was never far from my thoughts.

My junkyard hideout had become my home. My chin rested on the back of the Ninety-Eight hideout's front seat, just next to the headrest, my left eye hidden. In part, I was afraid he would glance up and see me staring out at him. But mostly, I don't think I could manage looking at him with both eyes. My hands couldn't touch him, so looking with just one eye— the other covered like I was a pirate—was all I could endure.

It wasn't even a question for me. There wasn't a tug between the examples I saw around me and what my body and mind and heart wanted. I wanted him. Not a boy, not a girl. Him. I wanted him. I was gay, though I didn't have a word for it yet. Knowing what I was didn't require a name. I wanted to touch this boy. I wanted this boy to touch me. I wasn't ashamed. It could not be wrong to feel this. When I wasn't hypnotized by him standing in front of me and wasn't dreaming of him, I wondered why more boys didn't feel this way about other boys. Why did all the boys around me want girls and never seem to think about boys that way. I had that in common with the girls. I loved a boy like they did. Ached to feel his cheek pressed against mine as he hugged me and whispered in my ear.

What would he whisper? Anything would do. "Gasoline." That's a good word, a beautiful word. Like a French name that rolls softly off the lips and into an ear, my ear. A perfect word because he smelled of cars. "Cinnamon toast." That's even better. It's two words. Two words to prolong the time the side of his face would be pressed against mine. "Cinnamon toast." So warm and buttery that his breath would melt the space between his mouth and my ear. I stared and longed to sneak out of the hideout, crawl along the space between the cars in the graveyard, reach up to where he hung his shirt now dangling off the radio antennae of an old Ford Falcon.

I'd snatch it down as the wind whipped it up, and then sneak back to the hideout and put his shirt up to my face and breathe in the next best thing to him. I'd take up my safe space in the back seat, peeking out next to the headrest, and think not of cinnamon toast, but cinnamon buns—because the cap of his arm, where the shoulder joined it to his body, looked like a glistening cinnamon bun. The sunlight glinted white in the sunshine just as the creamy white frosting does as it melts on a fresh-from-the-oven breakfast pastry. I closed my eyes and imagined butter and cinnamon and sugar and Knox.

And I said a prayer to Jesus to never let me forget what this felt like. And to let everything be okay. Because I felt I was right, not wrong. And I also felt a little sad that someone as beautiful and comfortable and perfect as he was would never want a broken thing like me, especially if he was like all the other boys who wanted a girl. And almost every day, if I heard the GTO growl awake, I was in my hiding spot next to the road before he even turned out of his driveway. "Please let him come this way. Please let him come this way. Please...."

And the GTO stopped on the road just on the other side of the pines. "You gonna get in, Keebler, or are you gonna let somebody come around the curve and run into me out here in the road?"

I held my breath. Was he talking to me?

"Keebler...Keebler, get in."

I slowly climbed out from between the branches and stood there on the side of the road.

"Want a ride?"

I just looked at him slack-mouthed.

"Come on, Keebler. I know you want to ride in the GTO."

My lungs felt squishy and full of water instead of air.

I reached for the door handle, and the car lurched forward about a foot. Was he making fun of me? I almost ran and teared up a little.

"Keebler! I'm sorry, man. You just look like it's a snake that's gonna bite you. It's just a car. It's a cool car, but it's just a car. Get in!"

I got in. I was sitting in the GTO, and I hadn't sneaked in. I was sitting here, and it was running, and we were about to ride in it.

"Keebler, it's a four-on-the-floor, wide-ratio Hurst," he announced, and then left a peel mark on the road in front of our house, and I weed in my pants a little before I caught myself. The mark was still there five years later.

I was numb. We just rode, up and down almost deserted paved country roads, and I wondered the whole time if this is what he did all those days when he peeled out of the drive and took off like a rocket on its way to someplace, a world I'd never been to and thought I'd never visit. But I'd been there now. I'd been out in the GTO with Knox. Just Knox and me.

"I figured you were never gonna just come out and ask me for a ride, so I figured I'd stop." He looked over at me with his head down and left eyebrow raised up under his hair, which had fallen down into his face. God help me, I wanted to reach over and brush that hair back off his face and know what it felt like tangled in my fingers. I didn't care if I wrecked us and killed us both right there. I wanted to touch his hair.

"How did you know I was there?"

"Keebler, you're standing at the side of the road behind a pine tree. They give pretty good shade, but you can pretty much see right through 'em."

I was so embarrassed and felt like a stupid stalker. "I'm sorry. I didn't mean to be weird."

"Hey, weird's cool. Besides, one of those idiot Evans boys would have come along eventually and taken out that tree you stand behind, and you'd be dead. I had to stop so you'd stop standing there waiting for them to wipe out and take you out with 'em."

The head of the gear shifter was not from the factory. I had the 1972 GTO car book from Mabie Motors. And the shifter didn't look like this, which was a piece of pine carved into the shape of a heart and polished so that it was the color of honey with a big knot right of center on the heart. That upper right curve of the heart's shape and all the way down the side to the pointy-tipped edge was smooth and glassy-sheened where his hand fit perfectly on it.

"How'd you get it? How'd you get the GTO?"

"Brownie gave it to me."

*Wow, that's a good gift from somebody who isn't even your daddy*, I thought.

"He gave it to you? You don't have to pay him back or anything?"

"Owe him anything? No way. He was trying to bribe me when he wanted to marry Mama," Knox explained.

I didn't know what to say to that.

"He's a good guy, but he was trying to butter me up."

"For what?" I asked.

"So he could marry Mama!"

"Oh, right. Yeah." He was so cool.

"Like I had any say in what they did."

## CHAPTER FORTY-THREE

# Super Man

"You're little, but you're strong. You can reach in where most mechanics can't. Most mechanics have ham hands. Now they're gonna have an advantage over you, Keebler, 'cause they'll pull a motor a lot easier than you, even after you're fully grown into your man's body."

And when he said that, I felt it in my pants. The way he said "man's body" stirred my boy's body, right in front of him. My blood headed in two different directions, knocking the breath out of me as half headed to my middle and half to my cheeks. A glittery gold wave blinded me, and a roar took out my hearing for a few minutes.

When I came out of it, I was half on, half off a mechanic's creeper, floating an inch off the oily cement floor. What had happened? I lay there, not moving, trying to figure out where I was. I took long, sweeping looks at the many vertical red lines going up the wall. Or, no…they were horizontal drawers. I was lying on my side, not moving. At peace.

I was in the garage. The embarrassment came back, reminding me what happened. And then I saw the dark brown cowboy boot step into view next to me. I saw him, only an ant's view of him from the floor, an angle that played with my perspective with only his bottom half visible as he bent over the fender under the hood. Calm bathed over me, and I reached out toward the frayed hem of his jeans, almost tracing my finger over a gash in the heel of his boot. Almost. Tonight, when he takes off his boots, gets ready for bed, standing there in his shorts before he gets in bed or when he's wrapped in a towel tomorrow morning after his shower, this boot, this gash will be there in plain view of him, able to see him if it had eyes. Nothing between him and the boot. And he won't even think about it there on the floor. He won't know that as I lie here, I'm wanting to be the boot, wanting to be next to him, though he gives them not a second thought.

My hand near his leg was the closest I had come to touching him. Really touching him in a way that made me feel like I was turning into a new person. I wasn't ready to face him. What could I say that wasn't the truth? Did it make me sound perverted in some way? Someone, someone's hands, had filled each of the drawers with tools, thought about the order in which they were organized. Was it him? Had he organized the drawers for Brownie? And why did I care?

He noticed me as I leaned over the fender next to him, and all he did was smile briefly and touch my nose, leaving a dark grease smudge. Then he turned back to the engine and told me to hand him the lug wrench. And then he asked for, I don't know what it was, but I guessed right. It was heavy, but I managed to get it up to the fender of the car.

"Keebler, no, you'll break your back. Here, let's put it down here. It goes down here." And his hand touched mine as we lifted this round metal thing and set it on the floor. He'd noticed that I hadn't grown into my man's body; it was my boy's body that was betraying me. I had as little command of my boy's body as I did of the tools around us.

"No worries, you'll get it. A car is complicated, but you've got passion for it."

*I do have passion for it*, to myself.

"You could take a mechanics class at the tech center if you wanted."

"I'd rather *you* teach me," I said, not wanting to give up the chance to be with him, but realizing he might be getting tired of me slowing him down.

"Yeah, that's cool. I just don't know if I can teach you all you need to know."

"I really want to design. You know, the way the car looks, the shape, and the features."

"Hmm, I don't know about that kind of stuff. You'd really need to go to school for that. Are you good at math?"

"Yeah, I'm really good at math. Mr. Booth says I'm his best student and know more than he does."

"You probably do. He's an idiot. I'm sorry. I'm not surprised because you're really smart. But he's an idiot for sure."

"He seems okay…. How do you know Mr. Booth?" I asked.

"I had him."

"For math?"

"Yeah," he answered.

"You went to my school?"

"Yeah."

I thought you were from over…"

"I drove over here for school for a while when Mama met Brownie. She was thinkin' of marryin' him."

*How did I never see him?* I wondered.

"But they broke up, so we went back home."

*How did Aunt Loodie miss this?*

"Mr. Booth was an ass."

Mr. Booth was nice to me, I remembered, though he did get angry a lot and call people names. I was just glad to win at *something*, at *someone*. I guess I didn't notice so much that he wasn't very nice to others.

"It's more than that," Knox continued. "He doesn't know how to teach. If math doesn't come to a kid naturally, you're out of luck. He doesn't help you."

"I hate him!" I said, understanding Mr. Booth had not helped Knox figure out math.

"I hate him too."

"He's a jerk," I said.

"Yeah."

"He's a dick," I added.

"A shithead!"

"Yeah, a shithead!"

Not knowing why I started this, but loving it, I added, "He's a Ford Pinto."

Knox thought that was the funniest thing he'd ever heard. "A Pinto?"

"Yeah, that's a crappy car."

"He's a Dodge Dart," he said.

"Yeah, he's the baby of a Ford and a Dart. He's a Fart! Get it? Ford? Dart? Fart!"

"Yeah, I get it. You're a little weirdo."

"Yeah," I mumbled, responding more to how much of a misfit I felt than his comment.

"Keebler, that's a good thing."

"Yeah, I know."

"I think you're super funny. You make me laugh."

"I do?"

"Yeah, you're funny. And you know the craziest stuff about cars."

"I like cars. They're like flying," I dreamed out loud.

"Yeah, Keebler. They are. They're like flying."

"That would be cool, to fly."

"That your superpower?" he asked.

"Huh?"

"Your superpower. What you'd choose for your superpower?"

"No, that's not what I'd choose," I said, not wanting to say what I really wanted: to have the power to make him want me. If I had a superpower, I'd make him want to kiss me and do other things with me.

"Oh, that's right, your superpower is knowing what kind of car's coming just from hearing the engine," Knox said.

"That makes me sound stupid."

"No, it's cool, Keebler."

*He's so beautiful. He thinks he hurt my feelings. He's trying to say just the right thing to make it okay.*

"I'm just joking," his hand with wrench mid-air, stopping his work on the car.

I just wanted to touch him, hug him and have that hug tell him, without words, that he didn't hurt me at all and any time he talks to me he makes me feel special and alive. I'm like a balloon so tight that I think I'm going to explode with these crazy impulses to reach out and…and look inside his ear. That's nuts. Just try to see what's in there like it's the most private part of his body. I mean, nobody in the whole history of the world would ever look at someone as sweet and beautiful as him and think, "I'm going to lunge at you and peer inside your ear, touch it, kiss it because all your private thoughts come from right there just behind your ear." It was so stupid, but it made me sweat behind my knees and under my arms.

"Keebler, you can't really be upset. I was joking."

"Um, yeah, I'm fine. I'm just wondering, um…if knowing about cars is my superpower, what's yours?"

"Oh, that's easy. It's knowing about people. It's like I can see inside of people."

Blood heated me from waist to forehead, cooling at my suddenly moist hairline.

"That would be your superpower?" I asked.

"It *is* my superpower."

I didn't exactly know what that meant, but I was troubled by the idea that he knew what I was thinking. No, that couldn't be so. He couldn't see inside people.

Knox was motion, always wanting to go and do something in a place that wasn't here. In a rush, it was always "Let's go." "Come with me." "Follow me." "I have an idea." "You know what would be fun?"

"I want to show you something," is what he said this day, and he took my wrist. I remember it was my wrist because I felt my pulse hurry under his rough-padded fingers, which were scratchy and dry like a carpenter's rasp. I wanted them to slice me open from ear to throat hollow to ear. Not a deep wound, but just through the top, softest layer of my neck to release the me inside of me.

I followed him into his house, which I'd never been in. We went through the kitchen to the hallway and through a door all the way back down the hallway. Suddenly, I was in his room, the place where he slept, where he was alone with whatever he thought about when he was by himself. Where he undressed at night and yawned, scratching his belly, and crawled into his bed. These walls knew the sounds he made when he slept.

I imagined him lying there with a hairy, sun-browned leg peeking out from the covers with his foot pointing up toward the ceiling. The bed was unmade, the floor covered in a wildflower field of colorful socks and shirts and underwear.

*Before I leave this room, I'm going to pick one of these Knox flowers to take it home with me,* I promised myself. I'll keep it, some part of him, something he dropped without thinking, planted without knowing he'd done it. The same way he had no idea of what he stirred in me.

"Knox, is that you?"

"Yeah, Mama."

"Come here for a minute."

"I'll be right back," he assured me.

Now that I had my chance, I couldn't move. Finally, I bent over and picked up a sock, keeping my eyes on a pair of white cotton briefs. I couldn't touch them. They were too personal, having been as close as a second skin. It would be wrong to take something that had been right next to that part of him, that part of him I'll never see and he wouldn't want me to want to see.

Instead, I grabbed a sock, one that had covered his foot, his beautiful feet that touched the red clay every day. His sock would do.

No, it wouldn't do. I wanted something else. I wanted his shirt, one that opened in front with buttons, one that I could wrap around me and pretend he was standing behind me, hugging me. A dirty one that smelled of him after a day in the garage and a night of running through the woods afterward to jump in the lake. A shirt that he stripped off just before he broke the water's surface because swimming without a shirt is what boys do. Most boys do. The ones who are free and spend down their days running headfirst into them as though mid-air leaping into cool water. I could throw one out the window and try to come back later after dark. I couldn't hide a shirt on me. Why didn't I have a backpack or something with me? "Stupid," I whispered.

I stuffed the sock and a pair of underwear in my pocket. I can't help it. *God'll have to forgive me later*, I thought.

I heard Knox coming back. I flushed cold, and a wet, shiny sweat—that must have been in me all the while—suddenly traded places so that my skin was beneath it, covered over and drowned. The prosthesis started to give way, not around the edges but in the center. When I breathed, it made a little pop as if I had a little croupy cough down in my chest. *Dear Lord, don't let it fall off in front of this boy, this beautiful boy*, was all I could think.

I picked up a baseball cap hanging on the post of his bedframe. He came in past me, ripped it from my hands and put it on my head backward. Then he took one big swoosh with his foot and cleared his clothes from next to the floor of his bed, and he reached under and pulled out a wooden box that looked like the silver chest that held MawMaw's old silverware, the one thing Mama wanted when MawMaw died.

He put it on top of his bed and opened it. It was full of stamps and coins.

"My Daddy gave me these."

"Yeah?"

"*His* Daddy gave them to *him*."

"My Grandaddy collects stamps," I said.

"Yeah?"

"Uh huh."

"That's cool."

"How do you know if they're valuable?" I asked.

"Well, 'cause Daddy gave 'em to me."

"Where's your daddy?"

"He's dead."

He'd never said. I thought his parents were divorced or something. "I'm sorry, Knox."

He looked at the coin in his hand. Then he held it up halfway between our faces, and his eyes disappeared behind it for a moment. I guess I disappeared from his view too. And I wondered what it was like for somebody you love to disappear, die, with some barrier between you that you can't move as easily as a coin between a thumb and a first finger. Can't even get around that barrier at all. I suddenly missed him, wanted his eyes to come into view again, afraid of the day when I wouldn't see him.

"Do you miss your daddy?"

"Sometimes. I do miss him, but I'm not sad anymore," Knox replied.

"What's it like, him not being here?"

He sat, softly rubbed the coin along his lips and looked at the floor. He shook his head so slightly that it almost didn't move at all. "Lonely." Then he put the coin back in the box. "It's like there're no cars passing by. It's quiet, and you wonder where they all went and if another will ever come along."

He looked into his box and took out a stamp.

"This is worth the most money."

"How much?"

"Maybe a thousand dollars," he replied.

"No."

"That's what Daddy said."

"Why?"

"See the numbers on it?" He gave me a closer look.

"Yeah."

"They're double printed…like there is the real image and a kind of shadow of the image."

"Yeah."

"That's what makes it valuable. When they made a mistake, they usually caught it and destroyed all the mistake stamps. But if a mistake got out in circulation without getting destroyed, then it was different from all the others. Special, one-of-a-kind special."

"That doesn't make any sense," I offered.

"The thing that is wrong with it is what makes it special. Rare, even."

"Why wouldn't you want a perfect stamp instead?"

"Nothing's perfect."

"Okay, a regular stamp?"

"A bunch of stamps that are just like each other are boring. You can get those at the post office. Use them to mail letters. You keep a one-of-a-kind."

*He* was one-of-a-kind, my Knox. I wanted to go back to my room, close the door, sit in the middle of my bed and open a secret box and find him there.

## CHAPTER FORTY-FOUR

# Giving Up My Heart

Knox held onto the steering wheel with one hand—one finger, really. He propped his elbow in the opened window with his hand kind of extended, like that first day when he reached to take a cookie crumb off my lip. His middle finger barely touched the wheel, as if steering were secondary, and the real control was in his right hand on the gear shift. I imagined what he felt through the shifter, the deep groan and vibration of the motor. He looked like he was part of the car, like he and the car were connected through the stick. When I close my eyes and think of him, he's in a car, or leaning on one, as comfortable as a bird in a tree. I read about a guy in Texas who was buried in his Corvette. Boy, he must've really loved it. I bet anything somebody in his family could've used that car.

Grandaddy was just the opposite. I used to watch him drive as I sat in my spot in the back seat of his Galaxie 500. He had his left hand on the left side of the steering wheel and his right hand on the other side, at least one hand on the wheel at all times. When he turned left or right, his arms didn't cross, ever. He fed the steering wheel from his left hand to his right hand and then he put his hands back at 10:00 and 2:00 as soon as he was back on his path following the turn. Steady. That was Grandaddy. He lived like he drove—calmly, purposefully, patiently, and in no hurry to get to his destination.

I didn't realize I was staring at Knox's hand on the gear shift until it reached up and pinched me on the nose as if it were a wild, exotic species he'd came upon.

"Earth to Philbet! Earth to Philbet!"

"Oh, sorry. I was just trying to figure out how you know when to change gears," is what I said, when what I was really doing was wondering what his hands felt like. As with every time I was near him, I unconsciously locked in on some part of him. His ears, the soft indentation just below his Adam's Apple—any part of him that struck me as standing out from the rest of him in a particular way. Today? It was his hand on the gear shift.

"Want to try?" he asked.

"Try what?"

"Drive."

"Oh, no." I quickly added, "I'm not old enough."

"You can reach the pedals. You're old enough."

"I don't know. I should learn on an automatic."

"If you can drive a stick, you can drive anything," he said.

"I used to help my daddy drive."

"His truck?"

"Yeah, it was stupid." I admitted.

"So, you know how?"

"Um, I do sort of…halfway," I said.

"What does that mean?" Knox asked.

Suddenly, I was too far into it to back out, but I realized that sitting on Daddy's lap and steering while Daddy controlled the brake, clutch, and gas made me sound like a baby. And the fact that I was about five years old at the time didn't help. I hadn't steered since Daddy got shot in the head.

"Daddy used to let me drive on dirt roads." I told him part of the truth.

"Cool! So, you drove a stick?"

Evading, I muttered, "We haven't done that for a while. I'm too big to sit in his lap now."

We had never talked about Daddy getting shot in the head. It was embarrassing, White-trash embarrassing, even though Daddy was trying to help somebody. He wasn't White trash. He was trying to help White trash not kill each other.

"Give me…" Knox said, and in the same breath he grabbed my left hand and put it on the steering wheel. "You steer. I'll go slow."

Suddenly terrified, I tried to take my hand back, but he held it on the wheel under his own. All I could think about was his hand on mine. I couldn't reason, much less steer. But I couldn't let go because he held me there. My mind went to the day before, in school, when Mrs. Peabody said the Earth, way below the surface where we lived, increasingly forced more and more pressure on every square inch, so much pressure that we couldn't comprehend it. All that pressure turned minerals and rocks into other kinds of rocks. Callie said that diamonds came from coal that had been under a lot of pressure, and her mama had two diamonds. She was so irritating.

"You can do it. We'll get you back in the saddle, and then we'll tackle the pedals. Then the gear shift," Knox promised.

"You gonna let me drive your car?"

"You got a car?" he asked.

"No."

"Okay then," he replied, looking at the road.

He was so cool, and I was so uncool. I got jittery. I blurted out, "What's it like where you're from?"

"Just like here," he said.

I'd only lived in Alvaton and here, so I didn't know what it'd be like living someplace else.

"Nothing's different?"

"Looks the same. Trees the same. Same gas stations and grocery store."

"Do you miss your old friends?" I asked.

"Well, yeah," he said.

"They going to visit?"

"I don't know. I doubt it," he mused, taking a swig of his Coke. "I don't think of here as being different from there."

I put my M&Ms one by one into my Coke. This was the best way to eat them because it turned your Coke kind of milkshakey and made some of the bubbles go down so they didn't burn your throat and nose when you swallowed. And the hard shells on the M&Ms got all soft so you just got the milk chocolate.

"I didn't have a lot of friends," he said, kind of to himself.

I couldn't believe that. He was the kind of guy everybody liked to be around.

"I worked a lot and didn't have time," he added.

"At the garage?"

"Yeah. I was always so sleepy in class that everyone thought I was a goof-off and stupid," he said.

"Why'd you work so much?"

"We needed to eat. And all I have to do is get in my car and drive back there if I want to. It's not like it disappeared."

"I can't believe Brownie bought the GTO for you." As soon as I said it, I thought that was none of my business...too personal. "That's none of my business. Sorry."

"It's okay, Keebler," he replied. "Like I said, it was a bribe, so I'd like him."

"I wish he'd married *my* mama," I said.

"Nope, you can't have him. Plus, you've got a daddy."

"My daddy's a jerk," I whined.

"But he's here."

"I wish he wasn't."

"Don't wish that Keebler. When he's gone you'll..." Knox stopped, then continued. "What does he do every day, at work?"

"I don't know."

"Does he like it or hate it?"

That much I knew. "He hates it."

"So maybe that's a reason he can be a jerk sometimes."

Why was he taking Daddy's side? I just looked at him.

"I'm just saying," he said.

"He calls Mama 'Mama.'"

"So?"

"He lets Uncle Calvin and Uncle Kingston call me names."

"What names?" Knox asked.

*Why did I say anything?* I thought.

"Okay," Knox said, agreeing even though I hadn't answered the question, "He shouldn't do that."

"No, he shouldn't."

"What have you done about it?" he asked, challenging me.

"What?"

"Have you told them to stop?"

I hadn't.

I didn't say anything for the rest of the ride. I was really irritated with Knox. Uncle Calvin and Uncle Kingston shouldn't call me names. Why didn't he say that? Why should I be the one to say anything to them? He drove, sensing I was lost in my thoughts, and didn't say anything else until we got home.

"Okay, Keebler, here you go," he said, as he dropped me off in front of the house.

I got out, looking down at the ground.

"Keebler, you've had a rough time. I know. All I meant to say is you don't need to take shit from anybody. Tell your uncles to go to hell. I'll be there right next to you if you need help poppin' them in the chops."

I wanted to climb back in and put my head against his arm, take off with him again and feel the muscles underneath his skin as they pulled and pushed the shifter into gear.

"We good?"

I loved him. I wanted him.

"Yeah, we're good," I said. And now, instead of simply getting back into the front seat, I longed to climb into the back seat and into his arms.

## CHAPTER FORTY-FIVE

# Four on the Floor

"Keebler, you cannot eat ten Krystals."

"Bet I can too!" And I knew I could because I'd already eaten nine a few months ago, and I could have eaten another one easy. I only stopped because I didn't have any more money, and I'd already beaten Jeb, who could only eat eight.

"If you can eat ten Krystals, I'll buy all your Krystals for the rest of the year," Knox promised.

Well, I wasn't going to let this challenge get by me. He'd have to be there every time I went to Krystal, and that was reason enough to risk the stomachache and throwing up.

"You're on!" I practically shouted.

"Hey, wait a minute," Knox replied. "What if I win?"

If he won, I'd give him a kiss every hour on the hour for the rest of my life. I didn't say that, but I thought it. And then I thought, *That's not a good bet because I'd do it anyway*. I'd do it and feel like *I'd* won the bet. What I did say is that I'd buy his Krystals for the rest of the year, but I couldn't because I didn't have the money. But I knew I wouldn't lose, so it was okay.

As we headed to Krystal—a full forty-five-minute drive because there was no place to eat in Warm Springs—Knox said he was thinking about it, and my uncles really were dicks for calling me names. This was his way of saying sorry, again, for taking Daddy's side of the argument.

"What would your daddy have said if you got called names, Knox?"

"I have no idea."

"He wouldn't tell your uncles to leave you alone?"

"I don't know," Knox said. I was really curious about his daddy—his real daddy, not Brownie. Knox didn't mention him, so I wondered if he didn't want to talk about him. Here I was with a living daddy I didn't like, and he didn't even have a daddy.

When we got there, he didn't park. He went to the drive through and ordered ten Krystals. I said, "Hey, what are you gonna eat?"

"I'm gonna to eat the five you don't eat because you're a little bullshitter who can't eat ten."

I was going to show him.

"If you eat 'em all, then I'll drive back through," Knox smiled.

"You just don't know," I said, even more determined to down every last one of those burgers.

"Yeah, yeah."

About fifteen minutes later we were driving back through to order his dinner, and I wished we were heading home. I figured if we left now I'd be home by the time I started to get sick. But no matter how gross it got later, it was worth it. The look on his face was worth it.

But I didn't get sick. I slept and dreamed, probably because the next day was the driving lesson from Knox. In the dream, my stomach rumbled the soft hum of a well-tuned motor as I stared at the little sliver of onion that caught on the stubbly edge of his mouth as he ate his Krystal.

The next morning I was still full from the food and from the time with him. I skipped breakfast and took nourishment from what I could see staring out the kitchen window. Then he appeared. He drove up to the house and stopped in the middle of the road like he usually did, just long enough for me to get in. Then he took off like a rocket from Cape Canaveral. We didn't go far, only to the lake, a five-minute drive from launch to landing.

Nobody was there, which made me glad. I was nervous. He said we'd practice first outside, and if it went well, he'd maybe let me try in the

GTO. Sitting in the driver's seat, *his* seat, would be like lying in his bed. I imagined every contour of the mattress was an impression from his body molding to it night after night. I figured it would feel the same, then, knowing I was in the seat he sat in when he was most happy, most fulfilled—behind the wheel of his car.

"Go sit on that stump, and take this," he instructed, handing me an old steering wheel, one from a '60s-era Pontiac.

"Where'd you get this?"

"Um, where do you think, Keebler?"

"Oh, yeah," I mumbled, remembering he slept only a few feet from a car graveyard.

"And, if you crash and burn, no problem. That steering wheel's been through a worse crash than you can manage out here."

Then he stuck a long, skinny gear shift knob in the dirt, and next to that he stuck a piece of school-lined paper with a diagram of a shifter path: first, second, third, fourth, and reverse gears. I studied the shift map. It looked kind of like the dance-step diagram Mama got when she took that mail-order dance class back before she gave up on Daddy.

"You're going to pretend to shift following that pattern when I tell you."

"Okay."

"These rocks are your clutch, here on your left. Your brake is here in the center, and your gas pedal is here on your right."

"Okay," I said, grinning.

"So, what do you do first?"

I stopped grinning. "Um…"

"*You* know," Knox coached.

"Um…I, um, I push the…the brake?" I guessed.

"No, tell me. Don't ask me."

I was getting hot.

"Okay, if you turn the key and your foot is on the brake, what happens?"

"It'll buck?" I guessed again.

"Yep."

"So, I need to press the clutch," feeling more confident.

"Good."

I pressed my right foot on the middle rock.

"Nope. Nope, Keebler."

"What?" I asked.

"You tell me. What's wrong?"

"Um…" I wanted to pass this test more for him than me, so that he'd be proud of me. So that he'd know his hard work was worth it. So that I could be more like him, could join the cool club. But I didn't know where I'd messed up.

"You got it, come on."

I was frustrated.

"Okay. If you use your right foot on the clutch?"

"I can't use it for gas," I said, not guessing.

"Yes!"

Then I pressed my left foot down on the clutch rock, slid past it, and fell off the stump. He snorted, trying not to laugh.

"Knox, don't laugh at me."

"I'm sorry, but that was pretty good."

"I feel stupid," I said.

"Here." And he walked over, kicked the rocks away, and sat on the ground. He faced me with the soles of his feet in place of the rocks, serving as break, clutch, and gas. "Press against my feet. I'll be the pedals."

I thought I'd surely fall off the stump again with him right there, leaning back on his arms with his knees bent and…. *There*, right there facing up at me was a hole about the size of a dime where the seam from his zipper and the back of his jeans came together. I couldn't breathe. He was wearing underwear because he had a good mama like mine, and I knew no matter what any boy with a good mama got up to, he always wore good underwear. But the sweetness of it left me breathless. He was so earnest in trying to help me, and he didn't even know he had a hole in his pants. But I felt so bad that I didn't tell him. Didn't tell him that he had a hole and didn't tell him that that little hole in his pants undid me. I wanted to tell him it was there as much as I wanted to peek.

"Philbet."

"Yeah?"

"Pay attention. You're spacin' out again," he said. "Okay, you are at a standstill on a flat surface. What do you do?"

"I press the clutch with my left foot," I said, pushing the bottom of my foot against the bottom of his.

"Yep."

"I jiggle the gear shift to make sure it's out of gear."

"Yep, good," he said.

"Turn the key."

"Good, Keebler, good."

"Then, let the clutch out while…"

"Nope."

"No?" I thought I had figured it out.

"Are you going to go straight or back up?" Knox asked patiently.

"Oh, I put it in first gear."

"Right."

"Then I let the clutch out," I said, feeling the pressure of his right foot against my left, "and press the gas as I let out the clutch."

His left foot gave as I pressed it with my right. The sensation overwhelmed me. I pressed when he yielded. He pressed, and I felt him push against me. Then our soles slipped off each other, both of us losing balance. He didn't miss a beat. He reached down to pull off his boots with the excitement of a little boy seeing the ocean for the first time. I felt I was at the edge of something new too—that continually shifting border of sand and ocean where the waves could come and grab you and pull you under.

"Take your shoes off?" Knox said.

"Why?"

"The clutch is alive, Keebler. It pushes back, and there's a balance of clutch and gas pedal. You have to memorize the feeling if you're going to master driving a manual transmission."

While I was thinking about that, he pulled my laces and took off my shoes, then my socks, undressing my feet. When both our feet were naked, he pointed the bottoms of his feet up to me, pink and untouched by the sun.

"Put your feet up," he said.

I stayed silent and lifted my feet to rest on his. They looked soft like a little baby, or something I wanted to pick up and hold to my cheek, my eyes closed and just enjoying the sweet warm feeling you get when you cuddle a puppy—like they're so cute you can't help but want to kiss them a little. My heart felt like it was in two pieces. The side that belonged to me beat faster than the other side, which belonged to him. I had never, ever thought of a foot as being for anything other than standing, running, and walking. And here I was wanting to hold his to my face and breathe it in.

We operated at different speeds, in different worlds almost. He was flat out at full speed, already in a higher gear. I was at a standstill, grinding my shifter into first, hesitating. I lifted my feet slowly, putting them directly against his like I expected them to be as hot as the stove burner. But they were just right, the warmth of his just-freed feet, the pressure of his against mine. My skin and his skin literally finding footing, sliding. The tickling caress as we found solid footing against each other was something that I didn't have words for.

As his feet, his soft, strong feet applied pressure to mine, he whispered, "You got it."

## CHAPTER FORTY-SIX

# No Words

"You're lucky to have this car," James said. "In India, they screw door handles on the outside of cars and trains and buses for people to hold on and ride outside because there aren't enough cars to go around. They'd love to have a Doodlebug."

Well, that was about the stupidest thing I'd ever heard. I was being a brat, but the Bug was embarrassing. It had a lawn mower engine. It smelled like dog food because Daddy stored Radar's dog food in it before it was rehabbed. A car used as storage for twenty-five-pound bags of dog food smelled like dog food and always would. You could rip out the seats and carpet—if it even had carpet—and it would still smell like Radar's food pellets.

But the worst part is that Daddy insisted on teaching me to drive it. I didn't want to say anything about my sessions with Knox, so I drove the VW Bug around the side yard of our house. Distracted and annoyed, I popped the clutch and misjudging the stop, lurched into a full-in-bloom snapdragon plant, sending its terra-cotta pot off its perch and into pieces on the hot, dried-out earth beneath it. I ran out of the car, which Daddy stopped from its backward roll down the hill by pulling the hand break.

And Knox saw it. I was so embarrassed. I know every time he'd see me in that car, he'd think of me breaking the flowerpot. And he drove so well, so cool with his arm slung across the window ledge with only a finger touching the steering wheel and the other hand on the gear shift. He looked like he was born and grew up right there in that seat, in full command of the car. I wanted to be cool like that, so cool that he'd look at me and think without thinking that I was like him, so much like him that I was a part of him.

"Dude, what is wrong with you? This is the coolest car," James said.

"Don't make fun of me, James."

"It is. I'd take it in a second."

"No you wouldn't," I said.

"The motor's in the back where a regular car has a trunk."

"Yeah, that's because a lawn mower motor doesn't need a lot of room," I quipped.

"I'd take that front part and put a loveseat in it. There's room," James said.

I listened.

"I'd take Anne out to the country, open that hood with the loveseat under it, and I'd sit there with her."

"Sit?"

"I'd start with sittin'." James raised one eyebrow.

I went out to the Bug that afternoon as the sun set and walked around the car a few times, circling it to take inventory of the scratches and rust. I opened the hood, pulled out the flat spare tire, and stared.

It had been a long time since I crawled under Grandaddy and Jorma's living room and nested on the top step. I bet I could still fit, but I'd outgrown that, as if the transition from the steps to my Ninety-Eighty hideout were a graduation from preschool to high school. I climbed into the Bug and sat there on the lip of the opening, surveying the ground around me. A bunch of little doodlebugs had made inverted cones down into the red dust as they burrowed their way underground.

I wondered if doodlebugs paired off like people do. Maybe that's why the Doodlebug car got its nickname, because it was only big enough for two people. Mama says we doodle around town when we have free time. That's fun because we don't have to be anyplace. I can stop and look at a car if I see one I like. I decided "doodle" is a funny word. Maybe doodle didn't really mean anything. Like sometimes, I didn't have the words to explain how I felt. I was happy but aching inside. Or I didn't really feel happy or sad, but I felt something.

The red clay at my feet in the shade and the red clay over by the car tire were the same—the very same. But the clay at my feet looked as dark as a sweet potato pie. The shade was so deep and murky. The clay over next to the tire was bright as a persimmon. If I closed my eyes and trained them at my feet, then opened them and quickly closed them and opened them again, I saw two different colors in the ground next to the car. But if I slowly looked at the ground at my feet and followed the ground all the way over to the sun-covered clay, I could tell it's the same color. It was the light hitting it that made it look different.

I'd have to use different colored chalk to draw it, even though the ground was the same. I was the same person at home as I was in the woods or in the hideout. But at home I was sullen, hating every minute of it. But I didn't feel that way in the dark shade of the pines or the hideout. There I felt like I was in sunshine. I was happier there, though I still ached inside. That didn't make any sense. How could I be happy, but still feel bad? I don't know how to describe it.

I didn't tell James or Knox or Mama what I thought, what I wanted. And that was as much because I didn't have the words as it was that it was so personal. And I didn't want them to stop liking me. Me telling Mama how I felt around Knox would be as odd as me saying that I wanted to eat the skin Daddy stripped off a freshly shot deer instead of a long-cooked deer stew. She wouldn't understand. I didn't understand either, but I still wanted it, was hungry for it. Mama and Daddy seemed to want one thing and do another thing too. They weren't happy, but they keep on day after day doing and saying the same things.

## CHAPTER FORTY-SEVEN

# Big Suzie

The Christmas before I turned sixteen, we all gathered across the road at Uncle Kingston and Aunt Ease's. Mama's sisters and brothers and their families came by for a drop-in. Aunt Ease opened up her living room on these holidays. This was not the carport that had been closed in to make a den. This was the room with cream-colored carpet, a needlepoint pillow-covered loveseat she treasured—which was way too fragile for her roughhousing crew—and usually a stack of bills on a side table that had little knobs you could pull on to reveal small, hidden surfaces. I always meant to ask Aunt Ease what they were for, but then I'd forget. The pile of bills weren't unpaid or anything like that. She just put them there to work on and maybe to remind everybody that Uncle Kingston had a management job on the railroad making what Daddy called "good money." They could afford to buy a lot of stuff, and I think Aunt Ease was the only one who went in that room when it wasn't a company-coming holiday.

But during holidays, the table was clear of envelopes and every surface was overfilled with ham, cheese straws, sausage balls, deviled eggs, veggies, and a variety of Jell-O salads. I dreaded every minute of the day ahead, never knowing when I'd hear "Suzie, get me this" or "I wonder what Suzie got for Christmas," when Uncle Kingston had had too much to drink and thought I needed to be brought down a notch or two. And it was not just about me being slight of build and a little effeminate. I think they thought I thought I was better than them. But that wasn't so.

And it was around this time the family dynamic shifted even more. Uncle Kingston, emboldened by never having been reprimanded for calling me "Suzie"—at least, I don't think Daddy ever stood up to him—started calling Daddy "Big Suzie." I didn't think either he or Uncle Calvin would stop even if Grandaddy heard about it and came down and popped them both in the mouth. But maybe Mama said something after all, and this was Uncle Kingston's way of telling Daddy he was a weak sissy just like me. I can't be sure, but I think it started a few months earlier when cousin Claudette got married. Daddy got really drunk. I was used to being around drunk folks. There were alcoholics in my family, let me tell you. I could spot 'em, too, even if they weren't falling down or slurring their words, which they never really did.

But I could spot 'em—not just my uncles, but anyone. The eyes and nose gave them away, the ones who drank to slow excess. The nose was always a little too pink, as though lightly aggravated by too many passes of a Kleenex, or pink from a chill in the air. And the eyes. Alcoholism moistens the eyes with an almost dreamy glisten. I'd found that blue eyes especially developed a depth of color that make them more compelling and beautiful. Maybe it's the thin-as-thread ring of blood red around the iris that sets off the blue, making it bluer than it really is.

Daddy didn't have a drinking problem. For Daddy, cost was the biggest drawback to drinking; it's expensive to stay drunk. But that night, during Claudette's wedding reception, Daddy was really drunk, like a teenager gets who's new to it, or like a little kid gets drunk on chocolate bars or hard candy. Daddy was "stupid drunk," Mama called it. But he was also funny and free, not like he was at home around us. He made jokes. Good ones. Not rehashed, low-brow stuff like everybody usually spouted. He was that night a silver-tongued devil, a redneck raconteur. And he either said something Uncle Kingston didn't like, or he was getting too much attention for his well-observed wit.

Real drunks, the ones who sucked in the juice as if hauling around an invisible IV drip, didn't like a sloppy and loud display. Instead, a seasoned drinker would masterfully modulate intake to remain in that narrow space between unmedicated, unbearable reality, and messy, out-of-control sloshdom.

Alcoholics cannot bear the sight of a new drunk, a novice, weekenders who can't hold their liquor. It's anathema to those who expend ninety-five percent of their energy locking down, choreographing the effects of drink. It cold-sweat scared me to see Daddy stumbling around in his fog while Uncle Kingston watched from across the room, cigarette burning in his hand, too concentrated on Daddy to even take a drag off it.

Uncle Kingston stood and moved one step toward Daddy. Then he stopped. He looked like a murderous tiger, still and settled in the tall grass watching a wobbly-legged antelope prance around in play. But he didn't pounce. He growled deep and slow and announced, "Big Suzie's having a big night." And then he moved toward Daddy, faster with every step. "Big Suzie's showin' his ass." In our circle, "showing one's ass" meant acting up or talking back. And finally Uncle Kingston said, as he held himself about a foot away from Daddy, really low, almost a hiss, "Get yourself on home, Big Suzie."

Daddy's eyes had been bright, reflecting all the light from the candles lit around us. He blinked one time, and when they opened, the reflection was gone—as if he was looking inside himself and couldn't see any candle-light or any brightness at all. Then the rage in Uncle Kingston disappeared, and joy returned through his loud laugh, suddenly a joking, stupid cracker instead of a beast.

It was this persona, the stupid redneck, that Uncle Kingston inhabited when I spoke to him one day months later, on July 4th. The whole family was over at Uncle Kingston's, including the cousins from Atlanta. And he joked to the whole brood that I sounded like Paul Lynde when I talked. Well, that was ridiculous because I hadn't said a word to anyone since I got there. And I had news for Uncle Kingston, and I said it right to his face: "Well, Paul Lynde's on TV makin' a buncha money. He doesn't get up in the middle of the damn night to ride a train to Alabama for a paycheck."

I expected the pent-up tiger in Uncle Kingston to emerge, haunches forward and ready to pounce on me for challenging him in front everyone.

The whole room got quiet, like I imagined it would if I ever took my shirt off in front of everybody. They weren't just quiet—their mouths hung open. You'd think I had taken Uncle Kingston's tobacco-spit cup and tossed it in his face. And I guess I had kind of thrown something in his face. Just like Knox said, if nobody was going to say anything, I figured I'd have to do it myself. Then, he took a spit in his cup and laughed louder than I'd ever heard him. "Well, you got some backbone after all."

Then he walked over, making a big show of it in front of everyone, and bear hugged me. And while I was close to him, I said, meant just for him, "You leave me alone, you broken-down old man. I'm tired…I'm…just… *stop. Just stop.*" And I didn't look away. He stopped smiling and let me go, almost pushing me away. "I guess I need a new name for you, Smart-Ass White Boy." And there he went again, getting in a dig at me and Black folks at the same time.

And I turned to walk away, "I've got a name, Kingston. And it's a great name, part Daddy and part Mama. Try using it." And he laughed a forced laugh as if he didn't get a joke someone told.

"You're…" Uncle Kingston began. I should have kept walking, but the boy in me conditioned to please, to listen, turned me around to face him. He poked me with his finger in the same way you press buttons on the vending machine when you want a bag of Cheetos, and it caught me right there on the prosthesis. His eyes left mine only long enough to look down. I thought for certain that he'd poke me again, or worse, pull up my shirt in front of everyone.

As I walked off, he muttered, "Yeah, you're part Big Suzie for sure."

And then, not looking back at him I yelled, "And stop callin' Daddy Big Suzie!" I turned around, wanting to face him this time in case the tiger lunged, but he wasn't heading toward me. He was just standing there, still. I wanted to lie on the ground suddenly, my vision obscured by what seemed a bubble-filled wave of ocean water breaking on a shore. I felt my heart tip over on its side, as if losing its balance propped on a shelf high up and then roll slowly to the edge of the shelf only to fall below.

My vision restored, I stared. I would not be the first one to turn away. He was a bully, and I finally saw it. A drunk and a bully to cover the fact that he was a paper person who even a weakling like me could punch a hand through once I saw him for what he was. It felt like Knox was inside of me, filling the void that would be filled with flesh and muscle if my chest were full, making me do and say what I'd never have done and said on my own. To myself, I said, "I'm not wearing this thing on my chest anymore."

And Uncle Kingston, he looked like I'd released the parking brake on his truck, and it had just started to roll down the front yard toward the ditch, something he could have stopped if he'd started running a few seconds ago…but not now.

# CHAPTER FORTY-EIGHT

# A Test

One day, months later, I held Knox's baseball cap in my hands, trying not to dislodge the stray golden-brown hair caught in the lining. I wondered why I sneaked out of the house to get into my spot near the tree every time I heard his engine roar into life. Why was I embarrassed, expending so much energy hiding from Mama and Daddy and Adam that my tenth-grade longing had been to ride in his car? Not just inside his GTO, but inside of him, impossible as that was. I dreamt of nestling inside his chest near his heart, feeling the regular beat lulling me into a deep calm, completely satisfied with everything. Impossible, I knew.

How would I get in? Wait for that between-worlds space, just before sleep injects its paralytic juices into you, right before unconsciousness takes over? All I knew is that I wanted it. Needed it. I wanted to settle myself in, protected by his ribs, peeking out through the coarse hair on his chest, rendering me invisible, no one knowing where I'd sneaked off to, no one knowing my feelings, our feelings. It wasn't that I thought I was wrong to feel this way about him.... I was just embarrassed to have these feelings period, for anyone or anything. Caring for someone with such intensity was almost more than I could bear at fifteen. It's almost too much now.

"It's hot as hell. Let's hurry this up and get outta here. It's too hot to work today," Knox said, wiping his forehead with his arm.

That sounded great to me. I was thrilled with the idea of Knox stopping work and taking me for a ride. Most days in the garage, I sent him telepathic messages to give him the idea that we should cut out on our own, but he was committed to helping me restore the Bug. If we were going to have it ready by my birthday, we'd have to work every day I wasn't in school and even some evenings.

A boy's first car was a rite of passage, and I wanted it. I wanted the freedom a car would provide and tried the feeling on as a way to get used to it, willing my birthday closer. I imagined Knox as he charged down the road all those days I hid, watching in secret from the trees. We could use my car now sometimes instead of his.

The GTO was a sanctuary; time was on hold whenever we were in it. No matter where we headed, it was the best time of the week. "Let's go get a hamburger at the trolley." "Let me give you a driving lesson in the Colonial parking lot after they close." "Let's go see who's out fishing." "Let's get Big Chick." He always had someplace in mind. I thought he had the most active imagination, never taking a breath before coming up with something to do. But I wanted to spend some time with him in the Bug so that I'd have the memory of it, even when we weren't together.

"You want to put seats in the hood?" he asked.

"Yeah, just a couple of seats."

"Why?"

"'Cause then…" I couldn't tell him that I wanted to drive up to the edge of the lake and sit there next to him and hold his hand while the sun went down over the tops of the pine trees.

"'Cause then…then there's a place to sit," I explained.

"Yeah, that's what seats are for," Knox, laughing a little.

"But we can drive right up to the lake and have a place to sit when we fish."

"It's prob'ly easier to just take a couple foldin' chairs."

"Anybody can do that. I want a loveseat."

"A loveseat?" he repeated.

Quickly adding, "That's what they call two seats scrunched together. It'd have to be scrunched since it's a tight space." That was so stupid of me to call it a loveseat.

"Where you going to get the seat?"

"I don't know. There anything out here in the junkyard?"

He looked out the door into the yard, having never scanned the wrecks needing two small seats.

"Um…hmm."

"Even a couple of old milk crates would work," I apologized for even suggesting it.

"No, that's no good. Your butt'll be asleep inside twenty minutes."

"It can be last. The important thing is to get the car road ready."

"I'll think about it," he promised.

"Knox, I really appreciate you helping me get the Bug fixed up." He was so good to me. He spent all his free time helping me fix it up. When it was done and I was sixteen, I could really drive it on the road beyond the few hundred feet of road between his driveway and mine. But that little stretch of road where I struggled to have enough space to get it into second gear felt like flying around the globe on a solo mission. I thought I had really accomplished something monumental. There was no lifeline between his drive and mine. If I broke down, I'd have to get it a few hundred feet to my yard. I was an astronaut on the dark side of the moon, a solo pilot over the Atlantic, a grown-up out on my own.

It was hot outside, the worse kind of hot. The red clay dried out into hard crackled cakes in the driveway, ground to a fine dust under the weight of tires. It was so hot the dust felt liquid under bare feet. A fine orange dust climbed up each foot and ended in a sharp line around the ankles, marking how far the foot dragged forward through the dry, dirty slop before it plopped down again. Feet that enjoyed the dry, red clay dust would turn a bath into a deep red soup almost immediately. A favorite end to a hot summer day, stomach full on yellow tomato, white bread, and mayonnaise, was to step into the bath slowly. The tie-dye swirl slowly emerged, proof that the day had really happened.

I didn't know it then, but fascination with how dirt could color water was a sign that I was still, in some ways, a little boy.

"Let's go swimming," Knox said.

I avoided swimming because it's a shirts-off activity. So I said, "I don't swim."

"I'll teach you," he offered.

"That's okay."

"Everyone needs to know how to swim."

"I know how. I just don't."

"Why not?" he asked.

"Um…water gets in my ears," I replied.

"Earplugs."

"They don't really work," I countered.

"Come on, Keebler, it's so hot."

"You go, I'll stay here. I'm not that hot."

"Okay…you don't have to get in, but you're coming along. Let's go." With that, he pulled me out the door by the hand and then guided me toward the woods, his hand on the small of my back.

"Where are we going?"

"You're not the only one who sneaks around in the woods, Keebler." Knox raised his eyebrows and smiled.

"I don't sneak."

"Uh, yeah, you do."

How did he know? Had he seen me sneak into the yard?

"It's no big deal. Come on."

And we set off through the pines in the opposite direction from my house. I followed. He was fast, moving in a straight line, right through the briars and over fallen trees. He'd go right through a thick bush rather than step five feet in either direction. Not me. I ducked under limbs and found the cleanest path to get to my destination. It took me a full ten minutes to get from my backyard to the fence separating the woods from his junkyard. If the woods were razed, it would be a two-minute walk.

I followed him down a steep but not deep gully and into a mostly dried-up creek bed. Then we turned and were in the open, the sun suddenly making us squint after having been in the cool shade of the piney woods. A beautiful, dark green lake spread out with woods on all sides.

"See that little dark opening?" he asked, pointing across.

"Yeah."

"That's over next to Raleigh Road. I like to come through the woods because there's never anybody over on this side, but if I drive, that's where I come through. There's sometimes folks fishing or drinking."

He sat down on the bank. "Damn, should've brought some Coke." And he started to pull off his shoes. "Let's go in."

"No," I said, way too abruptly.

"You don't have to put your head under."

"No."

"Well, okay," he said finally.

I felt so stupid, like a six-year-old who needs to go to the bathroom but won't ask for a hall pass. Before I lost my courage, I admitted, "I don't want to take my shirt off," thinking the only thing worse than telling him about my deformity was to leave him thinking I was a total weirdo.

"Oh."

"I just…I've never done that. It's because my…."

"Keebler, it's no problem."

Then, before I could talk myself out of it, I took off my shirt, my chest fully exposed in the sunlight. I just stood.

"See?"

He didn't talk. He just stared. My teenage fantasy was looking at what I spent hour after hour trying to hide.

*Say something*, I thought.

"Does it hurt?"

"Only when you don't touch it," I said without thinking.

"What?"

"Nothing. Forget it."

I'd never felt more exposed than I was right then, shirt off with my white, pasty, skinny, malformed bird chest in full view of the boy I loved. I didn't even know if he liked boys, much less freaky me. The sun hurt so much because I couldn't hide. I hated this moment. I couldn't hide, and I couldn't take it back for it never to have happened. Why didn't I show him at dusk when he couldn't see so clearly?

The cavity in my chest, already a smaller space than my heart needed to function, felt more compressed and restricted than usual. Just like the garbage room walls closed in on Han Solo and Princess Leia. Or maybe my heart was just growing, overfilled with love.

But I cherished this moment as much as I hated it. I think I'd die if I had to keep up the secret for much longer. If I dropped dead or if I lived, at least I'd never hide from him again. But it hurt so much, both the blood-pumping heart in my chest and in my feeling heart, the one I wanted to give to him. Was I going to die right there in front of him? If I didn't take this chance now, I never would. If he didn't reject me after seeing my half-sunken chest, I could trust him—could believe anything that happened after that.

I couldn't face him, couldn't look at him. He stared at me, but I couldn't look back. As embarrassing as it was, as much as I wanted to trade bodies with anyone who was normal, the pain was not because I was disfigured, and all my organs were fighting for room. I ached because someone finally saw me. It was the first time I wasn't spending fifty percent of my energy trying to find the best angle so that no one could see the large indentation in my chest, not trying to pull at and adjust my shirt so that it didn't sink into the void.

I hurt because I knew what I wasn't. I was not like Adam, not like Daddy, not like anybody I knew. I was someone frightened of myself. I had hoped I was like Knox—not beautiful, not complete and whole in the flesh like him, but alike in that we both wanted to love another boy. And I wished that if he wanted to love a boy that he'd choose me like I had chosen him. And I knew, even at this young age, I knew that this was a test I set up for myself and for Knox and that it would shape me and every relationship I'd ever have or attempt to have for my entire life.

I had to find out if anyone would or could ever love me, could want me the way I wanted him. My Knox. As much as I wanted Knox to love me, I was old enough to know that whatever happened, for the good or bad, it may not last forever.

"Hey, Keebler?"

I loved when he called me that. It was just between us, nobody else. When he said it, I was on his mind. My name rumbled from his chest, up his throat, over his lips, and into my ears.

"Keebler."

"Yeah?"

"Look at me," he said almost in a whisper.

"Yeah?"

"What do you want?"

"To be happy," is all I managed. I couldn't bring myself to say, *To kiss you, for you to kiss me.*

"Why aren't you happy?"

"I want to be normal." *I want you to want me like I want you,* I thought.

"What's normal?"

"Not me." *Not in body or in mind.*

"You're as normal as anybody else."

I can't trust him. He wasn't telling the truth.

"You just don't know how messed up everyone else is." Knox said.

"I want to touch your chest," I blurted.

"What?"

I've gone too far.

"I want to know what a normal chest feels like," hoping I didn't sound like a little pervert.

He stared at me, thinking. He blinked. In a single move he pulled his shirt over his head. He was so comfortable—the opposite of me. We stared into each other's faces, me too shy to look at his body. I expected him to be too creeped out to look at mine. Finally, I walked slowly toward him, lifting my gaze. Motionless. I wanted to fill my eyes with him, not knowing if I'd ever get this close to him again.

"Go ahead. It's okay," he said so softly, as one speaks to a sleeping body, not wanting to startle yet wanting to rouse it. At first, I placed two fingers just below the hollow of his throat and touched the few brown hairs that had teased me for months, peeking out from his shirt collars. They were not alone but intertwined with others and spread all across his chest. Softer than I dreamed, they tickled my fingers like stray corn silk left behind after a hearty shucking. The sun dipping into the trees just over his shoulder cast light between us, turning the tips of his brown hair to gold, like small fires just alighting.

I looked up at Knox, and his eyes were on mine, steady, inscrutable. "It's okay," he said.

As I looked at him, I flattened my right hand directly over where I imagined his heart to be. His heartbeat, very fast, surprised me. I smiled weakly and brought my other hand up to rest next to it. I wanted to dig my fingers in the soft curls on his chest and reach up to swallow his breath. Instead, I forced my hands to remain flat as if pressed against a window that let me see close up, separating me from what I really wanted on the other side.

The hair pointed downward from the center of his chest in a line that disappeared into the blue denim of his pants, curling out and over into his belt buckle as a delicate climbing vine sends out tender tendrils to envelop anything in its path. It was a road map in bas-relief to a place south of even our Georgia town. The road led to the underside of his belt, below the fold of the map, and I didn't know how to get there. A car wouldn't make this journey. I'd have to make it there under my own steam. But I didn't feel like I was welcome there, so I wouldn't set out in that direction. I'd just look as if I were standing up on a hill from a distance, not able to see all the details of that place, my imagination filling in what I couldn't make out.

But I ventured no farther than his chest. I had gone far enough under this ruse, using my imperfection as excuse to explore him, his beauty. I was so glad to have been close to him, so close I was smothered by his scent; he smelled slightly of gasoline. I stepped back, saying nothing. He stood for a moment and then moved toward me. He touched me, first two fingers in the fold of my neck just below that delicate hollow, then both hands directly on my chest. At first his touch was like fire because no one except the doctor ever touched me there, and never like this. There was warmth. It was gentle. Then he just looked at me.

If he wasn't going to say, "I love you."—which he wasn't, I wasn't delusional—he said the next best thing.

"You're okay, Keebler."

How did this boy, every time I saw him, manage to do this to me? Every time I opened myself up to him, he melted my heart a touch more so that it changed shape just a little, just enough so that it slowly morphed from the one God made for me into a new heart, one that fit more comfortably in its tight little cavity.

## CHAPTER FORTY-NINE

# My Heart's Desires

The GTO would always be the coolest thing ever, but the Bug became the second coolest as Knox and I rebuilt it together every afternoon after school and every weekend. It was the kiwi-green color of the Cougar Matchbox, and the interior was black. For my birthday, Grandaddy bought new rims and tires that had raised white Goodyear letters on them. And after it got reupholstered in black vinyl, it didn't smell like dog food anymore. It was perfect, sounding every bit like Mama's Singer making curtains with long, straight seams, racing so flat out that it had rather throw a piston and bust wide open than slow down, even a little. The Bug was in a class of its own and had such a distinctive sound that once you heard it, you'd never mistake it for anything other than the green VW Bug, the one Knox helped bring to life.

"Let's celebrate," I said, almost pleadingly to Knox. "I'll drive us to Dairy Queen and buy us dinner. Then we can go to the lake and sit there in the rumble seat with our burgers."

"Okay, Keebler. It's your birthday. I guess we do need to celebrate, but I'm buying." And we were off. I had decided to call the loveseat a rumble seat. That just sounded better. And if calling it a rumble seat or a fishing bench or anything at all would make it easier for him to sit there with me, I was all for it. Knox had come up with the solution. He found the rear-facing third seat from a 1964 Chevelle station wagon. It was the perfect size, and the seat folded down when I needed to close the hood. We sat together in the back of the Chevelle before we took the seat out, and I felt the heat of his thigh touching mine, never taking my gaze off the horizon.

I thought to myself, *It's like shopping for a couch where we can sit together and hold hands.*

We sat there next to each other in the rumble seat. His side was the right, mine the left, just like I was in the driver's seat, and he was in the passenger's. I couldn't wait to take fishing rods down to the lake and sit there next to him. But, today, it was a hamburger, fries, and a Coke with Knox in my newly brought-to-life car. I felt like I would burst with joy.

Knox said, "Happy Birthday, Keebler." He was quiet. We were quiet. And then he said, "I guess now that you've got wheels of your own, you'll be heading all over the place."

No, I didn't want to go any place without him. "I'll drive to school, I guess."

"You'll be off with your friends all the time. You'll have the coolest car at school. Have you told anybody?"

*What is he talking about,* I thought. I want to ride around with him, not anybody else.

"I told James. He's the one who had the idea for the rumble seat."

"Yeah, that was a good idea. Fishing."

He didn't want to hang out anymore?

"Don't you want to hang out? I can drive now," I said.

"Um, well don't you want to spend time with your friends at school?"

*Why is he trying to get me to go away?* I thought.

"I…James is really my only friend at school." He knew that. I had told him. I wanted to turn and stare at him because then maybe I would understand what he was *really* saying. Instead, I just pictured that muscle in his jaw flexing as he chewed, just below his ear. Oh, how I wanted to reach over and touch that ear, look inside. What was he thinking? It was just there behind his ear, inside his head. Did he want me to stop hanging around? Did he help me with the car so I'd go away and leave him alone?

"I can still hang out with you," I said.

He shook his head slowly as if to say, "Yeah, okay." His mouth was slightly parted, as if he had something to say…but he didn't speak.

I knew, somehow, despite my inexperience that I had to say it now and that I had to be clear, cut to the heart of it. A preamble would muddle it all, giving him the chance to misinterpret my nervous rambling as indecision and too young for this experience. But more than that, I had the courage now, in this second, on this once-in-a-lifetime day that I had waited for what seemed like my whole life. I had to take my chance.

"I want to kiss you," I said, my voice steady.

"What?"

"Kiss me one time, Knox, just one time." I was suffocating, willing to do or say anything for air.

Pleading, using our friendship as leverage and admitting this was a condition plaguing only me and not him, I said, "I know you don't want to, but I've loved you for so long. I try to hide it. But I don't want to go through my life wondering what it would be like."

I'd settle for a moment of my own if he couldn't share it completely with me.

The last, small reserve of respect I had saved me from saying out loud: *I want to know how you smell close up. How you taste. I don't care anymore. I'm going to die if you don't touch me just once.*

I wanted…I wanted that first moment of real intimacy. Joy. Or I wanted it over with, so I could get beyond the disappointment of never having this experience and move past to the other side of it. It was like we were back at the pond, facing each other shirtless in the afternoon sun. Me asking, begging. Him listening, giving me no hint of what was on his mind.

He stood up and walked away from the car and me and then turned toward me. I knew he was thinking. I felt like I was being wordlessly inter-rogated, his technique an impassive stare. I stood, chin up, ready to take whatever he said like a man. Waiting. Just waiting. Every second of quiet that ticked between us was slow-motion agony. I didn't know what was behind his gaze. Didn't know what he was thinking.

He was becoming a stranger right in front of me. Like when somebody you love to death moves away in fifth grade, and you think you'll die not seeing him in class every day. And after you cry with the intensity of a three-year-old for a few days, you get used to him not being there. Almost as if the daily cries become your new, transitional friend, establishing new patterns, the first of many new habits. You make other connections, form other friendships, change your routine based on the changing landscape— evolving interests as you mature and grow, new friends' preferences, new experiences and insights.

I couldn't read my Knox. Right then, he could be someone I had just met on the street, the checker at the Dairy Queen waiting for me to order, a photograph hanging on the wall. His decision made, he embraced me. My face in his chest, his in my hair. I bit his shirt, tasting that intoxicating blend of him—Knox and gasoline. I can smell it now. And I can still feel his soft, moist breath press through the valley between my skull and ear and down into my shirt collar.

He kissed me, long, breath-filled, brotherly, on top of the head. Letting me go like I was a rescued bird he'd nursed and set back into the wild. And then he turned and walked away.

## CHAPTER FIFTY

# No Coming Back

I didn't cry, not one tear.

I felt like I did after Daddy let me have a swig of beer when we were little. "Drink at home, and you won't have to drink when you're not supposed to." I didn't know what that meant. I thought it was pretty questionable parenting to give your ten-year-old beer for any reason, just like when he gave Radar beer. Radar would slurp it out of a dish Daddy set on the bottom back step, and then he'd run around in circles and into the chain-link fence headfirst. But I drank my one swallow of beer anyway when he offered it. And I felt now like I did back when Daddy gave me that swig: deadened and numb and like somebody taped two toilet tissue rolls to my eyes so I could only see what was right in front of me. And what was right in front of me was not my Knox. He was gone.

I watched him disappear into the pines. I walked back home through the woods, slowly so that I wouldn't catch up with him. I couldn't face him. I was embarrassed and angry. I blew it. I had a choice and over-reached. Being friends with him was the most important thing in my life, and I ruined it. Why would I ever think he'd want to kiss me? I passed by the junkyard on the way home, and I crept up to the fence and peeked in. I didn't see him or anybody. I wanted to see him. Would he be laughing about me? I didn't think so. He wouldn't make fun of me. He wouldn't tell anybody what I had confessed to him.

I climbed through the fence and crawled up to the hideout, opened the door, and got in. I took his shirt from under the seat. I put it on and sat there, and that's when the tears came. At first, I screamed a lot of words, dirty ones, which I only said because I missed him so much, and "goddammit," which I apologized to God for immediately because I didn't really mean it. Then in one breath, one single move that I didn't even know I'd done until it was over, I got out of the Ninety-Eight—my secret, safe place for three years, my spying place to watch him—and I picked up a red brick and hurled it through the back passenger door window. It didn't occur to me until later that Knox or someone from his house might hear me and come out, but no one did.

I didn't want to have the option of coming back. I knew myself enough to know that given half a chance I would return, I would. As soon as the scab healed over the new, raw hurt, I'd sneak back through the woods, under the fence, and inside the hideout and long for him and wonder what a real kiss from the beautiful boy would have felt like, tasted like. What I would have seen if I'd opened my eyes so close to his. Would he look at me or close his eyes?

I knew that when I got used to it, to knowing he didn't want me, I'd long to return at least to my role of little buddy. A little buddy can hide in plain sight, close enough to steal looks, to smell him, to take his kind words and inflate them, infusing them with meaning he didn't intend. I knew the raw disappointment would give way, and I'd be willing to take the consolation instead of the full prize. But the brick saved me from myself. Breath caught in my lungs, I felt like those moments when you're kind of asleep, but you're really awake and paralyzed and feeling like your mind is betraying you, taking control of your body to remind you that neither your mind nor your body are really your own.

I was over the fence and crouched under a pine tree before I drew a breath, holding fistfuls of pine straw to my face, wishing we could relive the last hour because an hour ago he was a possibility—was turned toward me, not away. An hour ago my heart was full, happy within its small house inside my chest. And he was my friend, smiling when he looked at me, enjoying spending his day with me, working on my car, any car.

Sudden new sobs and the words, "You're gone," caught in my chest. Gone.

In my mind, I spoke to him, telegraphing a message I couldn't say to his face. *When you do kiss someone, what will you feel? Who will it be? Will she know how kind you are, how gentle you've been with me? Will she sit alone and close her eyes and imagine how you smell? I hate her, hate her so much. The one you'll say yes to. The one you'll kiss. The one you'll choose.* And then I felt bad; she hadn't done anything except be what he wanted.

All my energy was gone, like a baby at the end of a screaming fit. I felt drugged, lethargic, calmly dissatisfied. As I sat there in the woods, I said a little prayer to be forgiven for all the bad things I imagined. That girl he'll love, she and I are alike, I thought. Her heart will fill up with him just like mine. She and I are the same.

It was the middle of that night when I remembered the Bug sitting down by the lake with the trunk lid open, dew settling on the vinyl rumble seat. How did I just walk home and not think about the Bug by the lake? I got up early morning and walked through the pines back to the Bug and drove it to school before the first bell.

James saw me pull up. "Dude, this is so cool. Let me see the rumble seat!" He lifted the hood while I was at the stop sign and sat right down in it. The cars behind me made an awful racket beeping.

"Put it back, James. I can't see!"

"Drive!" he yelled. "I'll tell you when to turn."

"Get up and close the hood!"

"Naw, man, this will be fun."

"I can't see," I said. "Move. Don't be a jerk!"

He got out and shut the hood, and I drove off to the school parking lot.

He walked over and jumped up and down slowly, like he was trying to stamp out a campfire that was so hot he could only step on it once every minute. "Let's cut classes and go for a ride."

"No!"

"Philbet, what's wrong with you?"

"Nothing," I lied.

"Oh, that's just bull crap."

James was in love too. Anne had hair the same color as Knox's. I always remember her coming up from the left and standing on the right. It never changed. It was odd, sort of like when you talk to someone, and they won't quite look you in the eye, and they continue to shift ever so slowly to one side like the sun moves in the sky. They wiggle all the way over to the other side of you if you stay still. But in order to keep them in eyesight, you shift along with them in a sort of dance.

James would plant himself in the hallway on breaks, and she always came down the hallway from the left about a minute later. She usually moved on to her spot with her friends down the hallway to the right. James said nothing for months. He just obsessed over her. He really liked how the ruffles on her blouse ran along the seam from her shoulders over her chest and down to her waist. All of her blouses were the same style, skintight with ruffles and buttons up to the neck. Then, one day, he spoke.

"It's a spectacular day." She didn't stop moving. She didn't even look.

He did this for a week. "It's a spectacular day." He was such a goof. The next week, she quickly glanced at him but, again, didn't stop.

They did that for a week. Then, "It's a spectacular day." And she stopped and turned to face him.

"Is it?" she replied, with an air of high-school sophistication.

"Yes, today it is."

"And why is it a spectacular day?"

"Because you're speaking to me," James said, grinning stupidly ear to ear.

She pursed her lips, smiled, and walked on. Seeing this day after day was like being on the set of a TV show, watching actors rehearse the same scene over and over, changing it just slightly after hearing the director's notes at the end of each take. The next day, she stopped without him saying anything to her. "Hi, James."

"Anne." He smiled.

"How's your day going?"

As Anne walked past, James grinned, "Getting better and better."

Some can only see the past, what has been. Some can only see the present, and what is or is not. No one can see the future, but some sense it and know the future will be different, better. James was like that. James was about the smartest person ever, next to Grandaddy.

"Come on. I know something's wrong, Philbet," he persisted.

Fear. I knew fear. It was my past, present, and I guess it would be with me always.

"Just tell me."

The walls of the school were made of cinder block, just like our old house back in Alvaton down the garden path from Grandaddy. Our walls were white, painted, layers so thick that the hard, rough blocks were softened and no longer sharp, and the slick, textured surface was cool to a cheek or forehead pressed up against it, even during the summer. Being there was like sitting in a suddenly quiet church after everyone had left.

The school walls weren't the same. The blocks were painted, but rough. It almost looked like they were stained beige with the part of the toothpaste you send down the sink after you brush your teeth. I couldn't, wouldn't consider talking about Knox here. And it wasn't as much about Knox as it was me. Looking at James, I couldn't tell him here, where I felt on alert and didn't believe anyone would understand.

I whispered to myself, "Now that MawMaw is dead…"

"Philbet, what are you talking about?"

"…we can stick knives in her."

That was ten years ago, but I heard it in my mind some days, as if a shadow of myself stepped out from behind a tree and whispered it in my ear. I was never quick enough to turn in time to see myself. But were I to face myself, I know my shadow would come close—not nose-to-nose, but its mouth to my ear, my mouth to its ear. We'd say to each other at the same time, "Wallow in your self-pity for the rest of your life, little boy."

I repeated in my head, *Now that MawMaw is dead, we can stick knives in her*. It had become a sort of Bible verse to remind me to be a good boy, not irrational and ridiculous. A child's thought, but I wasn't a child anymore.

James always tried to help me. I trusted him as much as I did anyone. But I looked at him here, in front of me staring back, and knew he couldn't possibly know what I was thinking…nor I, his thoughts. None of us ever really know what others think. It's like we're walking through each day as if it was a closed-book test, and you didn't even have a copy of the book to study, no notes from class, never having heard the lesson. That's what life felt like, a never-ending test. I remember thinking we're all boats trying to stay afloat, but there's a hole in my heart where my blood drains out more than the water rushes in, sinking the heart and the rest of me with it.

I really want to know what goes on in everybody else's head, what they actually mean when they say something, their private thoughts when they don't say anything. What are people thinking when they catch your eyes on the street and look away? What do they think when they are alone at home with no one watching? Whatever it is, it's real, having more power in it than any physical thing. And all those interior worlds are more vast than our homes, the town we live in, the whole of our world. We keep all of it locked away from each other, even if we're just feet apart. An entire world existed only a couple of feet from me in James's head, just behind the bones of his skull.

*What makes him hate or love?* I wondered to myself. *Why did James want Anne? Desire her? What were his thoughts from 9:00 to 9:02 this morning, and every morning, as we walked from class to first break?* I couldn't figure out how it's possible to know someone when you just get a few pieces of information, and all the rest is locked inside. Do we remember it as it really is or as we want it to be?

"Philbet, tell me. You can tell me," James reminded me where we were.

"School's about to start. I'm okay, I guess."

## CHAPTER FIFTY-ONE

# My Sanctuary

I couldn't talk to Grandaddy. I should be able to tell him anything, but I couldn't tell him this. I wouldn't be able to face him if he knew my inner thoughts about Knox.

But the pull of Knox felt so okay, so right, fit me so well. It made me feel warm like a buttered roll on the kitchen counter right after Mama had taken it out of the oven, sliding it on a plate with her pancake turner. So comfortable and satisfying. So right that I had wanted to find an opening in him and crawl inside and nest there. I didn't understand why it was considered so wrong.

I had wanted to kiss Knox and talk to him at the same time. I'd wanted to swallow breaths of air, instead of breathing them in because taking the time to breathe took too much time. And the only reason I wanted air was so that he could take it from me, his mouth covering mine, words and kisses all one.

I couldn't tell James. What would I do if my one friend stopped being my friend? Not having somebody to talk to is a heartache of its own. James would say, "Man, you don't give me credit." It wasn't that I didn't trust him. I wasn't ashamed. I just thought other people would think I *should be ashamed.*

And suddenly, I knew what to do and where to go for help.

"Mama, I'm going out."

"Why are you in your suit?"

"I want to ask Beau for a job?"

"Oh. Why?"

I didn't want to work for Beau. I wanted to talk to him because if Beau loved a boy, too, he'd understand. And I wanted a hug. I wanted to cry while somebody who understood told me it was okay.

"I thought I'd ask if I could clean up, answer his telephone, stuff like that," not having really thought about it.

"I'll go too. I'd like to see him."

When we arrived, I turned to Mama and said, "I know you want to visit with Beau, but will you wait in the car? I think I should ask him on my own."

"Okay, Sweetheart."

And I headed inside, hoping no one was there except for him.

"Hi, Philbet," he said in his big-hearted way, heading toward me. "Well, you are looking sharp today. Love that tie." With that, he enveloped me in a welcoming hug.

And before I could say a single word, I burst into tears.

He tightened his arms around me, and it felt like he was that hollowed-out pine tree that I wanted to climb into like a baby owl all those years ago. He was about the warmest person ever next to Grandaddy.

"What's wrong?"

I had planned to tell him my story moment-by-moment, almost methodically, plus explaining that Mama was outside and that I had lied to her about why I was here. But I was too sad. My heart hurt so much I felt hungry, but I wasn't hungry.

"I want to be stronger."

He didn't know what to make of that.

"I mean, I'm sorry."

"What's wrong?" Beau asked.

"I told Mama I was coming here so that I could ask you for a job, but I really wanted to talk to you because I love somebody and that somebody doesn't love me back."

"Oh, Philbet. I'm sorry." And he hugged me again. He smelled like turpentine, like he was older than he was. Like he was a big old cabinet that was always there in the room with you. You always went to it, every day, and opened it up and whatever you needed was always there in the top drawer.

"I didn't mean to spy on you when I was here before. I just looked up and I saw," I blurted out.

"Saw what?"

"I didn't mean to be nosey," I explained, "when I saw you and Dean."

"You don't worry about that."

"I just wanted you to know." I didn't mean to cry like a little kid. "And I won't tell anybody if I'm right, I promise."

He smiled. It was the same smile from years ago when I gave him the picture of him in the pine trees just before he went to Vietnam. "Talk to me," he said quietly.

"My heart hurts," barely able to keep my eyes dry.

"Tell me, Philbet. It'll be just between us."

"I love a boy."

Nothing.

I repeated, "A boy."

"Yeah?"

"Do you love a boy too? I think you do, but I'm not sure. I don't know any boys who love another boy."

"Who is this boy?"

"Knox. He lives next door and drives a GTO."

"Cool car."

"He's like a GTO come to life. He's…. You love a boy, too, right? If you don't, you won't understand. I won't tell anybody," I promised again.

"Philbet, I do. I love a boy too. You saw us."

And my world doubled in size just knowing that he understood. If he loved a boy too, he understood.

"I'm glad."

"Me too. What do you want me to do, Philbet?"

"I just needed to tell somebody," I said, not really knowing what I wanted.

"Go ahead. Tell me more."

And I thought back to the day I saw Dean put his hand in Beau's back pocket. It wasn't quite like the times I caught Grandaddy patting Jorma's bottom. That always looked more like he was warning her that he was there and not to back up and step on his toes. But it was right then and there talking to Beau, knowing he also loved a boy, that it dawned on me that Grandaddy really loved Jorma, wanted her. That's what Grandaddy meant when he said, "What's cookin', Springtime?" And as sad as I was, I smiled a little knowing that Grandaddy and Jorma must have felt about each other the way Beau and Dean felt, the way I felt about Knox. Like every time I saw him, it felt like my cold heart melted, and it was spring all of a sudden.

"I'll tell you more later, if that's okay?"

"Sure."

I hugged him, wanting to cry just a little more mostly from relief, but I could do that at home.

"So, what are you going to tell your mama?"

"I'm not going to tell her, not yet. I don't know if she'd understand."

"No, about the job. You came in for a job."

"Um…I'll say you didn't have anything."

"No sir, you're not going to make me the bad guy. I'll see you every Saturday afternoon from one to five."

"What do you want me to do?"

"What can you do?"

"Clean. Run the register?" I offered.

"Hmm, maybe. You can draw. I want you to paint the storefront windows to draw in the tourist trade. And you can draw signs to highlight our stock, give them a personality and back story."

"Yeah?"

"Ten dollars, plus I'll buy you lunch every Saturday. I don't have much coming in yet, so that's all I can do. How does that sound?"

"Yeah, that's great. Okay."

"Come here."

He hugged me and said, "Don't be too sad. When you cry, you can't see so well. You just might miss seeing somebody standing right there who does love you back."

"Really?"

"Yep. One day you'll love somebody—"

"And he'll love me right back?" I interrupted.

"Yes Philbet. I promise. He will."

## CHAPTER FIFTY-TWO

# Tech

After a week of avoiding Knox, I stopped. It was too small a town, and he did live next door through the woods. I resigned myself to seeing him eventually.

I didn't get the idea on my own. Grandaddy helped. After I went to see Beau, I felt a little better, enough to get an idea to go up to Alvaton and spend the weekend with Grandaddy and Jorma. I knew I wouldn't see Knox up there. I felt kind of guilty because it had been so long since I'd spent the night with them. I'd only been thinking about myself, Knox and me, and I was ashamed to think I'd rather ride around with Knox in his GTO and sit in the Krystal parking lot and eat hamburgers with him instead of seeing my own grandaddy.

That's what I thought about as I lay there in Grandaddy and Jorma's guest room bed. It wasn't even dark yet because they went to bed so early. I felt like I wanted to do something special for them, so I decided to go out first thing the next morning and pick up pecans as an unspoken "I'm sorry" to Grandaddy. He had trouble bending over these days, so it would be a big help.

And that's what I did as soon as I woke up. There was a fog in the backyard, a cotton bunting rolled out on the ground that curled and crept off over into the railroad cut as I walked through it. My shoes had a fine mist of water on the toes as the fog cleared and revealed the pecans on the ground. I hadn't been out there five minutes when Grandaddy came out and joined me. We were silent with only the leaves rustling under foot and the tang of the pecan shells as they hit the side of our tin buckets. It surprised me that he could bend over as well as he did, and I could tell from the echo of his pail he was getting his fair share of pecans.

I was turned away from him, and my nose started to run because I was forcing my eyes not to cry. And I wanted more than anything for him to put his hand on the top of my head and look down at me and make it all better. I shut my eyes and imagined it was years earlier—me looking up at him, his face in shadow as it eclipsed the sun. And about that time I felt his hand, not on the top of my head, but on my shoulder. I slowly turned to him, and I realized for the first time that I was as tall as Grandaddy. We were passing each other with me growing up and Grandaddy going in the other direction, and I sensed that one day I'd put my hand on his head to soothe his sadness, his pain.

"Hey, Whoop."

"Hey, Grandaddy."

"What's the matter, boy?"

I wasn't crying, so how did he know?

"You can tell me."

But I couldn't tell him. How could I tell him that my heart...my heart belonged to a boy?

Instead, I said, "I miss Adam." And as I said it, I realized I wasn't lying to Grandaddy because I *did* miss him. But I missed Knox more.

He hugged me to him. Grandaddy was a healer. He could have hung out a shingle. But I'm glad he didn't. I had him all to myself.

Grandaddy said, "I miss him too." And then he said, "You need a routine? Not school, something else."

And I recalled Knox had said something months earlier about taking a class on car repair, and I decided that was a good idea. If I wanted to design cars, I had to start someplace. Since I couldn't shadow Knox in his garage anymore, I thought I'd take a weekend class down at the technical school. I didn't know it, but classes were free for high school students.

Soon, Saturdays at 8:00 in the morning, I was in class and at the front table, and Grandaddy was there by me at the same two-top. My Grandaddy got up at 5:00 every Saturday morning and was at our house in Warm Springs by 7:00, so we could go to class together. Always focused on the outside of the car—the lines of the fender, the tail lamps, the logo design even—I was not prepared for a class so focused on the inside of the car, specifically under the hood. I think Knox distracted me from looking more deeply into the car, and I only really appreciated the surface, not the heart of it. Each week we sat at tables, each with our own identical carburetor or some other amputated car part, examining it, trying to understand everything about it. Only when the subject matter turned to tasks like changing the power steering fluid did we all gather around an actual car.

It was really different from working on my car with Knox. My role with Knox was mostly to hand him tools. When he painstakingly explained to me what he was doing, I'd act like I understood, but often didn't, having spent most of my car-side-listening time just staring at him. I loved these tech-school Saturdays. The discipline and structure of the day helped keep me from moping around and indulging my teenaged angst, which I thought was going to eat me alive that first week after losing Knox. It felt good knowing that I was challenging myself, learning something that I had admired in him, his knowledge of cars, his command of the tools around him, his ability to soothe and heal cars of their maladies. He was like a surgeon in a graveyard, bringing long-dead vehicles back to long life and good health.

When I first took up residence in my hideout car, I had wondered why they kept these old wrecks around, hauling them in tow truck after tow truck, arranging them around that one 1960 Impala that was there all alone before Finley moved out and Brownie moved in. That Impala had been there for years with bushes growing up around it and that skinny pine tree taking over by growing up though where the engine once sat, the front-end housing now a planter, hood open and hyperextended back against the windshield.

Knox said these wrecks were donors. In fact, he called them donor cars. "We take pieces from them and use those parts on cars that come in to be fixed."

"Why don't you dismantle them, catalog the pieces, and stack them up so you'd know where they were when you needed them?" I regretted the suggestion the minute I got it out. I loved the old cars, and I'd be so sad if they went away—their parts pulled and stacked up like cords of wood near a fireplace. Not to mention that my hideout would have disappeared.

"Oh, Brownie would never do that. Too much trouble. He'd rather keep a whole car for a hundred years just to pull off a fender he might need. Even if he never used anything else, he'd say, 'See, that LTD came in handy.'"

Tech school was the opposite of Knox's garage. It was neat, scrubbed clean like a doctor's office. There weren't any wrecks around. The one car we worked on was a permanent fixer upper with pieces that class after class lifted on and off, screwed and unscrewed, dismantled and reconstituted. Emotionless, without feeling, an Operation Game with no batteries to buzz if you made a wrong move. No passion, with each transactional turn of the screw, and no Knox to distract me.

In a semester I'd have a basic grasp of automotive functionality. All accomplished without those hypnotizing stares at the soft skin that showed between Knox's belt and T-shirt when he stretched on his back to slide under a car, his bottom half sticking out, feet splayed.

And after class, Grandaddy went with me to my job at Beau's antique shop. He didn't get paid like me, but I don't think he cared. On those Saturday afternoons, it was almost like no time had passed for Beau, Grandaddy, and me.

## CHAPTER FIFTY-THREE

# Fresh Off the Truck

Looking back, I think of my family as innocent. Not in the way a newborn is innocent, before it grows up, makes decisions, has an impact on others' lives. Hurts them. No. My parents—the whole family, really—were innocents as in we were not equipped for life in the world beyond our small community.

After Knox, I was more aware; I was less innocent. Him kissing me on top of my head and turning away was like that day over a decade ago when Aunt Novella picked me up under my arms and asked Mama what was wrong with me. That day, I grew up a little. It hurt, like I was shedding a skin I had outgrown. My new skin was soft, tender, vulnerable. Leaving behind a shell that no longer fit me, sort of like the cicadas that come out of the ground and start crawling up the pine trees, getting too big for their shells half-way up and leaving their amber, translucent husks behind mid-climb.

This was my third skin, I guess. Less innocent at seventeen than Mama was at forty. She went with me to New York City when I had a visit with a college there. Terrified, we called an airline—a first. Then we stumbled through buying plane tickets, after which we took off for the library to look at a telephone book so we could call and reserve a hotel room near the school. Turns out, somebody had walked off with their phone book, so we called information and located a hotel we thought was near my screening interview.

Uncertainty. If uncertainty had a smell, every breath we exhaled would have smelled of it. For Mama, it was an expensive trip, but she also must have been coming to terms with my eventual departure for college—if not in New York City, then someplace other than Warm Springs. She knew I couldn't stay home. She didn't know about Knox, but she knew something was not right with me. Mama could sense it. She somehow knew it, like mamas do.

The day after Knox, she said, "Your eyes used to have flecks of yellow." That's all she said, a tight smile on her face that turned downward instead of up like a smile should. And then she put her cheek to mine.

But she was different too. When we were looking for my birth certificate so I could get my driver's license, a photograph fell out of the metal firebox she kept in the closet. It was her. "Christmas 1969" was in someone's hand I didn't recognize. It was in black and white, but Mama wore a dress I remember well, red as a mid-summer tomato with a white bib and Peter Pan collar. Her hair was teased so high, she reached as tall as Uncle Calvin and taller than all of her sisters, though Mama was really a good six inches shorter.

Even with the black and white filter, I could see her pretty, clear face shining, so young. I had always thought of Mama as being about thirty. When I wasn't with her or if I closed my eyes and thought about her, that's how old I thought she was. This photo made me rethink that because she looked younger in it. She was about twenty-five, I guess, but she looked so, so shiny, smiling. I imagined all my cousins and Adam and me playing just outside the frame of the picture, pumped up on Christmas cakes, cookies, and candy, even the pretzels covered in waxy white chocolate, as gross as they were.

The time was from before Aunt Novella drove me to shed my skin that first time, the last day I didn't know I was different in my body and in my heart. It was before that day I found Mama standing on a chair with grief so raw she made sounds that didn't sound human. It was before we knew

that baby corn was a real thing and not unnatural and deformed, something to scare us, challenge our thinking, our expectations—that little can
of mislabeled baby corn on my mind all these years later.

I had no idea what to expect or what to do during a college visit. I
wasn't even sure how I got a chance to visit a college campus. It was a
few years before I understood that anybody can go and walk the grounds,
imagining that first real step toward what will be, turning away from what
is. I didn't even realize that I wasn't going for an interview and that they
based admission solely on scores, recommendations, and connections. I
had pretty good scores, but no connections, for sure. Night after night as
the New York City date approached, I imagined what a college interview
might be like. How might they want me to answer their questions? And
then Beau and Dean said they'd help. They'd pretend-interview me and get
me ready.

"Okay, we're not going to interrupt you, Philbet. This is practice, like
acting almost," Beau said.

They had reassured me that we'd practice so much between now and my
interview that my lighting-round responses would be like second nature to
me by then, and I was determined to concentrate and excel.

Dean followed up with, "Mr. Lawson, your scores are excellent. Your
essay is insightful, honest, charmingly bucolic, even."

I smiled, never having heard the word "bucolic" before. It sounded
like alcoholic, but I'd never heard of a charming alcoholic, so I figured it's
meant to be positive. I nodded and muttered, "Thank you."

"Okay, tell us about you, about Philbet."

"Um, I love to draw. I love numbers and spatial relationships, the way
things, anything at all, relates to other…things."

"Can you give us an example, Mr. Lawson?" Beau asked in his best
interviewer voice.

I froze. I should have been ready for that question, but my throat
locked up like I'd swallowed sand.

"Cars," I blurted out.

They waited.

"Cars are living beings, in a way. They are just like us. Um, they are fundamentally a machine. I mean, we're not. Cars evolve, based on need, like people do."

*What is wrong with me?* I thought to myself, blushing.

"There is order in good design, well-designed things. You—well, I don't mean *you*—a person…um. Or a car."

I was blowing it, I figured, but I charged forward.

"A larger car is not necessarily stronger or safer than a small car. The smaller car may well have design elements that transfer the energy of a crash away from passengers and toward other parts of the car's frame. It's just like…a body with sturdy muscles isn't necessarily better at lifting heavy objects. Body position is important. That's what interests me—how things work, how design and common sense can help us achieve more."

I had no idea if that made sense, especially as I attempted it in my best non-Southern accent.

"Tell us why you want to study here," Beau said, still in character.

"Your program is the best in the country. I want the best education I can get."

I took a good breath and continued, "May I…?" I had just learned to use "may" instead of "can" when asking permission.

"May I tell you about myself, again? I can answer who I am and why I want to study here way better than I just did."

"Yes, of course. Take your time, Philbet," said Dean. "We know this can be unnerving."

"Thank you," I said, breathing deeply.

"I'm pretty smart, and I have some natural talent. You must have seen something in my application that you liked and wanted to know more about. But what you didn't get from the application is who I am."

I kept going. "You've never met anyone as stubborn and determined to accomplish something as me. I know it's just words right now, but I'll prove it to you if you let me come here. I promise, you'll remember me in a good way, even years after I graduate because I am my grandaddy's boy.

He should have gotten this opportunity about sixty years ago. But since he can't, I will," I said, nodding my head for emphasis.

"Uh, you should meet him," I continued. "He's just about the best person ever. Did you read *The Fountainhead*? It's by this lady with the last name Rand, but I swear, nobody where I'm from would know how to pronounce her first name, and it's only three letters long. I don't think it's pronounced 'Ann.' Anyway, that's my grandaddy, the guy in *The Fountainhead*, except my grandaddy's smarter. And he's happy. He's able to be smart and capable without destroying everything around him, and without holding his feelings back. He loves all of us more than anything."

Telling my favorite Grandaddy story, I said, "I swear, when I was a little kid, I'd scoop up every drawing pencil he had on him, like a pickpocket. And when I came back to visit him the next day, there'd be more pencils right there for me to take. And he never got sore or anything. That's how he taught me to think. Gave me the tools, asked me questions without telling me what I should think about it. That's what my grandaddy taught me. If I'm even half as good as he is, I'll be a great addition to your program. He's been sick lately, so it sure would make him proud to know that we—the two of us, in a way—made it into this school."

They look back at me, hard to read.

"I want to design cars. I've always loved them. They were my friends almost, having personalities, a lifeline to the future, a way to get out of where I was. Now, I don't think of them as my way to get out. My mind is the way to get out. And I don't really want to get out. I want...I want to live a full life."

It struck me then that I didn't think Mama had lived a full life. It meant so much to me that she'd been able to find the courage to take me to New York. She had never been to such a place. At home, we talked about New York City like it was another planet. I mean, she was so scared during our one night at the hotel, she made me help her drag the dresser in front of the door to our room so no one could get in. That was love. Deep-inside-the-heart love. She'd take it as a personal success if I was admitted.

"Yes, Philbet, we understand about cars now. Anything else you feel compelled to say?"

Knowing nothing else to do, I pressed on. "I'm not my mama, and I'm not Grandaddy. I am not afraid of New York. I'm not afraid. I'm determined. And if what I'm saying backfires, I can live with that."

But there was no interview. We joined a group of about twenty other kids and some parents to take a walking tour of the campus. Then they gave us lunch, and we heard rising sophomores make only vaguely informative presentations about the school. And I didn't fit in.

## CHAPTER FIFTY-FOUR

# Truth Be Told

Mama didn't say much on the flight back home. I caught her biting her lip and, I don't know, trying not to cry as the plane was just lifting its nose into the air. Fearful flier? Dream forgone? Resignation? I couldn't tell. And I couldn't ask.

When we got back home, I continued to draw my designs and work at the garage. Not at Knox's, but another one in town. Knox hadn't spoken to me since that day, and I hadn't spoken to him. It didn't so much hurt any more as much as it felt like nothing. Numbness. I didn't feel anything.

I didn't have a not-getting-into-school back-up plan. I wanted to go to school to design cars. I'd written off New York, though I hadn't gotten a letter one way or the other. I had another application in though, over in LaGrange. It was a pretty good school, but I had thought getting out of Georgia was my best option. It would help to be away from Knox; still seeing him drive by every now and then pierced my numbness with a passing jab in my chest. But that would mean having to move a long way from Mama and Grandaddy.

I pondered our visit to New York City every day for about a week after we returned home. We went to see Grandaddy and Jorma to tell them about the trip that next Sunday afternoon. After a quick rundown, we all sat around eating our tomato sandwiches and were quieter than the soft wind in the pecan trees. I was staring down into my sweet tea, and it was like my head burst and tingled like an orange when you stuff your fingers in it. A thought materialized. Come this time next year, Grandaddy might not be here.

When I looked up, everyone was sitting, staring off into the breeze or looking at their plate of food. Grandaddy was off sitting on the back steps, looking at me, expressionless. Then he smiled and winked. He hadn't winked in years, and then, only when he was trying to make me feel better, letting me know everything was okay. But that wink didn't make me feel better. It wasn't one of his patented "everything-will-be-okay" winks, and it scared me. He was everything. Without him, none of us would be here— not because he was our Grandaddy, but because he led us, through trouble, through loss, through being lost.

Later that afternoon, he and I sat on the front porch swing as it creaked from old age and rusty chains. The orange and blue Gulf sign over at Pick's gas station was black, obscured as it sliced into the bottom edge of the big round orange sun that was falling faster than usual into the horizon. Grandaddy explained, "Your Jorma is afraid, Philbet. She's afraid. So's your daddy, and your mama."

The sun was almost gone, the orange and blue of the sign returned, glowing from the bulb inside. "I've led a small life. Them too. But I led the life I wanted. They didn't," Grandaddy continued in a low voice that cut through the night in little sparks just like the lightning bugs. "I want to tell you something, and I want you to listen. Okay?"

I nodded.

"And always remember this, even if you don't remember anything else about me. Even if you don't remember anything I ever did or said." He was quiet for a while. I waited, alert.

"I should have said this a long time ago, but...nope, I don't regret. I'm saying it now because I think now is the time. You weren't ready to hear it earlier. I hope you're ready now. I think you are. I think you'll understand what I mean."

Again, I nodded, a little uneasy.

"Don't be afraid, Philbet. If you let fear make your decisions, you'll never be what you are meant to be. You're a good boy, and you'll be a good man. You do have a lot of growing up to do, and the next couple of years are going to be tough. You're going to have lots of decisions to make, grown-up decisions, and I'm not going to be here."

"Grandaddy—" I couldn't stand this.

"Hush up and listen," he said, stopping me. "No matter what you do, there's going to be pain. You're gonna get hurt, and you'll hurt others. You can't get around it, so don't try. Just get on with it and do what you know is right. You don't do that usually. It's the safe choices, the ones that don't frighten you, that leave you wanting more."

It always felt like we didn't have the set of instructions on how to live... how to survive. The user manual existed. We knew it did. It seemed only misplaced in a stack of mail or shoved in a drawer in a hasty dash to straighten up before company arrived. But Grandaddy had the manual memorized. It was surprisingly straightforward in many ways, but for some reason Grandaddy's wisdom was lost on a bunch of my family. Grandaddy was the one among us most sharply attuned to the best way forward.

"Your mama and daddy both are making you a little soft, that's why you get called a sissy."

But I wasn't called a sissy. *They called me Suzie*, I thought. Grandaddy was saying more in one stretch than he usually said in a month. I didn't want it to stop.

"I love you, boy, so that's why I'm telling you this. A sissy isn't what you are. It's a name scared people call other folks they think are afraid and weak. It's something a bully calls somebody else so the bully can feel bigger. Sissies can be anybody; it's a name for people who aren't truly themselves."

I loved him so much at that moment. "Own up to who you are, Philbet, and honor your responsibilities in this world. Be brave. That's what it means to be a grown-up. Be a grown-up, no matter what. That's a man I'll be proud to know. This family wants the best for you. They want to help you, but they don't know how. Adam does. If you need a clear head, go to your brother. He gets it." And then he paused.

"I can't talk to him," I whispered.

"Yes, you can. He's a good boy too. He doesn't know how much you need him. He thinks you think you're better than him, so he's not gonna knock on your door with advice. But you're brothers. He'll never turn his back on you. Just remember that he needs you, too, or he will one day. Be there for him. Life is long, and the weak are eventually the strong if they try real hard to do what's right."

Silence.

"Take care of yourself first, Philbet, so you can be a good goddamn to anybody else. Get right with yourself." He stopped again.

"Do you hear me?" he asked.

"Yes sir, I do."

"Do you understand me?"

"Yes, Grandaddy, I do."

"Do you promise me?"

"Yes, Grandaddy. Yes, I promise."

"Do you have anything you want to talk about?"

"No."

"Anything you wanna ask me?"

I wasn't ready. "No."

"Okay." He touched the top of my head so lightly, almost as he touched the hood of the old white Galaxie when he traded it in on the Maverick all those years ago. A parting. A good-bye of sorts.

"One more thing. You're half happy. I gave you that. And you're half miserable. You can thank Jorma for that. I'd worry about leaving her behind if she weren't the second meanest woman ever to walk the red clay of Georgia."

Playing along, I asked, "Grandaddy, who was the meanest?"

"Her mama."

Grandaddy was funny.

"Philbet, you and your daddy are just alike. He never overcame his Jorma side of the family. You can. You have to. Don't be the second unhappiest man to walk the red clay of Georgia."

"Grandaddy, who's the unhappiest?"

"Your daddy."

## CHAPTER FIFTY-FIVE

# Counting Breaths

He didn't say anything, but Grandaddy didn't always need words to teach me something. The way he grasped the handle of a hoe showed me how to use it. He'd point to the hundred martins perched up on the telephone lines and then move his finger in a straight, steady line to the gourds on the tire-tie high up on the post to let me know that these were the birds that would live inside.

But it was that first lesson I think about now, remembering his hand on my head rubbing off the hot Georgia sun. And I returned the kindness, rubbing my palm on the crown of his head, his cool, vellum-thin skin that had soaked up no warmth from the hospital's drop-ceiling fluorescent lights. And I listened to the wordless sound he made, the last thing he'd ever teach me.

A death rattle doesn't rattle. At least not Grandaddy's. It's not a sound I'd ever heard. Not exactly.

Grandaddy sounded kind of like the sharp, high-pitched scream from the opening of a blown-up balloon if someone pinches it closed and then purposely, slowly lets the air out. *I can't stand this*, I thought. *Please just end*. That ear-splitting torture of a balloon in the hands of a child, a child who stands there next to you, taunting, letting the air peel out, holding it in with a grin, letting it out again.

Death is a child with a balloon.

If a balloon had somehow gotten sucked into Grandaddy, down his throat, down his lungs, that was the sound he made. It hurt my ears; it had to hurt him. His mouth was a baby bird's. Not a cartoon baby bird, but a starving, abandoned baby bird, head and neck awkwardly arched up and back toward the hospital bed headboard as if there was something on the wall behind him he longed to see.

If I didn't know better, I'd think the bed had grown one long scary finger out of the mattress about where Grandaddy's shoulder blades were, and it was poking him, making him arch up that way. He breathed once every two minutes for over an hour, about thirty breaths an hour. I counted. I didn't know what else to do after I called Mama and Daddy. So, I counted. Thirty breaths in an hour. That's all. I held my breath after one of his to see if I could hold mine for that long. I couldn't. That was just like always—Grandaddy doing something extraordinary, even as he lay dying. Went a whole hour with only thirty breaths. Quiet. Unbelievable. Extraordinary, even at the end.

Often people revert to childhood as they get older and closer to death, becoming childlike, innocent, smiling, and docile. But not him. He didn't look like a child, not childlike. He looked like he hurt, an old man who hurt. He'd never been childlike, always grounded. A real grown-up. I wondered if he ever pitched fits and held his breath as a little boy. Knowing Grandaddy, I couldn't picture it. He was steady.

He picked cotton as a child, the burs cutting into his fingers, his little-boy hands. By the time he was my age, his hands were the texture of Mama's oven mitt. When I was little, giggling breathlessly to shimmy out of his tickling clutch, his hands were like 40 grit sandpaper. When he was nine, he and his friend Benny rode bikes up the road twenty miles to pick up free puppies from the Garners. Grandaddy carried his pick, Butterbean, in his left hand, this hand I held all these years later, and he steered the bike with his right the whole way home. I remembered sitting on the back steps of Grandaddy's house, must've been about four years old, while he cut a peach up with his pocketknife and handed it to me one slice at a time because peaches stain clothes.

"Why'd you call him Butterbean, Grandaddy?"

"Him and his brothers and sisters reminded me of a buncha butter beans just shucked from their shell."

"They did?"

"Philbet, puppies don't come one at a time. They come in litters, like butter beans come three or four to a shell."

Butterbean lived seventeen years and licked my daddy's face the day he was born.

"Butterbean was a once-in-a-lifetime dog," Grandaddy used to say. "I got the good one. Benny's wadn't too smart. Sweet dog, but no common sense. Got out on the train track that first year."

How, why, does a body start with such a force, live a full life, and end up sounding like a leaking balloon, looking like a bird at the very end? A smart-alecky kid wanting to take lessons in breath holding could have learned a lot from Grandaddy that last hour.

He was leaving, going somewhere I couldn't follow him. I mean, he was right there in front of me, but he'd already gone all slack, life and will moved on to someplace else. I wondered if Jess sounded the same way when she died, if she went from being okay to not okay so quickly. Did Mama see it coming? It happened so fast with Grandaddy. We were talking. We were laughing, and I left to go to the bathroom.

I'd spent many days and nights in the hospital. I knew it well, especially the emergency room desk where I had often played on the ice-cold floor, while Grandaddy was being checked in. Back then, Adam's job was to watch me, mine to be a good boy and not need anything while we waited. I remember one night when I was on the way to the bathroom, Adam had pointed to a sign on the wall that I couldn't read.

"That's where you were born."

"I was?"

"Yeah, that's what Jorma said one time."

Another time, during another one of Grandaddy's nighttime hospital visits, Jorma walked me to the bathroom when I needed to go, and I asked for confirmation. "Jorma, is that where I was born?"

"Yeah," was all she offered.

"How do you know?"

"How could I forget?" she said as we passed the sign. "Your mama pitched a fit sum'um awful."

Jorma kind of giggled as I went through the bathroom door, and she never giggled. As the bathroom door slowly closed, I heard something I don't think Jorma really intended for me to hear. "Betty Tom really showed her ass when you didn't turn out to be a girl."

That hospital had been a nighttime adventure until then, the night I fully understood just how sick Grandaddy was. Jorma helped me realize then that wrong things happened in hospitals—hospital-born me, Grandaddy's heart.

Tonight, as I came out of the bathroom and headed back to Grandaddy's room, I saw Delia just out there in the hallway. She had become a constant, the nurse on duty every night since we'd checked Grandaddy in. No matter what was going on, Delia was cheerful and kind, dispensing goodwill along with the multi-colored pills she carried around in white paper cups.

I had been gone twenty minutes, maybe, but when I returned, it was as if I'd walked into a hospital room on a movie set, and actor Grandaddy had just unhooked his fake IV, thrown back the covers, and walked away. And the prop people had put a mannequin in his place, and yelled, "Rolling, action," just before I walked back in. His face was tight and yellow, like cold, hard wax, and his mouth was open like a fledgling reaching up to its mother for food. I didn't do anything at first. I really thought I was in the wrong room. He looked that different from just a few minutes ago.

"Grandaddy?"

Grandaddy's face was now a mask. I touched it to be sure he was real and not hard plastic, but it was the softest surface I'd ever felt. Grandaddy's face was the opposite of a marble statue. It told me his body was too weak to hold an expression. The slack pooled where his face met the pillow. Skin lay in small, fine rolls, looking like where the hot Georgia summer sun melted an asphalt highway into folds where the bottom of a hill meets the flat. Grandaddy had already rolled out of his own body.

"Wink at me, Grandaddy. Wink at me again."
He didn't respond.
"Grandaddy?"

## CHAPTER FIFTY-SIX

# Loss Is Rust

Mama and Daddy hadn't gotten to the hospital yet when they came to remove Grandaddy from his room.

"Sir, we're sorry, but we need you to step outside. We need to move your grandaddy."

Sir? Why did she call me that?

"It won't take us long," Delia repeated. "I'm real sorry. When we're done, you can go back in."

But I had to get out of there, so I headed to the car. I started the engine, but I didn't know where to go, so I got out. I couldn't bear to sit in the rumble seat because it was meant for two, and I'd never felt so alone. I sat on the ground under the glare of the headlights, right into a river of shallow mud that slid off the naked slope and into the parking lot. I just stayed there, the mud a comforting distraction. The red clay of Georgia was probably all the way through to my underwear by now. I knew it would never come out, but I didn't care.

Although I was a teenager, I still had my hand-sized Mercury Cougar Matchbox car in my pocket. I always had it with me when we visited Grandaddy in the hospital. It was easy to slip into my pants pocket. I put a lot of miles on it from tracing it back and forth over my knee as I sat in hospitals and doctors' offices, more than any real Mercury Cougar ever clocked on real roads. Over time, it became a talisman, a good luck charm to keep us safe—Grandaddy for sure, but all of us. As long as I had the Cougar in my pocket, we would all be okay. I kept thinking to myself, *I have the car; how could this have happened?*

Then I heard Grandaddy's voice in my head, *You're almost eighteen. You get up from there and act your age.* And when I didn't move, *You hear me?*

Through tears I answered, "I hear you, Grandaddy." People had been hauled into the crazy ward for less, but I swear I didn't care one bit.

I put that much-loved Matchbox up to my face. Its cool metal felt good on my forehead, hot from a crying headache. It smelled like a penny tastes when you put it in your mouth, so I impulsively licked it, licked it just to see how it tasted. After all the years with it, tasting the now rusting metal was probably the only thing it and I hadn't been through together. Then I kissed it, memorized it in my hands, closed my eyes, and hurled it into the dark. I didn't want it anymore.

Mama and Daddy weren't there yet, but because I knew I should, I got up. I leaned into the car, turned off the lights, beat my hand on the steering wheel, screaming the dirtiest words I could think of and wished I could back up a couple of hours.

I went back inside the hospital, and for some reason started thinking about Nebula Road. It was the straightest stretch in the county, save for the hairpin that took you back into town. Drunk teenaged boys don't anticipate the turn, imagining the road goes on forever, like life seems to at seventeen. I thought about the view of the pine trees in the hairpin, receding a few trees' depth each time someone missed the turn and five or six came down after catching a hood or door or teenager up high in one of their limbs. The trees, too, were casualties that I imagined comforted each other underground, roots intertwined together like the enlaced fingers of held hands and the loss they felt when a hand isn't there to hold anymore.

Death was an ordinary, everyday event. It must have been. Everybody died. Everybody knew someone who died or was going to die someday. But it didn't seem ordinary to me. It was the opposite of ordinary—not like waking up or having breakfast or breathing.

It hurt so bad that Grandaddy was gone that I thought my eyeballs would split open like the scuppernongs do when it rains too hard, and the husk can't take on any more water. They split just a little bit where the stem holds them on the vine, and that tear widens, aching as it splits, the more it rains until the whole side is opened up like it's trying to give birth to the heavy, sweet-sour pith inside. Then the yellow jackets are there to suck up the juice and drain the whole thing down to a gooey mass that hangs there and becomes raisin-like until the leaves turn brown and shed, until a new crop of scuppernongs grow in right next to it this time a year from now.

*I want to keep this grief until this time next year,* I thought. *I owe it to Grandaddy. As much as it hurts, if I can keep up the hurt, I'll show him how much he means to me, to all of us. How much a heart has the capacity to love. How much my heart can love.*

A child can't keep a temper tantrum going, and a thunderstorm plays itself out fairly quickly, but loss doesn't evaporate. It's always there. After the raw pain of getting through the loss, it turns numb. Grief is active. You throw things and change your life and tell people you love them and need them. Loss is rust. Unless you work against it, loss corrodes you, slows you, makes you leaden.

But I wanted to hurt. I didn't want it to stop.

## CHAPTER FIFTY-SEVEN

# Life and Death

After they took Grandaddy away, nobody was acting up or making a thing out of their grief. However deeply felt, that part was private. That's the way Grandaddy would have wanted it, I guess. But it was to an extreme. No one cried. Not a drop. And it started as soon as Mama and Daddy drove up to the hospital, right after he died. They were both red-faced, but not crying. Daddy didn't even have on shoes. It was like he put the phone down when I called him, got out of bed, put his pants and shirt on, and just took off.

After tossing my Matchbox into the dark, I felt a Zotz candy-sized hole in my chest, a mix of cold and hot oozing through my skin. I missed that little car. It was too much of a burden to place on it to think it could save Grandaddy or protect him from what happens to us all.

I turned on the Bug's headlights and looked in the direction I tossed the car. I climbed over the fence and saw that the space beyond was the scrawny twin to Grandaddy's full and lush plants. The potato plants were brittle and small; the few home-grown corn stalks were dry and stunted. I bent down and felt my way through and around every plant. They were planted in the red clay, not carefully cultivated rich brown soil. The plants still grew, but they struggled.

When they saw me climbing back over the fence into the hospital parking lot after retrieving the Matchbox, Daddy got out of the car, walked over, and stood in the headlamps like he was in a music video or something, and gave me a little verbal slap across my face, "Get off that fence. You're a grown man." It had the same effect as if he'd picked me up by the scruff of my neck and dipped me in quicksand. I still moved, still walked, but I felt as though I was standing still. I could have told them why I was climbing the fence—why I *had* to do it—but I didn't say a word. He was right. I was grown, but I wanted him to say something else. Maybe "You okay, son?" or "We'll get through this, son." But he didn't. He didn't know how.

Blank-faced, I thought, *Is it gonna be like this? We're gonna pretend this didn't happen?* I tried not to react or snap back at him. After all, Grandaddy was his daddy, not mine. Maybe I should have been saying those things to Daddy instead of wanting him to say them to me. Instead, I stood up, remained wordless, and we all walked toward the hospital to dance the survivor dance.

The hospital felt like the inside of a bottle of rubbing alcohol, almost bitter and unbearable. I'd never noticed that before, not in all the years we'd been in and out of there. It was like the day after Christmas when you realize school is just around the corner, and you've got to find a place for all this stuff you got from your family, hating the holidays because they have come and gone. Hating them because you let them mean so much to you, and no one around you seems to care it's over, not even talking about the great time you had, or the food, or the carefree days with no school or work. And all you have is your family getting back into the usual routine, eager to start the new year and put Christmas behind them. And you're left with only the certainty of a cold New Year with winter storms and homework.

I wondered what they were doing with Grandaddy. He'd been gone about an hour. They wouldn't be working on him yet, I guess. I mean, he was probably just lying on some stretcher somewhere in a room by himself. But I think the part of him that made him Grandaddy was probably floating up in the corner of the room, looking down and watching over us, still. Adam told me, back when he had me convinced that he knew everything there was to know about the world, because he was ten and I was six, "When you die, they embalm you, and that means they take all your blood out of you and put formal hides in you instead."

"Na-ah," almost breathless.

"Ah-ha. They take all your clothes off you and hang you on a hook over a concrete floor with a drain in it."

"Why?" I whispered, afraid of asking out loud, but not sure why.

"They hang you up and the undertaker takes a deer knife and cuts a slit on the bottom of both feet from your heel down to your toes so the blood'll run out."

I'd seen Daddy hang a freshly killed deer upside down in a tree behind the house on a cold November night, lit by the floodlights on the corner of the house and the headlights of his truck, which he'd pulled around the back side of the house, way beyond the driveway. The knife he'd sharpened earlier that day on his whetstone catching the headlamps and throwing them back in my eyes, temporarily blinding me, only seeing the negative image of the knife under my lids as I closed my eyes to block the glare. It was just like seeing an image on the TV screen in the dark and then closing my eyes, so I could see the same image from the television burned onto my closed eyelids.

The bright knife looked like it was made of fire because when he used it to rip that upside-down deer open from his most private parts downward to its throat, the steam rushed out like smoke from a campfire. Sometimes the cavities groaned like a train horn in the distance as the knife punctured the skin. The first time you see a deer dressing, you think it's crying out in pain. It's not. It's just the sound the already dead body makes as it's pulled apart, the outside-the-body and the inside-the-body air changing places.

I went deer hunting with Daddy one time. I was just a little kid, and I hadn't yet seen a deer dressing. All I knew about deer hunting was Daddy got up really early, put on a variegated, green-patterned suit that didn't have separate pants and coat, but was all one piece that sealed him in with a long zipper that ran from the bottom of his torso to his throat. Mama, barely awake, gave him breakfast, and then he went out to his truck, carrying his gun and a lunchbox, and drove off. Sometimes Adam went with him, and a lot of the talk the day after was about being in the woods, looking around in the quiet for the mythical twelve-point buck.

I figured if there were points involved, I wanted to play. It sounded like the Cherry Tree game that Adam played with me sometimes, accumulating points as you spun the wheel and tried to pull the cherries off the tree. And Adam enjoyed it, talking about killing his first deer. I wanted to give it a try.

For me, the reality was traumatizing and nothing close to what I had figured it to be in my head. Sitting completely still, not making a sound while up in a tree in the cold, dark morning air, was the oddest experience of my life to that point. We climbed down earlier than Daddy had ever ended a hunting trip because I couldn't stop fidgeting and asking questions.

As Adam described the embalming process, my young boy's feet wanted to curl up in my shoes just like how the Wicked Witch of the East's feet curled up when the house fell on her. I remember wondering if she knew what was about to happen.

## CHAPTER FIFTY-EIGHT

# The Aftermath

A few days after Grandaddy died, Jorma sat herself down in a chair in the big, wide hallway of her house. Nobody ever sat there. It was a pass-through only, too wide to be a hallway, too broken up by doors, six of them, to be a room. She just sat there. She didn't eat her peppermints. She didn't eat anything. She didn't cry. She just sat.

"You okay, Jorma?" I didn't know what to say.

I went and sat on the arm of the chair, and then Adam, on leave from the Navy for the funeral, sat on the other arm. We looked at each other over her head, gesturing for the other one to do something.

Adam said, "Jorma, what's your favorite color?"

"I don't have one," she replied flatly.

I didn't know why he asked her in the first place, but her reply brought me back to that conversation just a few weeks earlier when Grandaddy had told me she was the second meanest woman to ever walk the red clay of Georgia. I guess it's hard to be happy if you can't even find the joy in something as basic as a color. I bet blind people have favorite colors, I reasoned. Why shouldn't color be something they could enjoy like everybody else? Maybe they'd say yellow or orange because of the way the sun feels on their face, or green because they feel more alive as they reach out and pull the sweet shrub into them and suck that smell in, the fragrance that is the baby born of just the right amount of clean air, sunshine, and Georgia soil.

One of my favorite things to do when I was little was to pick a sweet shrub bud, small as a peanut M&M, and put it in the hollow between my head and ear. It fit there perfectly, and I didn't lose it even if I ran around. It was hiding, but close enough to my nose so I could smell it. And if Grandaddy ever saw me with a bud stuck there, he'd call me over with no expression on his face and walk me over to the sweet shrub and pick off another bud and put it behind the other ear.

"Send Adam over here," he'd say.

And Adam would come back with buds behind his ears, seeming like he didn't enjoy it.

There, sitting with Jorma on the day of Grandaddy's funeral, I could hear what Grandaddy must have said to Adam.

"Just wear 'em for a little while, and let him see you wearin' 'em. It'll make him happy."

Adam had gotten up at some point after Jorma didn't have an answer to what her favorite color was, and by the time I visited my sweet-shrub memory, Adam walked back up with three of Jorma's aluminum cups.

"Here, Jorma. Here's your new favorite color." He gave her the purple aluminum cup and inside was a milkshake, a purple milkshake. The green cup had green milkshake for me, and the blue cup had a blue milkshake for Adam.

Adam said, "Philbet used to love these." And he kind of smiled and breathed out a little air is if to say, *Huh, Philbet is grown up. My baby brother is all grown up, and I wasn't here to see it happen.* And if my throat hadn't been closed shut from overwhelming love for Adam and sadness from losing Grandaddy, I would have raised the glass and said, "To Grandaddy."

And we looked at each other over Jorma's head, the first time we'd *really* looked at each other in I don't know how long.

"Jorma, come and eat something. There's lots of food," Adam said.

"In a minute," she replied listlessly.

Jorma must have been sitting there wanting to be called Springtime again. And I wondered how she managed to make Grandaddy feel like it was spring, even when it was December or a hot and sweaty July day. Maybe it was because his heart felt like it was coming alive, just being born every time he saw her. Or maybe he remembered seeing sixteen-year-old her that first time sitting in her daddy's wagon. Though I never heard him say it, I imagined Grandaddy's voice: *I thought she looked like a May flower just opening. Her name was Springtime before I ever knew it was Georgia Mae.* He called her Springtime because of all those things and other reasons I didn't know and would come to understand in bursts all through my life, sudden realizations as unexpected as the cracks of thunder just before the warm, heavy sky opens and cries.

Adam and I headed back to the kitchen. There was a big bowl on the table. It was Adam's idea, and it was a good one.

"Everybody put something in, some kind of food, something that makes you think about Grandaddy. And we'll eat it."

It was turning out to be a salad with fresh vegetables from the garden, a way to remember Grandaddy always out there in the rows, puttering away. I dug up some baby-sized potatoes and boiled them. I tried to find the very best ones, the ones that were a little messed up and a little broken and malformed because they had all the good nutrients and more flavor. *I remember, Grandaddy.* I pulled them out of the water and set them on a towel to drain before I cut them into cubes. I tossed them in salad dressing and put them in the bowl, making a wish with every toss. "Let Grandaddy be okay. And please let me see him again one day."

I didn't realize I was thinking out loud until Adam put a hand to my shoulder and leaned over to peer inside the bowl. He turned me around and held me at arm's length, and just looked at me.

"I'll always be here," he said.

I'd have given anything for a cool summer night with a hundred thousand lightning bugs all around us, just fifteen minutes with two mayonnaise jars and Adam and me running around with our lives and our world as big as we'd dare make it in front of us while Mama, Daddy, Jorma, and Grandaddy watched from the back porch. But we had to find our own way now. There was no Grandaddy to guide us, and no lightning bugs to light the way.

## CHAPTER FIFTY-NINE

# None-my

Grandaddy left me his brown 1974 Maverick, which he must have done because I loved cars so much. I never had the heart to tell him that Mavericks were crappy cars. But that gift started a chain of events that really set Daddy off.

"You did what?" Daddy asked, astonished, I guess.

"I gave the Bug to James."

"Why?"

"I don't need two cars."

"No. You don't just give a car away. What is wrong with you? Do you owe him money?"

"No, Daddy, he just doesn't have a car."

"Who is this?"

"He's my best friend."

"Do I know this boy?" he asked.

"Mama knows him."

"Mama!" He called out to her. Then, to me, "Get that car back."

Calmly, "No, I gave it to him."

"It ain't a goddamn welfare Cadillac."

It wasn't a Cadillac at all. It was a VW Bug. But I knew what he meant. If Daddy ever saw a poor person driving a nice car, he'd reflexively say, "He's got him a welfare Cadillac."

The air caught in my lungs and felt stuck as if I had a mouth full of peanut butter and someone pinched my nose shut. I wanted to say some version of "You take that back!" James was my friend, and I was so angry. I hated Daddy so much right then. I hated him because he was hateful, and James hadn't done anything except be my only and best friend for over ten years.

And finally I breathed, but I still couldn't talk because something made me not so much angry at Daddy, but ashamed of myself. All those years that I hid James, pretended he was just a boy from school, and I let Daddy think he was a White boy because I didn't say otherwise.

I whispered, "It's not a Cadillac. It's a Bug," all the while hearing *coward* in my head.

"Did you look at the title?"

"The what?" I asked.

"Mama!" Daddy yelled for her again.

"The piece of paper that says who owns it?"

"I don't...have that," I said.

"That's because I own the goddam car."

"I thought it was *my* car."

"What?" Mama said walking in.

"This dumbass—"

"Phil," she interjected, lightening ready to take him on.

"He gave the Volkswagen away."

"What did you do?" Mama asked.

"I gave the Bug to James."

"Philbet, sweetie, you can't do that."

"Why not? I'm the one who worked on it."

"And I paid for it," said Daddy.

Mama was calm. "Philbet, let's go over to James's and talk to his parents."

"I'll pay you both back," I promised.

"For God's sake!" The doorknob made a dent in the sheetrock from the force of Daddy opening the front door as he stormed out.

"No," Mama breathed deeply. "It would take you years to pay that back."

"But—"

"Stop, Philbet," Mama said.

"But James—"

"Just listen. We're goin' on a ride. I don't know, just ride for a while. And when we come back, we'll tell your daddy that James's parents paid us. I have some money put up that he doesn't know about."

"Mama, I—"

She stopped me. "Friends are important."

"James was so—"

"But you have to pay me at least part of it back, no matter how long it takes," she said, finishing her thought.

"He was so excited when I gave it to him, Mama."

I remember how big his eyes got when I held out the keys and said, "I don't need two cars, James."

"Dude, that's crazy!"

"And it was your idea for the loveseat." I could call it a loveseat again if a boy and a girl would be using it.

"No way."

"Maybe you can get Anne to sit in the loveseat with you."

"Philbet, are you sure?" James asked.

I wanted to give it to him now, before I told him what I was going to tell him. I knew that if I told him first, I might never, or he might never, speak to me again.

"Yeah, I am."

"Wow. Thank you, Philbet."

"But I want to tell you something."

"Huh?"

He wasn't paying attention. He was opening the hood and sitting down.

"James, I have to tell you something."

"What? Man, this is so cool."

"I'm in love," I said.

"Huh?"

I wasn't in love—well, I guess I *was*, but Knox wasn't. "I liked somebody, but that somebody didn't like me back."

"You had a girlfriend?" He seemed confused. "When?"

"I didn't, I don't have a girlfriend." I should've known that he'd be too interested in the car to listen to me. But if he thought I was a freak, he might not ever talk to me again, like Knox. And I wanted to give him the car because he'd been my dearest friend for years and years. No matter what he said now, he was my best friend.

"I didn't tell you."

"Why?" He looked at me and not the Bug.

"I didn't know what you'd say?" I replied.

"You're such a weirdo. Tell me. Who?"

"You know I've been working on the Bug."

"Yeah."

"And a neighbor, Knox, helped me."

"Yeah."

"I..."

"What?"

"I..."

"You like him?" James said.

My throat was tight in a way I didn't ever remember feeling before. It didn't feel the same as when Grandaddy died. It was closer to how I felt the day Knox walked away from me on my sixteenth birthday. As if my eyes and my throat struggled to reach out and give each other a comforting, loving hug. The result was that I didn't answer him, so he answered for me.

"Yeah," James replied, without a hint of judgment.

"How did you know?" I finally managed.

"'Cause first you liked Wright, and I knew you'd like somebody else one day."

*Wright. Did I like Wright the way I like Knox?*

There was only the sound of the whip-poor-will in the trees, although it was way too early for him to be singing since the sun wasn't all the way down yet. Without the whip-poor-will it would have been completely silent. And in the quiet, there between James and me, I realized that James knew me. He knew me and what was in my heart before I knew it myself.

"Why didn't you say something?" I asked.

"None-my."

"What?"

"None-my-business," James said, matter-of-factly.

"You don't have anything else to say?"

"Nope."

"You don't mind?" I asked.

"Mind what?" he asked.

"You don't mind that I liked a boy?"

"No."

I couldn't believe it.

He continued, "Hey, as long as you don't try to kiss me or stick it in me, I don't care."

Why did James say that? Here I was, hadn't even kissed a boy, and he was talking about sticking things in things. I wasn't talking about sticking anything in anybody. I was talking about how I loved Knox, and how I felt, and how I wanted to know how Knox smelled and what he thought, and how my heart hurt from wanting to be around him, and how I wanted him to want to be around me.

"My cousin Jermaine lives up in Atlanta," James said, "and he's always got a boy around him."

"So?"

"We just let him be."

## CHAPTER SIXTY

# By Design

"You can't make a living drawing," Daddy said.

"Yes, I can."

"What are you going to draw?"

"Cars."

"Who's going to pay you to draw cars?" Daddy asked.

"Car companies."

"What are they going to do with your drawings of their cars?"

"I'm not going to draw their cars."

"You just said you were going to draw cars, and the car companies are going to pay you for 'em." Daddy was not happy.

"They're going to make the cars I draw, the cars I design."

"Huh," he muttered, as he thought about it.

"They're not really paying me for drawing. They're going to pay me for imagining, for designing." I tried to help Daddy understand.

"Hmm." He sounded as if it was a pretty good idea that he hadn't considered.

"I have some good ideas," I went on.

"Uh-huh," Daddy listened.

"Cars should have cameras, so you can see all around."

"You're gonna mount cameras on cars?"

"Not like Polaroid cameras, Daddy."

"What's the point?"

"So you can see if there's anything around that you don't want to drive over."

I think he was imagining how you'd get the film developed.

"Like a closed-circuit video camera, so you can see right then and there."

"Where do you…? Oh, never mind."

Daddy had backed his sky-blue Chevy truck over my pedal car years ago, and if he'd been able to see behind him, maybe he wouldn't have run over it. I mean, I think he would have gotten out and moved my little car and not just run over it if he had known it was there.

"I ain't payin' for you to go to school and draw shit. You need to learn how to do somethin' you can get paid to do."

Mama said from the kitchen, "Phil, he's a smart boy. He's got some good ideas."

"Yeah," I seized on this welcome support from Mama, "and cars should have tires that can't go flat."

"How?"

"I don't know, but it's a good idea."

"You need air in a tire. A solid tire would be too rough a ride."

"There's a way to do it. I just don't know it yet."

"If you do away with inner tubes, folks won't have anything to float in on the river."

"Maybe a tire that won't go flat would be better for that too," I countered, though I'd never gone inner tubing, so I didn't know too much about it.

*That's a good idea*, I thought to myself. A car that floats so that you don't sink if you drive off into the river.

"And one day, cars will drive for you," I continued. "You'll just get inside and sit down and tell it where you want to go." That would have been good to have when Daddy had to get on the airplane and go to Florida when Uncle Rudy got so sick all of a sudden. Daddy hated flying, and if he'd had a car that did all the driving, he could have put a sleeping bag on the floor while the car drove him to Florida and just woken up when they arrived.

But I didn't tell Daddy the real reason I was going to design cars. I couldn't. He wouldn't understand. Cars in the future would be parts poetry, music, and art. They would be objects over which people, even two boys, could find each other, could fall in love—just like people do over art and food and literature. I couldn't say that to Daddy. I didn't have the words, and even if I had, he wouldn't understand. He couldn't understand that for me they were magical machines that pulled my half-working heart out of my body, looked at it, and decided what it needed to work at full force. To really do its full job, my heart needed more than blood. It needed another boy. A car did that for me; it found me a boy who made my heart pump with purpose.

But I did tell Mama, kind of, earlier that day.

"Philbet, why don't you be a pharmacist or something like that? You can make a good livin' doin' that. You could pay the rent just dispensing to my side of the family."

That was true. Filling Aunt Novella's painkiller prescriptions would be enough to pay the light bill, I was sure of that. "But I don't wanna be a pharmacist, Mama. I want to design cars, be an artist."

"Oh, Lord." Shaking her head as if she had caught me swinging from a light fixture.

"Mama, cars talk to me."

"Philbet...you are...."

I didn't want to talk to her anymore. Mama took my face in her hands and pointed it up to hers.

"I know you want to leave," she said, tearing up. "It breaks my heart, but I know you want to." And then she got hold of herself, the tears left, and her voice came back.

"Cars are nothing but machines to catch a ride out of town." As she turned away, she said under her breath, "I wish I'd never bought you those goddamn Matchbox cars."

Then she turned back to me, "You're on your own to convince your Daddy to pay for you to go off to learn how to draw." But to me, it sounded like she was saying that I had to convince Daddy to let me leave—leave Mama behind while I went off to begin my life.

I said after her, softly enough that I knew she couldn't hear me even if she were listening, "Mama, I can't live here anymore. I can't live next to the boy I love if he doesn't love me back."

Mama didn't say anything to me for the rest of the day, but she piped in from the kitchen with something I couldn't make out. Only Daddy heard her, and whatever she said helped push him to see it my way, one step closer to leaving her.

Daddy walked up beside me and looked down at his shoes, "Okay, Philbet. Okay. Go."

## CHAPTER SIXTY-ONE

# Clearing the Air

"Yeah?" James answered his telephone.

"I…"

"What's going on?"

I blurted, "I don't want for anybody to just let me be."

"Huh?"

"You let your cousin just be, like he's a harmless thing that you can't change so you just tolerate him."

"Philbet, I don't know whatcha talking about."

"You said your cousin, who likes boys…your family just lets him be."

"Yeah," James said.

"Why does anybody even care?"

"I don't care," James explained.

"You *do* care. You just let him be."

"But I let everybody be."

"But you don't let your other cousins be, like a boy cousin who likes a girl. Have you ever thought, or said, 'We just let him be, 'cause he likes girls?'"

Silence.

"Have you?" I insisted.

"No," James admitted.

"I'm not some weirdo."

"Oh, you're a weirdo, Philbet, but not because you like boys."

"I'm serious. That made me mad."

"I'm sorry, buddy."

I choked out, "I'm so lonely," no longer in a conversation with James.

"I'm sorry."

"I live my whole life inside my own heart. I feel like my heart gets squeezed inside me 'cause I'm all deformed, and then I've got to squeeze it down even more because it wants to love a boy and even if people say it's okay, they have to say it's only okay because they're looking the other way and letting me be this way because they're being real big about it and, I don't know, tolerating freaky little me." I didn't know how to stop talking after having said nothing for long. "I can't stand—"

James interrupted. "Let's get together today, Philbet."

And all of a sudden, I couldn't talk, my throat a hard, dry knot.

"I'm okay," I finally said.

"No, let's get together."

Silence.

"I'm sorry I didn't realize that there were two entrances at the doctor's office."

"What?"

"There shouldn't be two front doors at the doctor's office or the dentist's office...or actually, front doors and side doors."

"Liking boys isn't like being Black."

"It is too. Nothing's wrong with either one of them. They're just as good as anything else."

"You can't change this stuff, Philbet."

I didn't want to hear that. I couldn't make Knox love me, but I could do something about the other. "C'mon James, the next time you're sick, go to the White waiting room. I'll go with you."

"I don't want to go to the White waiting room."

"Then I'll go with you to the Black waiting room."

"Philbet."

"What?"

"I don't want you to."

"What? Why not?"

"You don't have to prove anything to me," James said.

"I'm not."

"I don't think White people are better than me. And nobody in my family does either."

"But you're treated different," I said.

"We treat *you* different too."

All I knew to do was try to get a good deep breath in me because I felt like I hadn't breathed, hadn't really tasted how beautiful and crisp air could be. I didn't have anything to say.

"It won't always be like this," he said. "Let's just be good to one another and finish growing up."

# CHAPTER SIXTY-TWO

# Happy Birthday to Me

I was about to head to LaGrange College. It was my birthday, and I wanted to spend it with Grandaddy.

I set a slice of birthday cake down on the ground next to his grave, careful not to put it on or step on Grandaddy. We never stepped on graves, the first rule of etiquette and respect Adam and I ever learned. It was a lesson even before, "Kids can't get in to see anybody at the hospital, and they can't kiss people in coffins." Adam explained that people in coffins were dead people who wore makeup to make them look asleep instead of dead. But now, grieving for my Grandaddy, I wanted to kiss him goodbye, to feel his soft skin and white stubbly beard against my cheek for one last hug with his three big, heavy pats on my back.

He wasn't a big man, but his hands were so warm and strong. No wonder he was so good at building things. It was as much a passion sparked by creative impulse over the years as it was out of need and lack of money. And when he fake-spanked you to make you laugh, or gave you a hug, patting you on the back, it was a comforting, flat-palmed sound.

Kneeling at his grave, I waited until sadness released my throat from its clenched, dry hold. Then I lit the single candle and sang, just as Grandaddy and I did every year since I turned three. "Happy Birthday to me, Happy Birthday to me." And I surprised myself because I laughed. The slice of Mama's cake I'd brought was good—pound cake with a sad streak. Then I pulled some weeds from the grass around his headstone. I liked pulling weeds. I couldn't make things grow, but I was really good at weed pulling. I liked that it took a lot of time to pull weeds one-by-one. Gave me time to think and not have to do anything else.

Finally, I said, "Grandaddy, I'm leaving tomorrow. I got into college. I'm going."

I could almost hear Grandaddy's voice in my head, expressing his pride, congratulating me with just the right words he always summoned. I broke the rule and lay on the ground, face down, half on Grandaddy's grave, pretending I was a little boy again, Grandaddy holding me on his lap with my hand grabbing onto his shirt pocket just above his heart, testing my luck at seeing if I could take one of his drawing pencils for my own.

And then my heart felt like it was in an elevator that suddenly dropped two floors. Grandaddy was the reason I loved to draw. It'd never crossed my mind before. Never dawned on me. Every time I took a pencil from his pocket, another appeared the next time I saw him. We didn't draw together. We never talked about it. But he was encouraging me, setting me on a path.

Finally, for the first time since Daddy told me to be a man out in the hospital parking lot, I didn't feel...well, nothing. I didn't even try to hold it in. "Grandaddy, I'm gonna miss you so much. I love you so much, I don't know what to do." I thought my chest would burst.

"I wish we could talk again. I wish we had drawn together. And I wish I knew you thought this was the right thing to do." I picked up a leaf that landed on his grave, put it in my pocket. "Four. Zero. Four. One. Three. Two. Five. Four. Three. Two." And I turned to go.

"Oh, Grandaddy," I said, turning back to his resting place, "I brought you a birthday present," and I pulled my favorite Matchbox car out of my pocket, my green with red interior Mercury Cougar, and set it on the headstone. "It's my birthday, but I wanted to give *you* something." And then, needing his guiding hand, I said, "I know you were so sick, and you must still be so tired. But if you can, help me know you're still here.

I'm not sure how I'm going to make it not knowing you're okay, or you're someplace near."

I said under my breath, "Bye, Grandaddy."

Then I looked up, and there was Knox.

## CHAPTER SIXTY-THREE

# And Then This

About the length of a four-door sedan away, Knox was standing under a tree, not leaning there like he was waiting on me to finish talking to Grandaddy, just standing there with his arms down by his sides, looking at me like there was no tree next to him or anything else in the world except for him and me.

I wondered, *Grandaddy, is this you letting me know something?*

To Knox, I simply said, "Grandaddy."

It wasn't a question like, "Did you know Grandaddy died?" It was a breathless statement, an embarrassing repeat of when I first spoke to him, and he first spoke to me in Daddy's truck all those years ago. With a single word, I revealed that he completely unraveled me with one look.

"Hey, Keebler." Knox paused and then continued. "Your grandaddy… I'm so sorry."

I no longer wanted to go out to the road, waiting for him to race by. I hadn't been to my hideout in two years. Knox looked the same, except his hair was longer, as if he worked too much to bother to get it cut. It was long enough for it to reach out and wrap itself around my fingers if my hands got too close to his face. So long that if we stood nose to nose, staring into each other's eyes, his hair would shade my face like a veil, making what we do, what we say, secret.

I had not seen him these two years since the lake, my birthday, the day he kissed me on top of the head and turned and walked away. Well, I had, but only from a distance and only by chance.

I didn't know what to say, so I said nothing.

"He was a good man," he said awkwardly, trying to comfort me.

I wasn't trying to be unkind, but I couldn't believe he was standing in front of me, speaking to me, looking at me. I was angry.

*Grandaddy, what does this mean?* I thought to myself.

"I hear you're going away."

"Yeah," I managed finally.

"When do you leave?"

"Tomorrow."

"Oh," he said and then nothing for minutes. "Do you have time to talk?"

I didn't know what to say to him.

"I won't take long," he promised.

"Why are you here?" I managed evenly, not sounding as upset as I was, or as excited.

"Come with me?"

"Leave me alone, Knox. Please," I pleaded. I couldn't believe I was telling the boy I love to go away. "I don't want to talk to you," I lied, determined to stand my ground.

"Keebler, let's not end angry with each other."

I thought, *What does he mean? He hasn't spoken to me or even looked at me sideways in two years. It ended. Two years ago.* I turned back at Grandaddy's grave, partly for one last look, partly out of nerves, but mostly because I didn't want Knox to see my eyes turn so red with the strain of holding back tears. Then I walked past Knox as I made my way down the hill.

"Keebler," he said, following me. His GTO wasn't there. Instead, he had a motorcycle. Running around in front of me, "Here. I promised him I'd give this to you." He held out an envelope.

I didn't take it. He took my hand, put the envelope securely in it, and as he let go of it his hand reached toward me, resting on my upturned wrist. His calloused fingers scratched my skin. It felt like a candle had dropped wax on me, like he had touched through and below my skin.

Then he got on his bike and rode off. The envelope had my name written in open, broken, peaked angular letters. It was from Grandaddy.

I thought, *This is Grandaddy's work.* He never let me down. I didn't open the envelope. I got in Grandaddy's car, my car now, and headed off in Knox's direction.

Beeping my horn when he was in sight, he looked around but didn't stop. He kept going, heading back in the direction of the road where we both lived, just walking distance from where we both slept each night. It was torture being so close to him, only several hundred feet through the woods. At night the world seemed smaller. It was the still, quiet country nights that made the space between us feel closer than in daylight. We were so near, we could hear the same sounds, even hear voices from each other's yards if we'd been out early in the morning before any cars ventured out.

And I was out there, sitting outside late into the night, unable to sleep, worrying about Grandaddy, thinking about Knox. If I managed to go to bed, I'd often wake up, quietly creep out early and pad out on bare feet to crawl into the hammock between the pecan trees, my substitute for the cover of my Ninety-Eight hideout. The dark nights were my answer, concealing me, lit only by the stars. There, I'd wonder if Knox were awake or asleep. Wonder if he'd forgotten about me and wouldn't even speak to me. I must have really disgusted him for him to just walk away from me. It felt worse, in a way, than losing Grandaddy.

Death is natural, even if it hurts like you're going to die yourself. But in some ways rejection hurts worse. There's no reason for it. If everyone lived forever, there'd be no room for new babies. All those people who come after us would never get to come and follow the cycles of their lives, their first love, their losses, their coming of age. But rejection doesn't take up any space in the world; it only takes up space in our hearts, leaving scarce room for anything else.

As he headed away with me following, the length of several cars separating us, I thought, *He's just up ahead, and I'm here, with only the shortest distance between us, just like it's been these two years. Why did I never sneak over to his bedroom window or go back to my hideout in the junkyard? Why did I let him leave just now? He came to see me. He gave me a letter from Grandaddy. That's a sign if there ever was one.*

But two car lengths apart didn't matter. We were apart and had been for a long time. Then he pulled off the road, near our houses, but before he got to the road that took us home. The day wasn't over, and the sun was bright and low in the sky, hung almost shoulder level, half hidden behind the pine mountains.

As I got out of my car, he said, "Get on," and handed me his helmet.

"When did Grandaddy give you the letter?"

I didn't need him like I used to. I'd gotten used to the idea that he didn't want me. Still holding the helmet out to me, he said, "Take it. Okay?"

I took the helmet.

"Put it on, Keebler."

"What do you want, Knox?"

"Just come with me. I'll bring you back as soon as you tell me to."

Not thinking, I put the helmet to my face, and I closed my eyes when I smelled the gasoline scent that came from him. The underside of my eyelids looked blue, that perfect shade that is the same color as the sky during one of the five perfect days in mid-September every year. This was one of those days. The air was exactly the same temperature of a person's skin, like swimming in a stream during that moment when it transitions from too warm to too cool.

But his helmet, with its intoxicating scent, suddenly made me hungry, and thirsty. The kind of thirsty when you've been out in the sunshine all day long and just want to swallow big gulps of sweet tea, one after another. The smell of his helmet….

*Dear Lord, don't let this happen. Don't let me fall back into this. I'm going to melt right into the ground. He gave me the letter. Why couldn't he leave me be?* I thought all in the space of a single breath.

I got on behind him, holding onto the bottom edge of the seat. He reached back, took my hands, and pulled my arms around his waist. His belt, the one with the buckle I sneaked stares at for years was under my hand, and I grabbed onto it, touching it for the first time. My other hand on his stomach, feeling it expand and contract with his breaths, the fabric lightly moving across his skin. Two years and a Grandaddy ago I loved him. I didn't feel anything now. I couldn't. I was leaving in the morning.

We cut into the pines, down a trail I didn't know was there, invisible just five feet from the road. Once we were under the tree canopy the old, familiar calm returned. The forest floor lightly carpeted with pine needles made the motorcycle slide and slip when he turned or leaned too far in this or that direction. Before long, we emerged at the edge of the lake where we last spoke on my sixteenth birthday. It was a small camp filled with a seat from the back of a Chevy Suburban, overturned milk crate table, a hole that previously held a campfire, and a cooler. He pulled the sides of the helmet back just enough to pull it off my head. His thumbs brushed my cheeks, and I suppressed the impulse to incline my face toward his hand. The day was perfect. My birthday was always on one of those perfect September days; the sky as blue and clear as it's allowed, so blue it needs another name.

He walked over to the cooler, opened it, and pulled out a little cake, a birthday cake about the size of a mega-muffin from the Minute Mart. It had a big plastic, green "18" stuck right on top of the green icing.

"Happy birthday, Keebler."

Not wanting to smile, I asked, "How did you know it was my birthday?"

"Um, we were best buds for a few years." And after a slow beat, he admitted, "Okay, somebody told me."

"Who?"

"Your Grandaddy."

"Oh."

"Keebler, I want to explain."

"When did he give you the letter?"

"A month or so ago."

"Why?"

"He wanted me to give it to you after he was gone. He wanted you to have it without anyone in your family knowing."

I stared at the envelope, wondering what it held. He knew about Knox. He must have known.

"You talked to him?" I asked.

"Yes."

"What about?"

"Lots of stuff. He was a really good guy."

"You talked a lot?"

"Yeah, Keebler, about once a week. For over a year. Close to two years."

Knowing why, but needing him to say it, I asked, "Why were you talking to my grandaddy?"

"Keebler."

"Why were you talking to Grandaddy? He didn't tell me. *You* tell me."

"He wanted to talk to me about—"

"What?"

"Us. You and me."

"You told Grandaddy?" I asked, with no air in me, only managing a whisper.

"I'm sorry. I didn't know what to do. I mean, I was a grown man," he said.

"Yeah, a grown man who kissed me on the top of my head and walked away."

"A twenty-year-old man cannot, should not, kiss a sixteen-year-old boy."

"I'm not sixteen."

"You *were* sixteen, Keebler."

"But I'm not sixteen now."

His arms sprang out, and with both hands he pulled my face to his. It was my first kiss, *our* first kiss. A first kiss from a boy I first loved. And I kissed him back, wrapping my arms around him and up his back like I was grabbing a pull-up bar with my hands full of his shirt and him in it, having never done a chin up and having never been kissed. I'd felt nothing like it before. It was a new sensation between taste and smell that I didn't know, one I didn't and couldn't imagine existed.

There, in his arms, I knew I'd die if I never felt it again. Die as sure as if I held my breath too long. It was so overpowering that I felt like I was crying, except I wasn't. The best part of it was how he looked at me when he stopped and took a deep breath.

"Keebler."

He didn't say it like, "Keebler, can I ask you a question?" Or "Keebler, are you okay?" Or. "Keebler, I'm sorry I walked away."

He said it like, "Keebler, I love you."

"I love you too." I responded to what he hadn't said, what I hoped he meant.

And he kissed me again, but it was different from the first one. It was more gentle, slower, and he moved his hands from my face down my shoulders to my chest, my twisted, sunken chest.

I pulled away, and he took my hands. He put one under his shirt and set it on his chest, right on top of where his heart beat below. The last time I touched him was two years ago, almost to the day, and this is the place my hand touched him. Then he let go of my other hand and put his finger under my chin, lifting it so gently until my face was pointed just toward his.

He offered his free hand to me. I didn't know what to do. All I could think was I felt so free, like I hadn't felt in years. Not since I was four or five and running around the living room without any clothes dancing to "C'mon Get Happy." Then I knew he was waiting to see if I'd put his hand to my chest.

"My chest. I'm so—"

But he stopped me with another kiss.

"But that's where your heart is. It's the best part of you."

He tapped the back side of his fingers to my shoulder, as if he were knocking on a door asking permission to come inside. "Your heart is in there under your chest. You've got the strongest heart of anybody."

Who was this boy? He was suddenly a poet after not speaking to me for two years. He was speaking poetry, and I didn't even know I liked poetry until this very second.

"I want you to want to look at me the way I want to look at you," I said.

He almost laughed and caught his breath. "Keebler."

"Please don't laugh at me," I whispered, and I tried to pull away.

"Keebler, I do."

"Do what?"

"I want to look at you. And I do," he admitted, and we kissed again.

This kiss was different again from the first ones. It was like…it was like his Mama gave him the beaters off the mixer after she had finished making the cookie dough, and he was licking those beaters like he hadn't had breakfast, lunch, or dinner, and all he wanted was that sweet, gooey dough. And I was the dough, the last remnants of what was left clinging to the beaters. I felt my breath leave me and go into him. It was magic. My heart woke up and realized that all along it was supposed to pump Coca-Cola and peppermint through my veins.

"I spent the last couple of years wanting to look, but you were too young. And now…now I want to know how to love like you do," he whispered to me.

I never knew exactly what happened when two people gave themselves to each other, which were the words the preacher used every time we went to a wedding. The preacher even asked the bride's father, "Who gives this woman to this man?" Judy, who lived down the road, went off to school and came back here for her wedding a few years ago. They had different words for that wedding, and her parents walked in on either side of her from one door, and his parents walked in with him from the other door. And nobody gave anybody to anyone, and nobody took anyone. And when the preacher told them they could kiss, it was different from other weddings. The kiss wasn't funny, wasn't part of a show put on for the audience, and her brother and cousins didn't whistle or hoot. I'd never seen anything like it. It made me cry because I thought I shouldn't be looking. They acted like they were alone in a room with only themselves and nobody else. And that was the first time I saw real passion, real intimacy, right there in front of everybody.

And I wanted to know what that was like for myself, wanted it more than air, more than a car.

What came after a kiss like that was unclear. I knew sex existed, and I knew generally how it worked, what went where. I didn't want to do that, not exactly what Judy and her husband would do, but I couldn't ever tell anybody. They'd think something was wrong with me for even saying such a thing out loud, much less not wanting somebody as pretty as Judy. I wanted the kiss though, just the kiss. If Knox and I could just kiss like this all the time, that would be everything, more intimate than anything I could imagine, more than enough for me.

I imagined him lying next to me on my bed, on me, with his lips on mine, with his head next to mine, his breath in my ear. I didn't, couldn't, think of words we'd share. My imagination wasn't developed enough, not mature enough yet, to project actual love for me into his heart and mind. The most I could manage to conjure was lying there, kissing. It was a step-by-step seduction, almost a paint by numbers project. After I filled in color number one, the kissing, I could fathom going on to color number two, the words and feelings. And I guess color number three would be some boys-only version of what Judy and her new husband shared.

Now that Knox had come to me, and we had finally kissed, colors two and three joined color number one on this canvas all of a sudden, together, like the scene painted itself. It happened as soon as he touched me, kissed me very hesitantly, pulled back to look at me in the eyes, directly into them.

"Keebler."

*Maybe if I kiss him each time he says my name, I'll condition him to expect and want my touch every time he thinks or says my name, whether I'm actually near or not.*

His rough thumb reached up to touch my lips, which felt like they were buzzing, vibrating, almost like they had come to life, just born. I almost knocked him over, lunging for his mouth.

"You taste like honey," he said.

"You taste like life." That was corny, but it came out of me before I thought about it.

"Keebler, I've always tried to watch out for you."

I didn't want him to feel sorry for me like I was so helpless. *Please don't ruin this. Don't talk,* I thought.

"Sometimes I didn't know how, how to protect you...from me. I'd never hurt you for the world."

It dawned on me that it wasn't him who didn't like me. It was *me* who didn't like me. And, slowly, I felt like we were equals. Me graduating from a broken little boy to a man. Him not so godlike, a real person, but not so far past being a boy himself. Suddenly, we were both men in his eyes, walking on a level playing field. But I still wasn't sure what came next.

"Do you know what it says?" I whispered, looking at Grandaddy's envelope.

He shook his head "no" and turned away to the little green cake, not looking at me. I opened the envelope, careful not to rip it because I'd never get another letter from Grandaddy.

*Dear Philbet,*

*I'll miss you more than anyone. You're the strongest little fella I ever knew. You're brave, and I'm so proud I got to be your grandaddy.*

*I need you to do some things for me. I wrote them down because I won't be here anymore to talk with you about them when the time comes. So, now has to be the right time. Now, and any time you pick up this letter and reread it in years to come.*

*Try to talk to your Mama and Daddy more. They're not perfect, but they are your family.*

*Give Adam some time. He'll come back around and be a good big brother if you let him in. I expect it wasn't easy for him to leave home, even one that isn't happy. The only way he could leave was to break a few things as he went. He thought it would make the leaving easier for you if he tried to push you away. He'll realize his mistake one day.*

*You don't have to go through life all by yourself. Your heart is closed off, and that broke my heart to see because you weren't afraid of anything when you were just a little fella. Open that heart back up, Philbet. It gets tougher as you get older. No matter what, you'll be okay. When a heart breaks, it mends in time and grows stronger and wiser.*

*Don't be angry with Beau. He told me about your broken heart because he was worried about you. You can always trust Beau, and you can always trust Adam. Beau understands better, but Adam loves you just as much.*

*And don't be angry with Knox. He knows he hurt you, but he was trying to protect you. I made him visit me. He didn't want to. I made him. I needed to find out if he is a good boy. He is. He loves you, Philbet. He's older than you, but he's more of a boy than you in some ways. He'll make a fine man. You can help him become that man.*

*And when you give your heart to somebody, know that I did the same thing when I was about your age now. I gave mine to Jorma. If nobody understands what your heart wants, it doesn't matter. If you know what your heart wants, no one else has to understand except you and the one you love. And here's the thing, Philbet, you have to give your heart away for it to be any good to you. That's how hearts work. The one you love, the one you give your heart to may not accept it, but give it anyway. That's a lesson you might have to learn on your own. I won't be there to guide you, but you're ready.*

*Go after what you want. And don't let anybody tell you what you should want. You decide. You deserve as much as anybody else. And don't grieve too hard, Philbet. Remember, I'm always with you. Every time you hear a Ford head down the road, I'm right there. Every time you pick up a pencil to draw, I'm watching you.*

*"Four. Zero. Four. One. Three. Two. Five. Four. Three. Two." Just say those numbers to yourself, and I'll always answer you in your heart.*

*Philbet, you are okay, just like you are. I think you're just about as perfect as any man can be. Happy 18th birthday.*

*My sweet boy, be happy.*

*Love,*
*Grandaddy*

Knox walked up to me with a plate full of cake, "Open up, birthday boy." And he held out a pinch of cake to my mouth. It was sweet, and it filled my nose with vanilla and butter. He put the plate down and held a napkin up to my eyes.

Then he took my hand in both of his hands and put it flat on his mouth, and I thought he was kissing it at first. Multiple kisses. But he was talking, barely above a whisper.

"Keebler. Keebler. I miss you," he said, as if my ears were in the palm of my hand, and he'd just this very minute realized it. Then he kissed each finger like I had cinnamon-toast sugar on the very tips, the pads. He didn't lick them clean, but whatever he did, I didn't know there was so much feeling right there in the ends of fingers. My other hand felt left out, so I lifted it to his hair, his hair the color of Robert Redford in 1973, like spun sugar from fresh maple syrup. It was warm, like a blanket just after you get out of bed in the morning, so inviting you just want to crawl back in face-first.

The only thing better than a warm blanket is one that smells like this boy, the boy I'd loved for so long, whatever I may have told myself from time to time. The one I had willed myself to love no more, here in front of me again, looking at me and touching my hand to his face.

My mind drifted back to the letter. Grandaddy knew about us. He knew I wanted Knox like Judy wanted her husband, like Beau wanted his love. He said it was okay. He liked Knox.

"Why didn't he tell me?"

Knox looked at me, but he didn't speak.

"Tell me. He knew."

Knox raised his shoulders slowly, gently. And then, "I think he…I think he hoped you'd come to him when you were ready."

I stared down at the letter. It was one of Grandaddy's lessons. There was a gulf between Grandaddy and me—a gap of the unspoken, of what had been left unsaid. He had always been there to reach out and squeeze the heat out of my hair after a day in the Georgia sun, there to hug the chill off my shoulders when the gas heater couldn't quite reach across the whole of the room. And all I had to do was reach back and tell him what he already knew.

"I want to show you something," Knox said quietly. "Come with me." And he gently pulled me along, leaving the bike behind.

He did not let go of my hand. His rough, calloused hands gripped mine. He was strong, and it felt like the hand of a much older person, reminding me of the differences between us. As young as we were, as close as our homes were, his life was so different from mine. The soft, pink pad of my hand against his rough palm was a symbol of how our lives had begun to go down different roads in the two years since we stood here.

As he pulled me along—me next to and slightly behind him—I fantasized about how his hands would feel if I lifted his fingers to my own lips, tasted them just as he had mine. How would they feel on my body, on my neck, just below where my hair met the collar of my shirt? On my back, pulling me close to him? *My heart will explode*, I thought.

*I want...I want....* I couldn't finish because I was sure I'd burst from wanting him if I found the end of that thought. He turned to smile at me as he rushed us along. I'm changing, and I'll change more over the years, more than he will. I don't know how I knew, but I knew. *Will this difference matter?*

And then, from my place just behind and to the side, I caught sight of his ear, that beautiful little curve that stood out from him, his golden-brown hair protecting it from me, obscuring it. I didn't watch where we were headed, didn't know how long it had been since we set off. Then he stopped and turned to me, pushing us both low on the pine straw-covered carpet beneath us. I thought he'd read my mind, my wordless request to stop so that I could touch his ear, look inside.

He started to speak, but I stopped him with a kiss as I reached my right hand to his left ear. Turning his head, I put my mouth to it, my nose, my fingers. I could see inside, finally. The old urge to reach out, to climb inside. For a half second, I let reason interrupt me, but I pushed that away and breathed him in, his delicate little ear that made me burn, made me aware of the impossibility of ever really being inside him, knowing what he thought and felt, being a part of him.

He turned toward me, looked, our breaths held, our heads cocked at angles, as if we were unsure how we came to be in such an odd embrace. We were still for a moment, as though the other was a rare, wild woodland creature that would bolt away with any sudden movement. Finally, I moved first, a simple, primal lick of his ear. And he pulled me into an embrace with his big, strong arms wrapping me like a winter coat. Behind him, I saw we were at the fence to his yard, just behind my Ninety-Eight hideaway. I hadn't been here in a very long time, not since the day I threw a red brick through the window.

"Quiet," he said. "Nobody's home, but you never know." He climbed through the fence and held the wire while I climbed through as well. We sneaked up the side of the Ninety-Eight to the back door.

"I fixed it," he said, watching me while I reached up to feel the glass. "I fixed it…in case you ever came back."

"How did you know?"

"Keebler, you little weirdo. I know this junkyard like I know my own room. And I saw you. You didn't think you could sit out here, and I wouldn't see you?" He opened the door for me, and we climbed inside and onto my beloved brown velvet seats, the place I had spent so many hours drawing, watching him work in the yard.

"You don't know how hard I worked to keep a clear path from here to the shop. They'd haul a wreck in and try to park it right out there. We didn't park anything there. I always managed a reason."

*I was the reason*, I thought.

"We couldn't touch, but we could look," he said. "I like that you looked. It made being here bearable, knowing you were here." And my own true love pressed me against the door like we were regular boy and girl teenagers parked out on Nebula Road on a Saturday night.

I'd never made out in the back seat of a car before. But then, I'd never made out before period. I'd never even been kissed until about twenty minutes ago. Entangled with him was the oddest sensation, like traveling in a cocoon to a new world that seemed really small, a world with a population of only two. But that small world was bigger than the whole Earth to me.

I wasn't sad in that world of two. I didn't feel lonely while we were in it. Because it was only meant for Knox and me. I didn't look for Grandaddy, which was the first time since he'd died that I'd gone five minutes without hoping to turn and see him standing there. It probably sounds weird, thinking about Grandaddy in this private, intimate moment with Knox. But it didn't feel weird. Grandaddy knew. He knew I loved Knox. He knew I wanted Knox, and it was okay with him.

Grandaddy and Knox in the same room, talking. I'd give just about anything to have been there just one time to hear them, hear their voices in the same room. To see them shake hands hello and goodbye. To walk into the garden with them and check out the plants and hear Grandaddy's update on how they are doing and then hear him give Knox some plant care tip, which was really a life lesson if you paid close attention.

"Those funny-looking potatoes are the tastiest...the best ones. They have to work harder to survive."

To have a picture of the three of us would be the most special thing ever. I'd put it in a frame and take it with me everywhere. And if I ever get to be a grandaddy, it'll be okay with me, too, if my grandchild loves somebody everybody else thinks is wrong. I won't send a messenger. I'll tell my grandchild myself.

Knox's kisses rubbed my face raw, clean. All the crying, all the ache of losing Grandaddy was washed off, for now. And I breathed deeply and steadily, better and deeper breath than I had drawn in a long while. Here, around my mouth, I still smelled his breath and felt his touch, where his soft lips met the many pins of his stubble. It felt like I started to split open, my skin a thin, translucent shell cracking down the middle, starting at the corner of my mouth. And I, without moving, felt myself crawl out of that small husk of my old shell. The old me, the boy who stood there at Grandaddy's grave when Knox walked up, was breaking open so that a newer me could emerge. My old skin fell away, lifeless where it lay.

"I have to go," I said suddenly.

"Yeah, it's getting dark. I'll take you to your car."

"No, Knox. I have to go. I have to leave. Tomorrow."

He didn't say anything. He reached out his rough hand to my face. I wanted so much to turn toward it, breathe into it, press it into me. He took my hand in both of his and pressed it to his open mouth. I don't know what he said into it. I think it was only for him to know.

No promises of anything to each other. We sat there, holding hands with our fingers interlaced, layered like we were playing Church and Steeple, which felt right.

I wanted to visit a church with him, a church with no people except him and me. Just go inside, together, and in that church we'd promise ourselves, give ourselves to one another forever and always with nobody looking, because it was private, intimate, and meant for only the two of us.

Some day. One day.

# Acknowledgments

With grateful thanks to my family, whose care and love have made me the man I am today, and to the family I have created around me for their unfailing kindness, extraordinary patience, and caring guidance when the world, from time to time, has overwhelmed.

My first readers (alphabetically!)—Claire Green, Elaine Greenstone, Terri Nimmons, Alice Powers, Jennifer Swift, and Jane Vandenburgh—gave me insights that only improved, enlivened, and polished my prose. Marie Arana, Levon Avdoyan, The Authors Guild, Jag Bhalla, Emily Barrosse, Emi Battaglia, Nicole Caputo, Christopher Castellani, Becky Clark, Robin Ervin, W. Ralph Eubanks, Hank Heflin, Susannah Greenberg, Brette Goldstein, Meredith Goldstein, Willa Greenstone, Michael Gross, James Hart, Rachel Hoge, Anne Holmes, Ismita Hussain, Josie Kals, Heather King, Lambda Literary, Joanne Leedom-Ackerman, Willee Lewis, Will Lippincott, Paul Lisicky, Rachel Mears, Meg Metcalf, Monica Mohindra, Liz Nealon, Muriel Nellis, Claiborne Smith, Ben Stockman, Lindy Woodhead, Van Van Cleave, and Alyona Vogelmann provided incalculable help as I navigated the world of literary agents and the publishing industry in general, a foreign landscape at the start. My brilliant agent, Mona Kanin of Great Dog Literary, believed that mine was a story that needed to be told. Each word of encouragement shaped my confidence and sharpened my courage to put it out there, come what may. And the wonderful Debra Englander saw straightaway that my manuscript was a book-worthy tale of life on the fringes.

To each of them I offer my deep-from-within-the-heart gratitude for every act, however small, that brought me to this moment. To anyone I have failed to name by inadvertence or faulty memory, I ask for your forgiveness and give my abundant thanks. And to Erich, my life partner, I am curiously without words to express my outsize devotion for his abiding love and unshakable faith in me and my talent, such as it may be; he is my bedrock in all things.

# About the Author

Jeffrey Dale Lofton hails from Warm Springs, Georgia, best known as the home of Roosevelt's Little White House. He calls the nation's capital home now and has for over three decades. During those early years he spent many a night trodding the boards of DC's theaters and performing arts centers, including the Kennedy Center, Signature Theatre, Woolly Mammoth, and Studio Theatre. He even scored a few television screen appearances, including a residuals-rich Super Bowl halftime commercial, which his accountant wisecracked "is the finest work of your career."

Ultimately he stepped away from acting for other, more traditional work, including providing communications counsel to landscape architects and helping war veterans tell their stories to add richness and nuance to historical accounts. At the same time, he focused on pursuing post-graduate work, ultimately being awarded Master's degrees in both Public Administration and Library and Information Science. Today, he is a senior advisor at the Library of Congress, surrounded by books and people who love books—in short, paradise.

Red Clay Suzie is his first work of fiction, written through his personal lens growing up an outsider figuring out life and love in a conservative family and community in the Deep South.

JeffreyDLofton.com